DC SUPER HERO GIRLS™

SPACED OUT

a graphic novel

WRITTEN BY
Shea Fontana

ART BY
Agnes Garbowska

COLORS BY
Silvana Brys

LETTERING BY
Janice Chiang

COVER BY
Yancey Labat and Monica Kubina

SUPERGIRL BASED ON THE CHARACTERS CREATED BY JERRY SIEGEL AND JOE SHUSTER.
BY SPECIAL ARRANGEMENT WITH THE JERRY SIEGEL FAMILY.

MARIE JAVINS Group Editor
DIEGO LOPEZ Assistant Editor
STEVE COOK Design Director - Books
AMIE BROCKWAY-METCALF Publication Design

BOB HARRAS Senior VP - Editor-in-Chief, DC Comics
BOBBIE CHASE VP & Executive Editor, Young Reader & Talent Development

DAN DiDIO Publisher
JIM LEE Publisher & Chief Creative Officer
AMIT DESAI Executive VP - Business & Marketing Strategy,
Direct to Consumer & Global Franchise Management
MARK CHIARELLO Senior VP - Art, Design & Collected Editions
JOHN CUNNINGHAM Senior VP - Sales & Trade Marketing
BRIAR DARDEN VP - Business Affairs
ANNE DePIES Senior VP - Business Strategy, Finance & Administration
DON FALLETTI VP - Manufacturing Operations
LAWRENCE GANEM VP - Editorial Administration & Talent Relations
ALISON GILL Senior VP - Manufacturing & Operations
JASON GREENBERG VP - Business Strategy & Finance
HANK KANALZ Senior VP - Editorial Strategy & Administration
JAY KOGAN Senior VP - Legal Affairs
NICK J. NAPOLITANO VP - Manufacturing Administration
LISETTE OSTERLOH VP - Digital Marketing & Events
EDDIE SCANNELL VP - Consumer Marketing
COURTNEY SIMMONS Senior VP - Publicity & Communications
JIM (SKI) SOKOLOWSKI VP - Comic Book Specialty Sales & Trade Marketing
NANCY SPEARS VP - Mass, Book, Digital Sales & Trade Marketing
MICHELE R. WELLS VP - Content Strategy

TABLE OF CONTENTS

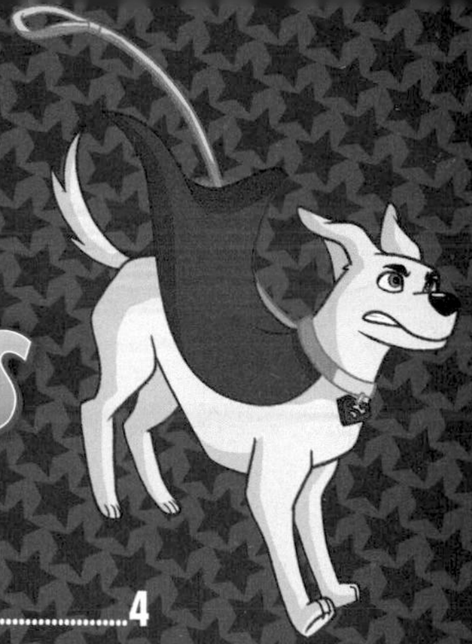

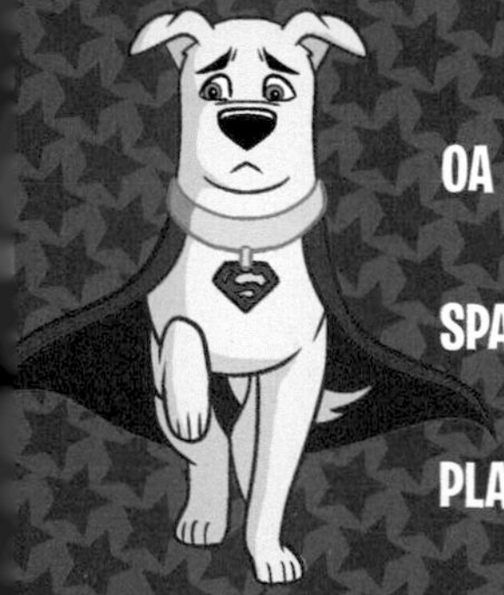

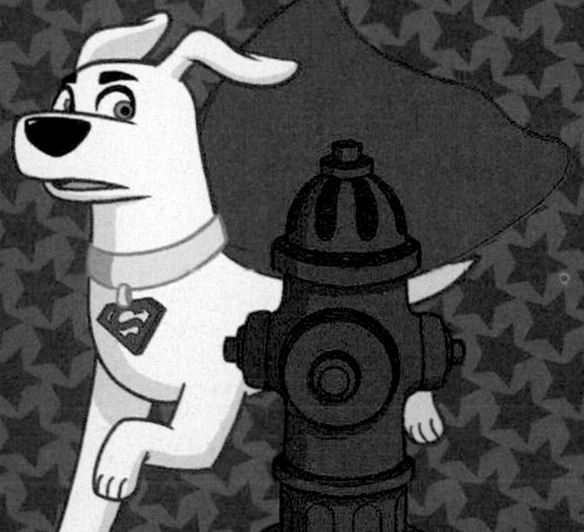

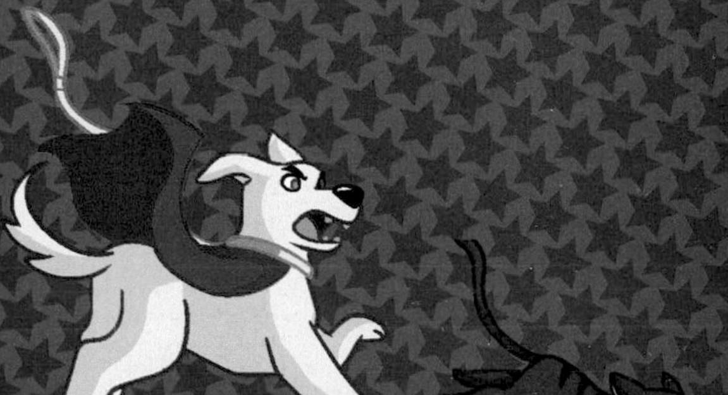

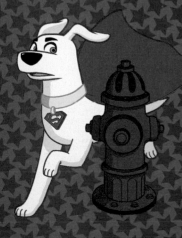

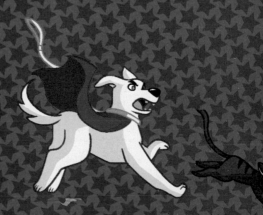

CHAPTER ONE

OA SNAP

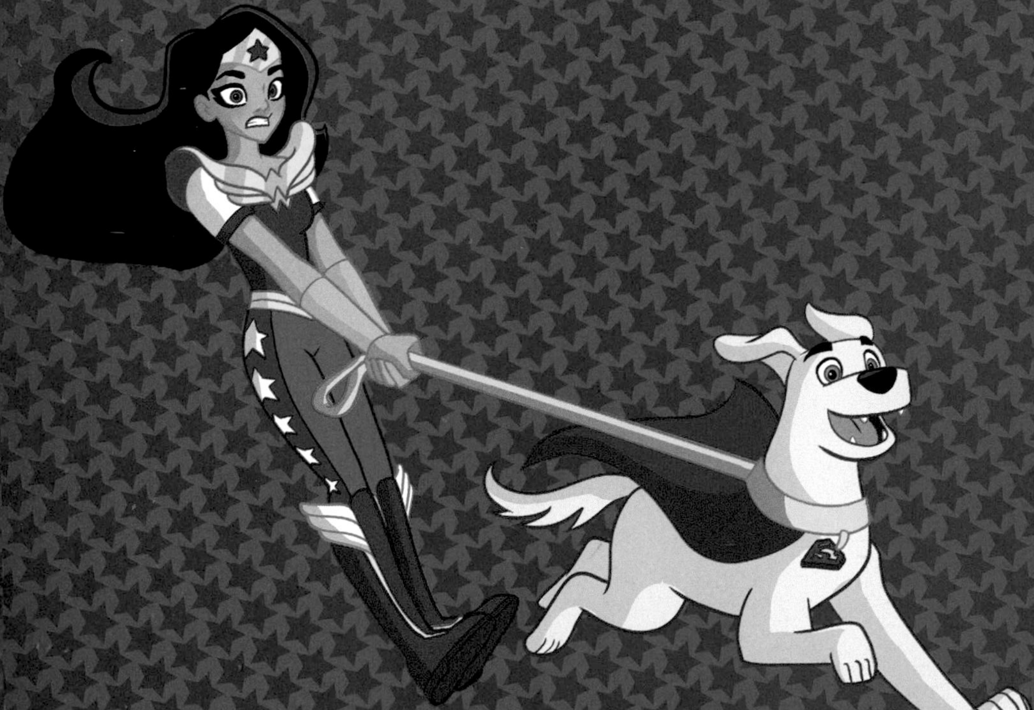

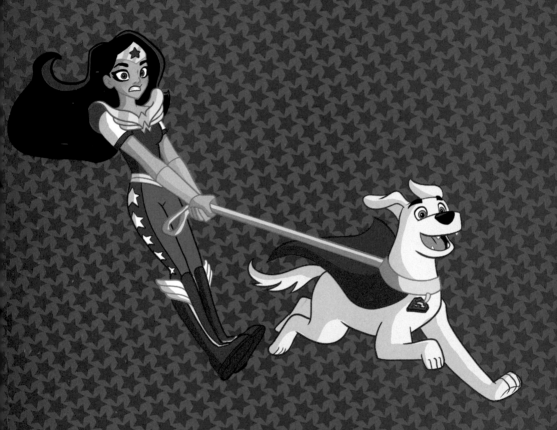

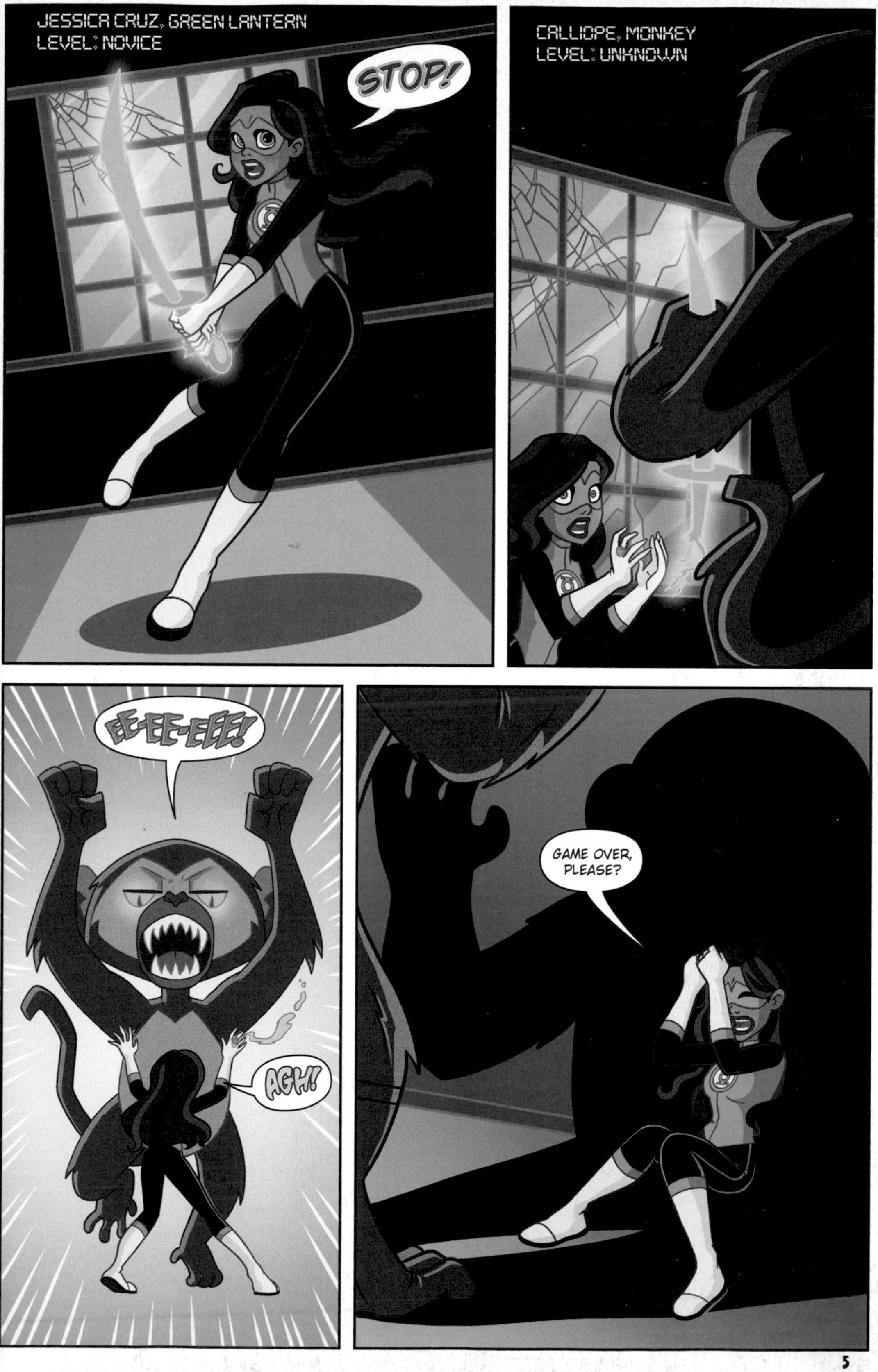
JESSICA CRUZ, GREEN LANTERN
LEVEL: NOVICE
STOP!
CALLIOPE, MONKEY
LEVEL: UNKNOWN
EE-EE-EEE!
AGH!
GAME OVER, PLEASE?

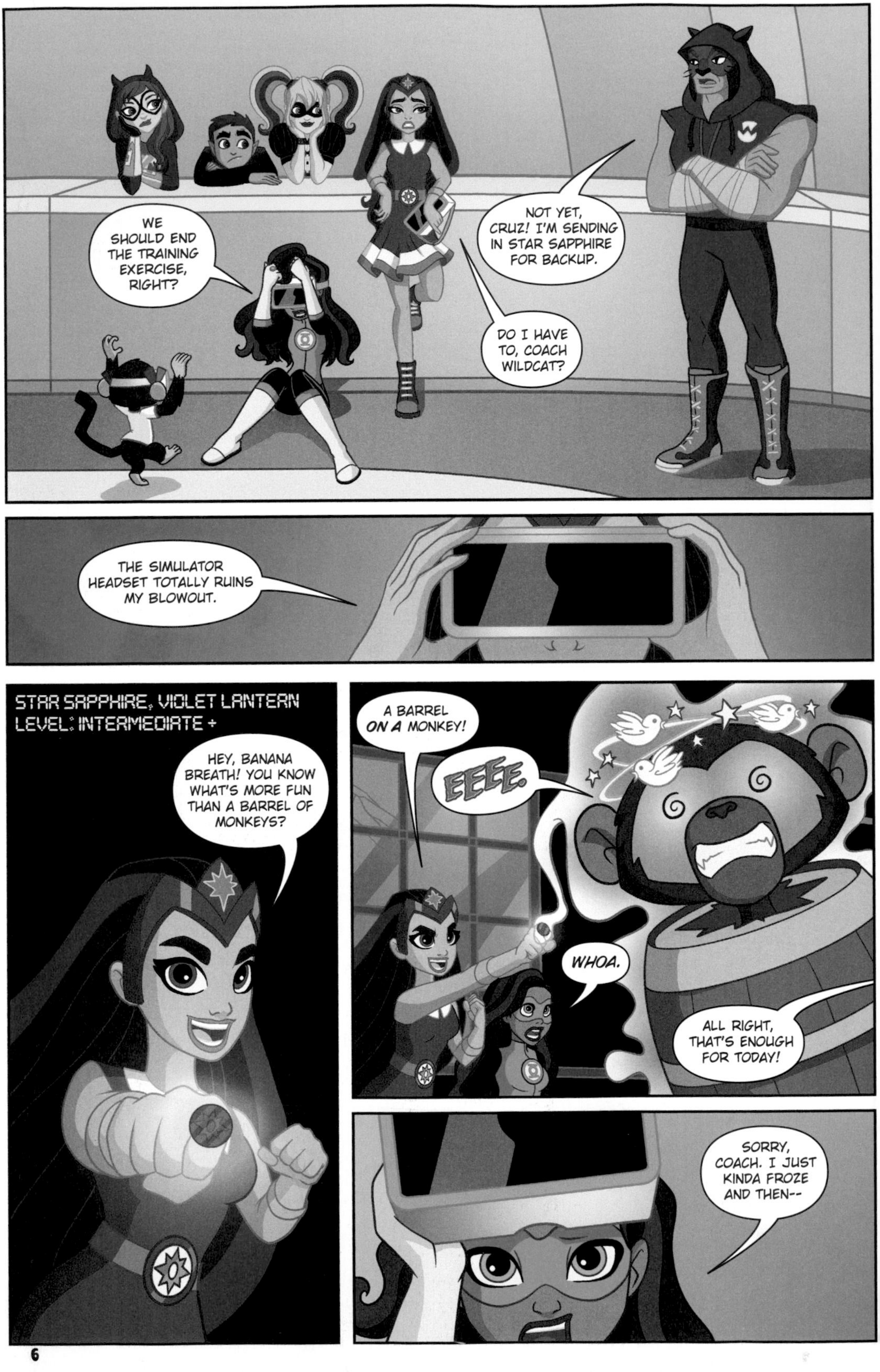
WE SHOULD END THE TRAINING EXERCISE, RIGHT?
NOT YET, CRUZ! I'M SENDING IN STAR SAPPHIRE FOR BACKUP.
DO I HAVE TO, COACH WILDCAT?
THE SIMULATOR HEADSET TOTALLY RUINS MY BLOWOUT.
STAR SAPPHIRE, VIOLET LANTERN
LEVEL: INTERMEDIATE +
HEY, BANANA BREATH! YOU KNOW WHAT'S MORE FUN THAN A BARREL OF MONKEYS?
A BARREL ON A MONKEY!
EEEE.
WHOA.
ALL RIGHT, THAT'S ENOUGH FOR TODAY!
SORRY, COACH. I JUST KINDA FROZE AND THEN--

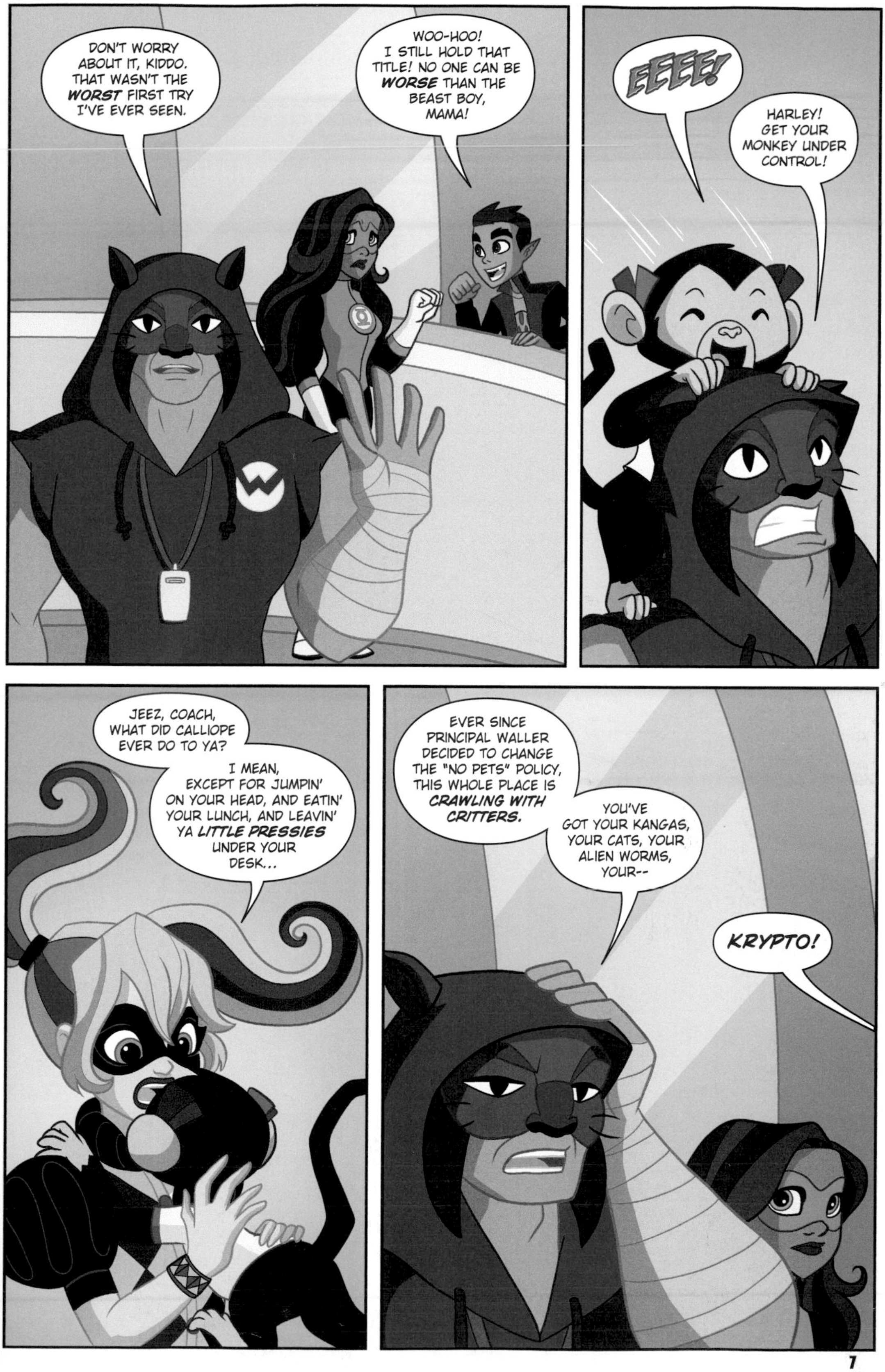
DON'T WORRY ABOUT IT, KIDDO. THAT WASN'T THE *WORST* FIRST TRY I'VE EVER SEEN.
WOO-HOO! I STILL HOLD THAT TITLE! NO ONE CAN BE *WORSE* THAN THE BEAST BOY, MAMA!
EEEE!
HARLEY! GET YOUR MONKEY UNDER CONTROL!
JEEZ, COACH, WHAT DID CALLIOPE EVER DO TO YA?
I MEAN, EXCEPT FOR JUMPIN' ON YOUR HEAD, AND EATIN' YOUR LUNCH, AND LEAVIN' YA *LITTLE PRESSIES* UNDER YOUR DESK...
EVER SINCE PRINCIPAL WALLER DECIDED TO CHANGE THE "NO PETS" POLICY, THIS WHOLE PLACE IS *CRAWLING WITH CRITTERS.*
YOU'VE GOT YOUR KANGAS, YOUR CATS, YOUR ALIEN WORMS, YOUR--
KRYPTO!

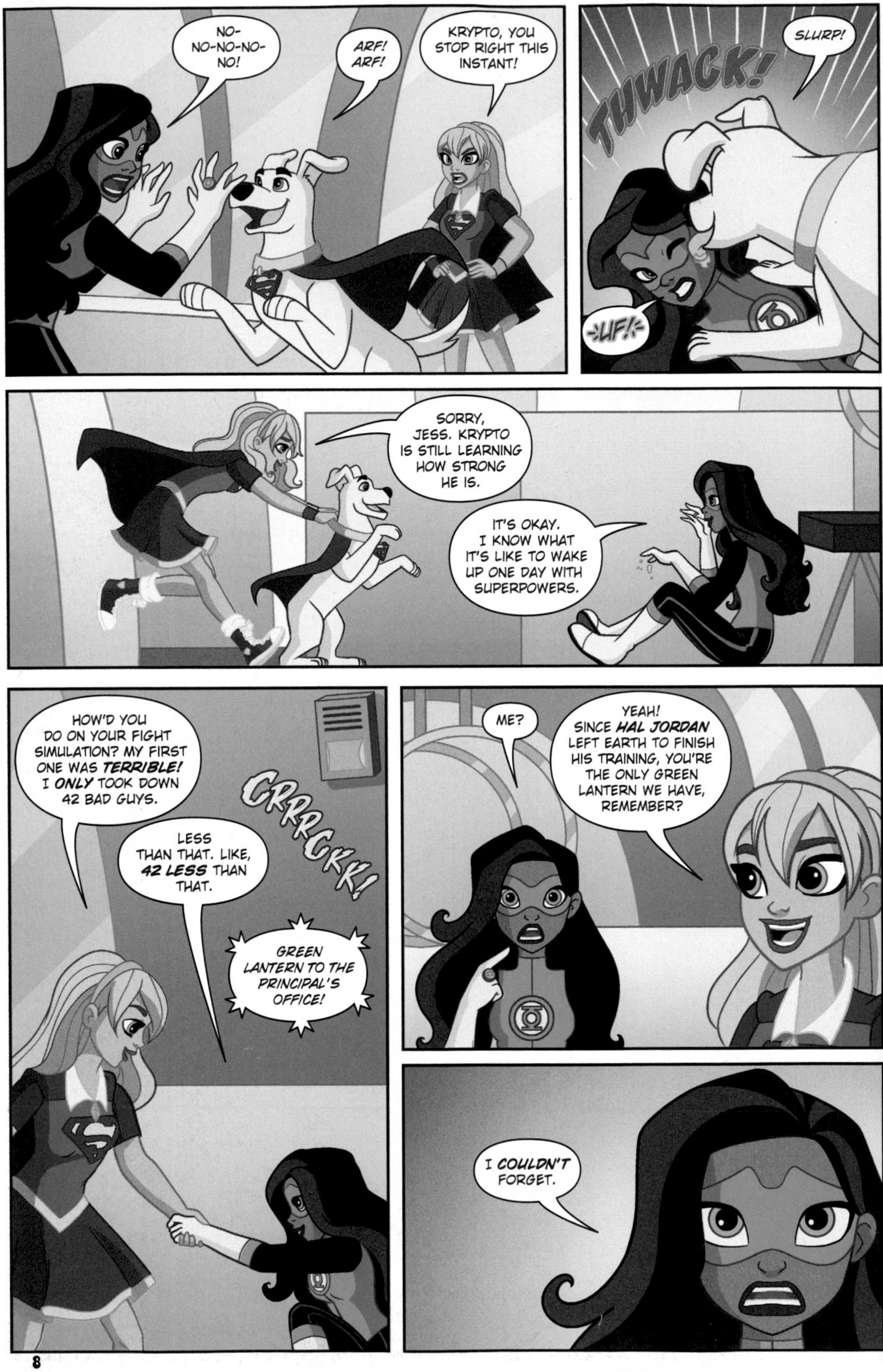
NO-
NO-NO-NO-
NO!
ARF!
ARF!
KRYPTO, YOU STOP RIGHT THIS INSTANT!
THWACK!
SLURP!
UF!
SORRY, JESS. KRYPTO IS STILL LEARNING HOW STRONG HE IS.
IT'S OKAY. I KNOW WHAT IT'S LIKE TO WAKE UP ONE DAY WITH SUPERPOWERS.
HOW'D YOU DO ON YOUR FIGHT SIMULATION? MY FIRST ONE WAS TERRIBLE! I ONLY TOOK DOWN 42 BAD GUYS.
CRRRCKK!
LESS THAN THAT. LIKE, 42 LESS THAN THAT.
GREEN LANTERN TO THE PRINCIPAL'S OFFICE!
ME?
YEAH! SINCE HAL JORDAN LEFT EARTH TO FINISH HIS TRAINING, YOU'RE THE ONLY GREEN LANTERN WE HAVE, REMEMBER?
I COULDN'T FORGET.

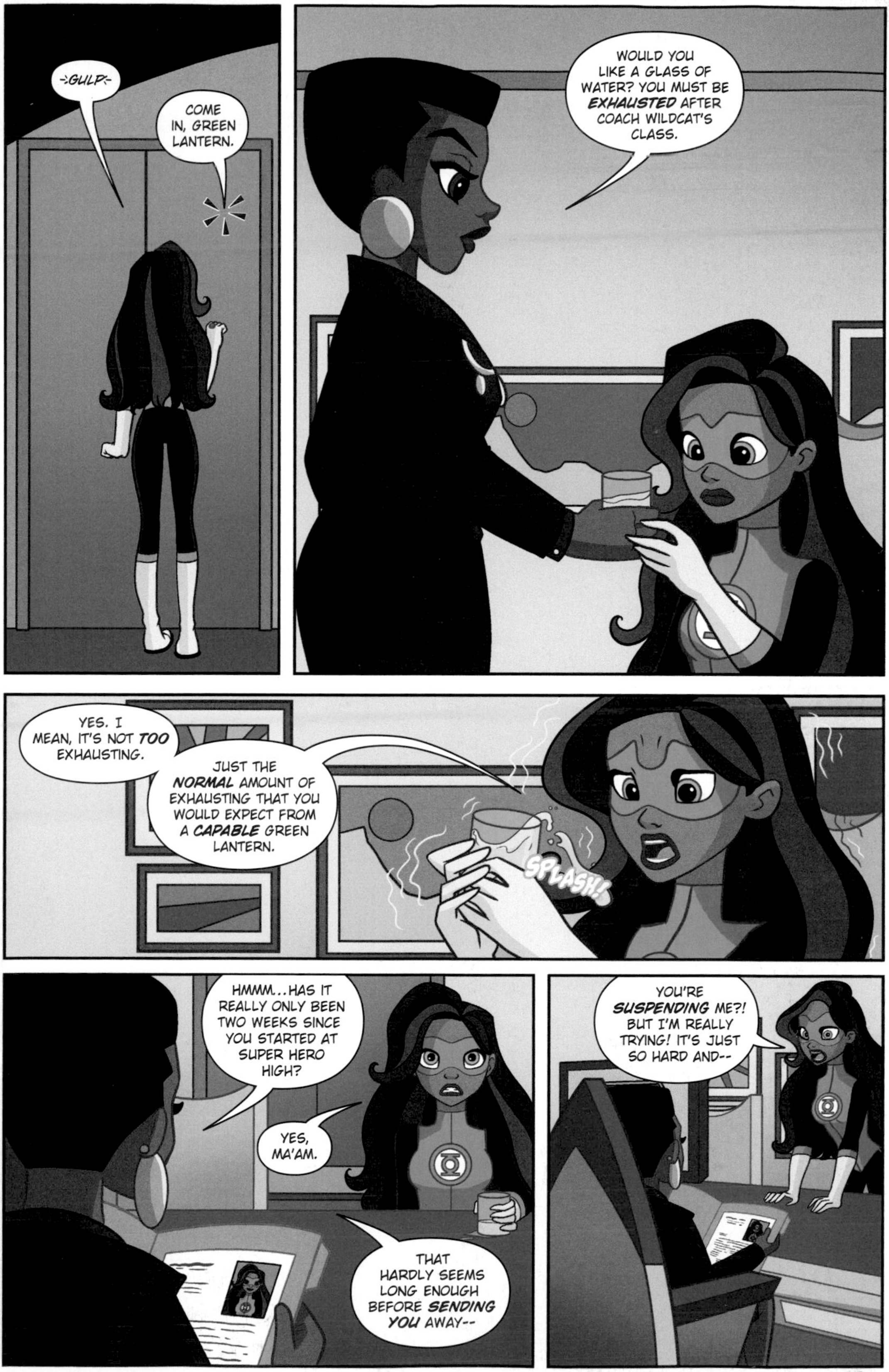
-GULP-
COME IN, GREEN LANTERN.
WOULD YOU LIKE A GLASS OF WATER? YOU MUST BE **EXHAUSTED** AFTER COACH WILDCAT'S CLASS.
YES. I MEAN, IT'S NOT **TOO** EXHAUSTING.
JUST THE **NORMAL** AMOUNT OF EXHAUSTING THAT YOU WOULD EXPECT FROM A **CAPABLE** GREEN LANTERN.
SPLASH!
HMMM...HAS IT REALLY ONLY BEEN TWO WEEKS SINCE YOU STARTED AT SUPER HERO HIGH?
YES, MA'AM.
THAT HARDLY SEEMS LONG ENOUGH BEFORE **SENDING YOU** AWAY--
YOU'RE **SUSPENDING** ME?! BUT I'M REALLY TRYING! IT'S JUST SO HARD AND--

HA! SIT DOWN, SIT DOWN. YOU'RE **NOT** BEING SUSPENDED.

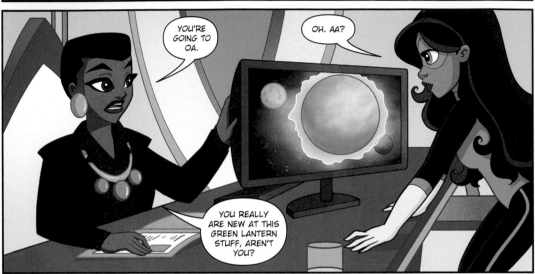

YOU'RE GOING TO OA.

OH. AA?

YOU REALLY ARE NEW AT THIS GREEN LANTERN STUFF, AREN'T YOU?

"OA IS THE PLANET HEADQUARTERS OF THE GREEN LANTERN CORPS.

"OUR PREVIOUS GREEN LANTERN, **HAL JORDAN**, IS CURRENTLY FINISHING HIS TRAINING ON OA.

"AS YOU KNOW, THE GREEN LANTERN RING CHOOSES ITS BEARER WITHOUT ANY GUIDANCE FROM THE CORPS. THE RING SENSES WHO WILL USE IT TO **SPREAD THE LIGHT**."

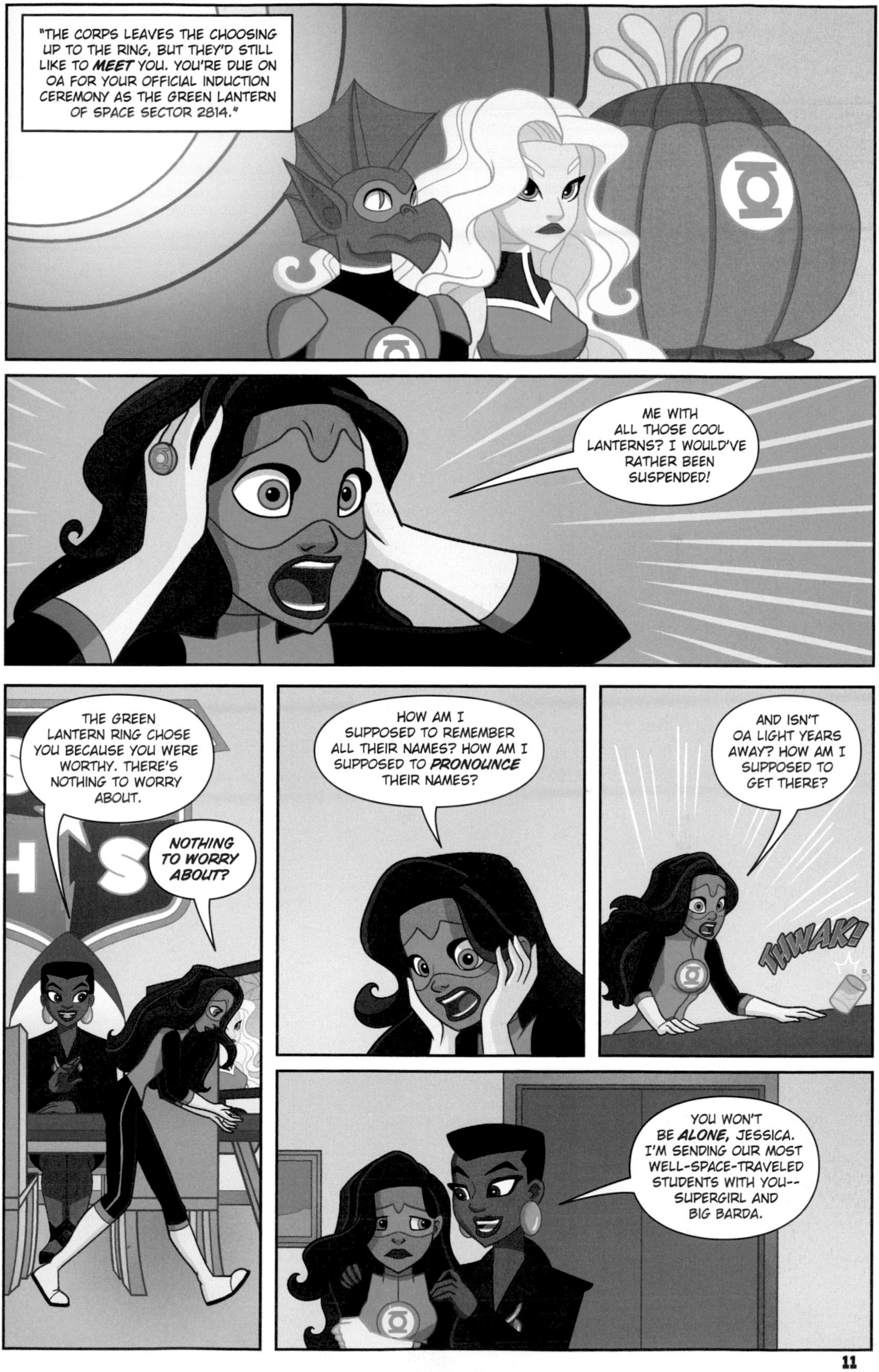
"THE CORPS LEAVES THE CHOOSING UP TO THE RING, BUT THEY'D STILL LIKE TO MEET YOU. YOU'RE DUE ON OA FOR YOUR OFFICIAL INDUCTION CEREMONY AS THE GREEN LANTERN OF SPACE SECTOR 2814."
ME WITH ALL THOSE COOL LANTERNS? I WOULD'VE RATHER BEEN SUSPENDED!
THE GREEN LANTERN RING CHOSE YOU BECAUSE YOU WERE WORTHY. THERE'S NOTHING TO WORRY ABOUT.
NOTHING TO WORRY ABOUT?
HOW AM I SUPPOSED TO REMEMBER ALL THEIR NAMES? HOW AM I SUPPOSED TO PRONOUNCE THEIR NAMES?
AND ISN'T OA LIGHT YEARS AWAY? HOW AM I SUPPOSED TO GET THERE?
THWAK!
YOU WON'T BE ALONE, JESSICA. I'M SENDING OUR MOST WELL-SPACE-TRAVELED STUDENTS WITH YOU-- SUPERGIRL AND BIG BARDA.

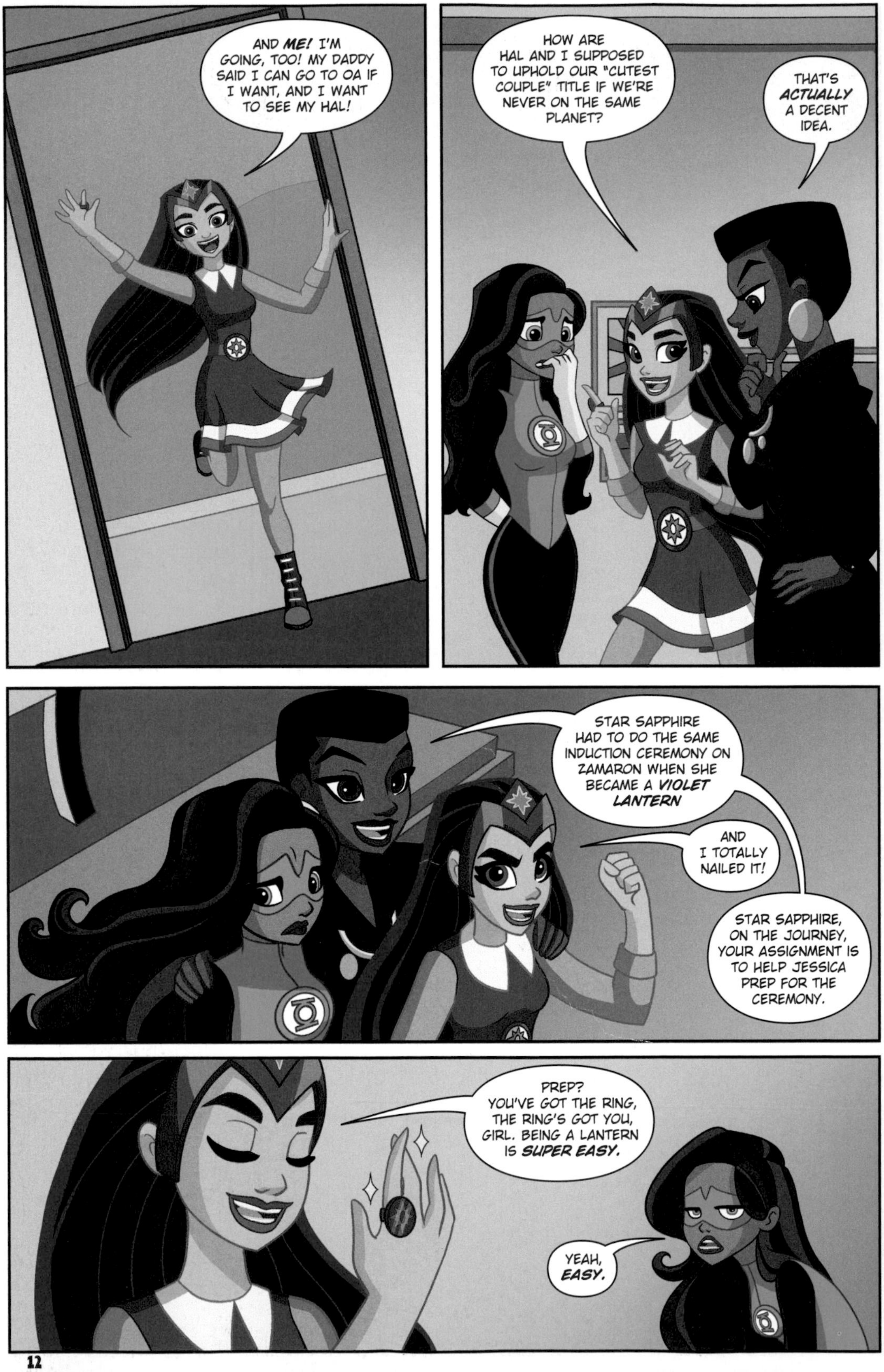
AND ME! I'M GOING, TOO! MY DADDY SAID I CAN GO TO OA IF I WANT, AND I WANT TO SEE MY HAL!
HOW ARE HAL AND I SUPPOSED TO UPHOLD OUR "CUTEST COUPLE" TITLE IF WE'RE NEVER ON THE SAME PLANET?
THAT'S ACTUALLY A DECENT IDEA.
STAR SAPPHIRE HAD TO DO THE SAME INDUCTION CEREMONY ON ZAMARON WHEN SHE BECAME A VIOLET LANTERN
AND I TOTALLY NAILED IT!
STAR SAPPHIRE, ON THE JOURNEY, YOUR ASSIGNMENT IS TO HELP JESSICA PREP FOR THE CEREMONY.
PREP? YOU'VE GOT THE RING, THE RING'S GOT YOU, GIRL. BEING A LANTERN IS SUPER EASY.
YEAH, EASY.

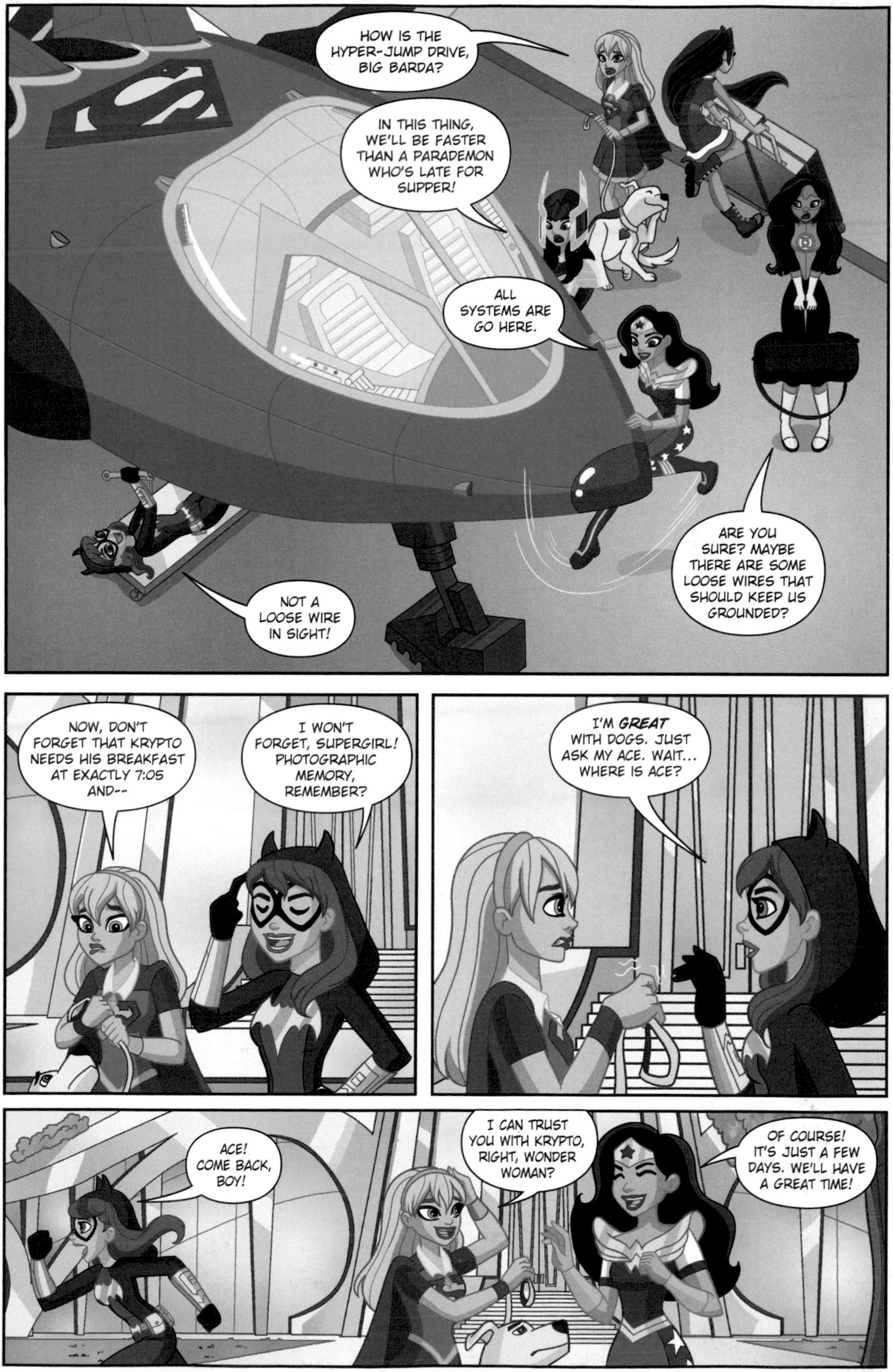
HOW IS THE HYPER-JUMP DRIVE, BIG BARDA?
IN THIS THING, WE'LL BE FASTER THAN A PARADEMON WHO'S LATE FOR SUPPER!
ALL SYSTEMS ARE GO HERE.
ARE YOU SURE? MAYBE THERE ARE SOME LOOSE WIRES THAT SHOULD KEEP US GROUNDED?
NOT A LOOSE WIRE IN SIGHT!
NOW, DON'T FORGET THAT KRYPTO NEEDS HIS BREAKFAST AT EXACTLY 7:05 AND--
I WON'T FORGET, SUPERGIRL! PHOTOGRAPHIC MEMORY, REMEMBER?
I'M ***GREAT*** WITH DOGS. JUST ASK MY ACE. WAIT... WHERE IS ACE?
ACE! COME BACK, BOY!
I CAN TRUST YOU WITH KRYPTO, RIGHT, WONDER WOMAN?
OF COURSE! IT'S JUST A FEW DAYS. WE'LL HAVE A GREAT TIME!

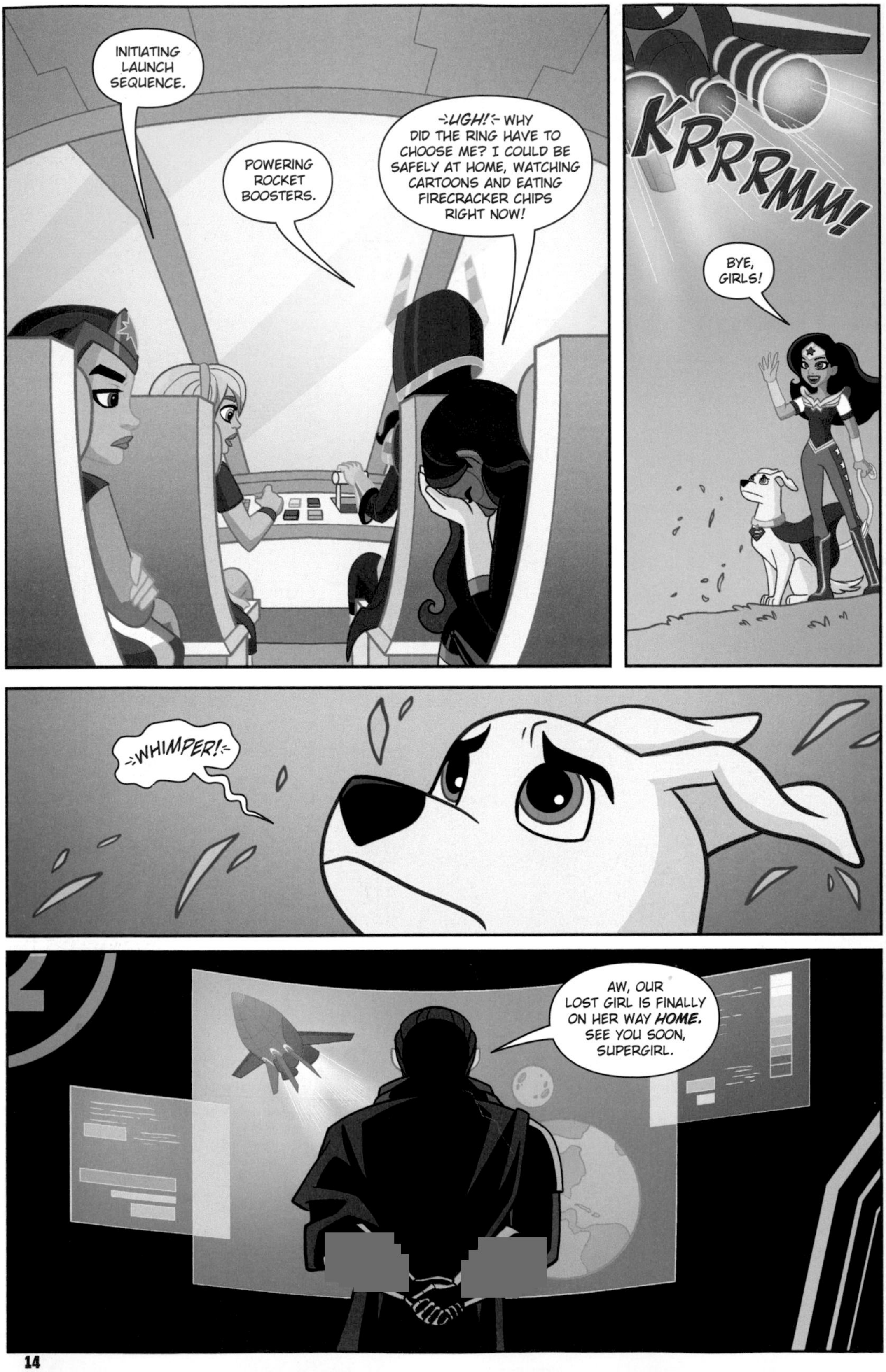
INITIATING LAUNCH SEQUENCE.
POWERING ROCKET BOOSTERS.
-UGH!- WHY DID THE RING HAVE TO CHOOSE ME? I COULD BE SAFELY AT HOME, WATCHING CARTOONS AND EATING FIRECRACKER CHIPS RIGHT NOW!
KRRRMM!
BYE, GIRLS!
-WHIMPER!-
AW, OUR LOST GIRL IS FINALLY ON HER WAY HOME. SEE YOU SOON, SUPERGIRL.

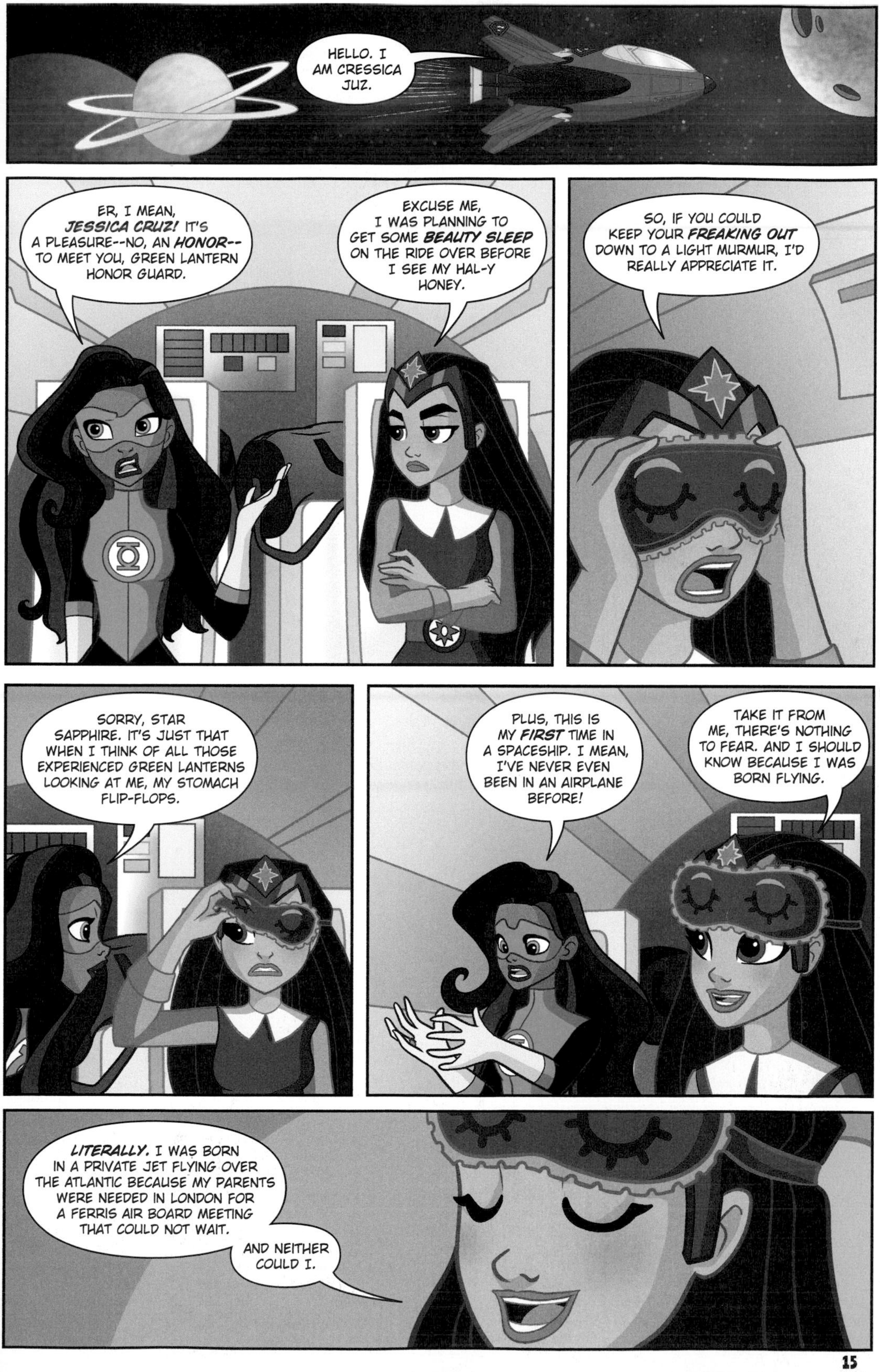
HELLO. I AM CRESSICA JUZ.
ER, I MEAN, JESSICA CRUZ! IT'S A PLEASURE--NO, AN HONOR--TO MEET YOU, GREEN LANTERN HONOR GUARD.
EXCUSE ME, I WAS PLANNING TO GET SOME BEAUTY SLEEP ON THE RIDE OVER BEFORE I SEE MY HAL-Y HONEY.
SO, IF YOU COULD KEEP YOUR FREAKING OUT DOWN TO A LIGHT MURMUR, I'D REALLY APPRECIATE IT.
SORRY, STAR SAPPHIRE. IT'S JUST THAT WHEN I THINK OF ALL THOSE EXPERIENCED GREEN LANTERNS LOOKING AT ME, MY STOMACH FLIP-FLOPS.
PLUS, THIS IS MY FIRST TIME IN A SPACESHIP. I MEAN, I'VE NEVER EVEN BEEN IN AN AIRPLANE BEFORE!
TAKE IT FROM ME, THERE'S NOTHING TO FEAR. AND I SHOULD KNOW BECAUSE I WAS BORN FLYING.
LITERALLY. I WAS BORN IN A PRIVATE JET FLYING OVER THE ATLANTIC BECAUSE MY PARENTS WERE NEEDED IN LONDON FOR A FERRIS AIR BOARD MEETING THAT COULD NOT WAIT.
AND NEITHER COULD I.

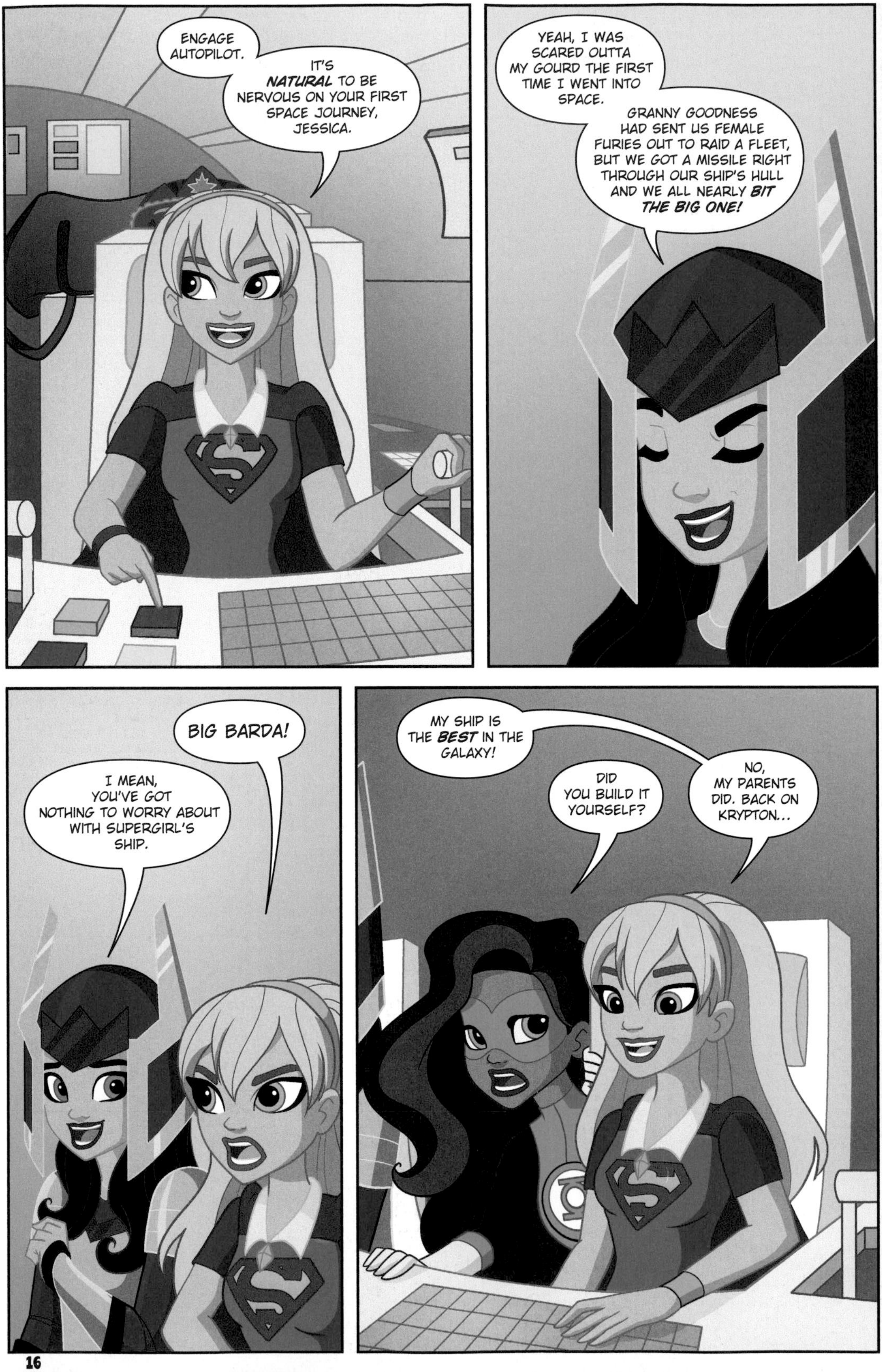
ENGAGE AUTOPILOT.
IT'S **NATURAL** TO BE NERVOUS ON YOUR FIRST SPACE JOURNEY, JESSICA.
YEAH, I WAS SCARED OUTTA MY GOURD THE FIRST TIME I WENT INTO SPACE.
GRANNY GOODNESS HAD SENT US FEMALE FURIES OUT TO RAID A FLEET, BUT WE GOT A MISSILE RIGHT THROUGH OUR SHIP'S HULL AND WE ALL NEARLY ***BIT THE BIG ONE!***
I MEAN, YOU'VE GOT NOTHING TO WORRY ABOUT WITH SUPERGIRL'S SHIP.
BIG BARDA!
MY SHIP IS THE ***BEST*** IN THE GALAXY!
DID YOU BUILD IT YOURSELF?
NO, MY PARENTS DID. BACK ON KRYPTON...

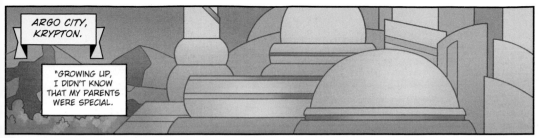

ARGO CITY, KRYPTON.

"GROWING UP, I DIDN'T KNOW THAT MY PARENTS WERE SPECIAL.

"I FIGURED EVERYONE'S PARENTS WERE AWESOME SCIENTISTS!"

<HURRY UP, KARA!*>

ARF!

<WE WANT TO BE FIRST IN LINE FOR THE GEOLOGY EXHIBIT AT THE SCIENCE MUSEUM!>

*TRANSLATED FROM KRYPTONIAN.

<SORRY, KRYPTO, I KNOW YOU LOVE SLURP-O-SWAP ICE CREAM, BUT-->

SLURP!

-:WHINE!:-

RRRUMMBLE!

"THE EARTHQUAKES WERE THE FIRST WARNING SIGN THAT SOMETHING WAS REALLY **WRONG** ON KRYPTON."

<GREAT RAO!>

ARF?

<ARE YOU ALL RIGHT, KARA-BEAR?>

<IT'S OKAY, KARA. WE'LL **NEVER** LET ANYTHING HAPPEN TO YOU.>

17

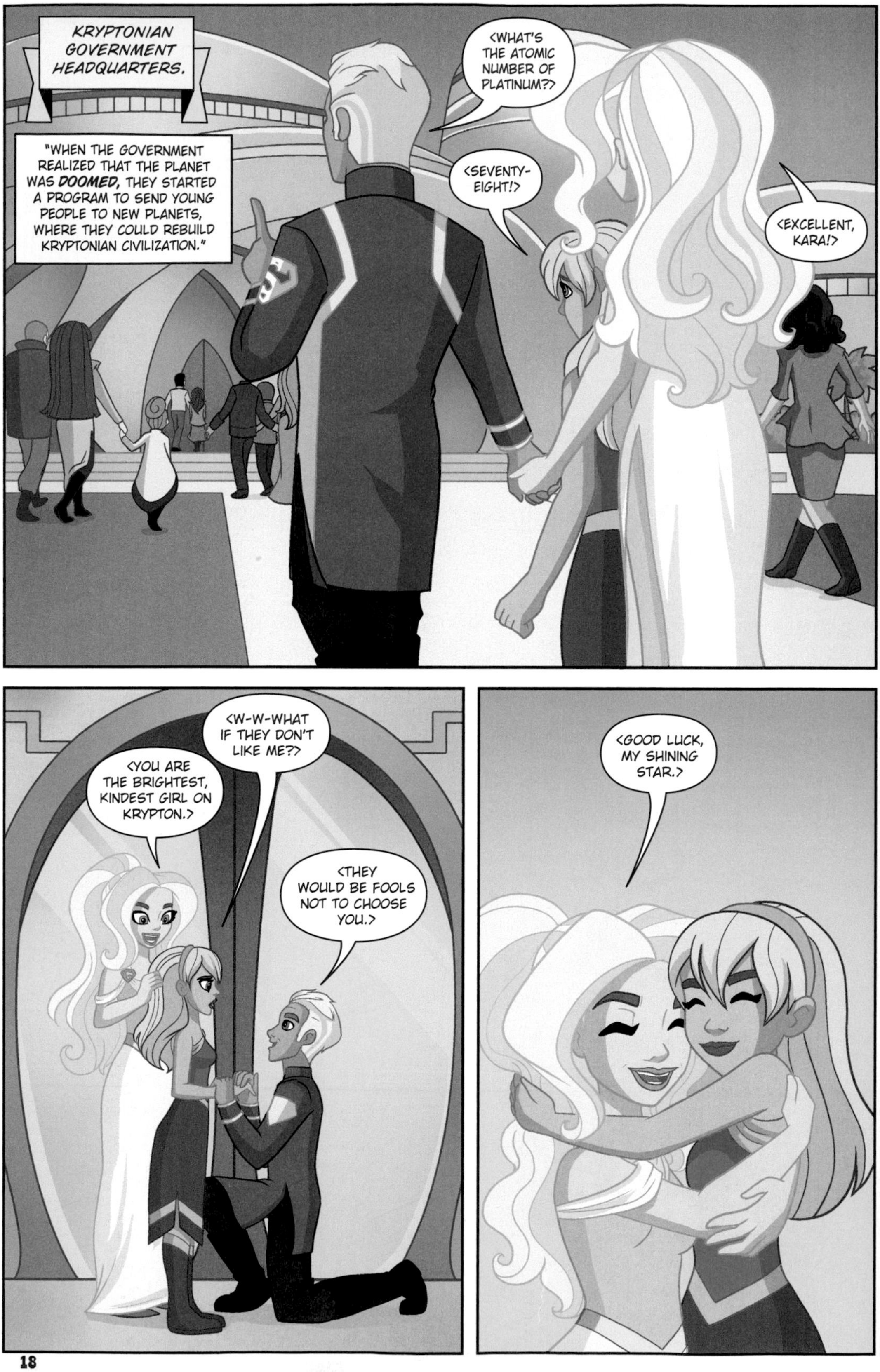
KRYPTONIAN GOVERNMENT HEADQUARTERS.
"WHEN THE GOVERNMENT REALIZED THAT THE PLANET WAS **DOOMED**, THEY STARTED A PROGRAM TO SEND YOUNG PEOPLE TO NEW PLANETS, WHERE THEY COULD REBUILD KRYPTONIAN CIVILIZATION."
<WHAT'S THE ATOMIC NUMBER OF PLATINUM?>
<SEVENTY-EIGHT!>
<EXCELLENT, KARA!>
<W-W-WHAT IF THEY DON'T LIKE ME?>
<YOU ARE THE BRIGHTEST, KINDEST GIRL ON KRYPTON.>
<THEY WOULD BE FOOLS NOT TO CHOOSE YOU.>
<GOOD LUCK, MY SHINING STAR.>

WOW.

<CONGRATULATIONS ON BEING A KRYPTONIAN COLONIZER SEMI-FINALIST!>

T○◇♀ ◇ii̇Ti̇◌♀ *

*"THE FUTURE."

<COLONIZERS WILL BE ASSISTED BY THE BEST TECHNOLOGY, INCLUDING *TERRAFORMING ROBOTS* THAT CAN TRANSFORM THE SURFACE OF ANY BARREN PLANET INTO A RICH, BEAUTIFUL WORLD LIKE KRYPTON!>

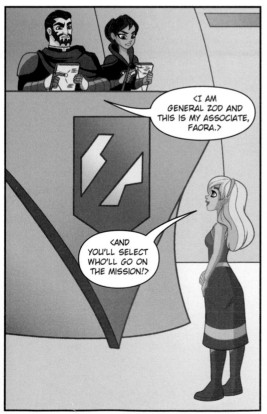

<I AM GENERAL ZOD AND THIS IS MY ASSOCIATE, FAORA.>

<AND YOU'LL SELECT WHO'LL GO ON THE MISSION!>

<YES, I'M QUITE AWARE OF MY DUTIES, MISS, UM?>

<KARA ZOR-EL, DAUGHTER OF ALURA AND ZOR-EL.>

"I THOUGHT MY INTERVIEW WITH THE SELECTION COMMITTEE WAS PRETTY GOOD..."

<THE MAD SCIENTISTS' DAUGHTER? LIKE SHE HAS A CHANCE!>

<I CAN'T WAIT TO BREAK THE NEWS TO THAT LOSER ZOR-EL.>

"BUT I WASN'T CHOSEN FOR THE MISSION."

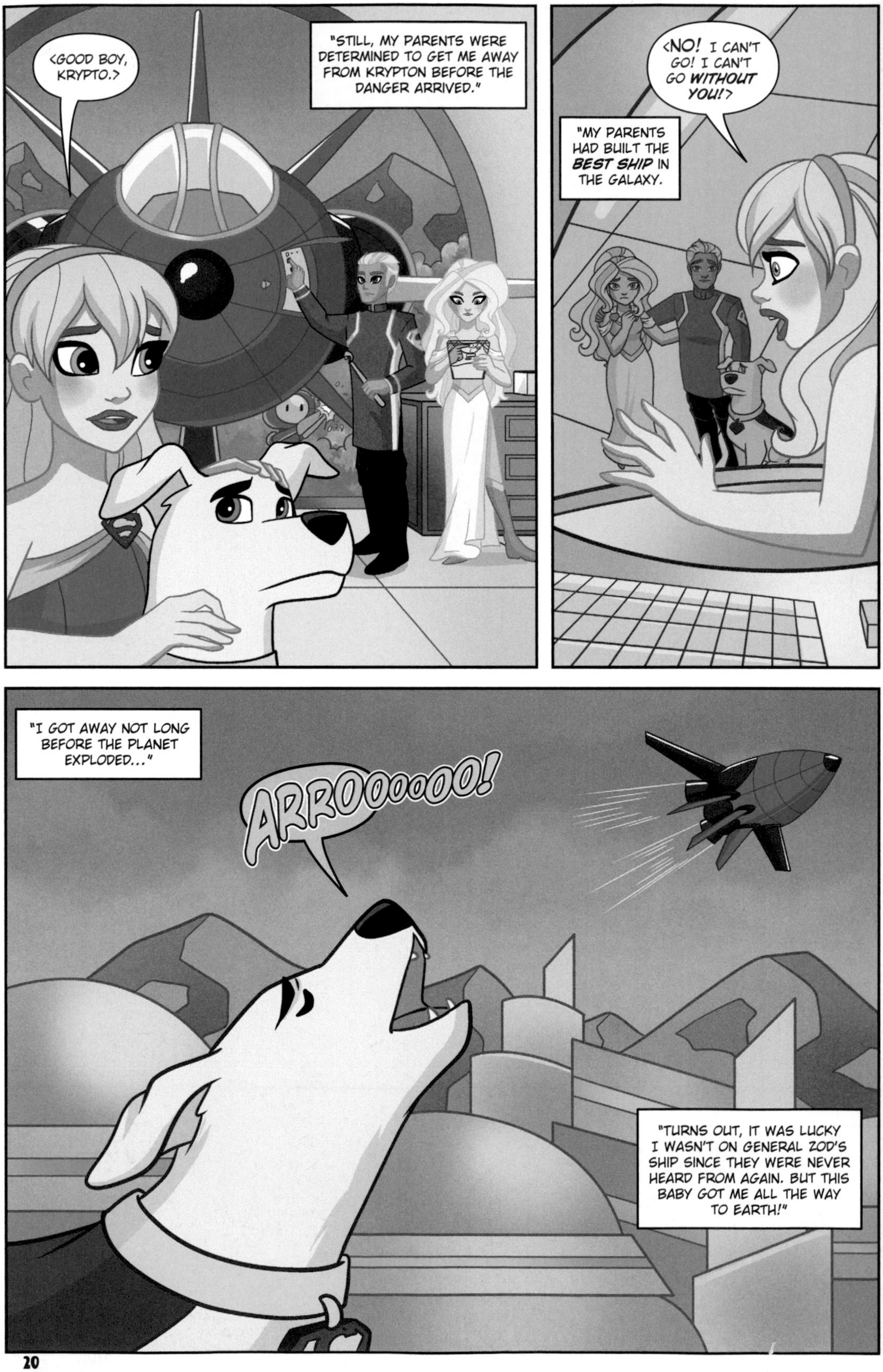

<GOOD BOY, KRYPTO.>
"STILL, MY PARENTS WERE DETERMINED TO GET ME AWAY FROM KRYPTON BEFORE THE DANGER ARRIVED."
<NO! I CAN'T GO! I CAN'T GO WITHOUT YOU!>
"MY PARENTS HAD BUILT THE BEST SHIP IN THE GALAXY.
"I GOT AWAY NOT LONG BEFORE THE PLANET EXPLODED..."
ARROOOOOOO!
"TURNS OUT, IT WAS LUCKY I WASN'T ON GENERAL ZOD'S SHIP SINCE THEY WERE NEVER HEARD FROM AGAIN. BUT THIS BABY GOT ME ALL THE WAY TO EARTH!"

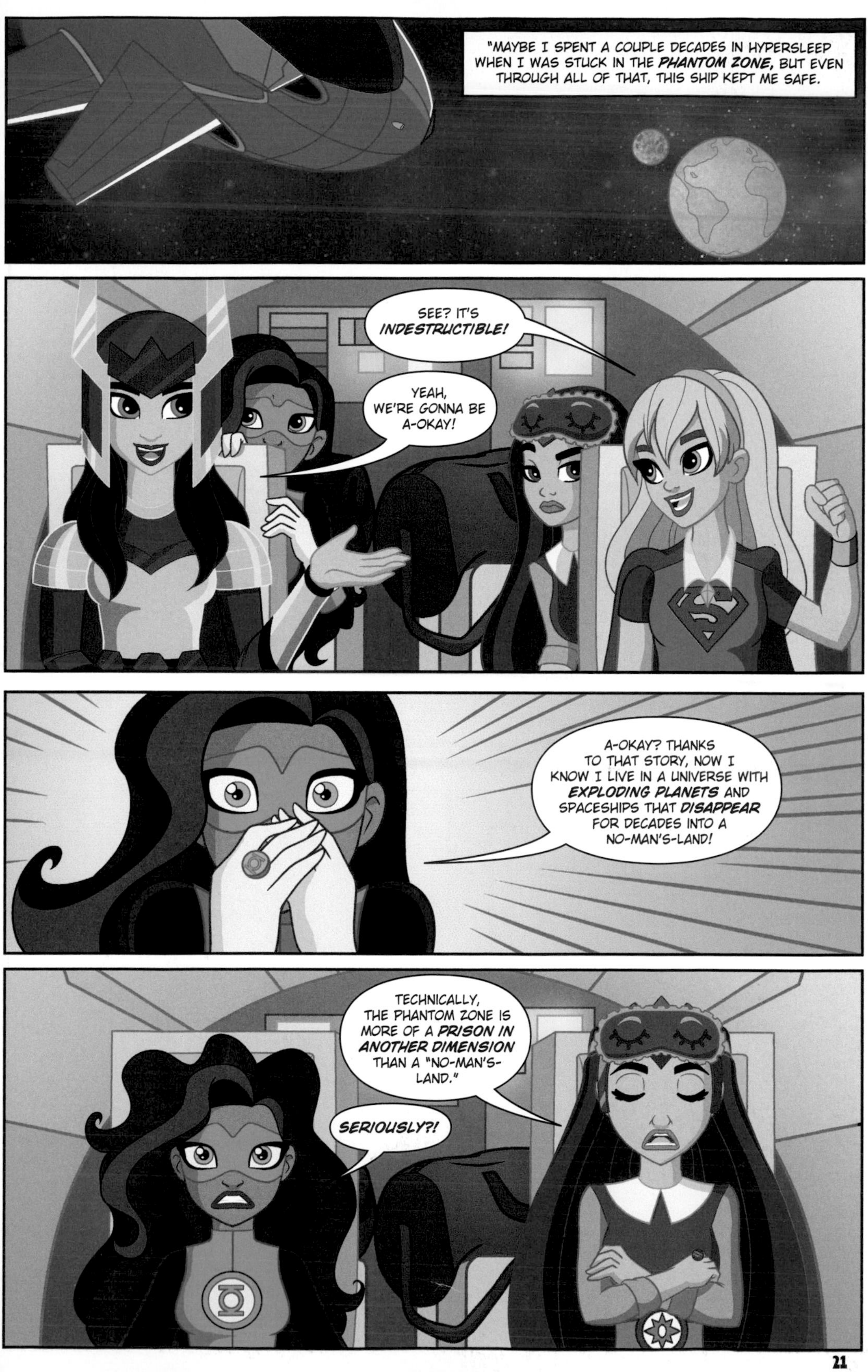
"MAYBE I SPENT A COUPLE DECADES IN HYPERSLEEP WHEN I WAS STUCK IN THE ***PHANTOM ZONE,*** BUT EVEN THROUGH ALL OF THAT, THIS SHIP KEPT ME SAFE.
SEE? IT'S ***INDESTRUCTIBLE!***
YEAH, WE'RE GONNA BE A-OKAY!
A-OKAY? THANKS TO THAT STORY, NOW I KNOW I LIVE IN A UNIVERSE WITH ***EXPLODING PLANETS*** AND SPACESHIPS THAT ***DISAPPEAR*** FOR DECADES INTO A NO-MAN'S-LAND!
TECHNICALLY, THE PHANTOM ZONE IS MORE OF A ***PRISON IN ANOTHER DIMENSION*** THAN A "NO-MAN'S-LAND."
SERIOUSLY?!

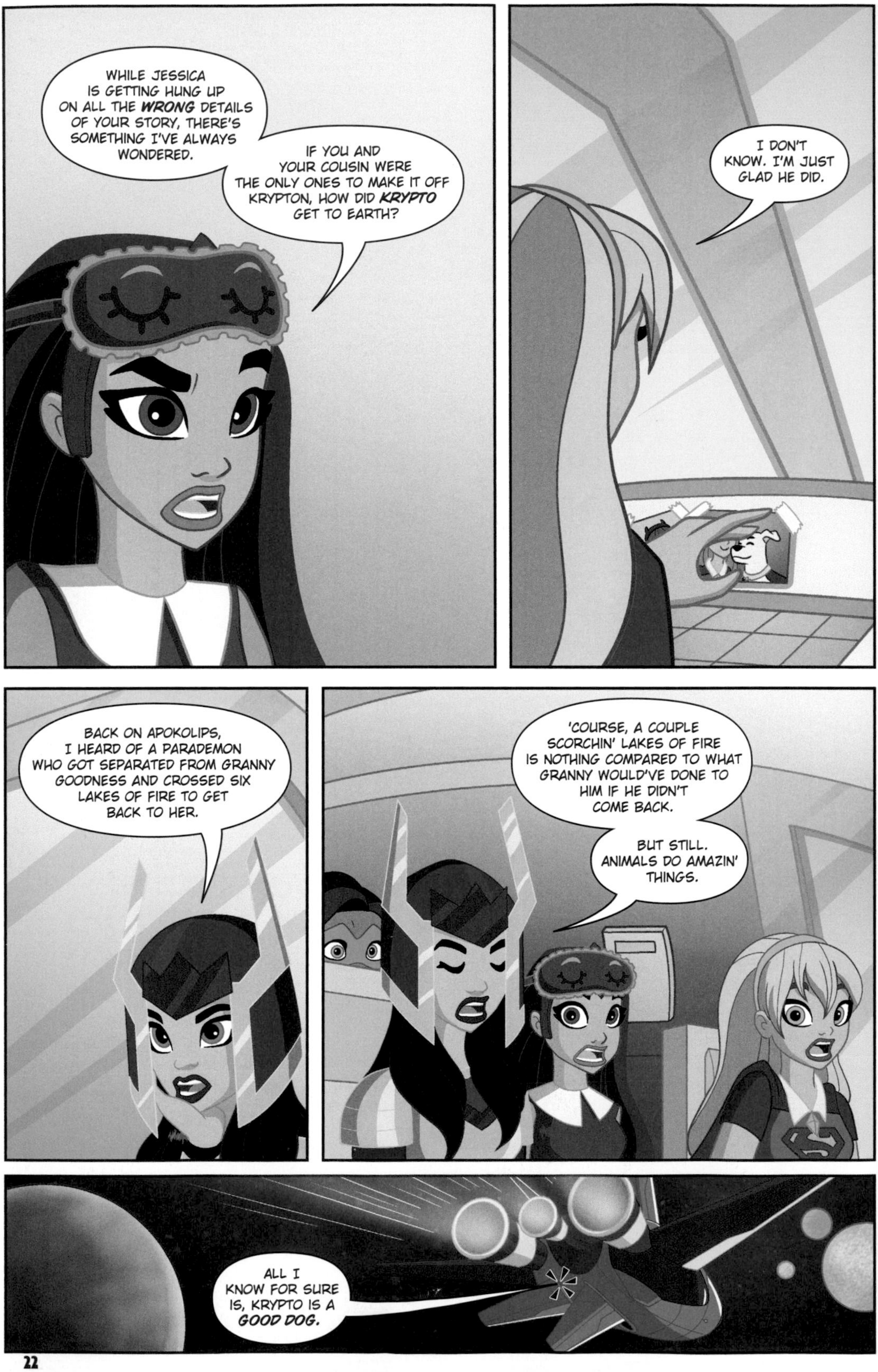
WHILE JESSICA IS GETTING HUNG UP ON ALL THE WRONG DETAILS OF YOUR STORY, THERE'S SOMETHING I'VE ALWAYS WONDERED.
IF YOU AND YOUR COUSIN WERE THE ONLY ONES TO MAKE IT OFF KRYPTON, HOW DID KRYPTO GET TO EARTH?
I DON'T KNOW. I'M JUST GLAD HE DID.
BACK ON APOKOLIPS, I HEARD OF A PARADEMON WHO GOT SEPARATED FROM GRANNY GOODNESS AND CROSSED SIX LAKES OF FIRE TO GET BACK TO HER.
'COURSE, A COUPLE SCORCHIN' LAKES OF FIRE IS NOTHING COMPARED TO WHAT GRANNY WOULD'VE DONE TO HIM IF HE DIDN'T COME BACK.
BUT STILL. ANIMALS DO AMAZIN' THINGS.
ALL I KNOW FOR SURE IS, KRYPTO IS A GOOD DOG.

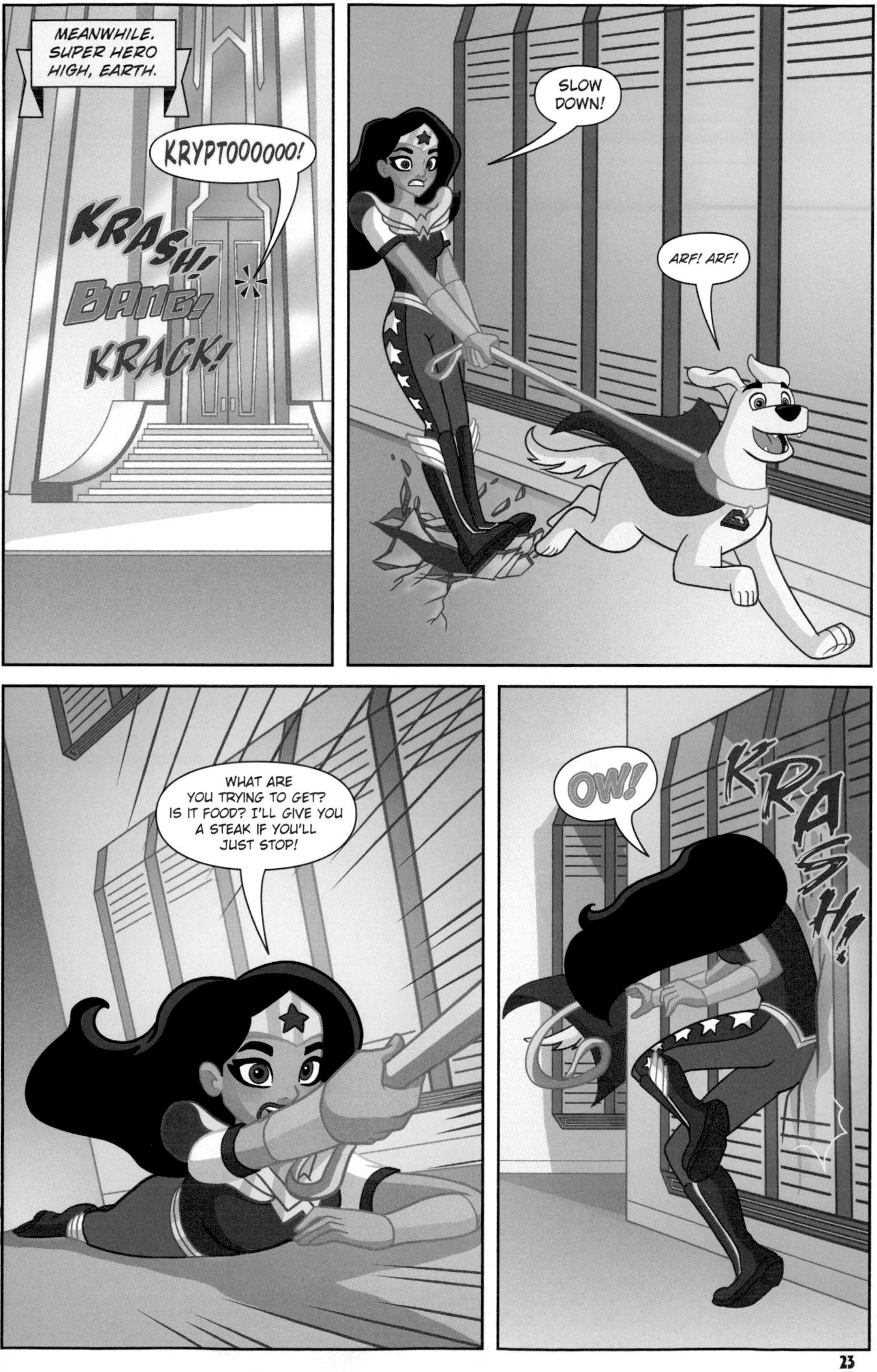
MEANWHILE. SUPER HERO HIGH, EARTH.
KRYPTOOOOOO!
KRASH! BANG! KRACK!
SLOW DOWN!
ARF! ARF!
WHAT ARE YOU TRYING TO GET? IS IT FOOD? I'LL GIVE YOU A STEAK IF YOU'LL JUST STOP!
OW!
KRASH!

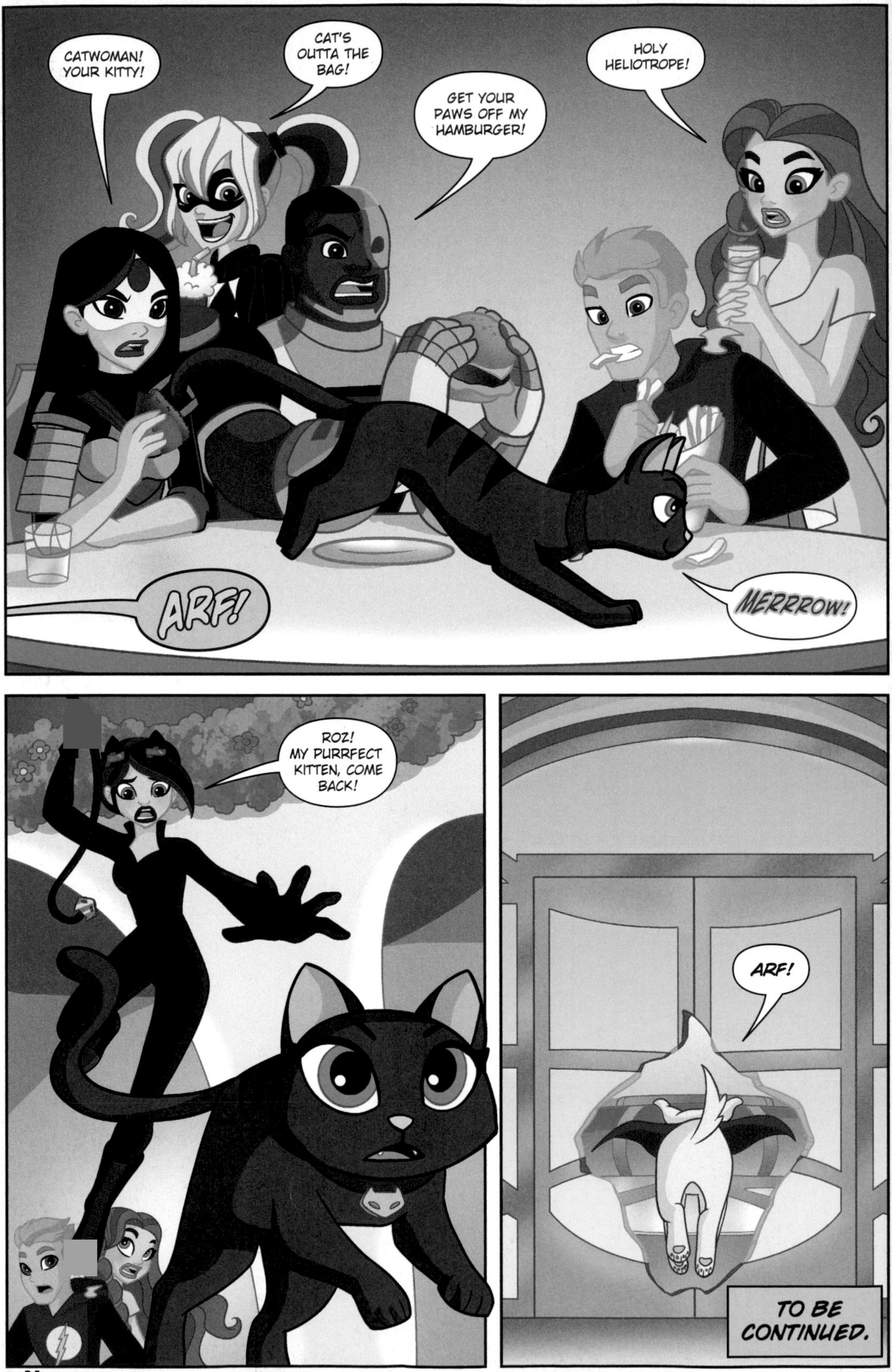
CATWOMAN! YOUR KITTY!
CAT'S OUTTA THE BAG!
GET YOUR PAWS OFF MY HAMBURGER!
HOLY HELIOTROPE!
ARF!
MERRROW!
ROZ! MY PURRFECT KITTEN, COME BACK!
ARF!
TO BE CONTINUED.

CHAPTER TWO

SPACE WALK WITH ME

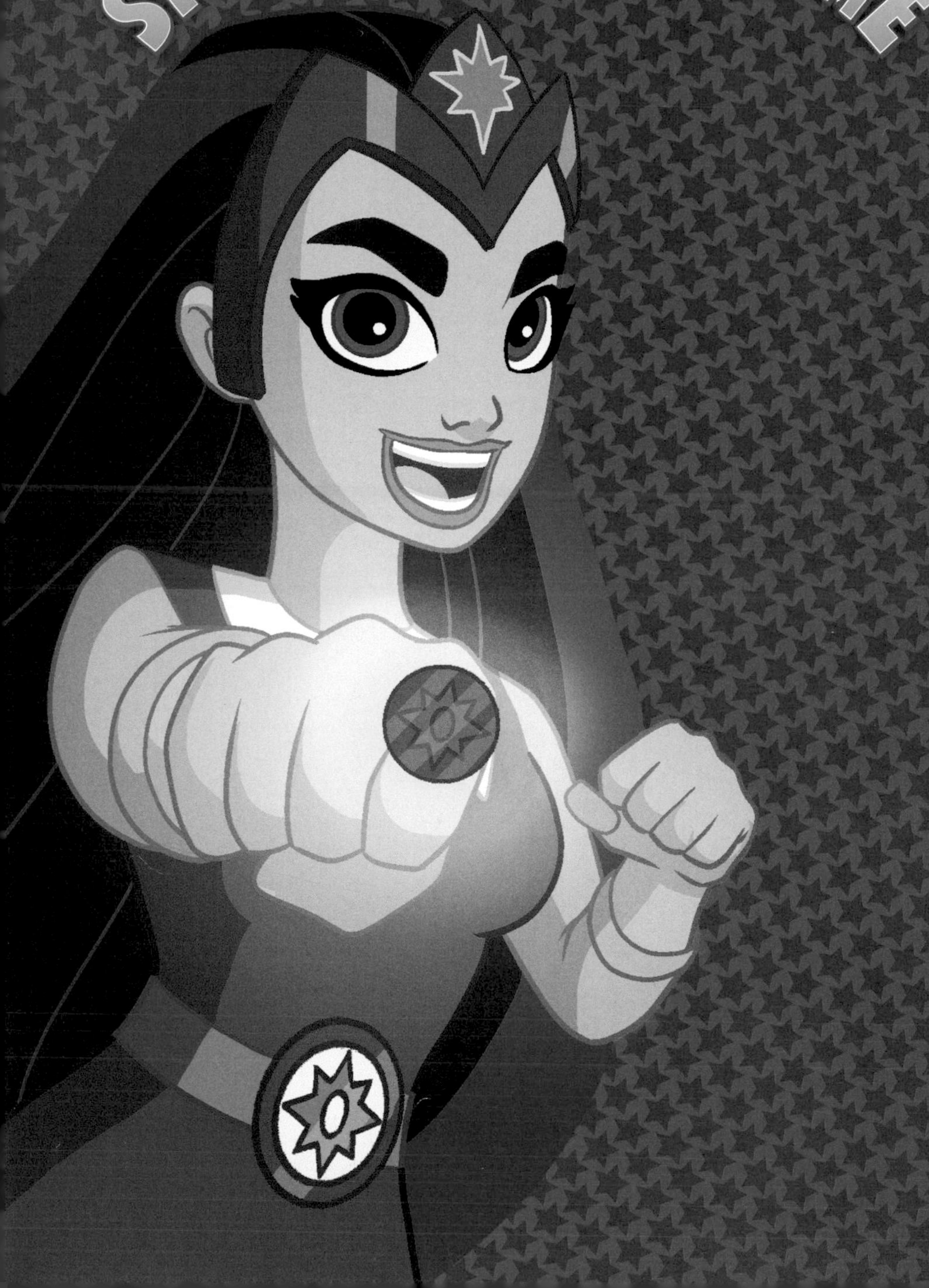

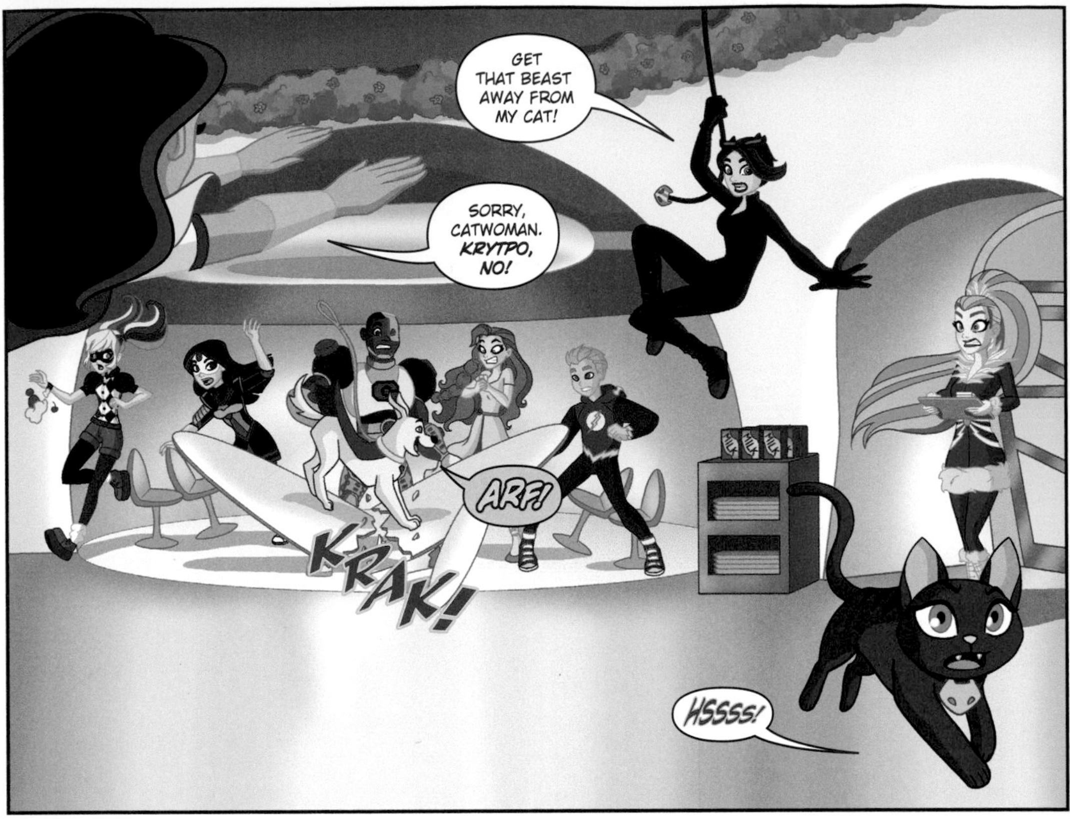
GET THAT BEAST AWAY FROM MY CAT!
SORRY, CATWOMAN. **KRYTPO, NO!**
ARF!
KRAK!
HSSSS!

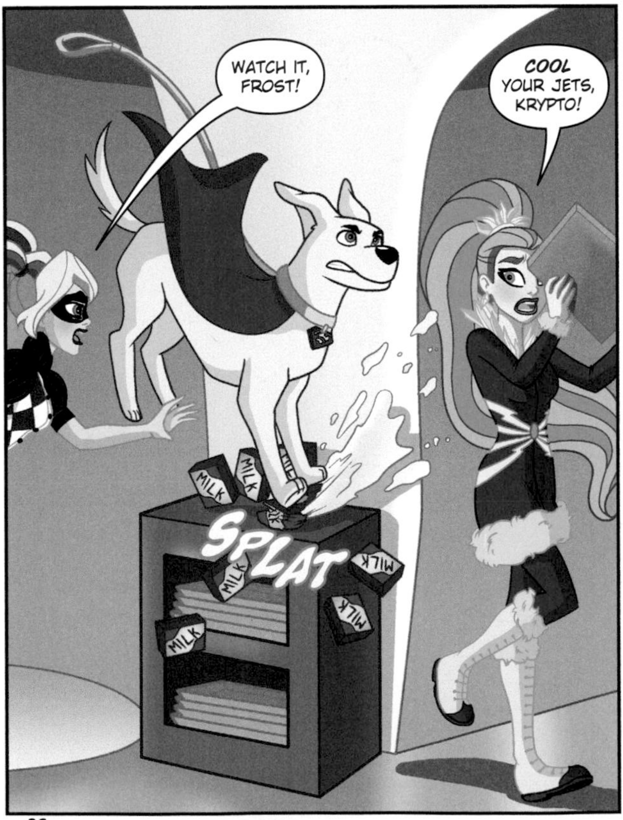
WATCH IT, FROST!
COOL YOUR JETS, KRYPTO!
MILK
SPLAT

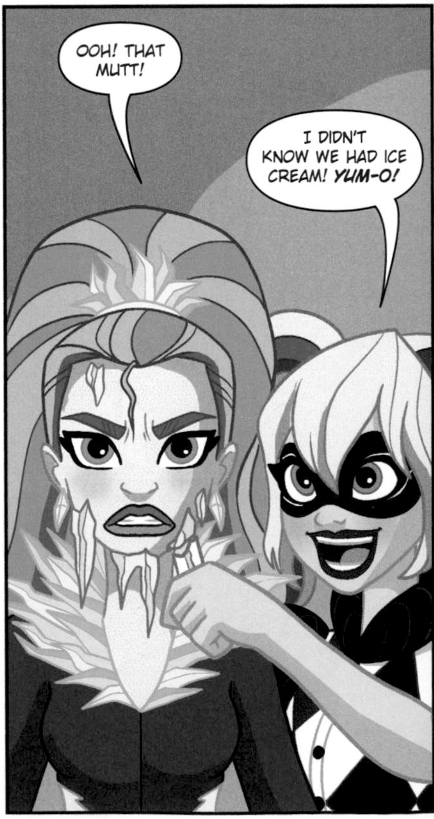
OOH! THAT MUTT!
I DIDN'T KNOW WE HAD ICE CREAM! **YUM-O!**

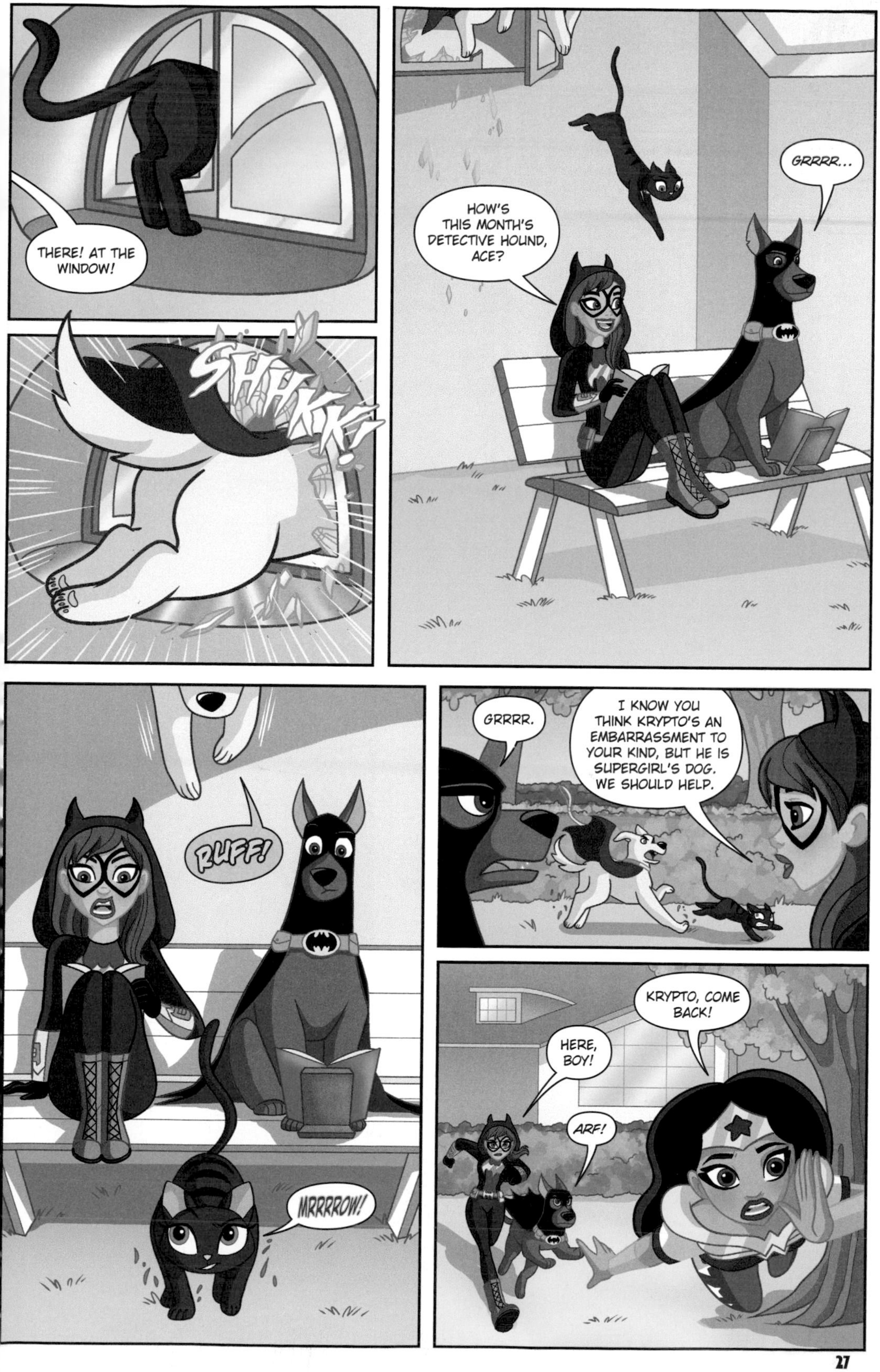
THERE! AT THE WINDOW!
SHHKKK!
HOW'S THIS MONTH'S DETECTIVE HOUND, ACE?
GRRRR...
RUFF!
MRRRROW!
GRRRR.
I KNOW YOU THINK KRYPTO'S AN EMBARRASSMENT TO YOUR KIND, BUT HE IS SUPERGIRL'S DOG. WE SHOULD HELP.
KRYPTO, COME BACK!
HERE, BOY!
ARF!

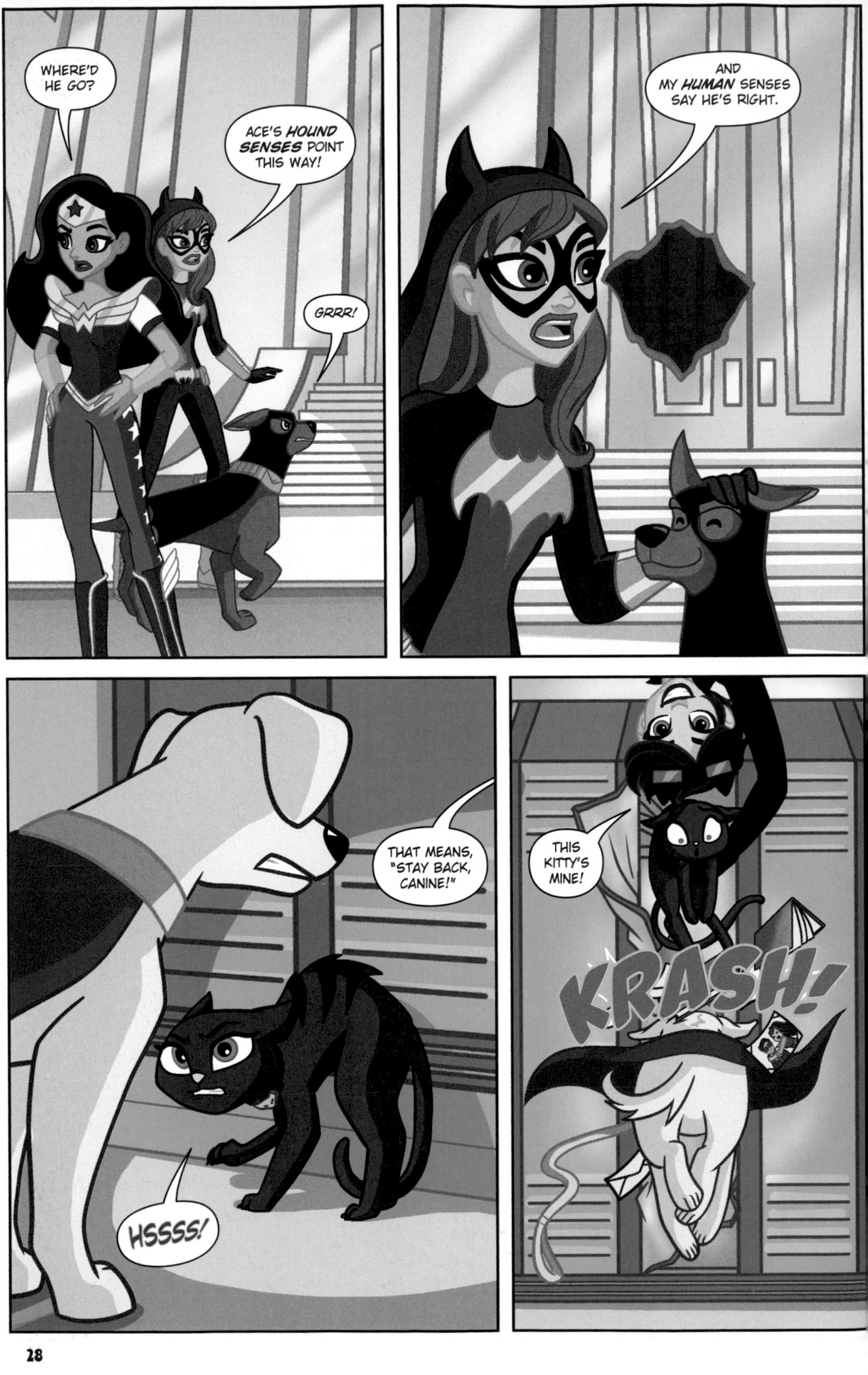
WHERE'D HE GO?
ACE'S HOUND SENSES POINT THIS WAY!
GRRR!
AND MY HUMAN SENSES SAY HE'S RIGHT.
THAT MEANS, "STAY BACK, CANINE!"
HSSSS!
THIS KITTY'S MINE!
KRASH!

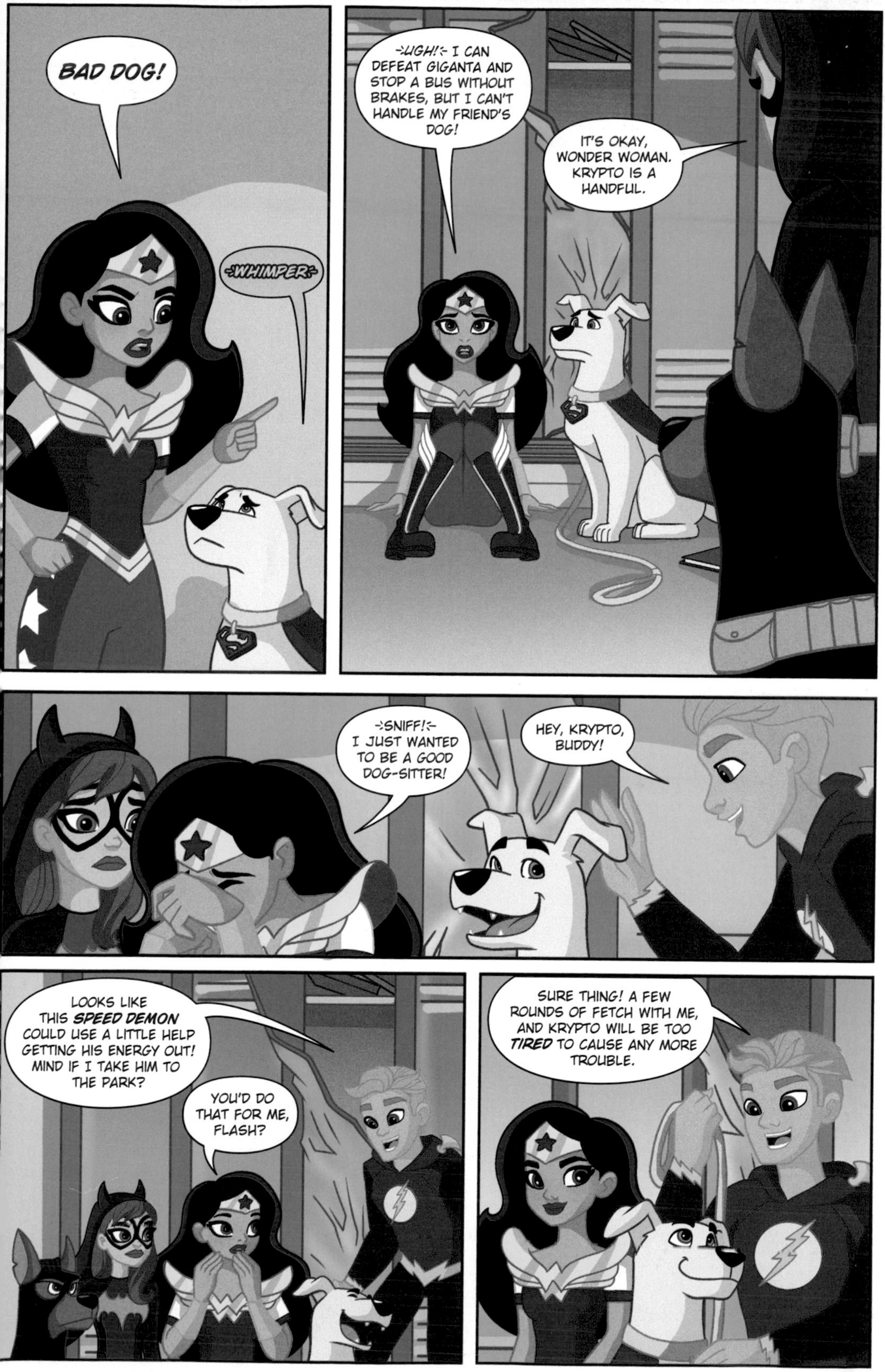
BAD DOG!
-WHIMPER-
-UGH!- I CAN DEFEAT GIGANTA AND STOP A BUS WITHOUT BRAKES, BUT I CAN'T HANDLE MY FRIEND'S DOG!
IT'S OKAY, WONDER WOMAN. KRYPTO IS A HANDFUL.
-SNIFF!- I JUST WANTED TO BE A GOOD DOG-SITTER!
HEY, KRYPTO, BUDDY!
LOOKS LIKE THIS SPEED DEMON COULD USE A LITTLE HELP GETTING HIS ENERGY OUT! MIND IF I TAKE HIM TO THE PARK?
YOU'D DO THAT FOR ME, FLASH?
SURE THING! A FEW ROUNDS OF FETCH WITH ME, AND KRYPTO WILL BE TOO TIRED TO CAUSE ANY MORE TROUBLE.

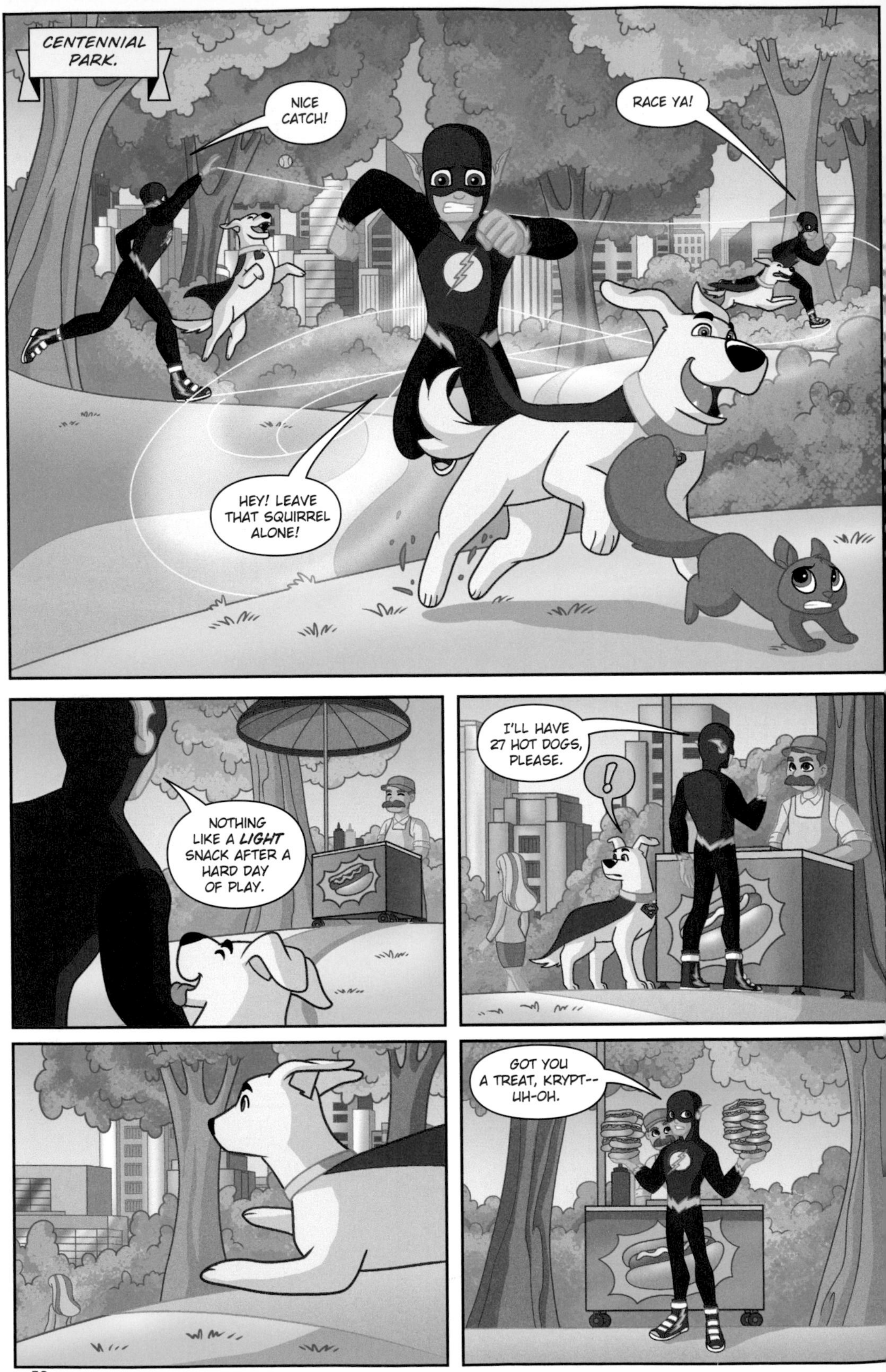
CENTENNIAL PARK.
NICE CATCH!
RACE YA!
HEY! LEAVE THAT SQUIRREL ALONE!
NOTHING LIKE A *LIGHT* SNACK AFTER A HARD DAY OF PLAY.
I'LL HAVE 27 HOT DOGS, PLEASE.
!
GOT YOU A TREAT, KRYPT-- UH-OH.

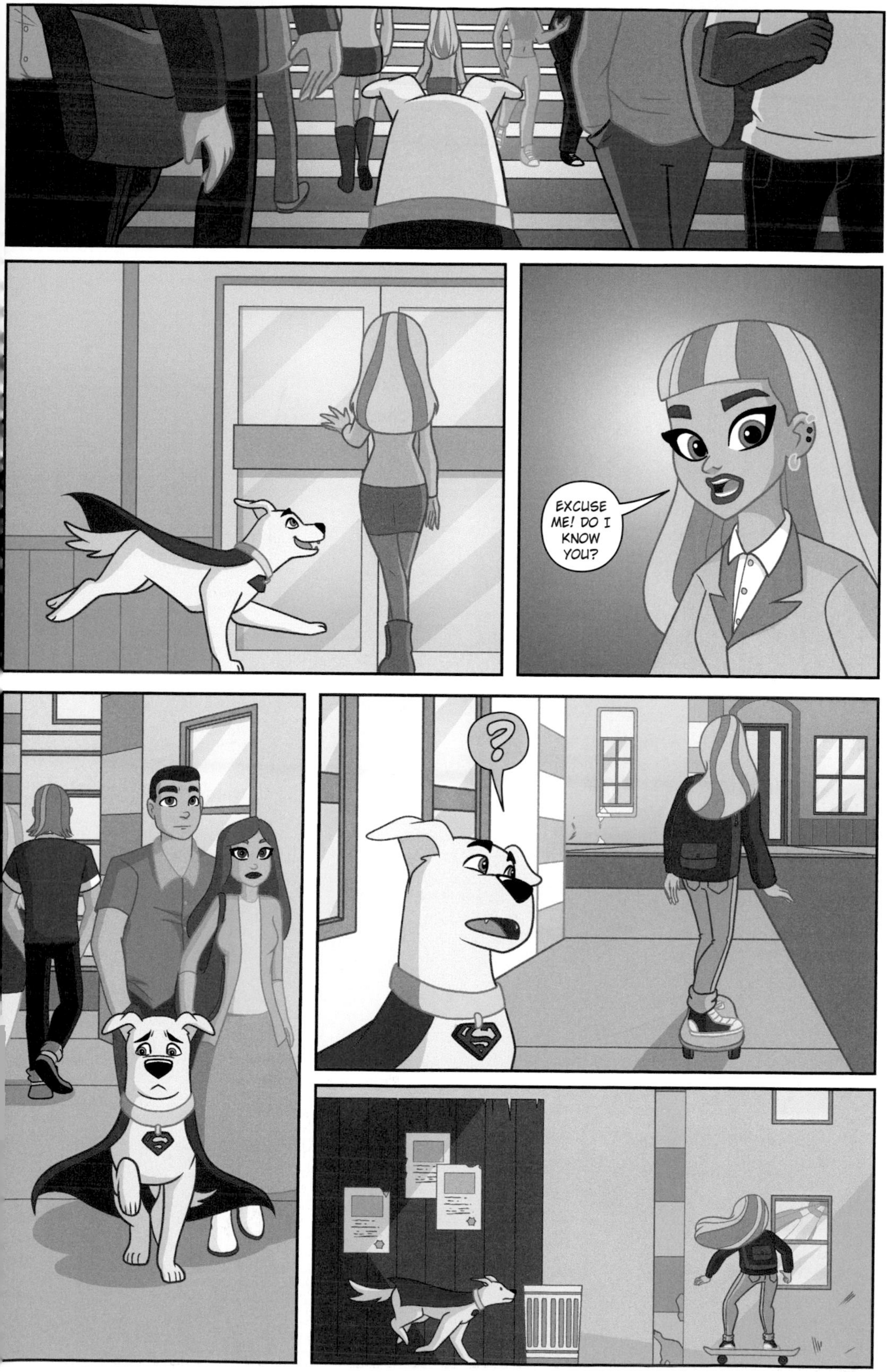
EXCUSE ME! DO I KNOW YOU?
?

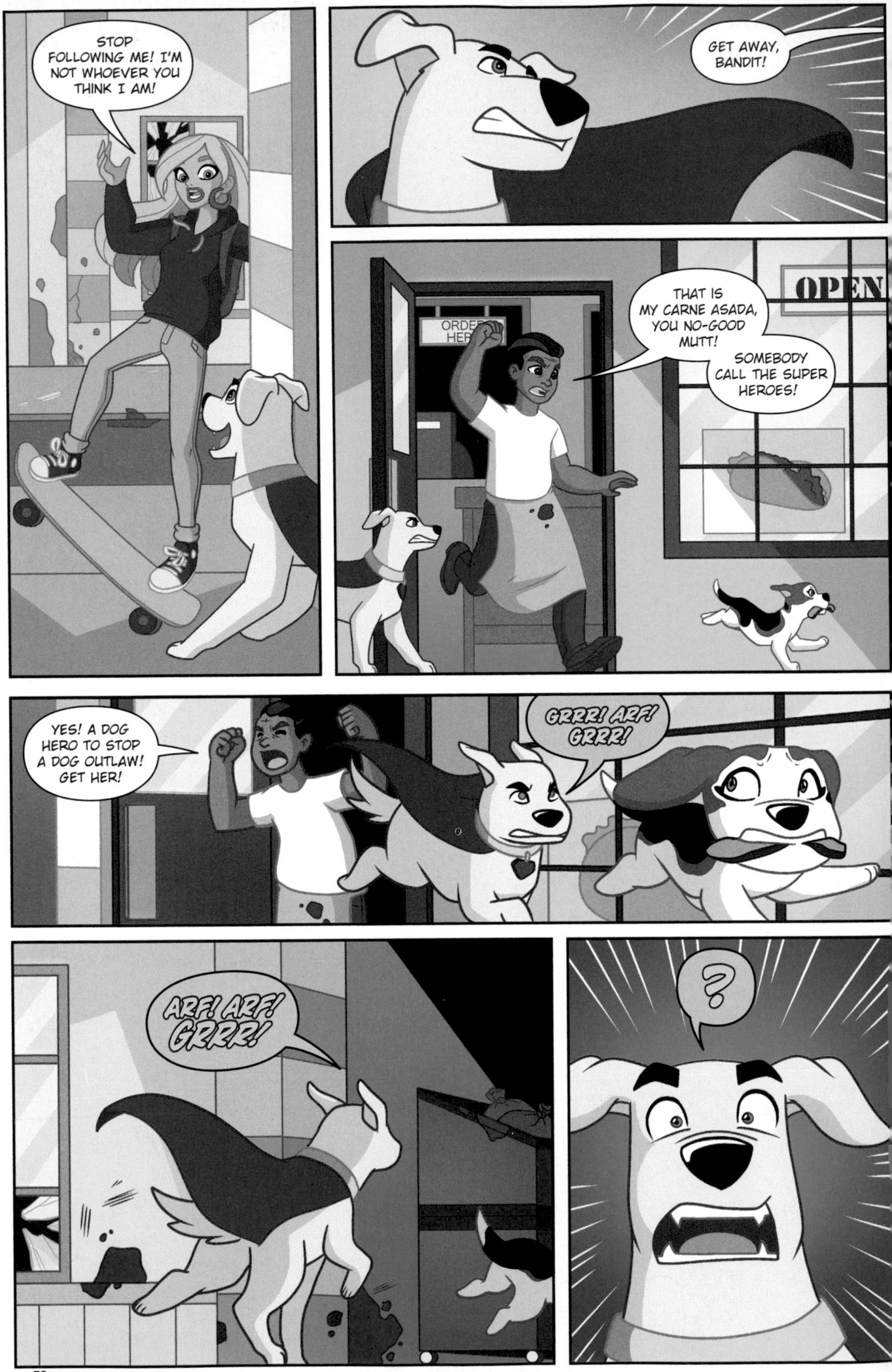
STOP FOLLOWING ME! I'M NOT WHOEVER YOU THINK I AM!
GET AWAY, BANDIT!
OPEN
ORDER HERE
THAT IS MY CARNE ASADA, YOU NO-GOOD MUTT!
SOMEBODY CALL THE SUPER HEROES!
YES! A DOG HERO TO STOP A DOG OUTLAW! GET HER!
GRRR! ARF! GRRR!
ARF! ARF! GRRR!
?

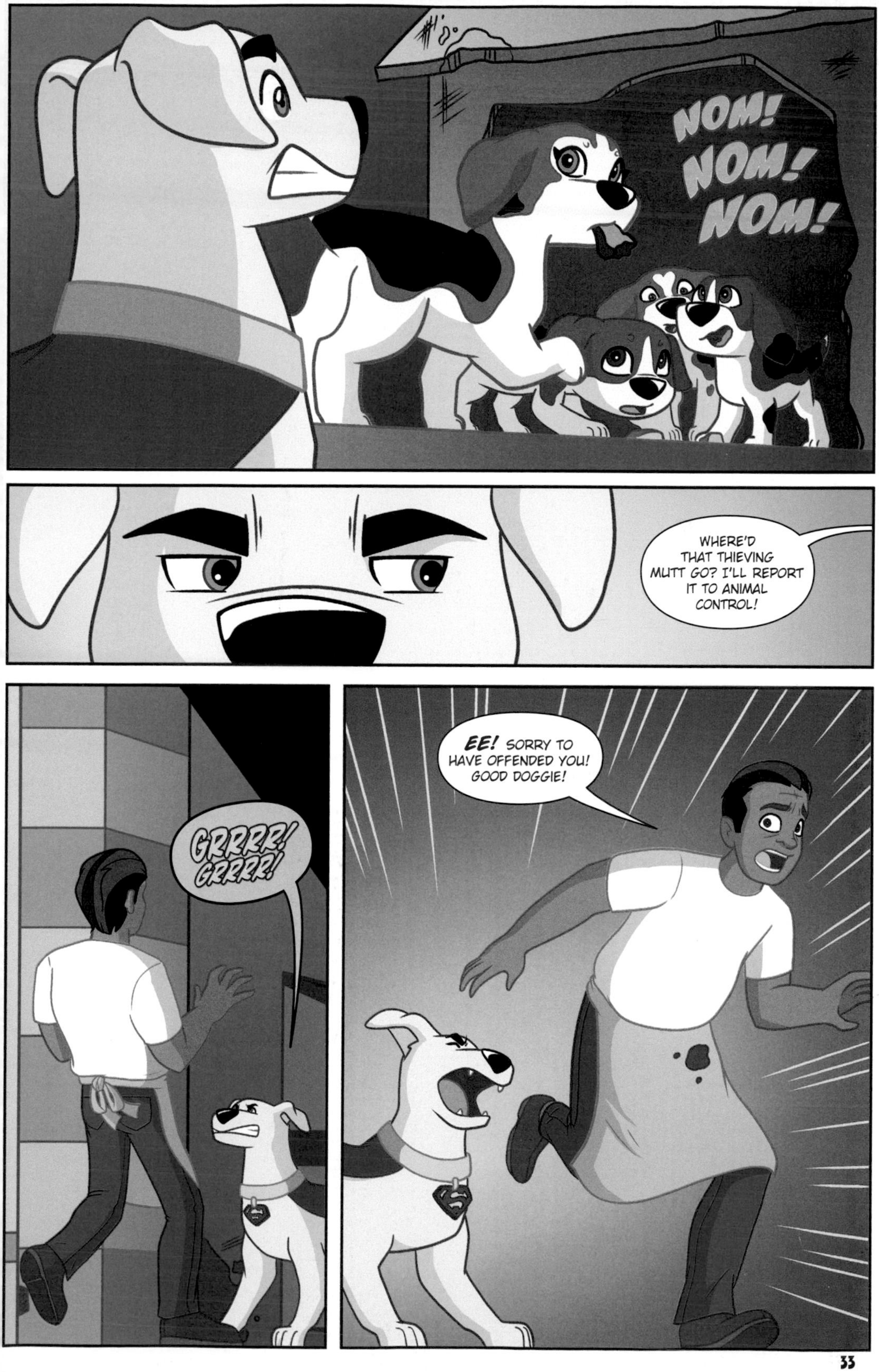
NOM! NOM! NOM!
WHERE'D THAT THIEVING MUTT GO? I'LL REPORT IT TO ANIMAL CONTROL!
GRRRR! GRRRR!
EE! SORRY TO HAVE OFFENDED YOU! GOOD DOGGIE!

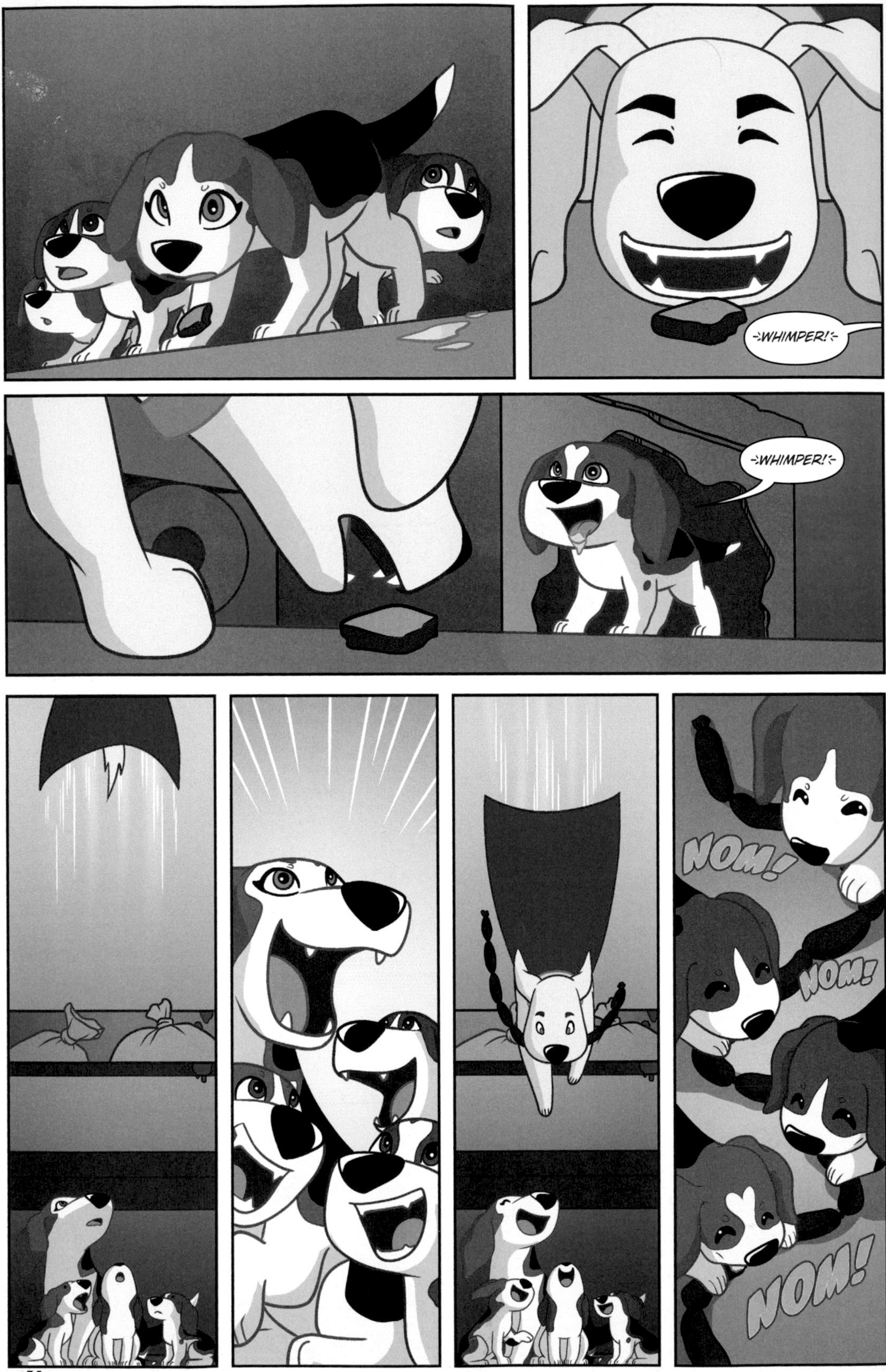
-WHIMPER!-
-WHIMPER!-
NOM!
NOM!
NOM!

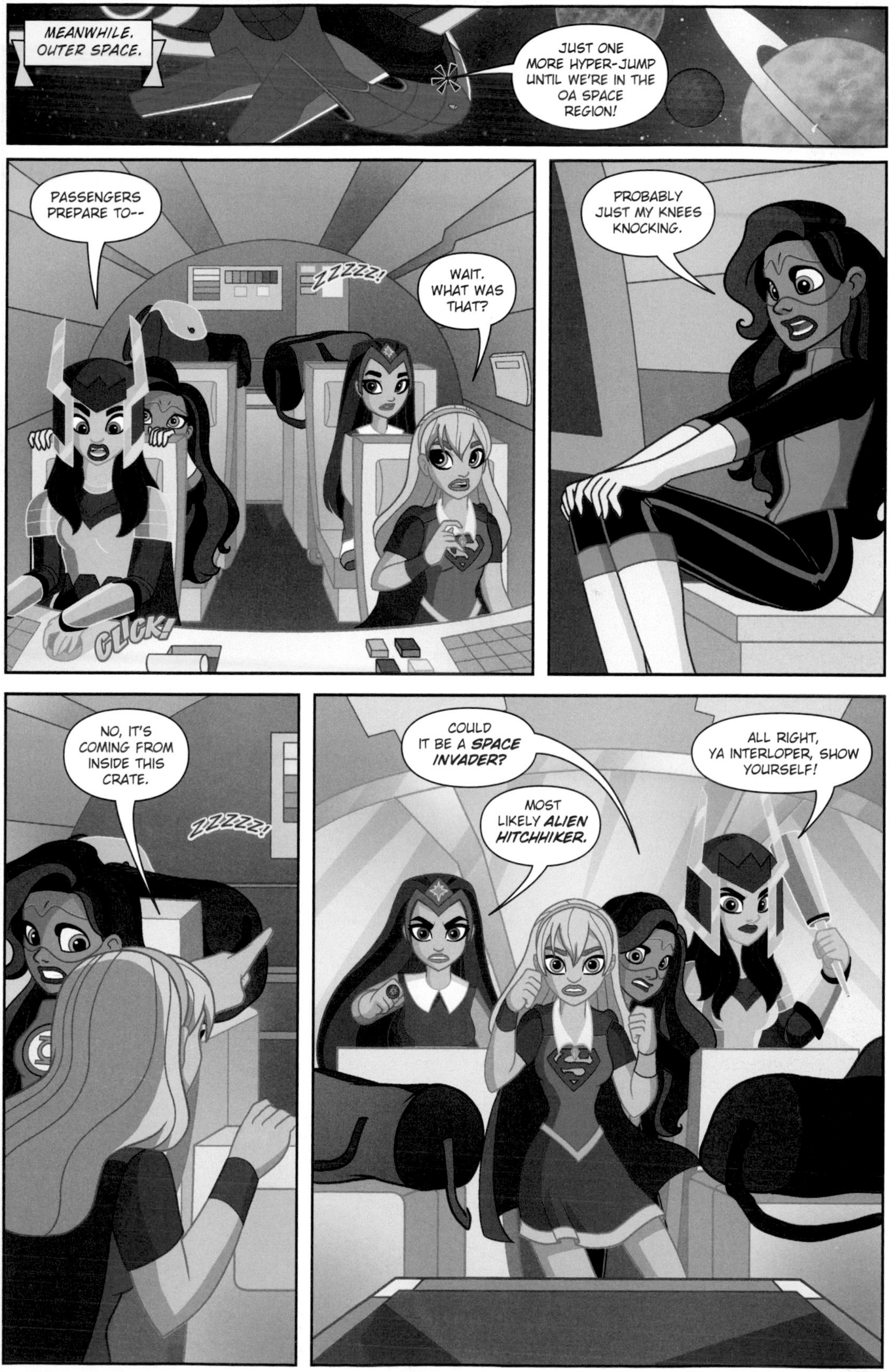

MEANWHILE. OUTER SPACE.
JUST ONE MORE HYPER-JUMP UNTIL WE'RE IN THE OA SPACE REGION!
PASSENGERS PREPARE TO--
ZZZZZZ!
WAIT. WHAT WAS THAT?
CLICK!
PROBABLY JUST MY KNEES KNOCKING.
NO, IT'S COMING FROM INSIDE THIS CRATE.
ZZZZZZ!
COULD IT BE A SPACE INVADER?
MOST LIKELY ALIEN HITCHHIKER.
ALL RIGHT, YA INTERLOPER, SHOW YOURSELF!

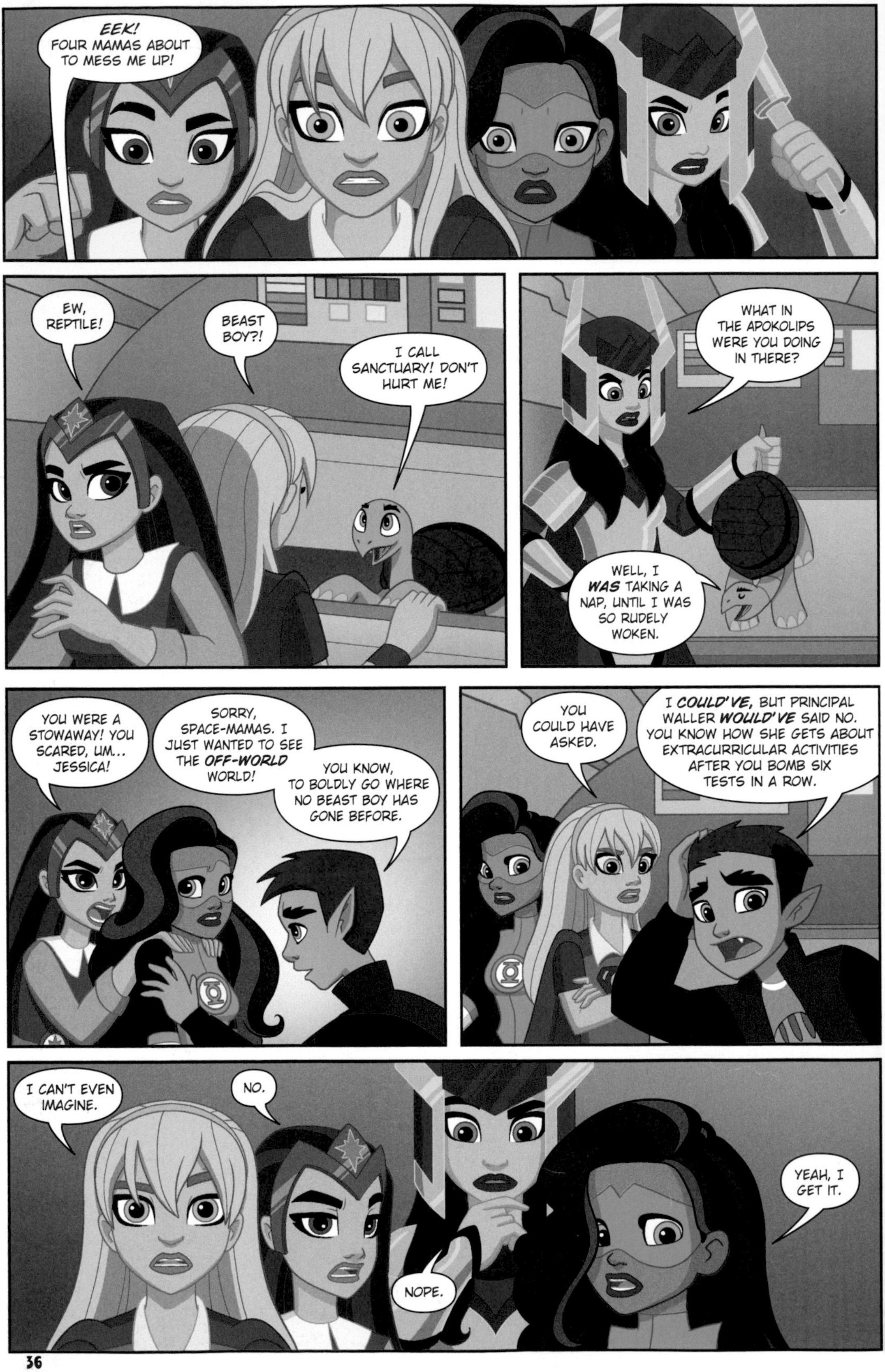
EEK! FOUR MAMAS ABOUT TO MESS ME UP!
EW, REPTILE!
BEAST BOY?!
I CALL SANCTUARY! DON'T HURT ME!
WHAT IN THE APOKOLIPS WERE YOU DOING IN THERE?
WELL, I WAS TAKING A NAP, UNTIL I WAS SO RUDELY WOKEN.
YOU WERE A STOWAWAY! YOU SCARED, UM... JESSICA!
SORRY, SPACE-MAMAS. I JUST WANTED TO SEE THE OFF-WORLD WORLD!
YOU KNOW, TO BOLDLY GO WHERE NO BEAST BOY HAS GONE BEFORE.
YOU COULD HAVE ASKED.
I COULD'VE, BUT PRINCIPAL WALLER WOULD'VE SAID NO. YOU KNOW HOW SHE GETS ABOUT EXTRACURRICULAR ACTIVITIES AFTER YOU BOMB SIX TESTS IN A ROW.
I CAN'T EVEN IMAGINE.
NO.
NOPE.
YEAH, I GET IT.

GUESS SINCE YOU'RE HERE, YOU BETTER STRAP IN, BEAST BOY.
NOW LET'S GET THIS LAST LEAP OVER WITH.
INITIATING HYPER-JUMP TO OA IN THREE, TWO--
--ONE!
SEE? THAT JUMP WAS SMOOTH AS--
ASTEROID!
AAAAGH!
ASTEROIDS? THAT'S ONE OF MY PHOBIAS!

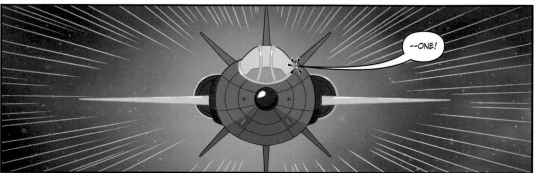

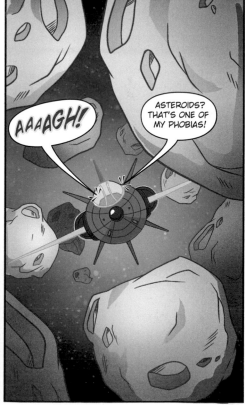

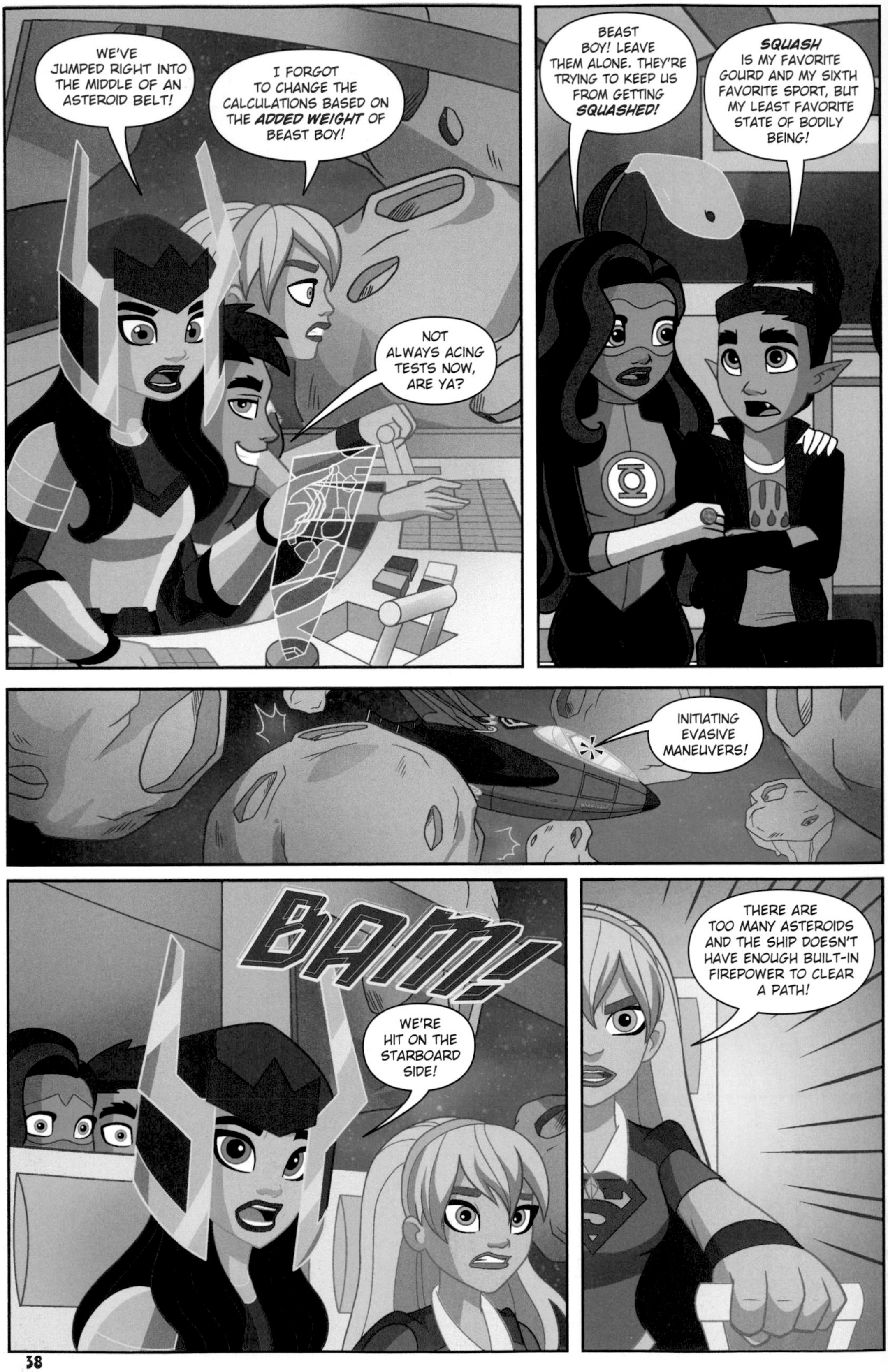
WE'VE JUMPED RIGHT INTO THE MIDDLE OF AN ASTEROID BELT!
I FORGOT TO CHANGE THE CALCULATIONS BASED ON THE ADDED WEIGHT OF BEAST BOY!
NOT ALWAYS ACING TESTS NOW, ARE YA?
BEAST BOY! LEAVE THEM ALONE. THEY'RE TRYING TO KEEP US FROM GETTING SQUASHED!
SQUASH IS MY FAVORITE GOURD AND MY SIXTH FAVORITE SPORT, BUT MY LEAST FAVORITE STATE OF BODILY BEING!
INITIATING EVASIVE MANEUVERS!
BAM!
WE'RE HIT ON THE STARBOARD SIDE!
THERE ARE TOO MANY ASTEROIDS AND THE SHIP DOESN'T HAVE ENOUGH BUILT-IN FIREPOWER TO CLEAR A PATH!

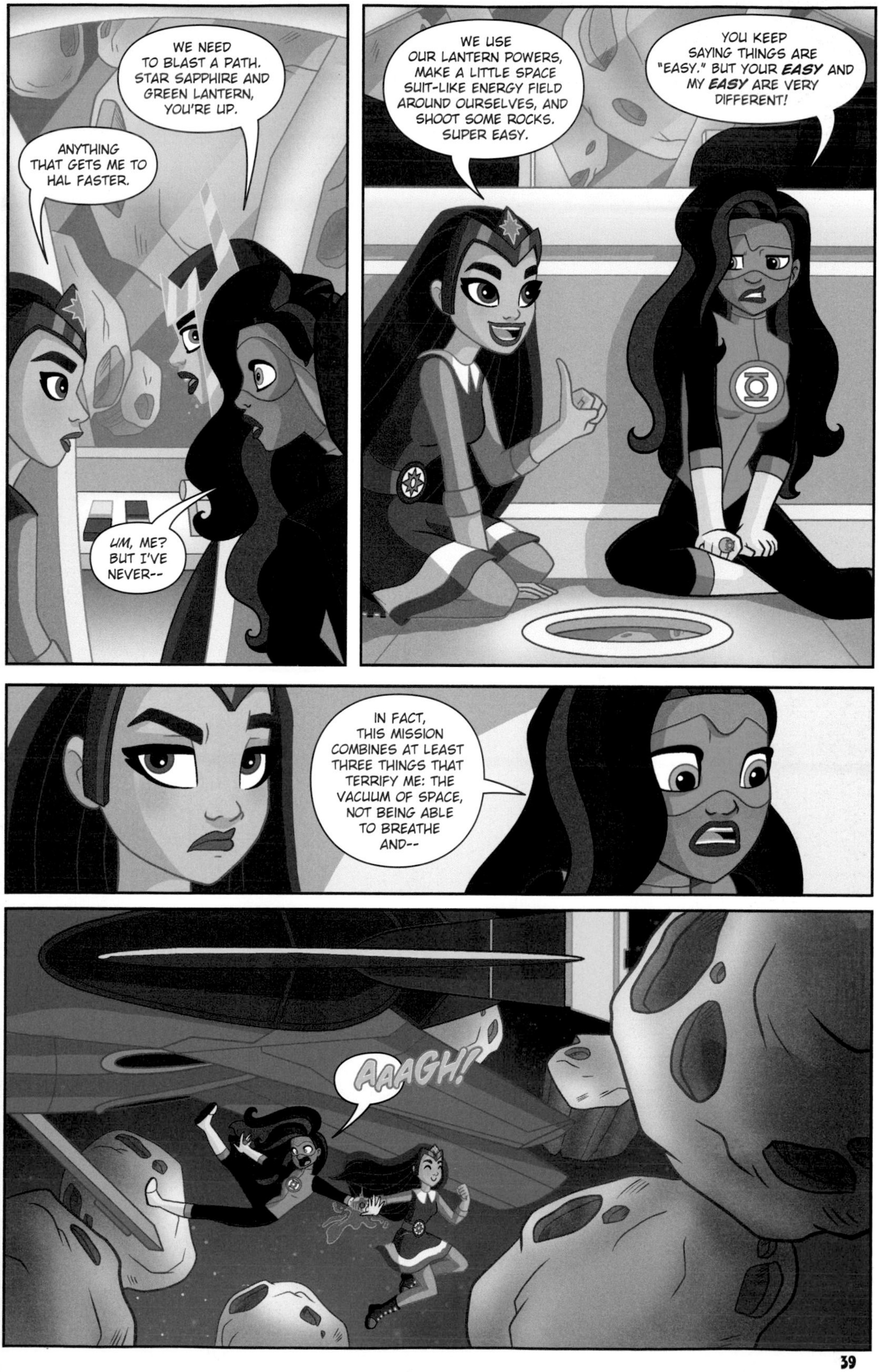
WE NEED TO BLAST A PATH. STAR SAPPHIRE AND GREEN LANTERN, YOU'RE UP.
ANYTHING THAT GETS ME TO HAL FASTER.
UM, ME? BUT I'VE NEVER--
WE USE OUR LANTERN POWERS, MAKE A LITTLE SPACE SUIT-LIKE ENERGY FIELD AROUND OURSELVES, AND SHOOT SOME ROCKS. SUPER EASY.
YOU KEEP SAYING THINGS ARE "EASY." BUT YOUR ***EASY*** AND MY ***EASY*** ARE VERY DIFFERENT!
IN FACT, THIS MISSION COMBINES AT LEAST THREE THINGS THAT TERRIFY ME: THE VACUUM OF SPACE, NOT BEING ABLE TO BREATHE AND--
AAAGH!

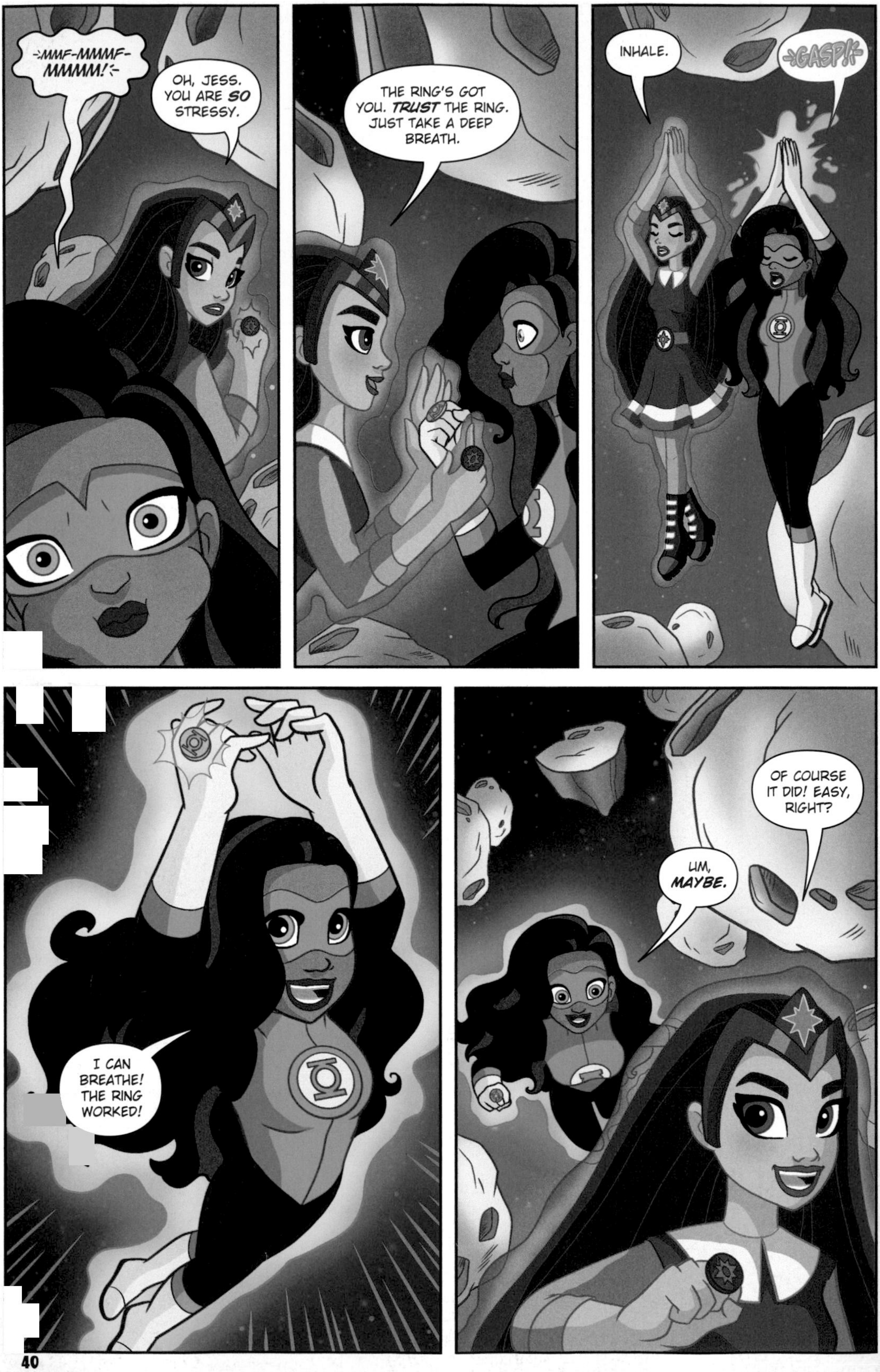
-MMF-MMMF-
MMMM!-
OH, JESS. YOU ARE SO STRESSY.
THE RING'S GOT YOU. TRUST THE RING. JUST TAKE A DEEP BREATH.
INHALE.
GASP!
I CAN BREATHE! THE RING WORKED!
OF COURSE IT DID! EASY, RIGHT?
UM, MAYBE.

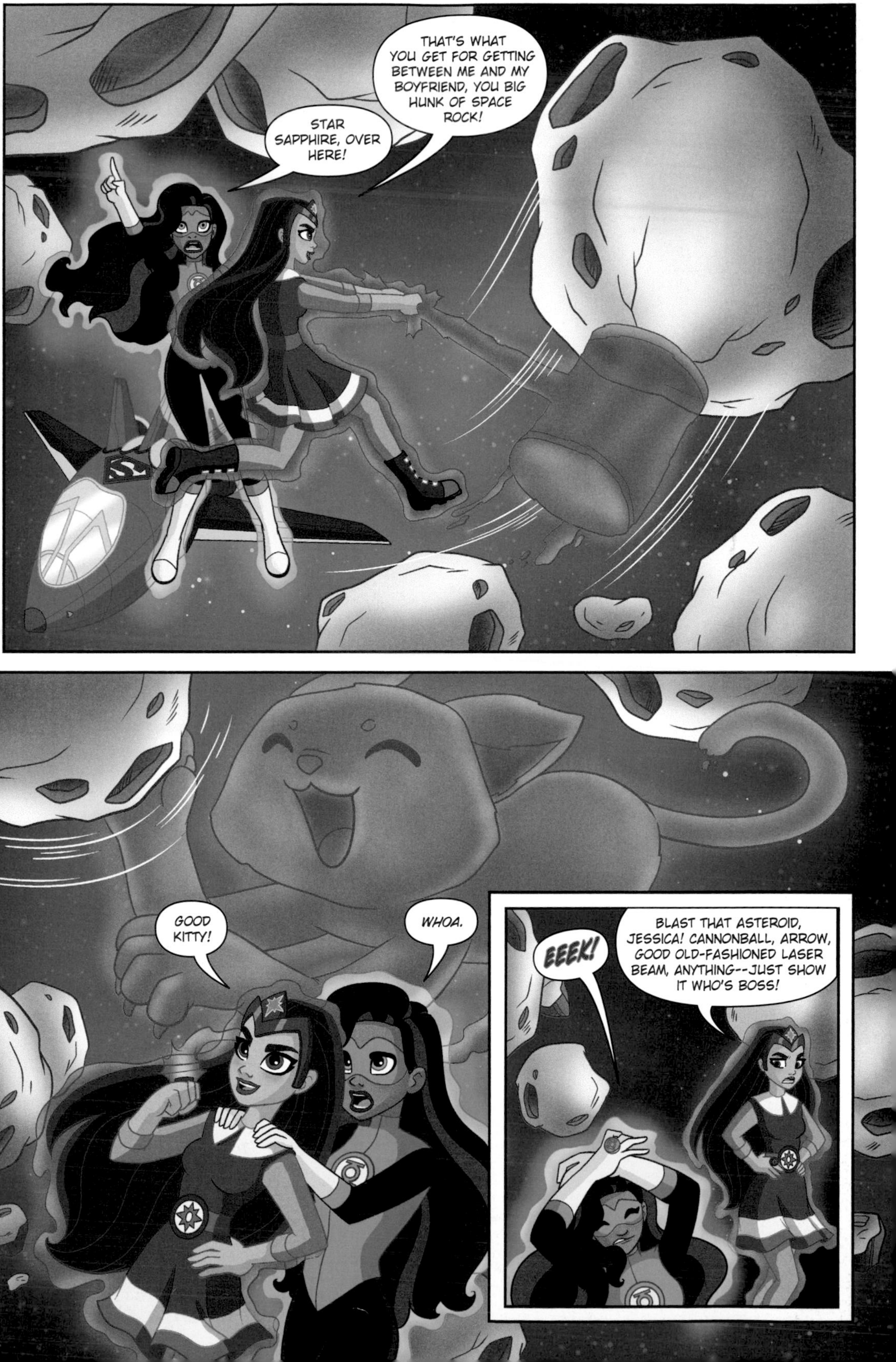
STAR SAPPHIRE, OVER HERE!
THAT'S WHAT YOU GET FOR GETTING BETWEEN ME AND MY BOYFRIEND, YOU BIG HUNK OF SPACE ROCK!
GOOD KITTY!
WHOA.
EEEK!
BLAST THAT ASTEROID, JESSICA! CANNONBALL, ARROW, GOOD OLD-FASHIONED LASER BEAM, ANYTHING--JUST SHOW IT WHO'S BOSS!

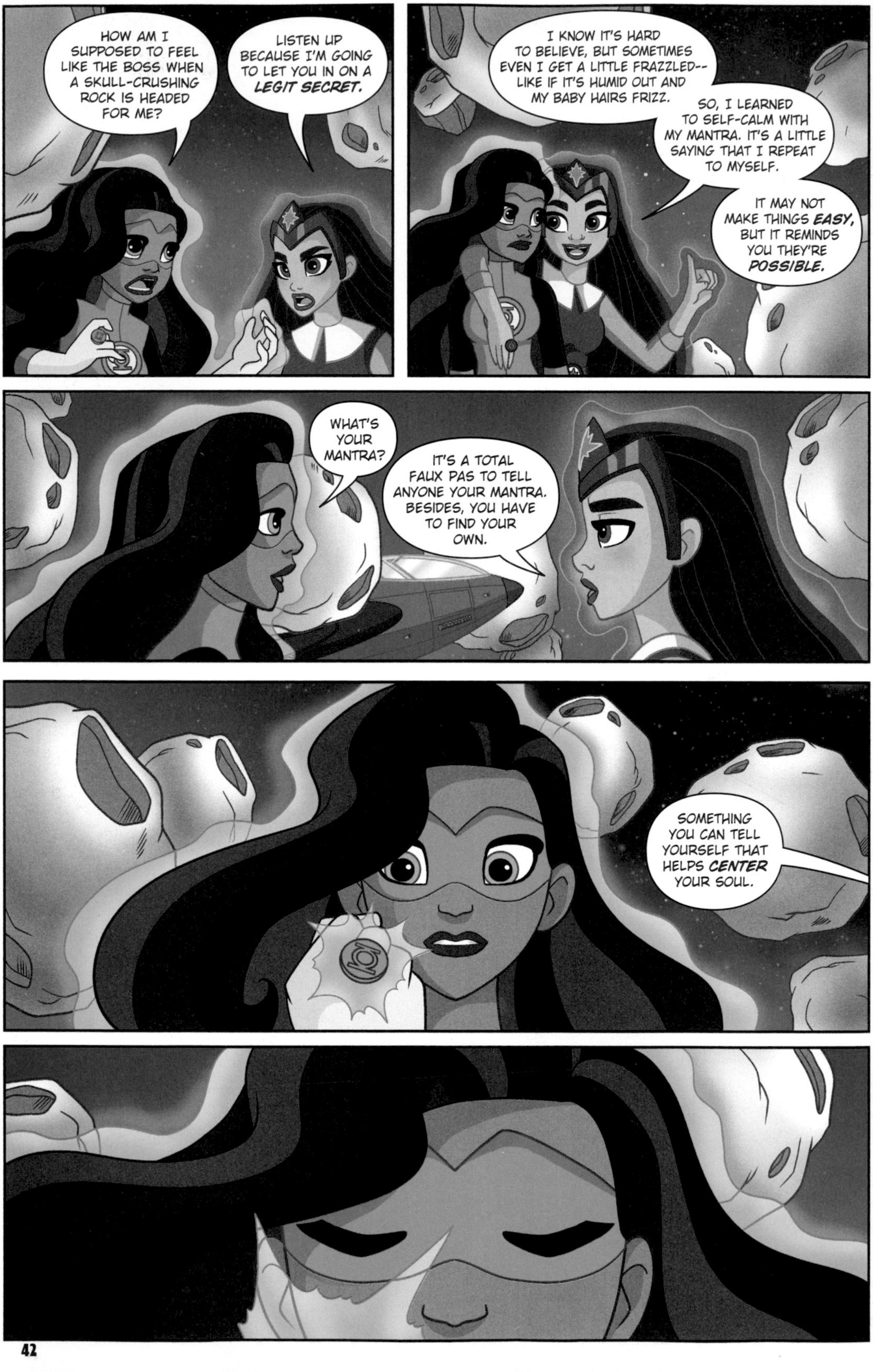
HOW AM I SUPPOSED TO FEEL LIKE THE BOSS WHEN A SKULL-CRUSHING ROCK IS HEADED FOR ME?
LISTEN UP BECAUSE I'M GOING TO LET YOU IN ON A LEGIT SECRET.
I KNOW IT'S HARD TO BELIEVE, BUT SOMETIMES EVEN I GET A LITTLE FRAZZLED-- LIKE IF IT'S HUMID OUT AND MY BABY HAIRS FRIZZ.
SO, I LEARNED TO SELF-CALM WITH MY MANTRA. IT'S A LITTLE SAYING THAT I REPEAT TO MYSELF.
IT MAY NOT MAKE THINGS EASY, BUT IT REMINDS YOU THEY'RE POSSIBLE.
WHAT'S YOUR MANTRA?
IT'S A TOTAL FAUX PAS TO TELL ANYONE YOUR MANTRA. BESIDES, YOU HAVE TO FIND YOUR OWN.
SOMETHING YOU CAN TELL YOURSELF THAT HELPS CENTER YOUR SOUL.

IN BRIGHTEST DAY...

IN BLACKEST NIGHT...

NO EVIL SHALL ESCAPE MY SIGHT...

GOOD SHOT, JESS!

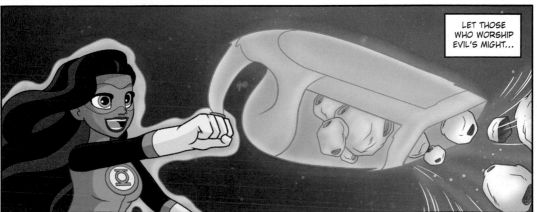

LET THOSE WHO WORSHIP EVIL'S MIGHT...

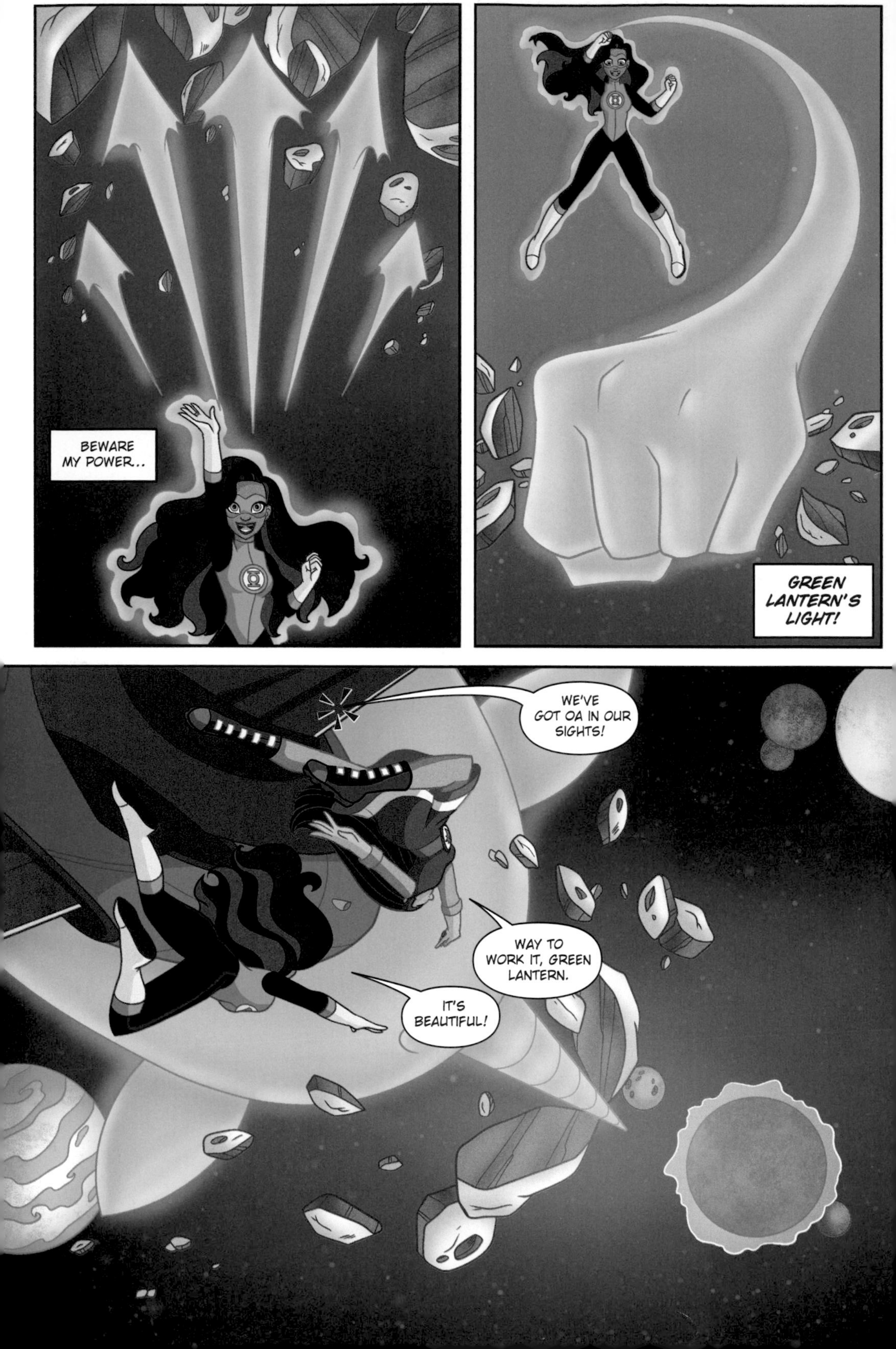
BEWARE MY POWER..
GREEN LANTERN'S LIGHT!
WE'VE GOT OA IN OUR SIGHTS!
WAY TO WORK IT, GREEN LANTERN.
IT'S BEAUTIFUL!

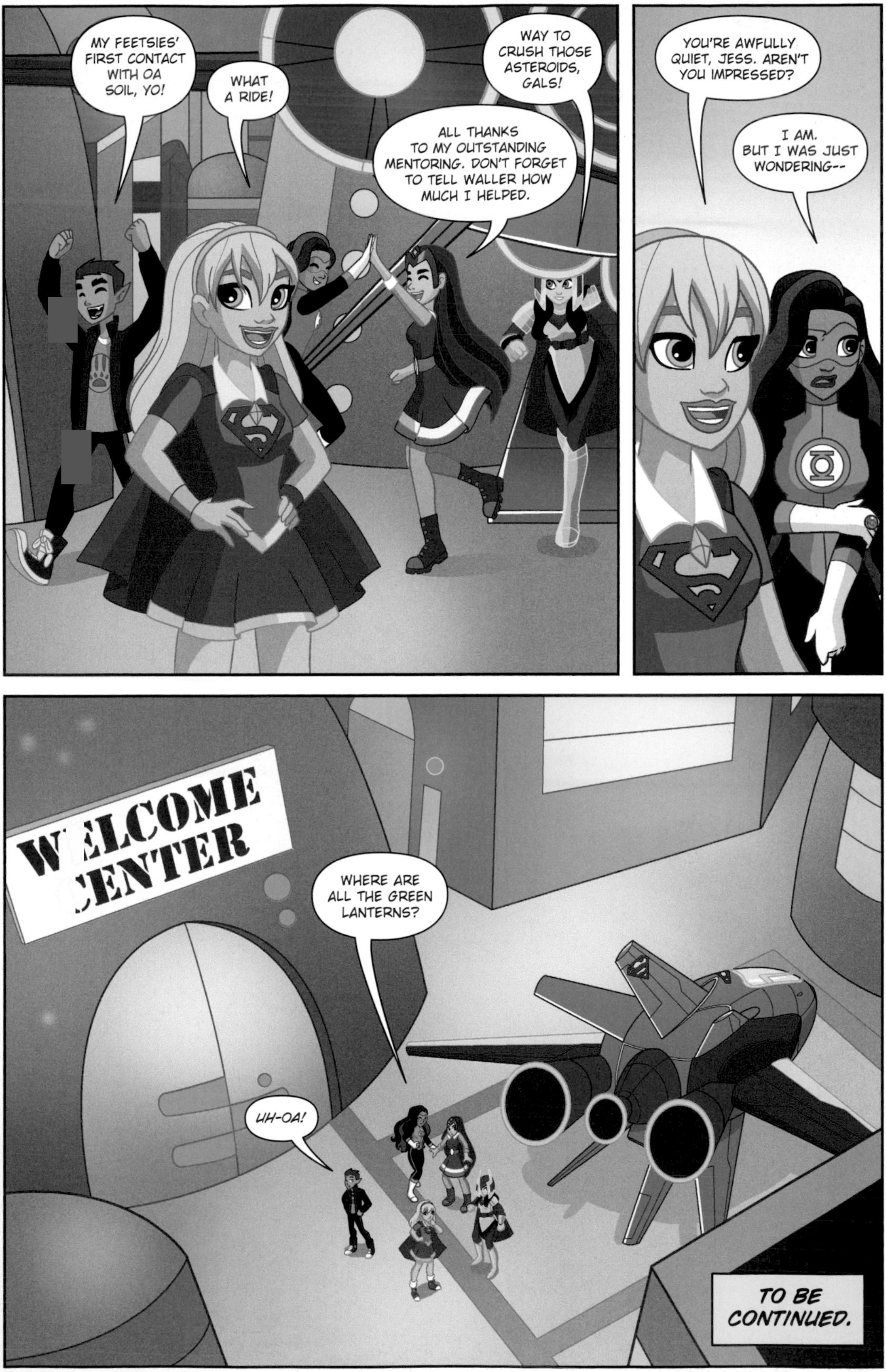
MY FEETSIES' FIRST CONTACT WITH OA SOIL, YO!
WHAT A RIDE!
WAY TO CRUSH THOSE ASTEROIDS, GALS!
ALL THANKS TO MY OUTSTANDING MENTORING. DON'T FORGET TO TELL WALLER HOW MUCH I HELPED.
YOU'RE AWFULLY QUIET, JESS. AREN'T YOU IMPRESSED?
I AM. BUT I WAS JUST WONDERING--
WELCOME CENTER
WHERE ARE ALL THE GREEN LANTERNS?
UH-OA!
TO BE CONTINUED.

CHAPTER THREE

PLANET OF THE BOTS

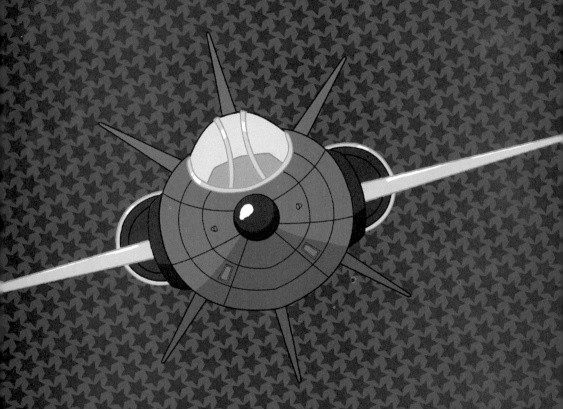

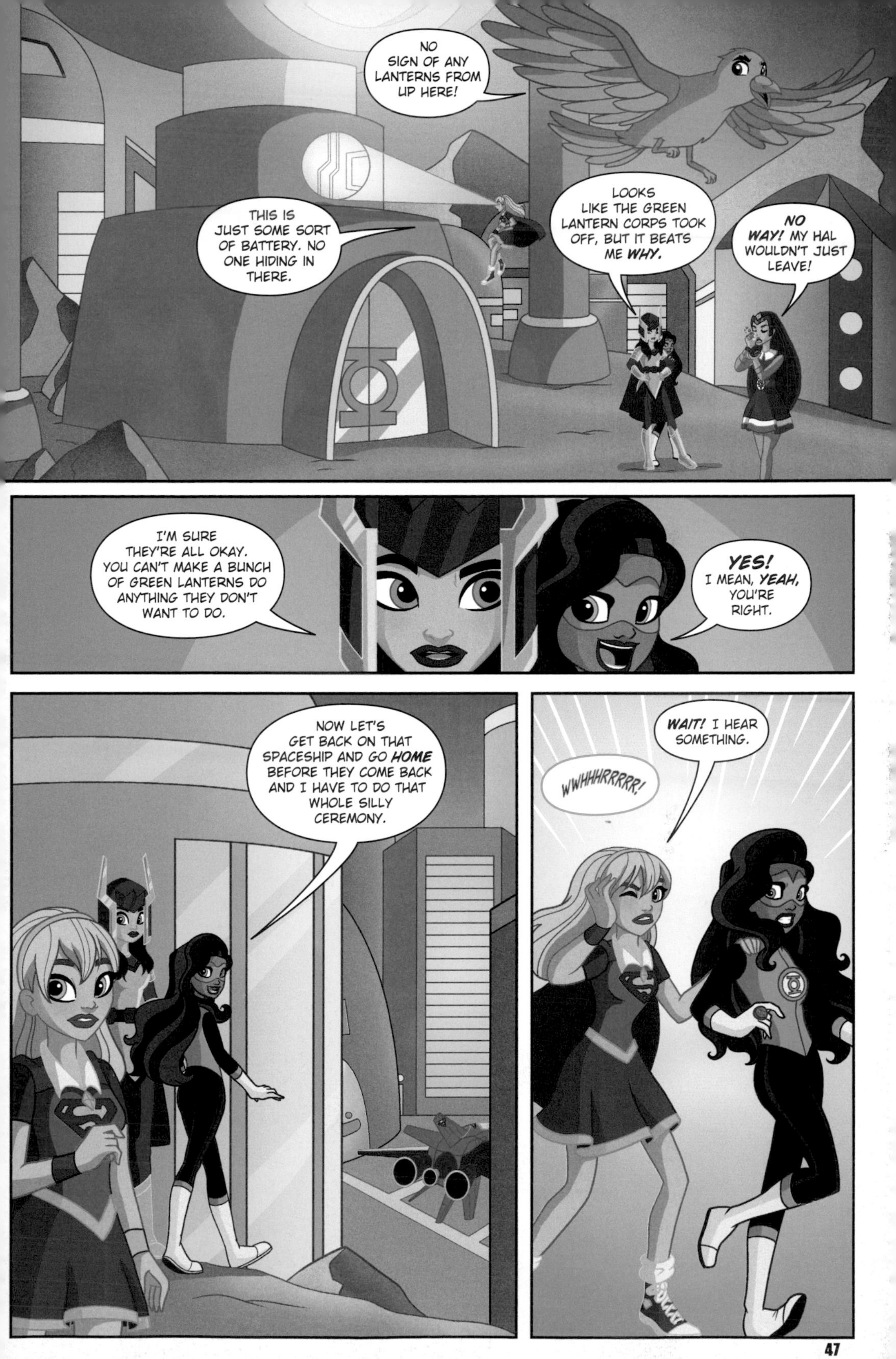
NO SIGN OF ANY LANTERNS FROM UP HERE!
THIS IS JUST SOME SORT OF BATTERY. NO ONE HIDING IN THERE.
LOOKS LIKE THE GREEN LANTERN CORPS TOOK OFF, BUT IT BEATS ME WHY.
NO WAY! MY HAL WOULDN'T JUST LEAVE!
I'M SURE THEY'RE ALL OKAY. YOU CAN'T MAKE A BUNCH OF GREEN LANTERNS DO ANYTHING THEY DON'T WANT TO DO.
YES! I MEAN, YEAH, YOU'RE RIGHT.
NOW LET'S GET BACK ON THAT SPACESHIP AND GO HOME BEFORE THEY COME BACK AND I HAVE TO DO THAT WHOLE SILLY CEREMONY.
WAIT! I HEAR SOMETHING.
WWHHHRRRRR!

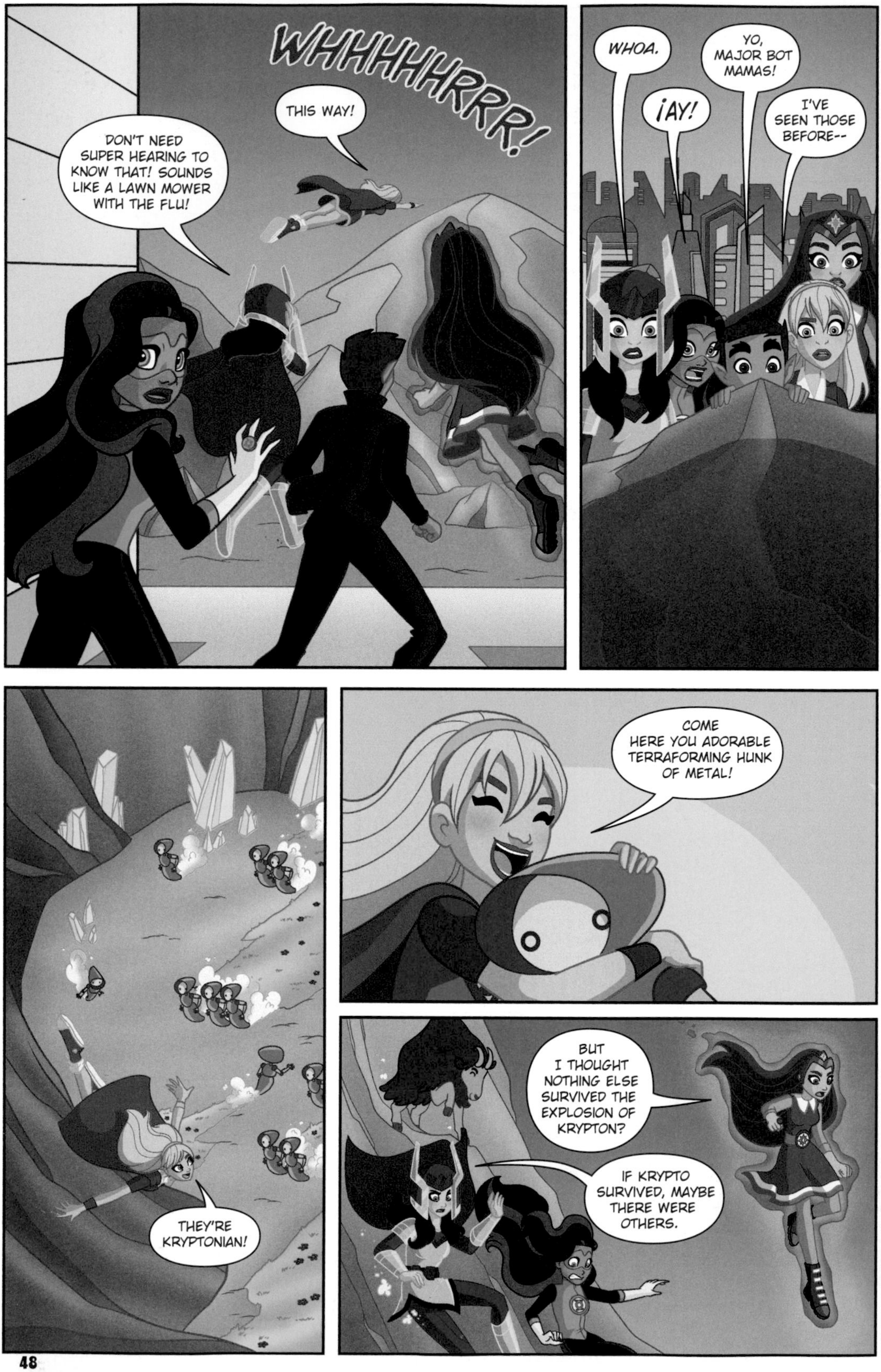

WHHHHHRRR!
THIS WAY!
DON'T NEED SUPER HEARING TO KNOW THAT! SOUNDS LIKE A LAWN MOWER WITH THE FLU!
WHOA.
¡AY!
YO, MAJOR BOT MAMAS!
I'VE SEEN THOSE BEFORE--
THEY'RE KRYPTONIAN!
COME HERE YOU ADORABLE TERRAFORMING HUNK OF METAL!
BUT I THOUGHT NOTHING ELSE SURVIVED THE EXPLOSION OF KRYPTON?
IF KRYPTO SURVIVED, MAYBE THERE WERE OTHERS.

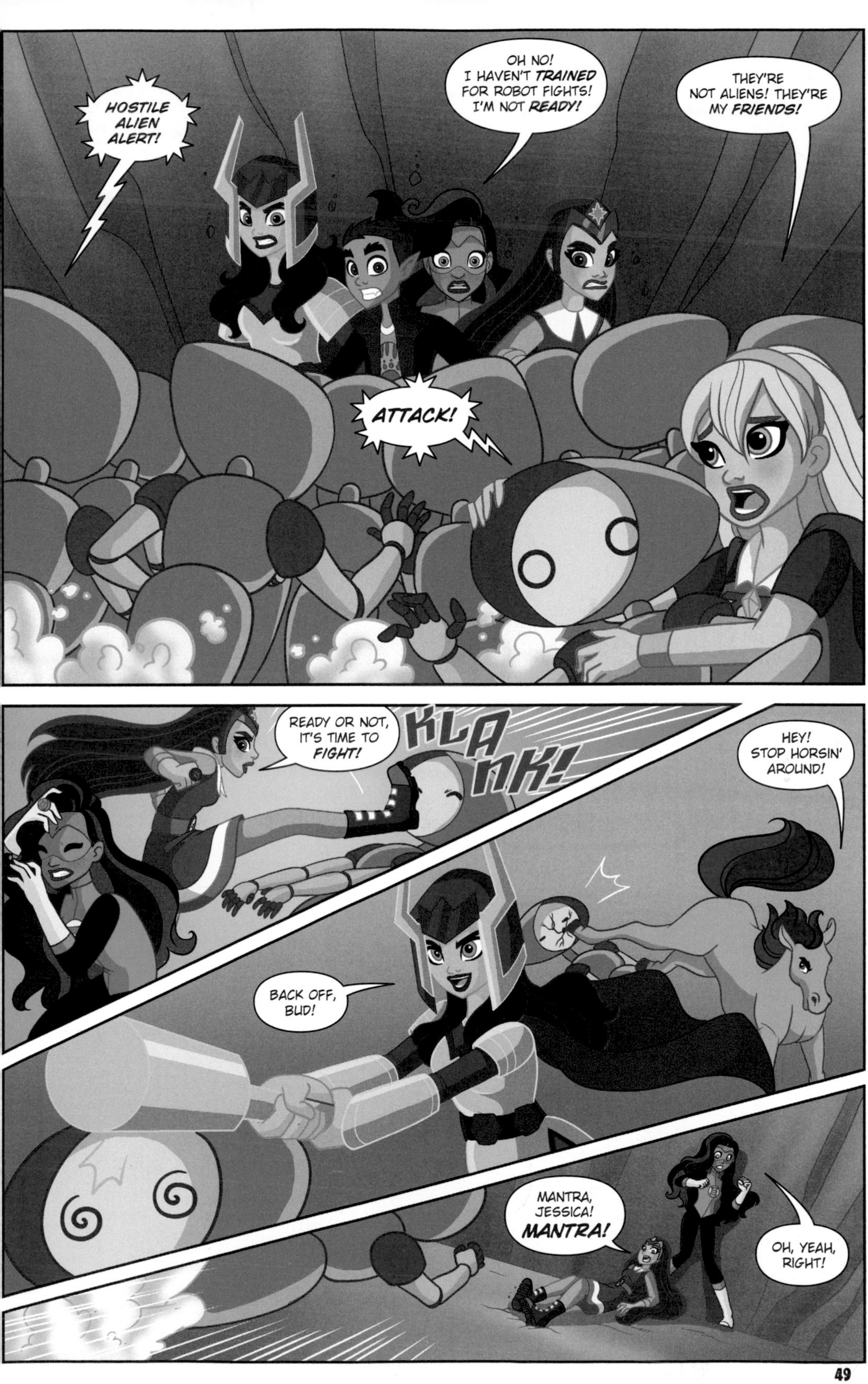
HOSTILE ALIEN ALERT!
OH NO! I HAVEN'T TRAINED FOR ROBOT FIGHTS! I'M NOT READY!
THEY'RE NOT ALIENS! THEY'RE MY FRIENDS!
ATTACK!
READY OR NOT, IT'S TIME TO FIGHT!
KLANK!
HEY! STOP HORSIN' AROUND!
BACK OFF, BUD!
MANTRA, JESSICA! MANTRA!
OH, YEAH, RIGHT!

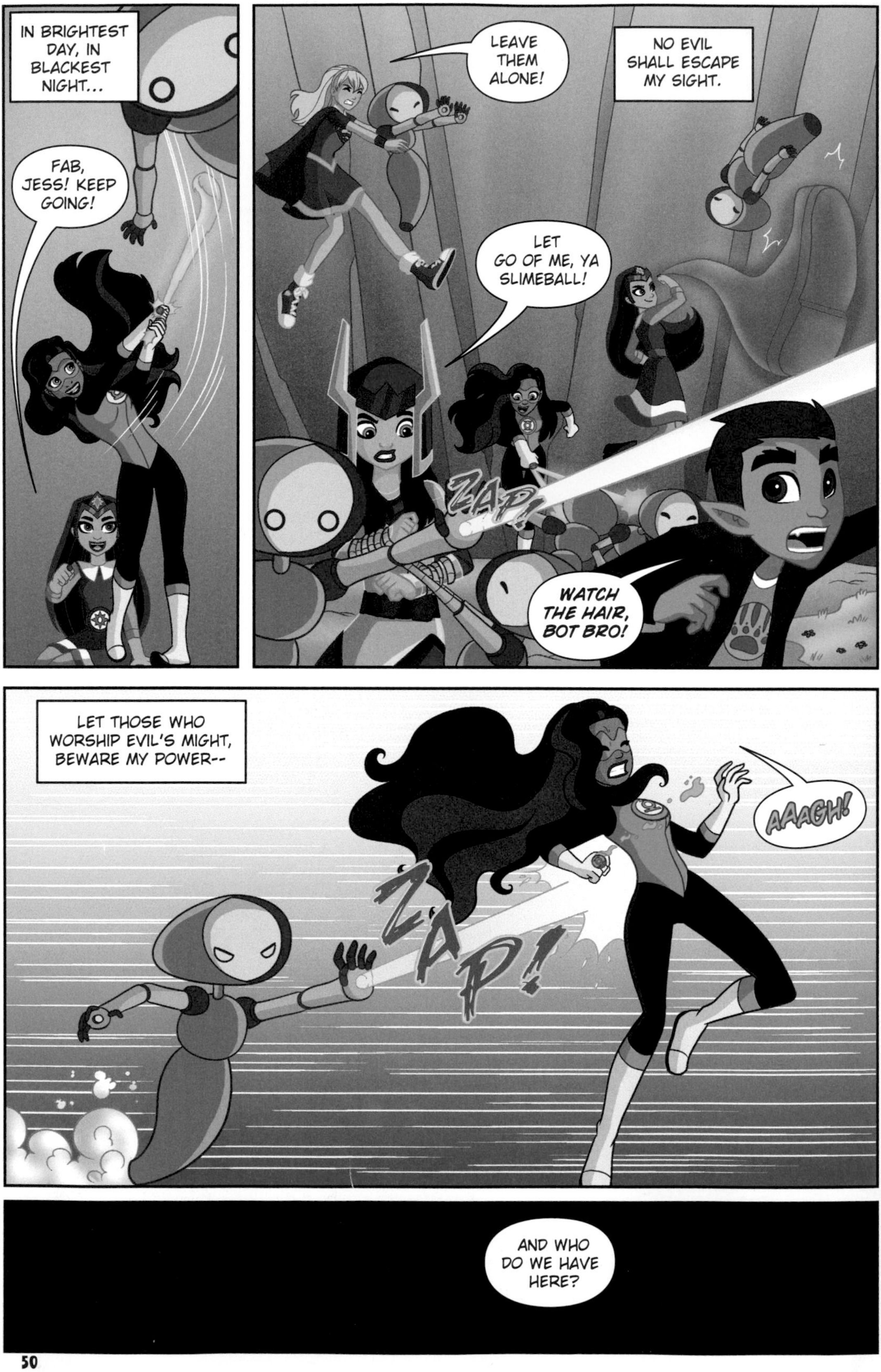
IN BRIGHTEST DAY, IN BLACKEST NIGHT...
FAB, JESS! KEEP GOING!
LEAVE THEM ALONE!
NO EVIL SHALL ESCAPE MY SIGHT.
LET GO OF ME, YA SLIMEBALL!
ZAP!
WATCH THE HAIR, BOT BRO!
LET THOSE WHO WORSHIP EVIL'S MIGHT, BEWARE MY POWER--
AAAGH!
ZAP!
AND WHO DO WE HAVE HERE?

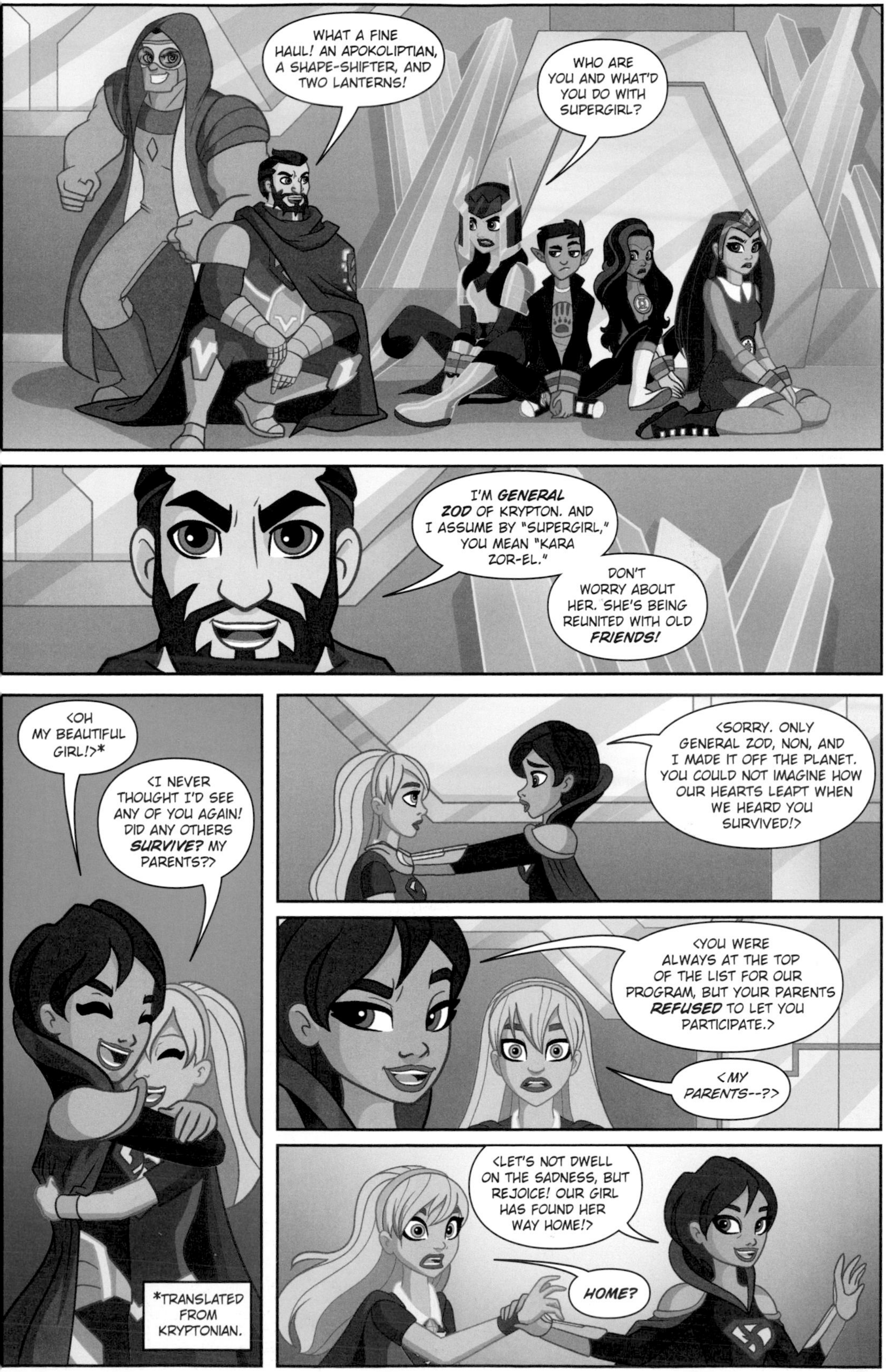
WHAT A FINE HAUL! AN APOKOLIPTIAN, A SHAPE-SHIFTER, AND TWO LANTERNS!
WHO ARE YOU AND WHAT'D YOU DO WITH SUPERGIRL?
I'M GENERAL ZOD OF KRYPTON. AND I ASSUME BY "SUPERGIRL," YOU MEAN "KARA ZOR-EL."
DON'T WORRY ABOUT HER. SHE'S BEING REUNITED WITH OLD FRIENDS!
<OH MY BEAUTIFUL GIRL!>*
<I NEVER THOUGHT I'D SEE ANY OF YOU AGAIN! DID ANY OTHERS SURVIVE? MY PARENTS?>
*TRANSLATED FROM KRYPTONIAN.
<SORRY. ONLY GENERAL ZOD, NON, AND I MADE IT OFF THE PLANET. YOU COULD NOT IMAGINE HOW OUR HEARTS LEAPT WHEN WE HEARD YOU SURVIVED!>
<YOU WERE ALWAYS AT THE TOP OF THE LIST FOR OUR PROGRAM, BUT YOUR PARENTS REFUSED TO LET YOU PARTICIPATE.>
<MY PARENTS--?>
<LET'S NOT DWELL ON THE SADNESS, BUT REJOICE! OUR GIRL HAS FOUND HER WAY HOME!>
HOME?

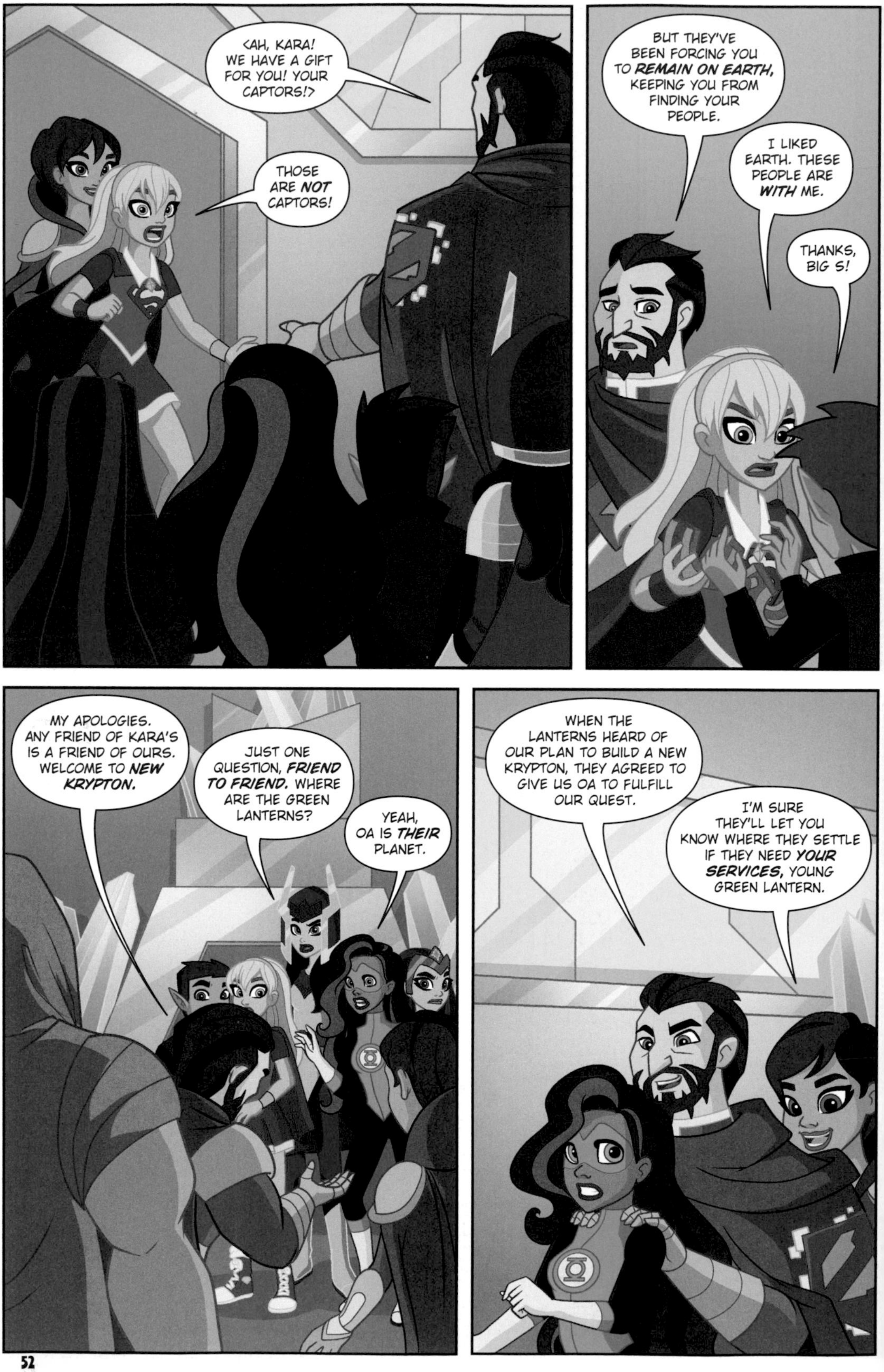
<AH, KARA! WE HAVE A GIFT FOR YOU! YOUR CAPTORS!>
THOSE ARE NOT CAPTORS!
BUT THEY'VE BEEN FORCING YOU TO REMAIN ON EARTH, KEEPING YOU FROM FINDING YOUR PEOPLE.
I LIKED EARTH. THESE PEOPLE ARE WITH ME.
THANKS, BIG S!
MY APOLOGIES. ANY FRIEND OF KARA'S IS A FRIEND OF OURS. WELCOME TO NEW KRYPTON.
JUST ONE QUESTION, FRIEND TO FRIEND. WHERE ARE THE GREEN LANTERNS?
YEAH, OA IS THEIR PLANET.
WHEN THE LANTERNS HEARD OF OUR PLAN TO BUILD A NEW KRYPTON, THEY AGREED TO GIVE US OA TO FULFILL OUR QUEST.
I'M SURE THEY'LL LET YOU KNOW WHERE THEY SETTLE IF THEY NEED YOUR SERVICES, YOUNG GREEN LANTERN.

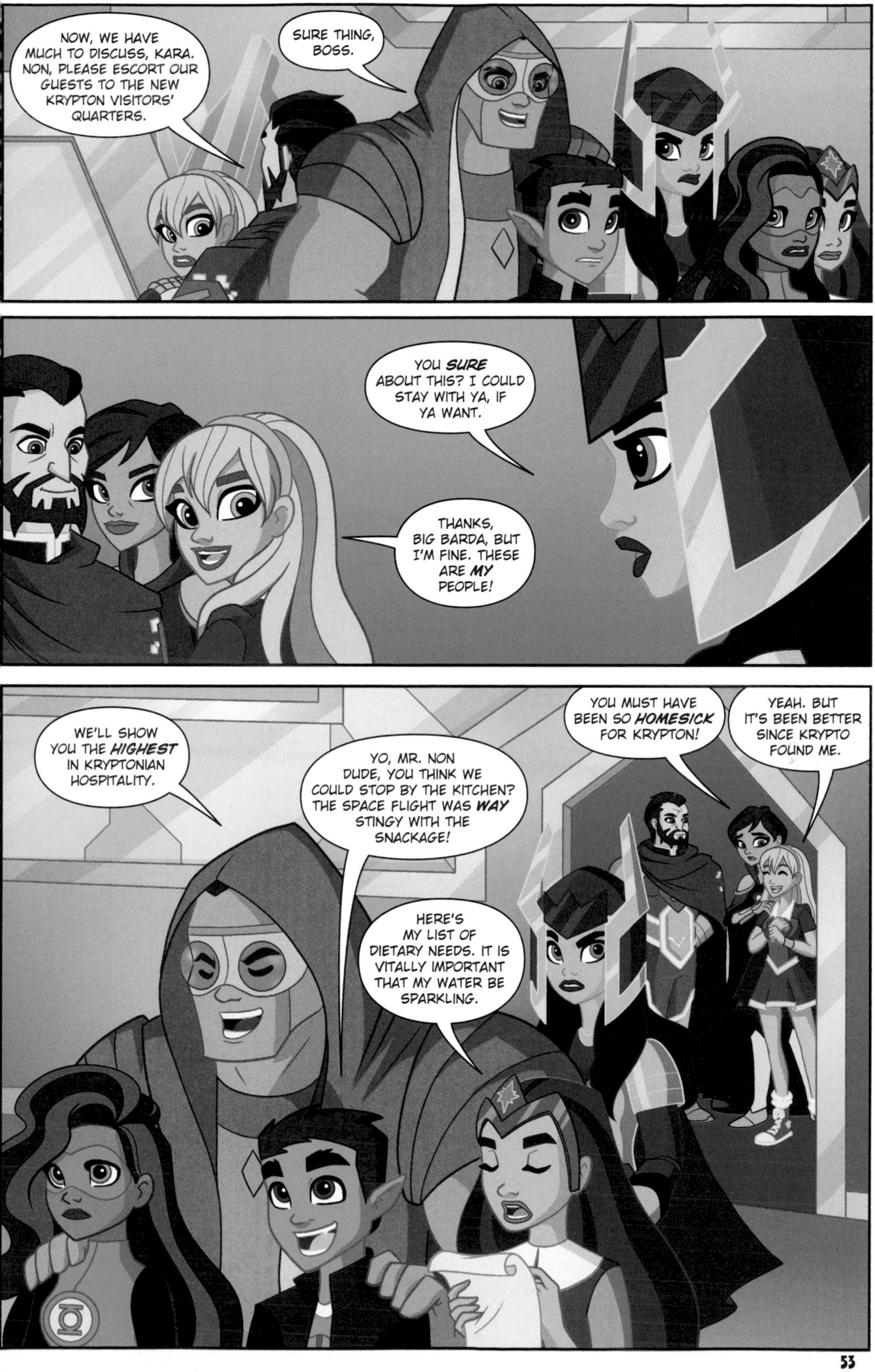
NOW, WE HAVE MUCH TO DISCUSS, KARA. NON, PLEASE ESCORT OUR GUESTS TO THE NEW KRYPTON VISITORS' QUARTERS.
SURE THING, BOSS.
YOU SURE ABOUT THIS? I COULD STAY WITH YA, IF YA WANT.
THANKS, BIG BARDA, BUT I'M FINE. THESE ARE MY PEOPLE!
WE'LL SHOW YOU THE HIGHEST IN KRYPTONIAN HOSPITALITY.
YO, MR. NON DUDE, YOU THINK WE COULD STOP BY THE KITCHEN? THE SPACE FLIGHT WAS WAY STINGY WITH THE SNACKAGE!
HERE'S MY LIST OF DIETARY NEEDS. IT IS VITALLY IMPORTANT THAT MY WATER BE SPARKLING.
YOU MUST HAVE BEEN SO HOMESICK FOR KRYPTON!
YEAH. BUT IT'S BEEN BETTER SINCE KRYPTO FOUND ME.

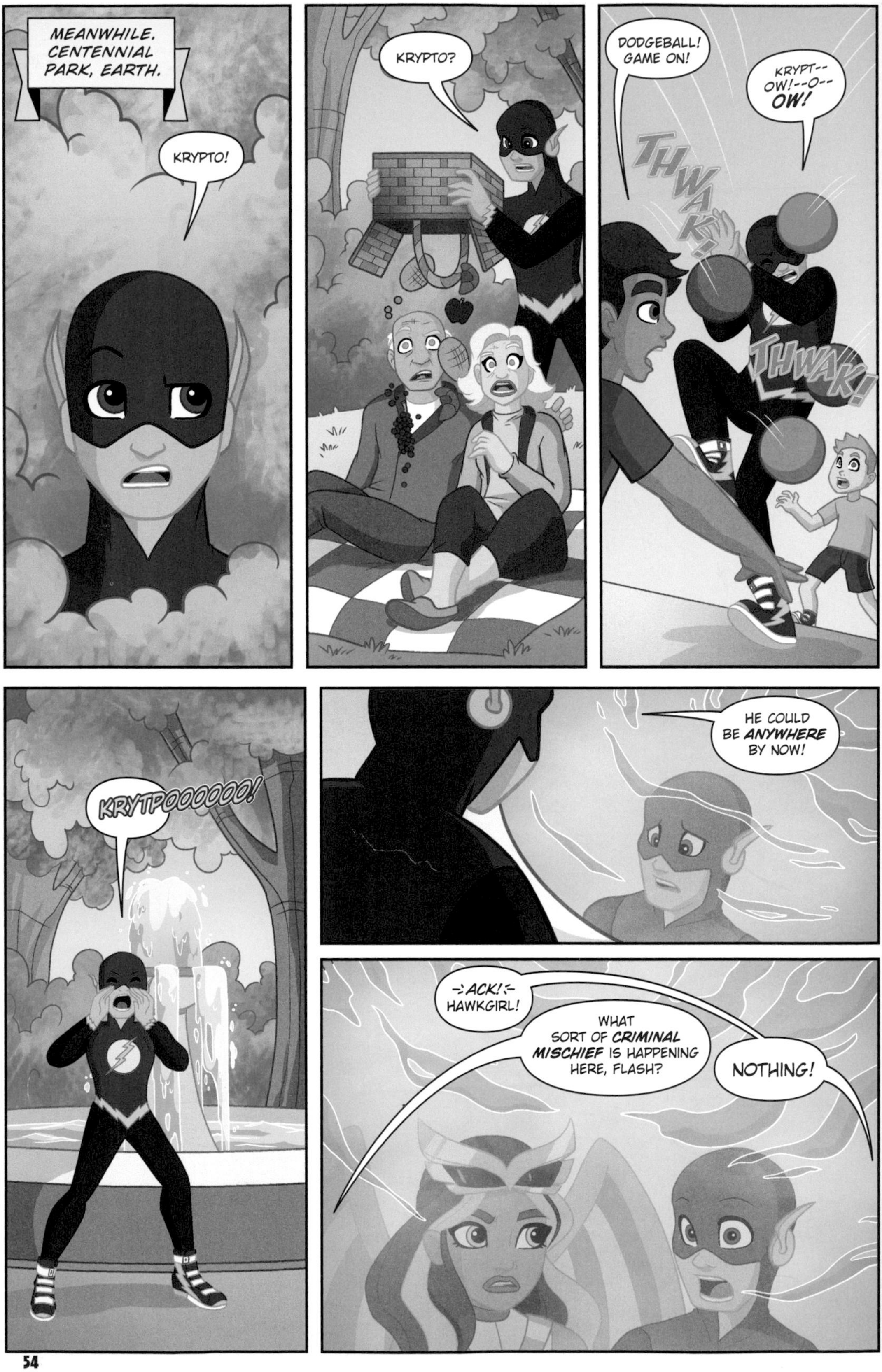
MEANWHILE. CENTENNIAL PARK, EARTH.
KRYPTO!
KRYPTO?
DODGEBALL! GAME ON!
KRYPT-- OW!--O-- OW!
THWAK!
THWAK!
KRYTPOOOOOOO!
HE COULD BE ANYWHERE BY NOW!
ACK! HAWKGIRL!
WHAT SORT OF CRIMINAL MISCHIEF IS HAPPENING HERE, FLASH?
NOTHING!

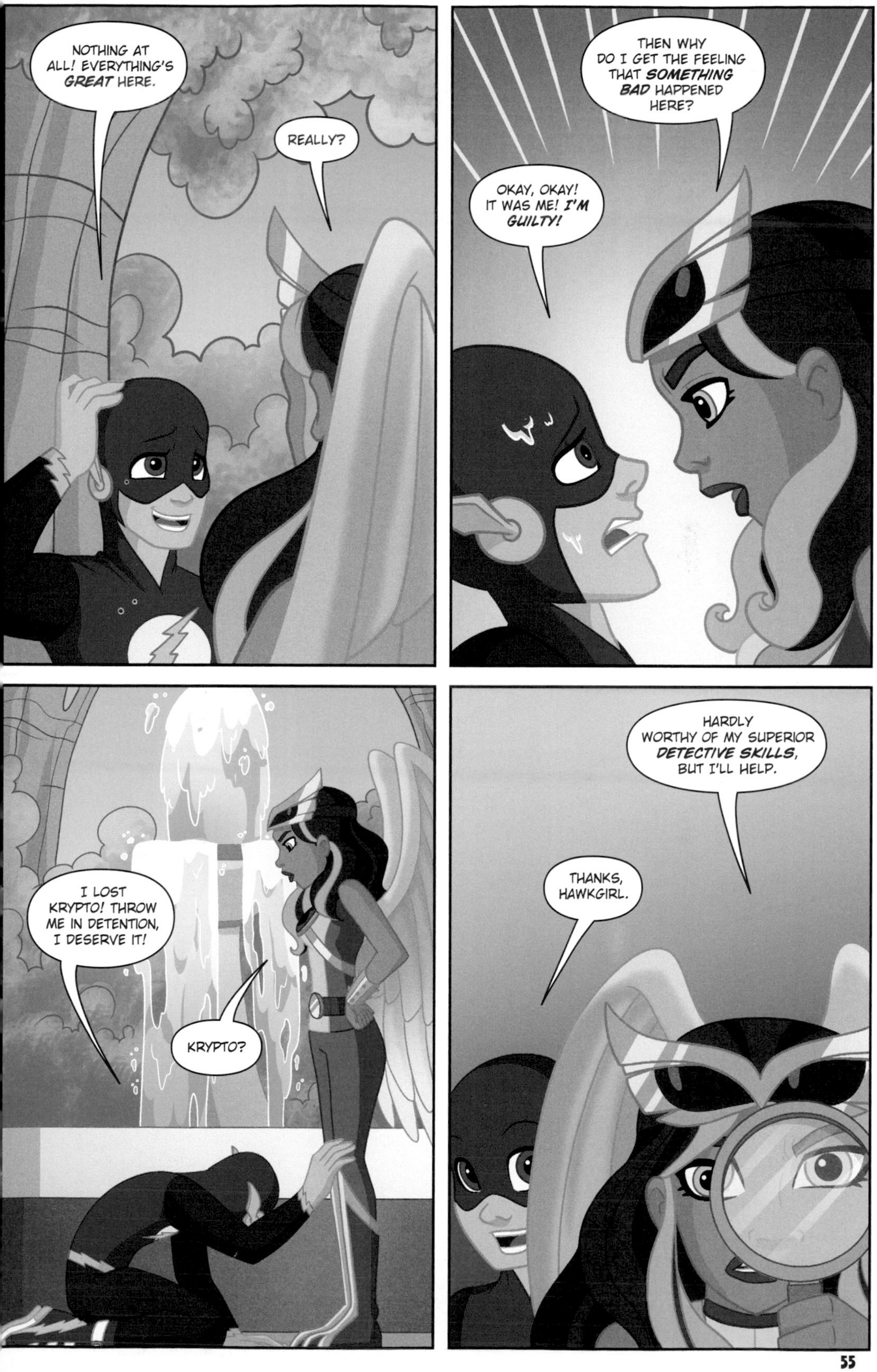
NOTHING AT ALL! EVERYTHING'S GREAT HERE.
REALLY?
THEN WHY DO I GET THE FEELING THAT SOMETHING BAD HAPPENED HERE?
OKAY, OKAY! IT WAS ME! I'M GUILTY!
I LOST KRYPTO! THROW ME IN DETENTION, I DESERVE IT!
KRYPTO?
HARDLY WORTHY OF MY SUPERIOR DETECTIVE SKILLS, BUT I'LL HELP.
THANKS, HAWKGIRL.

ARE YOU **SURE** THESE ARE FIVE-STAR ACCOMMODATIONS?

YEAH. ONCE YOU GET THROUGH THE DOOR, IT REALLY OPENS UP IN THERE.

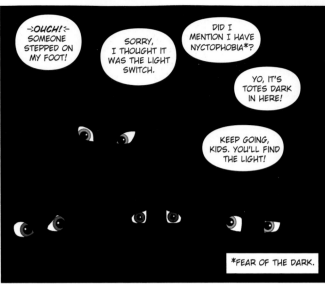

~:OUCH!:~ SOMEONE STEPPED ON MY FOOT!

SORRY, I THOUGHT IT WAS THE LIGHT SWITCH.

DID I MENTION I HAVE NYCTOPHOBIA*?

YO, IT'S TOTES DARK IN HERE!

KEEP GOING, KIDS. YOU'LL FIND THE LIGHT!

*FEAR OF THE DARK.

CLICK!

LAUNCH

HAVE A NICE TRIP! OR NOT. HA!

BOOM!

56

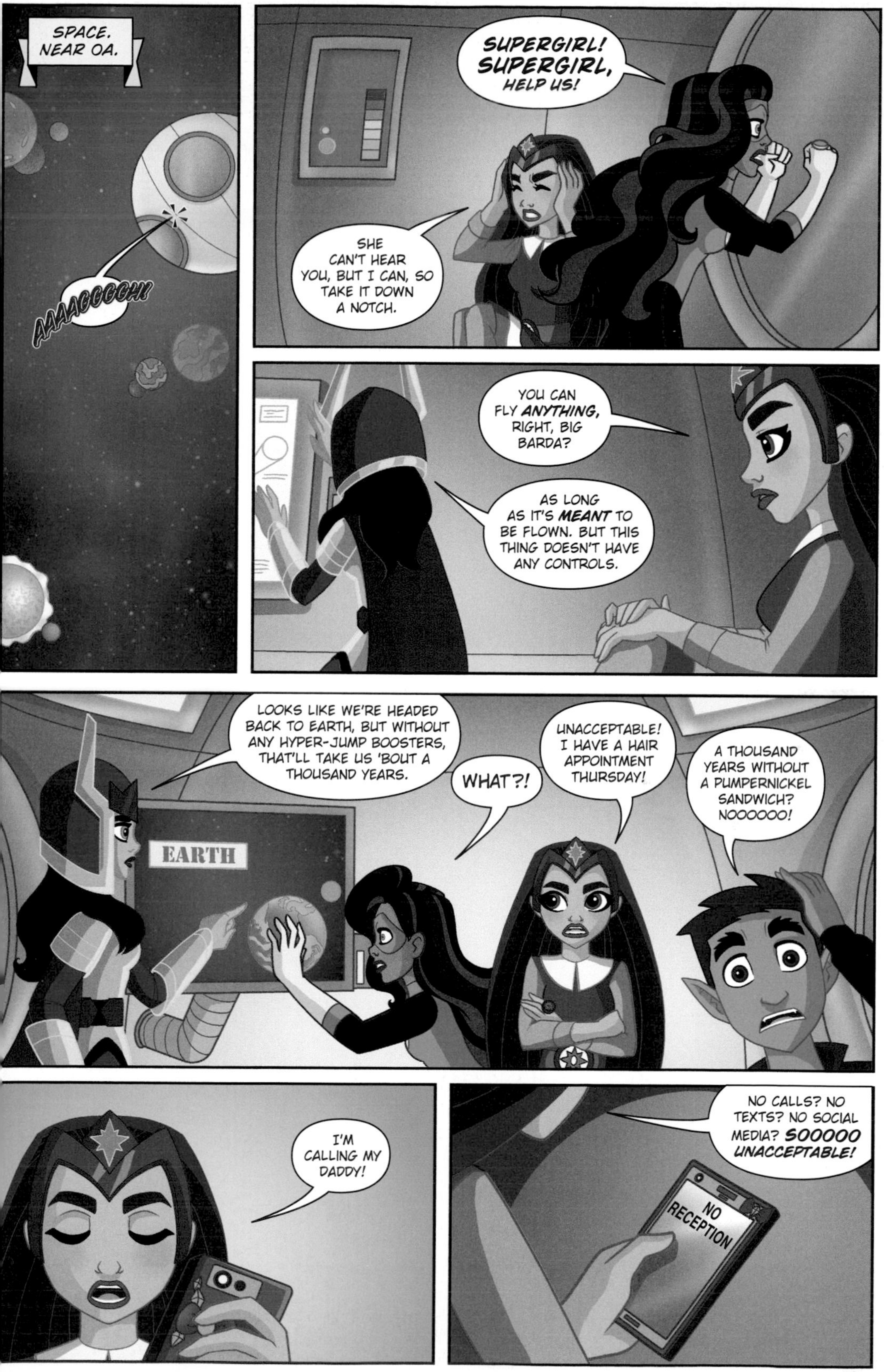
SPACE. NEAR OA.
AAAAGGGGH!
SUPERGIRL! SUPERGIRL, HELP US!
SHE CAN'T HEAR YOU, BUT I CAN, SO TAKE IT DOWN A NOTCH.
YOU CAN FLY ANYTHING, RIGHT, BIG BARDA?
AS LONG AS IT'S MEANT TO BE FLOWN. BUT THIS THING DOESN'T HAVE ANY CONTROLS.
LOOKS LIKE WE'RE HEADED BACK TO EARTH, BUT WITHOUT ANY HYPER-JUMP BOOSTERS, THAT'LL TAKE US 'BOUT A THOUSAND YEARS.
EARTH
WHAT?!
UNACCEPTABLE! I HAVE A HAIR APPOINTMENT THURSDAY!
A THOUSAND YEARS WITHOUT A PUMPERNICKEL SANDWICH? NOOOOOO!
I'M CALLING MY DADDY!
NO CALLS? NO TEXTS? NO SOCIAL MEDIA? SOOOOO UNACCEPTABLE!
NO RECEPTION

THERE'S *SOMETHING* OUT THERE!

WHAT IN THE APOKOLIPS?

IT'S--

A--

SPACE CAB!

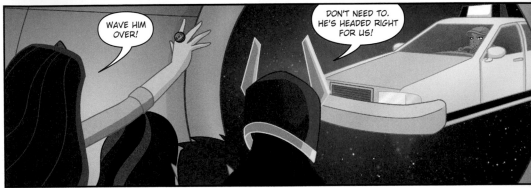

WAVE HIM OVER!

DON'T NEED TO. HE'S HEADED RIGHT FOR US!

BRACE FOR IMPACT!

CRASH!

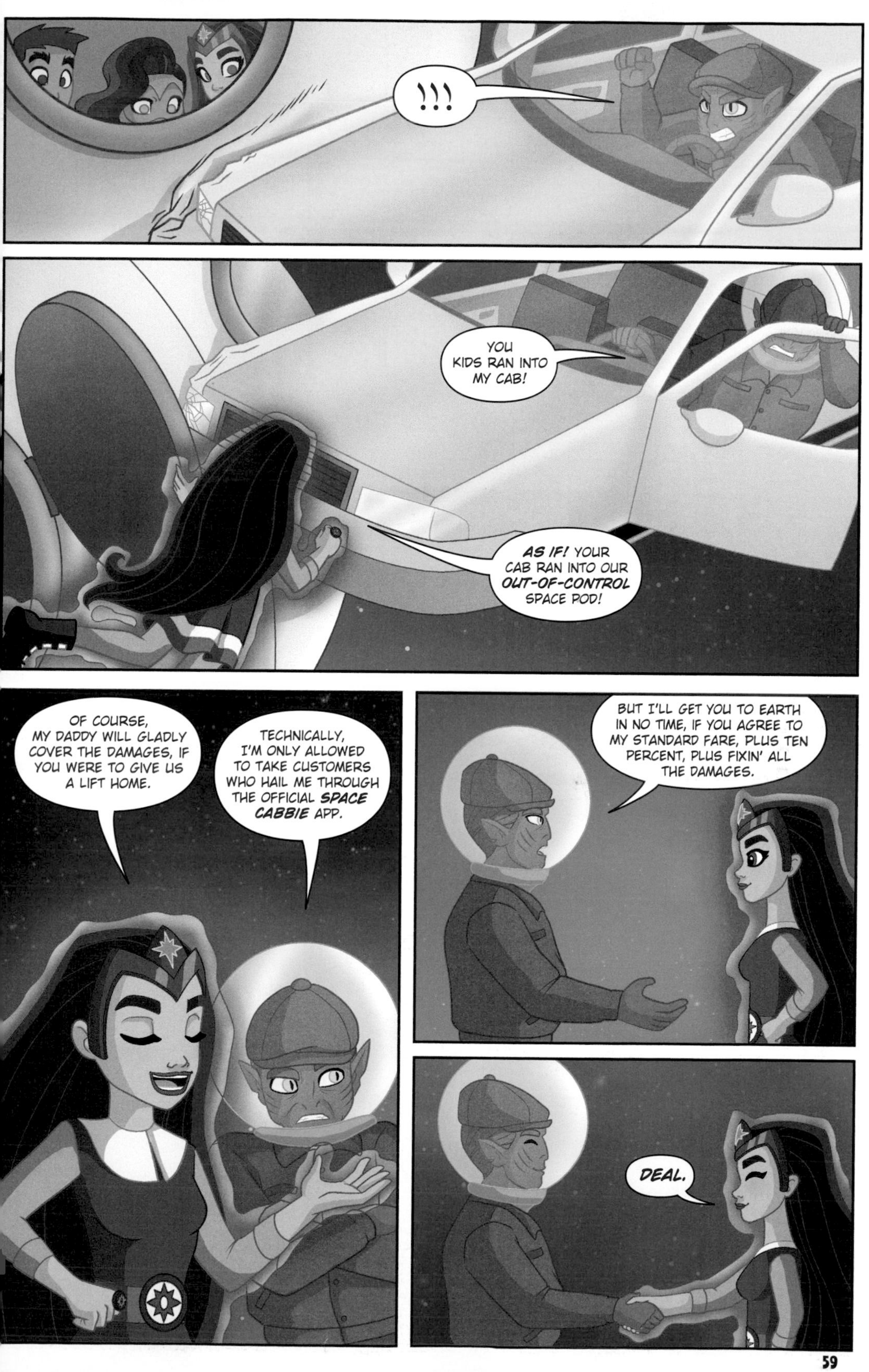
!!!
YOU KIDS RAN INTO MY CAB!
AS IF! YOUR CAB RAN INTO OUR OUT-OF-CONTROL SPACE POD!
OF COURSE, MY DADDY WILL GLADLY COVER THE DAMAGES, IF YOU WERE TO GIVE US A LIFT HOME.
TECHNICALLY, I'M ONLY ALLOWED TO TAKE CUSTOMERS WHO HAIL ME THROUGH THE OFFICIAL SPACE CABBIE APP.
BUT I'LL GET YOU TO EARTH IN NO TIME, IF YOU AGREE TO MY STANDARD FARE, PLUS TEN PERCENT, PLUS FIXIN' ALL THE DAMAGES.
DEAL.

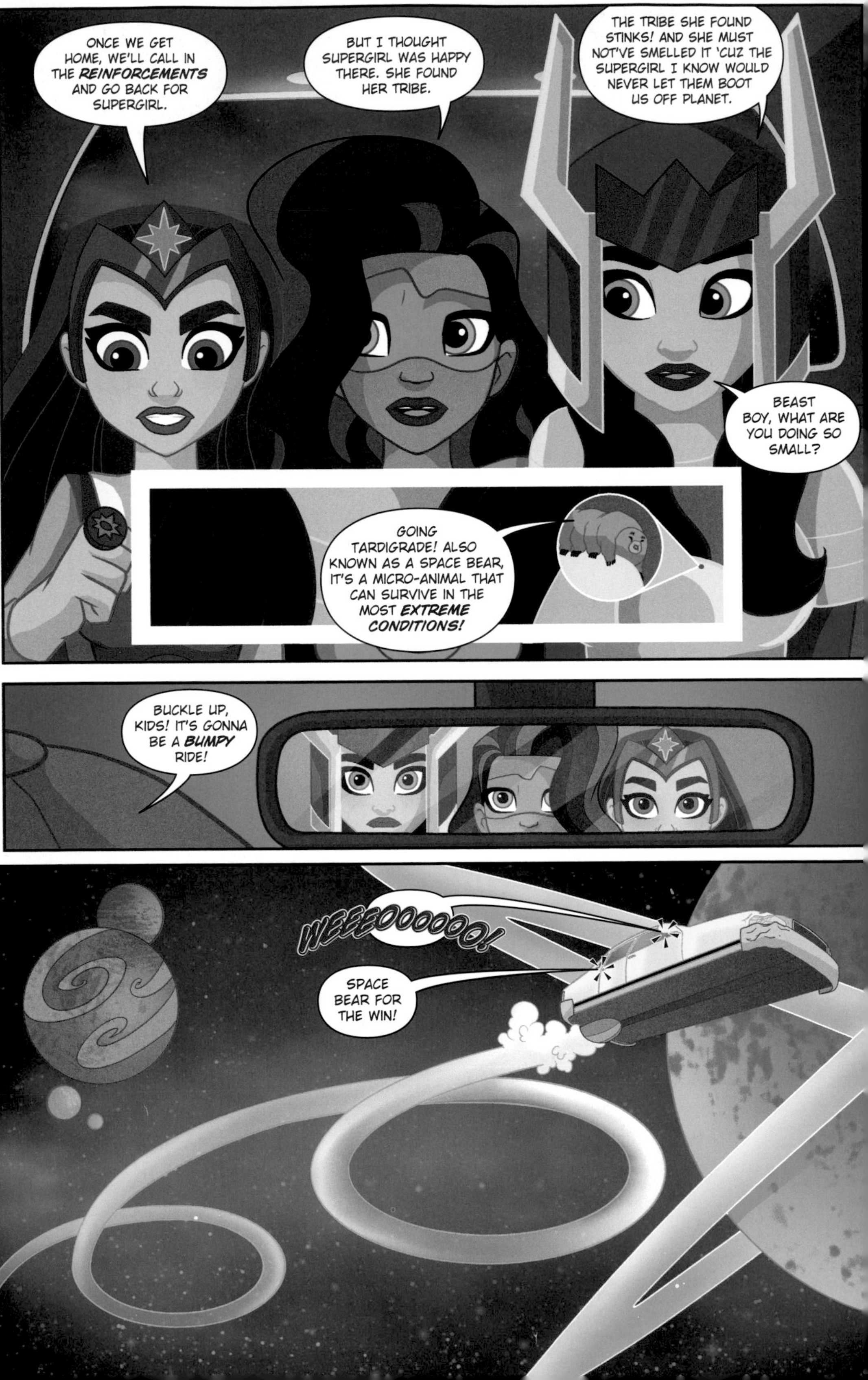
ONCE WE GET HOME, WE'LL CALL IN THE ***REINFORCEMENTS*** AND GO BACK FOR SUPERGIRL.
BUT I THOUGHT SUPERGIRL WAS HAPPY THERE. SHE FOUND HER TRIBE.
THE TRIBE SHE FOUND STINKS! AND SHE MUST NOT'VE SMELLED IT 'CUZ THE SUPERGIRL I KNOW WOULD NEVER LET THEM BOOT US OFF PLANET.
BEAST BOY, WHAT ARE YOU DOING SO SMALL?
GOING TARDIGRADE! ALSO KNOWN AS A SPACE BEAR, IT'S A MICRO-ANIMAL THAT CAN SURVIVE IN THE MOST ***EXTREME CONDITIONS!***
BUCKLE UP, KIDS! IT'S GONNA BE A ***BUMPY*** RIDE!
WEEEOOOOOOO!
SPACE BEAR FOR THE WIN!

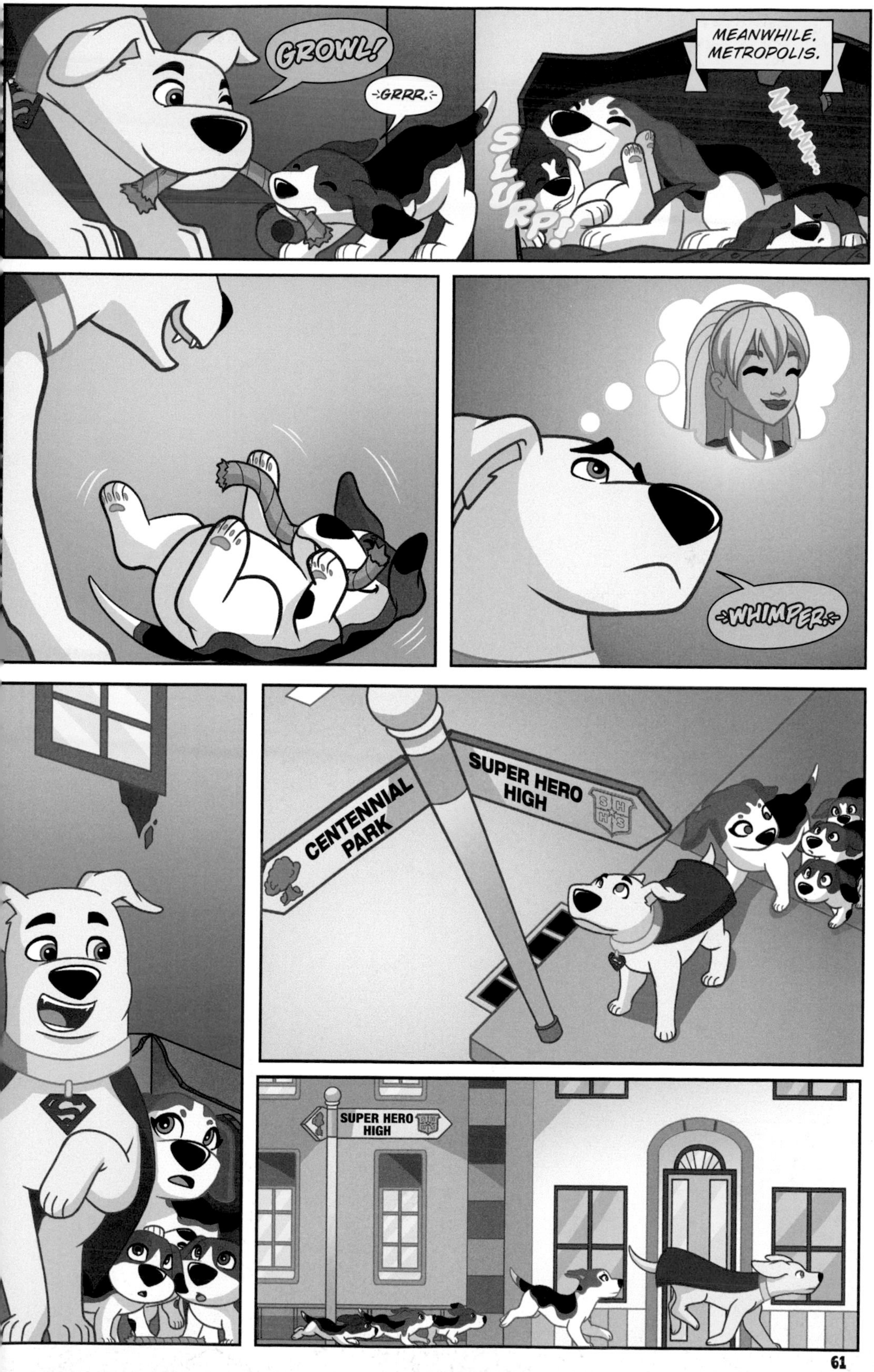
GROWL!
GRRR.
MEANWHILE. METROPOLIS.
ZZZZZ...
SLURP!
WHIMPER.
SUPER HERO HIGH
CENTENNIAL PARK
SUPER HERO HIGH

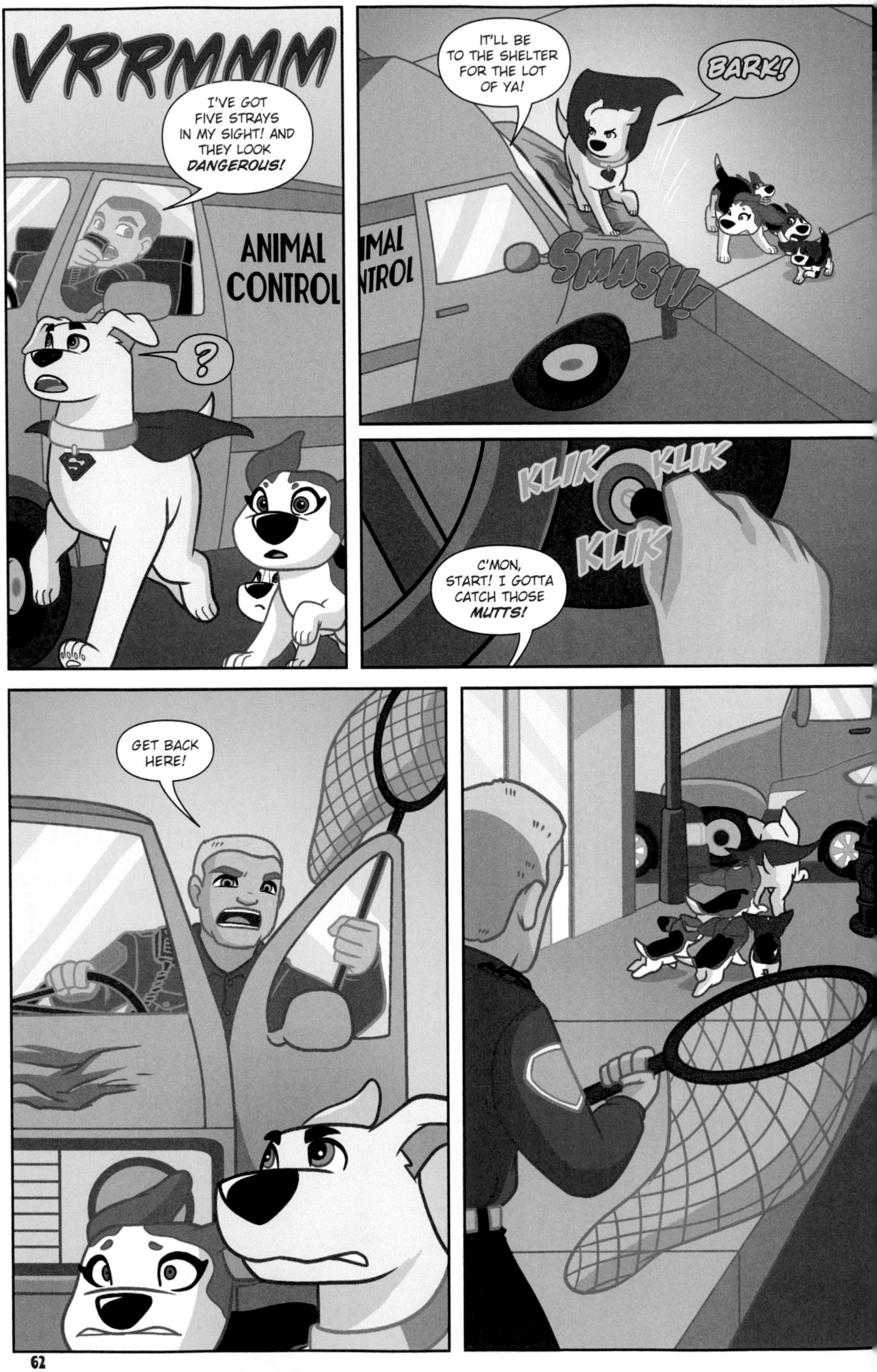
VRRMMM
I'VE GOT FIVE STRAYS IN MY SIGHT! AND THEY LOOK DANGEROUS!
ANIMAL CONTROL
?
IT'LL BE TO THE SHELTER FOR THE LOT OF YA!
BARK!
SMASH!
KLIK KLIK
KLIK
C'MON, START! I GOTTA CATCH THOSE MUTTS!
GET BACK HERE!

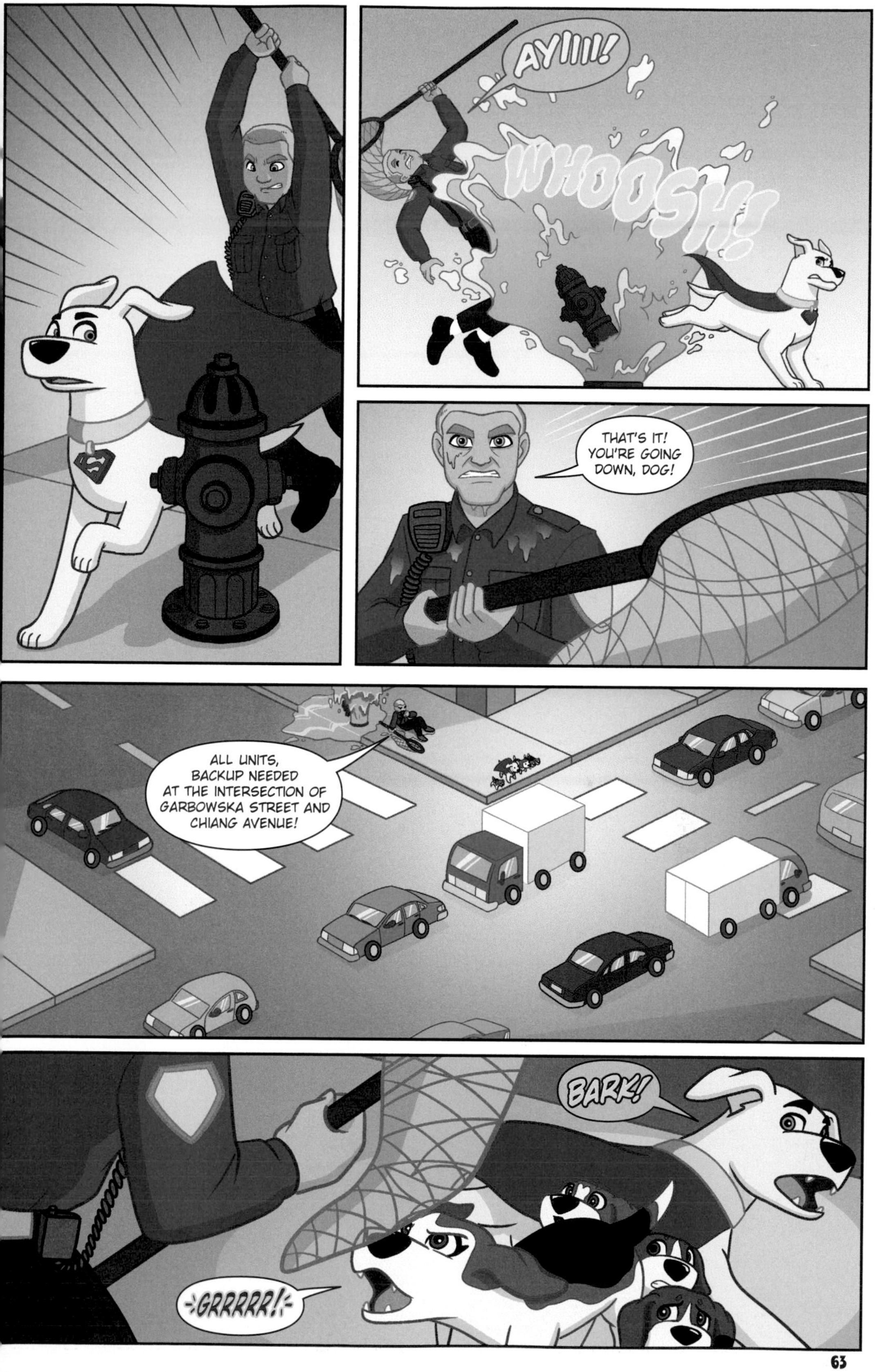
AYIIIII!
WHOOSH!
THAT'S IT! YOU'RE GOING DOWN, DOG!
ALL UNITS, BACKUP NEEDED AT THE INTERSECTION OF GARBOWSKA STREET AND CHIANG AVENUE!
BARK!
GRRRRR!

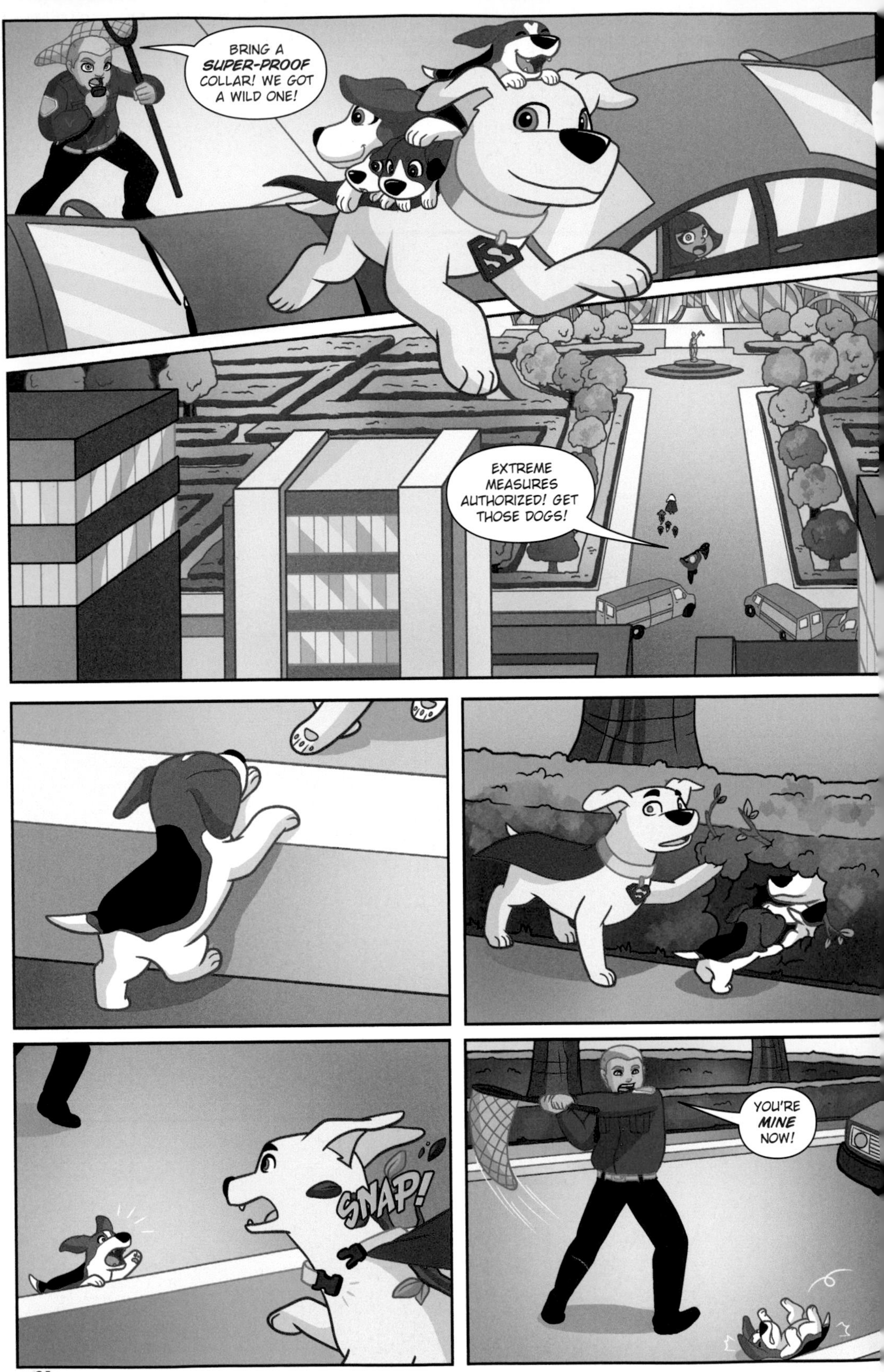
BRING A SUPER-PROOF COLLAR! WE GOT A WILD ONE!
EXTREME MEASURES AUTHORIZED! GET THOSE DOGS!
SNAP!
YOU'RE MINE NOW!

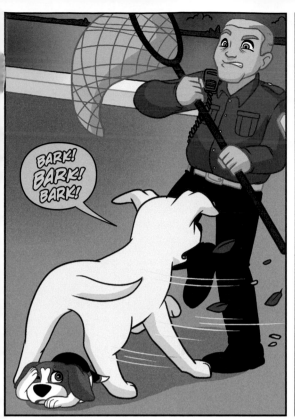

BARK!
BARK!
BARK!

YIII!
COLLAR THIS ONE! GO-GO-GO!

CRUNCH!

NOT SO **SUPER** NOW, ARE YA, MUTT?

KLANK!

AROOOO!

SPECIAL CRIMES K9 UNIT

AD035

≈WHIMPER≈

IF LOST CALL SUPERGIRL

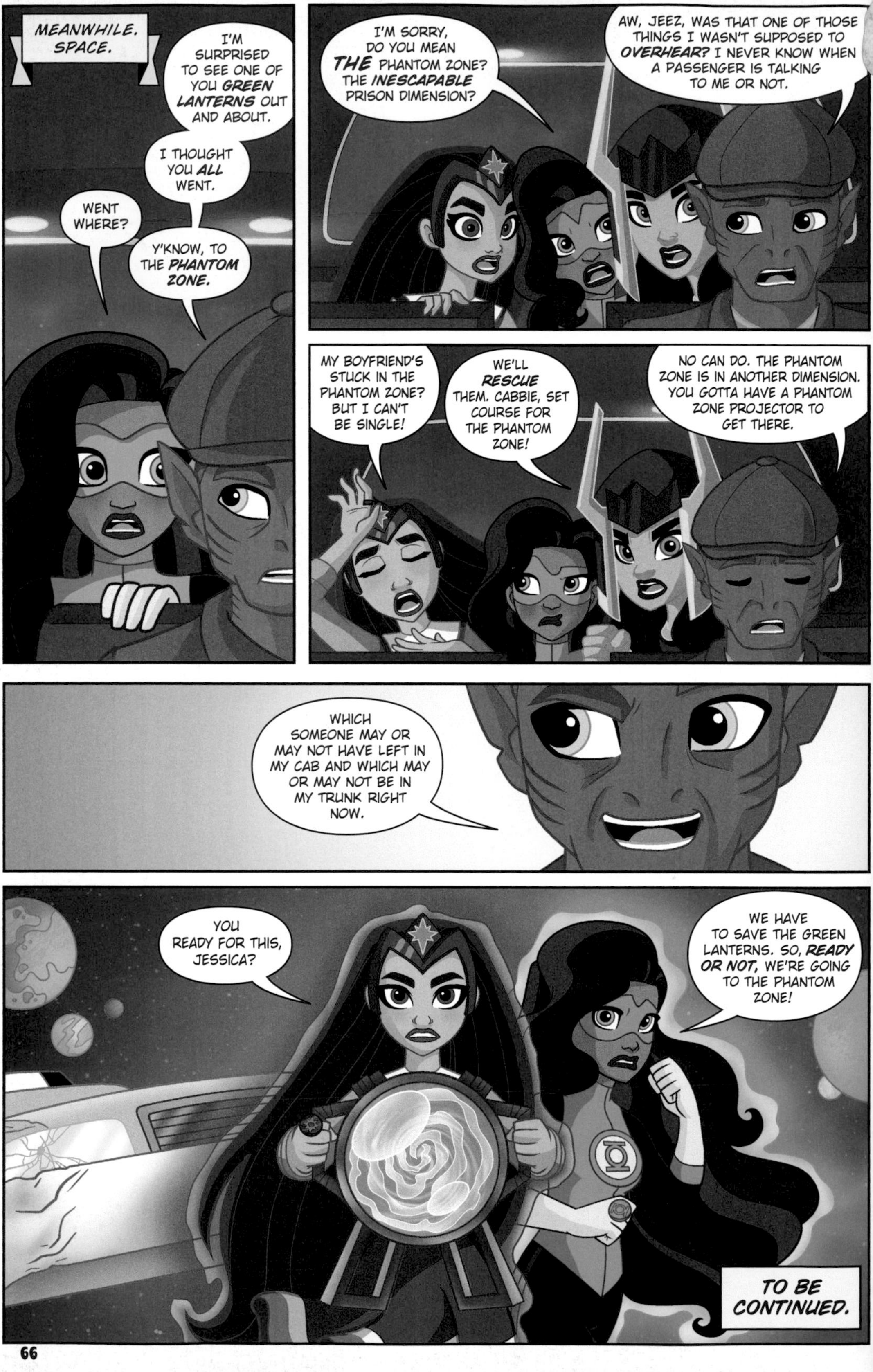
MEANWHILE. SPACE.
I'M SURPRISED TO SEE ONE OF YOU GREEN LANTERNS OUT AND ABOUT.
I THOUGHT YOU ALL WENT.
WENT WHERE?
Y'KNOW, TO THE PHANTOM ZONE.
I'M SORRY, DO YOU MEAN THE PHANTOM ZONE? THE INESCAPABLE PRISON DIMENSION?
AW, JEEZ, WAS THAT ONE OF THOSE THINGS I WASN'T SUPPOSED TO OVERHEAR? I NEVER KNOW WHEN A PASSENGER IS TALKING TO ME OR NOT.
MY BOYFRIEND'S STUCK IN THE PHANTOM ZONE? BUT I CAN'T BE SINGLE!
WE'LL RESCUE THEM. CABBIE, SET COURSE FOR THE PHANTOM ZONE!
NO CAN DO. THE PHANTOM ZONE IS IN ANOTHER DIMENSION. YOU GOTTA HAVE A PHANTOM ZONE PROJECTOR TO GET THERE.
WHICH SOMEONE MAY OR MAY NOT HAVE LEFT IN MY CAB AND WHICH MAY OR MAY NOT BE IN MY TRUNK RIGHT NOW.
YOU READY FOR THIS, JESSICA?
WE HAVE TO SAVE THE GREEN LANTERNS. SO, READY OR NOT, WE'RE GOING TO THE PHANTOM ZONE!
TO BE CONTINUED.

CHAPTER FOUR

ZONE IN

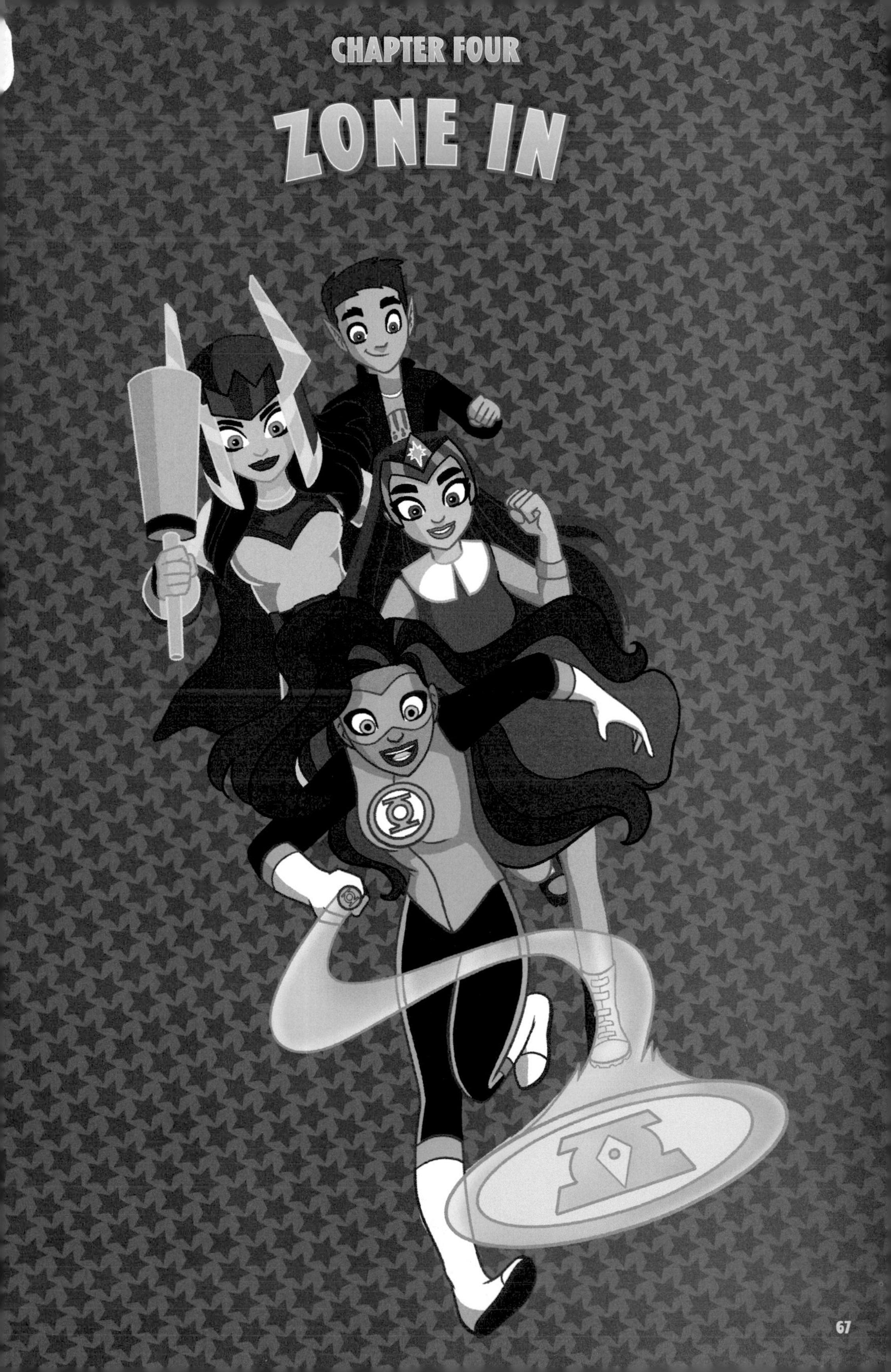

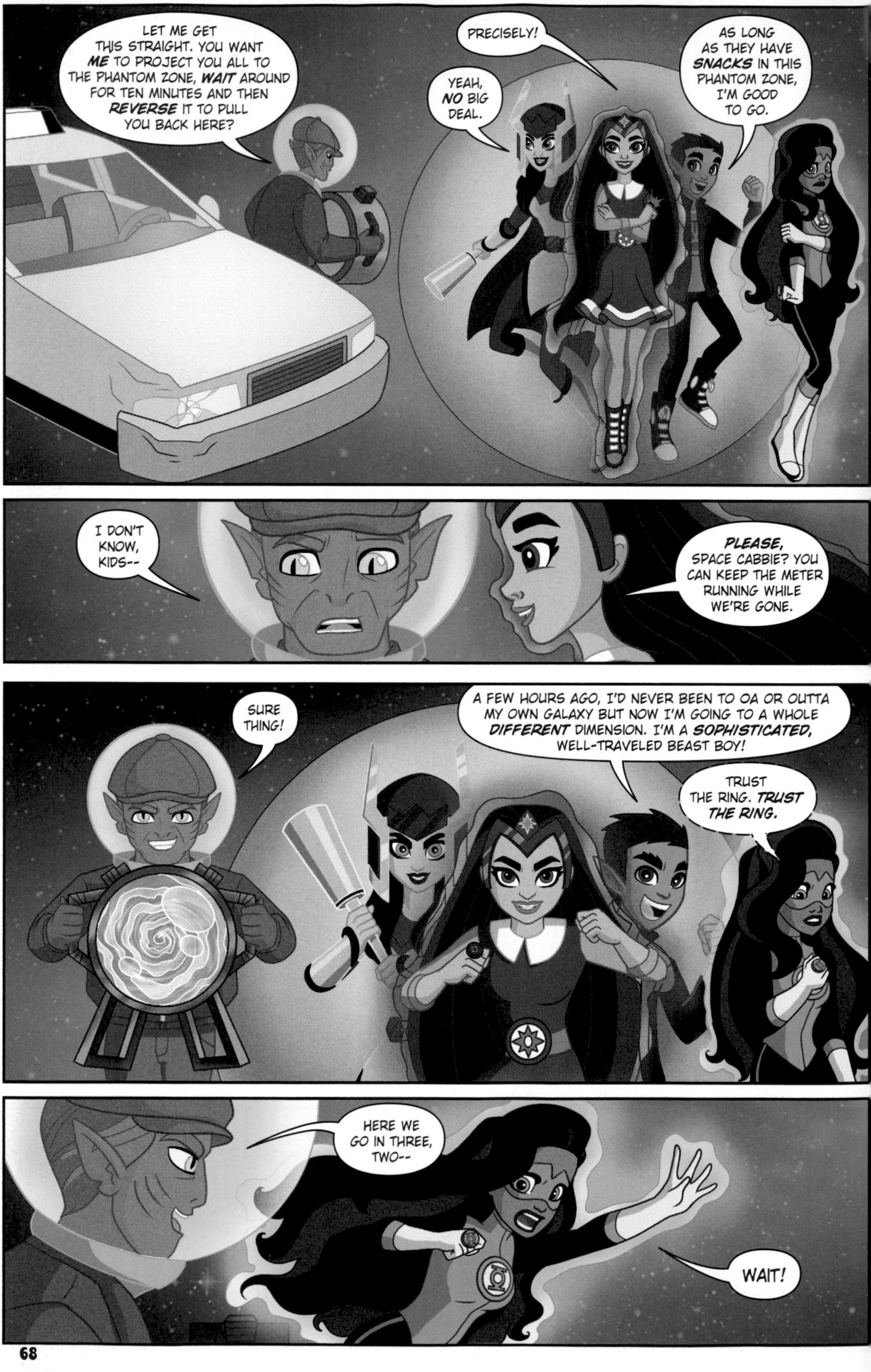
LET ME GET THIS STRAIGHT. YOU WANT ME TO PROJECT YOU ALL TO THE PHANTOM ZONE, WAIT AROUND FOR TEN MINUTES AND THEN REVERSE IT TO PULL YOU BACK HERE?
PRECISELY!
YEAH, NO BIG DEAL.
AS LONG AS THEY HAVE SNACKS IN THIS PHANTOM ZONE, I'M GOOD TO GO.
I DON'T KNOW, KIDS--
PLEASE, SPACE CABBIE? YOU CAN KEEP THE METER RUNNING WHILE WE'RE GONE.
SURE THING!
A FEW HOURS AGO, I'D NEVER BEEN TO OA OR OUTTA MY OWN GALAXY BUT NOW I'M GOING TO A WHOLE DIFFERENT DIMENSION. I'M A SOPHISTICATED, WELL-TRAVELED BEAST BOY!
TRUST THE RING. TRUST THE RING.
HERE WE GO IN THREE, TWO--
WAIT!

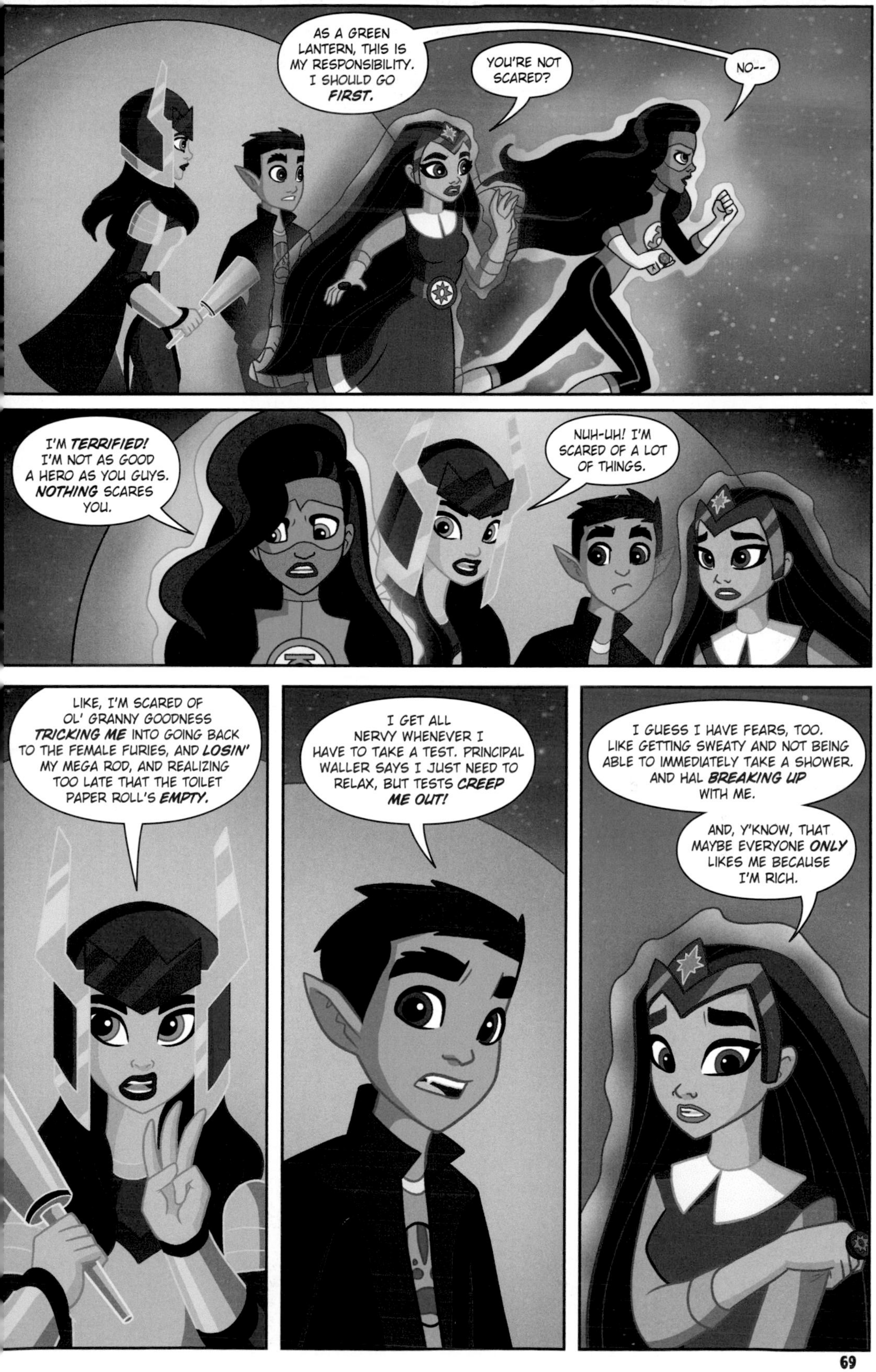
AS A GREEN LANTERN, THIS IS MY RESPONSIBILITY. I SHOULD GO FIRST.
YOU'RE NOT SCARED?
NO--
I'M TERRIFIED! I'M NOT AS GOOD A HERO AS YOU GUYS. NOTHING SCARES YOU.
NUH-UH! I'M SCARED OF A LOT OF THINGS.
LIKE, I'M SCARED OF OL' GRANNY GOODNESS TRICKING ME INTO GOING BACK TO THE FEMALE FURIES, AND LOSIN' MY MEGA ROD, AND REALIZING TOO LATE THAT THE TOILET PAPER ROLL'S EMPTY.
I GET ALL NERVY WHENEVER I HAVE TO TAKE A TEST. PRINCIPAL WALLER SAYS I JUST NEED TO RELAX, BUT TESTS CREEP ME OUT!
I GUESS I HAVE FEARS, TOO. LIKE GETTING SWEATY AND NOT BEING ABLE TO IMMEDIATELY TAKE A SHOWER. AND HAL BREAKING UP WITH ME.
AND, Y'KNOW, THAT MAYBE EVERYONE ONLY LIKES ME BECAUSE I'M RICH.

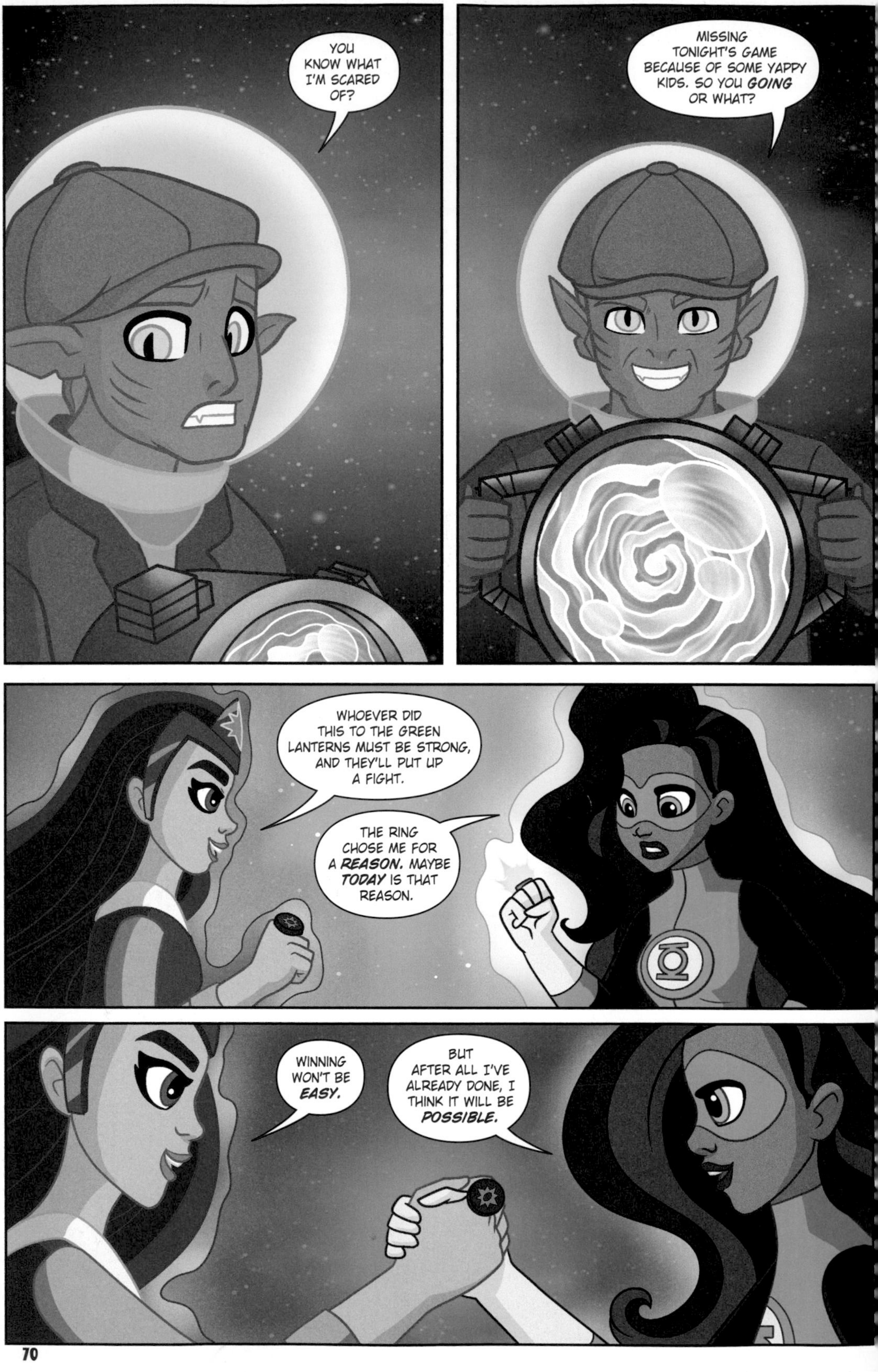
YOU KNOW WHAT I'M SCARED OF?
MISSING TONIGHT'S GAME BECAUSE OF SOME YAPPY KIDS. SO YOU *GOING* OR WHAT?
WHOEVER DID THIS TO THE GREEN LANTERNS MUST BE STRONG, AND THEY'LL PUT UP A FIGHT.
THE RING CHOSE ME FOR A *REASON.* MAYBE *TODAY* IS THAT REASON.
WINNING WON'T BE *EASY.*
BUT AFTER ALL I'VE ALREADY DONE, I THINK IT WILL BE *POSSIBLE.*

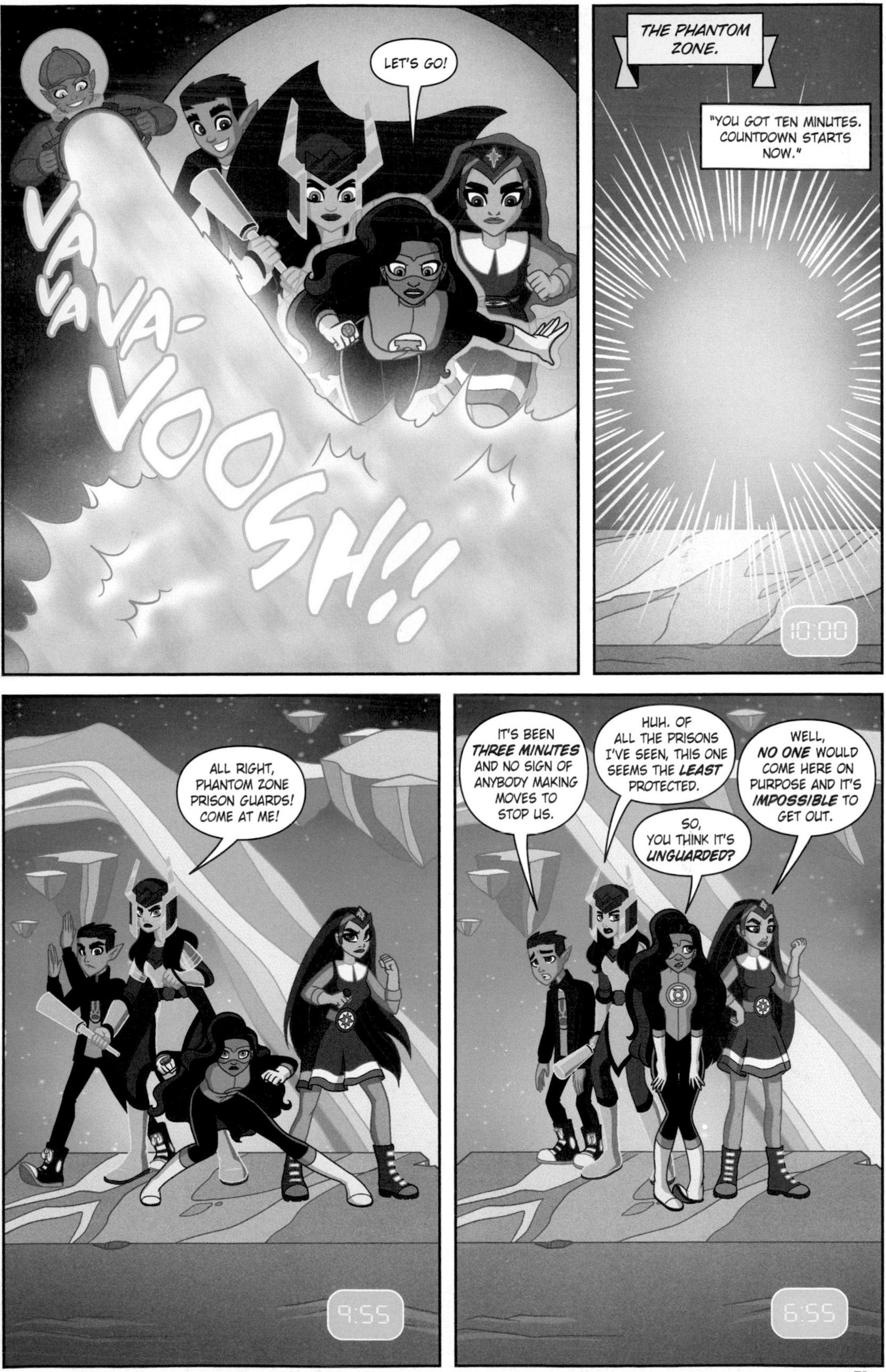
LET'S GO!
VA VA VA-VOOSH!!
THE PHANTOM ZONE.
"YOU GOT TEN MINUTES. COUNTDOWN STARTS NOW."
10:00
ALL RIGHT, PHANTOM ZONE PRISON GUARDS! COME AT ME!
9:55
IT'S BEEN THREE MINUTES AND NO SIGN OF ANYBODY MAKING MOVES TO STOP US.
HUH. OF ALL THE PRISONS I'VE SEEN, THIS ONE SEEMS THE LEAST PROTECTED.
SO, YOU THINK IT'S UNGUARDED?
WELL, NO ONE WOULD COME HERE ON PURPOSE AND IT'S IMPOSSIBLE TO GET OUT.
6:55

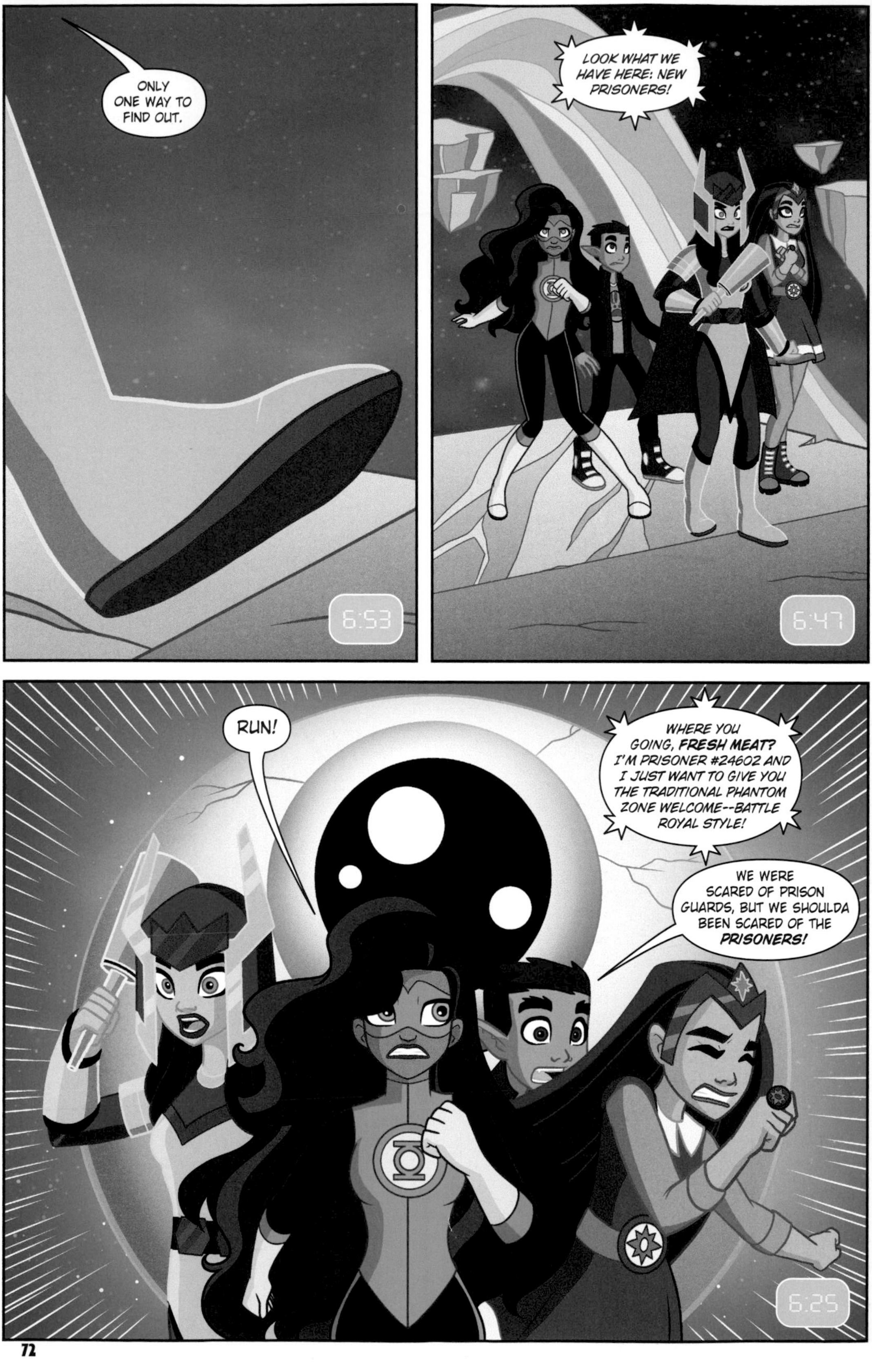
ONLY ONE WAY TO FIND OUT.
6:53
LOOK WHAT WE HAVE HERE: NEW PRISONERS!
6:47
RUN!
WHERE YOU GOING, **FRESH MEAT?** I'M PRISONER #24602 AND I JUST WANT TO GIVE YOU THE TRADITIONAL PHANTOM ZONE WELCOME--BATTLE ROYAL STYLE!
WE WERE SCARED OF PRISON GUARDS, BUT WE SHOULDA BEEN SCARED OF THE **PRISONERS!**
6:25

MEANWHILE,
METROPOLIS,
EARTH.

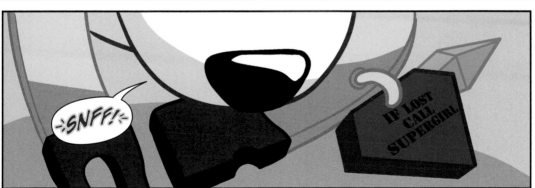

SNFF!

IF LOST
CALL
SUPERGIRL

SNFF!
SNFF!

SNFF!

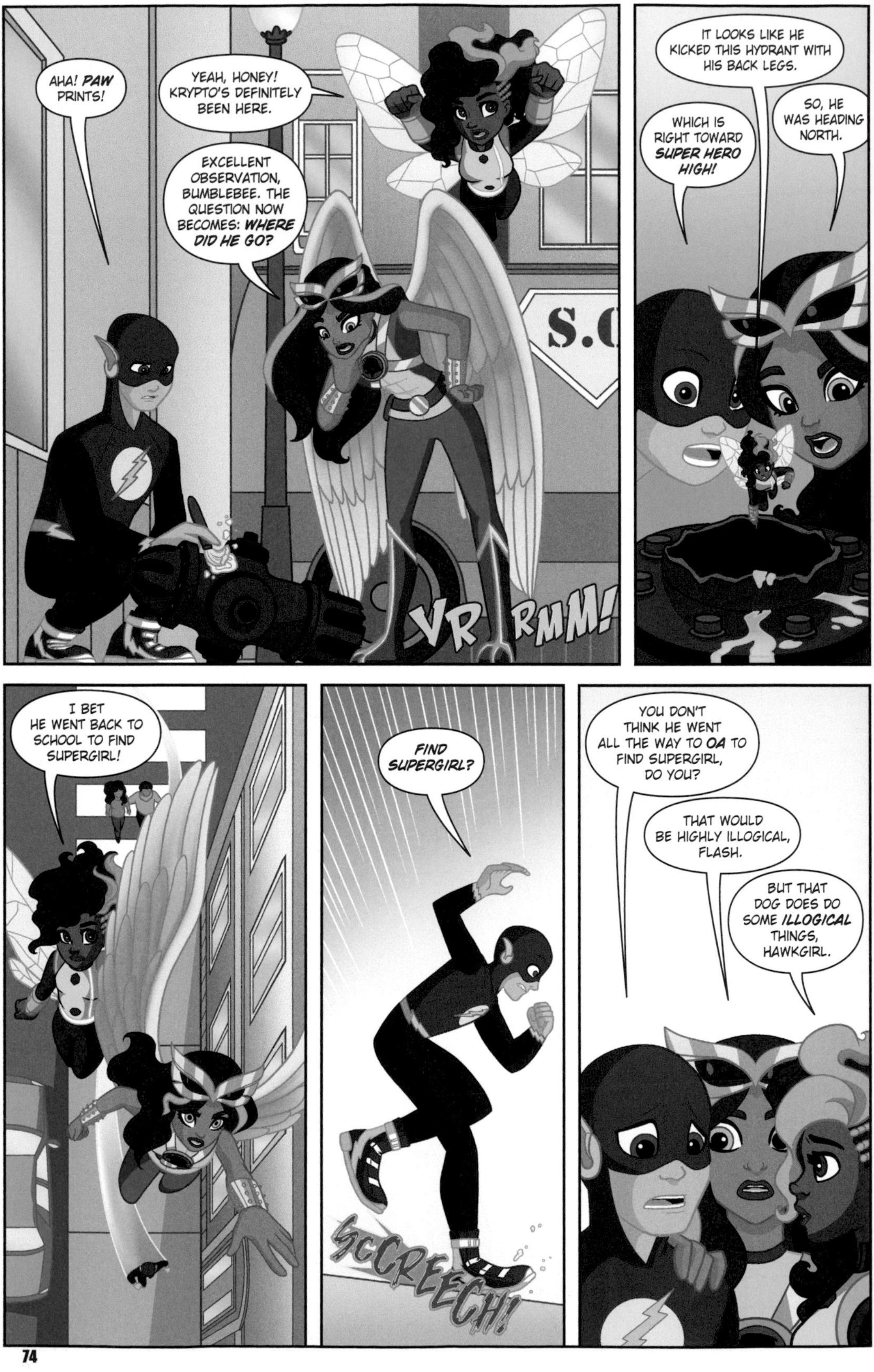

AHA! PAW PRINTS!
YEAH, HONEY! KRYPTO'S DEFINITELY BEEN HERE.
EXCELLENT OBSERVATION, BUMBLEBEE. THE QUESTION NOW BECOMES: WHERE DID HE GO?
S.C
VRRMM!
IT LOOKS LIKE HE KICKED THIS HYDRANT WITH HIS BACK LEGS.
SO, HE WAS HEADING NORTH.
WHICH IS RIGHT TOWARD SUPER HERO HIGH!
I BET HE WENT BACK TO SCHOOL TO FIND SUPERGIRL!
FIND SUPERGIRL?
SCCREECH!
YOU DON'T THINK HE WENT ALL THE WAY TO OA TO FIND SUPERGIRL, DO YOU?
THAT WOULD BE HIGHLY ILLOGICAL, FLASH.
BUT THAT DOG DOES DO SOME ILLOGICAL THINGS, HAWKGIRL.

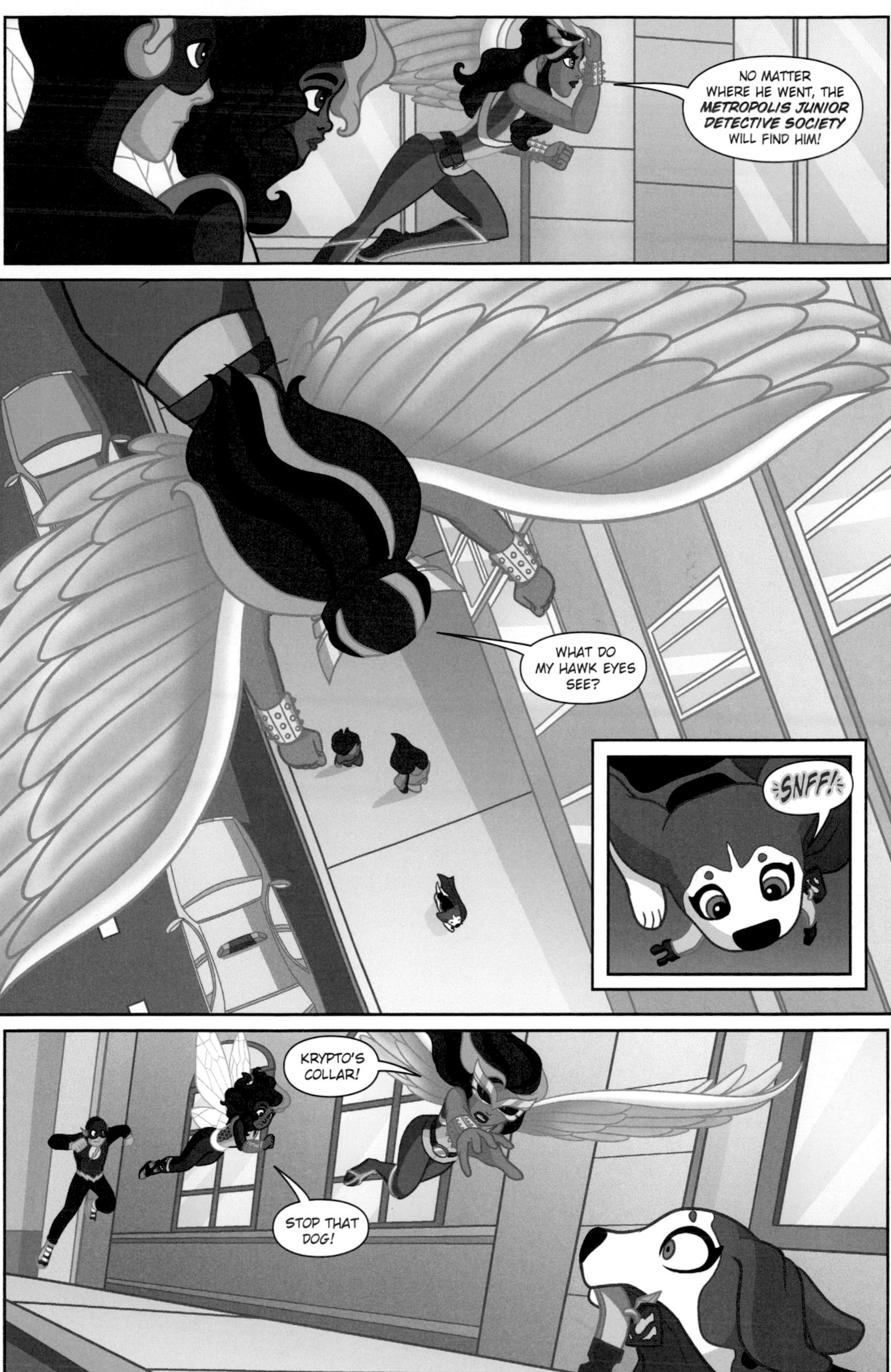
NO MATTER WHERE HE WENT, THE METROPOLIS JUNIOR DETECTIVE SOCIETY WILL FIND HIM!
WHAT DO MY HAWK EYES SEE?
SNFF!
KRYPTO'S COLLAR!
STOP THAT DOG!

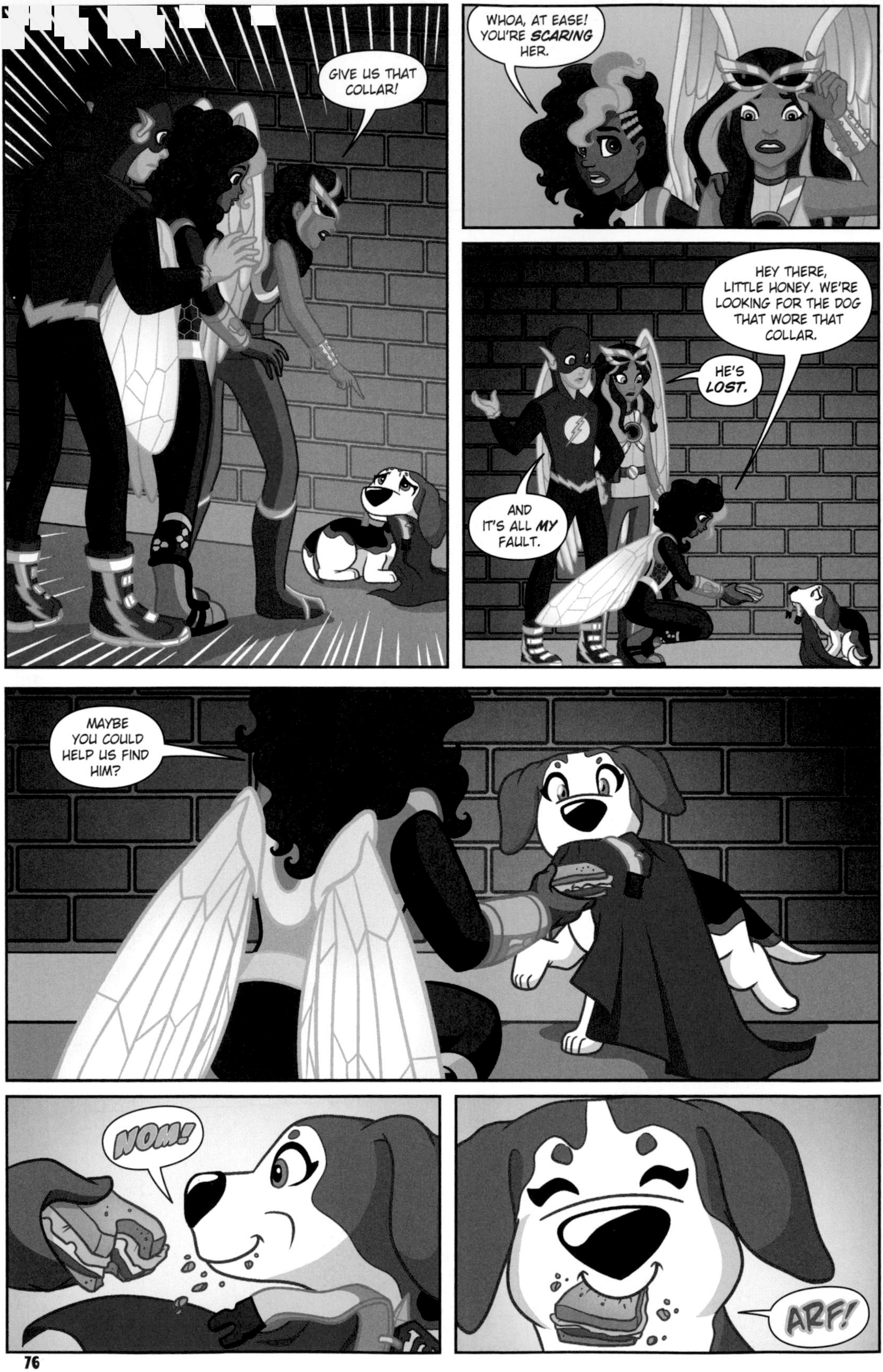
GIVE US THAT COLLAR!
WHOA, AT EASE! YOU'RE SCARING HER.
HEY THERE, LITTLE HONEY. WE'RE LOOKING FOR THE DOG THAT WORE THAT COLLAR.
HE'S LOST.
AND IT'S ALL MY FAULT.
MAYBE YOU COULD HELP US FIND HIM?
NOM!
ARF!

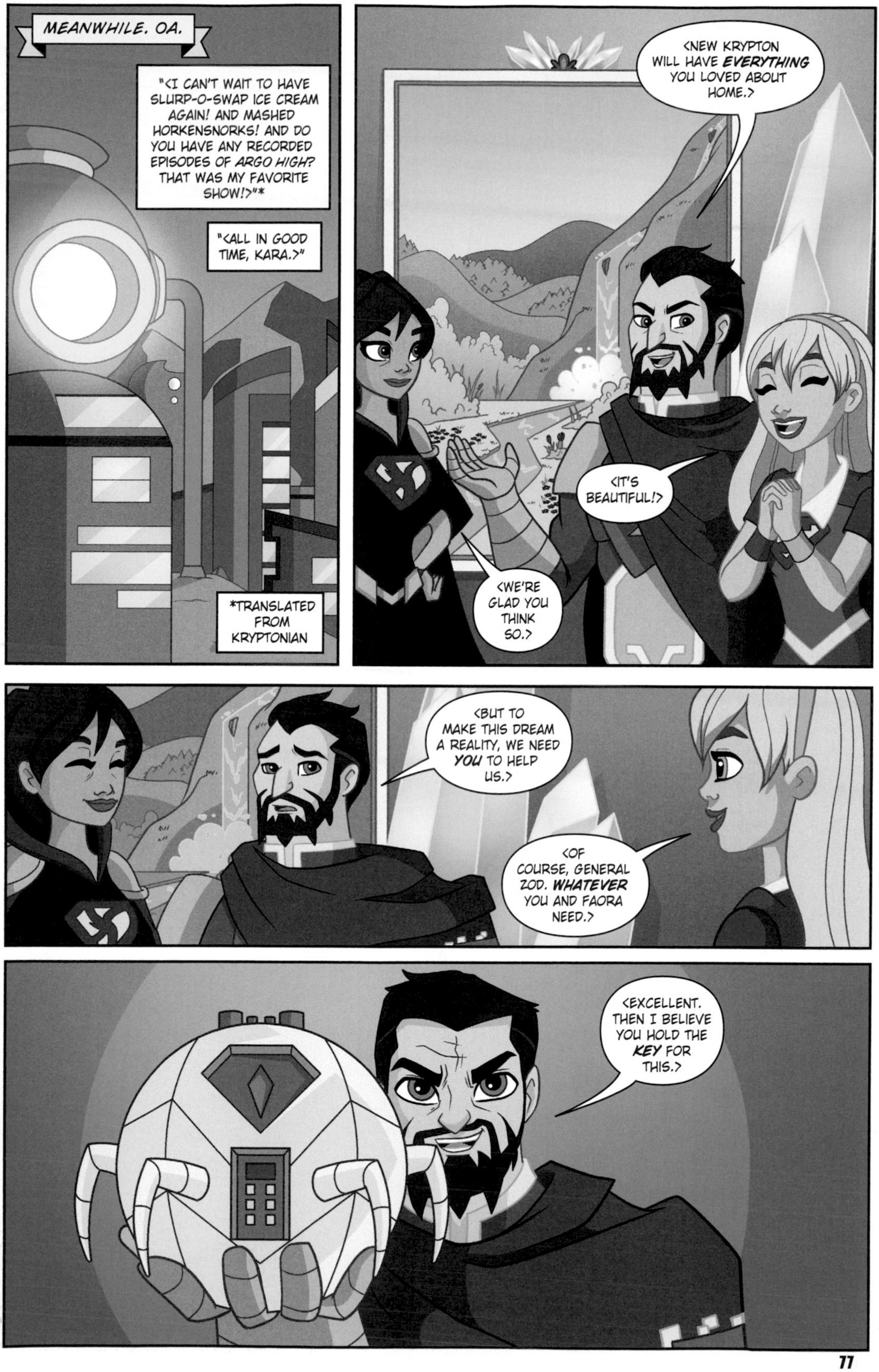
MEANWHILE, OA.
"<I CAN'T WAIT TO HAVE SLURP-O-SWAP ICE CREAM AGAIN! AND MASHED HORKENSNORKS! AND DO YOU HAVE ANY RECORDED EPISODES OF *ARGO HIGH*? THAT WAS MY FAVORITE SHOW!>"*
"<ALL IN GOOD TIME, KARA.>"
*TRANSLATED FROM KRYPTONIAN
<NEW KRYPTON WILL HAVE **EVERYTHING** YOU LOVED ABOUT HOME.>
<IT'S BEAUTIFUL!>
<WE'RE GLAD YOU THINK SO.>
<BUT TO MAKE THIS DREAM A REALITY, WE NEED ***YOU*** TO HELP US.>
<OF COURSE, GENERAL ZOD. ***WHATEVER*** YOU AND FAORA NEED.>
<EXCELLENT. THEN I BELIEVE YOU HOLD THE ***KEY*** FOR THIS.>

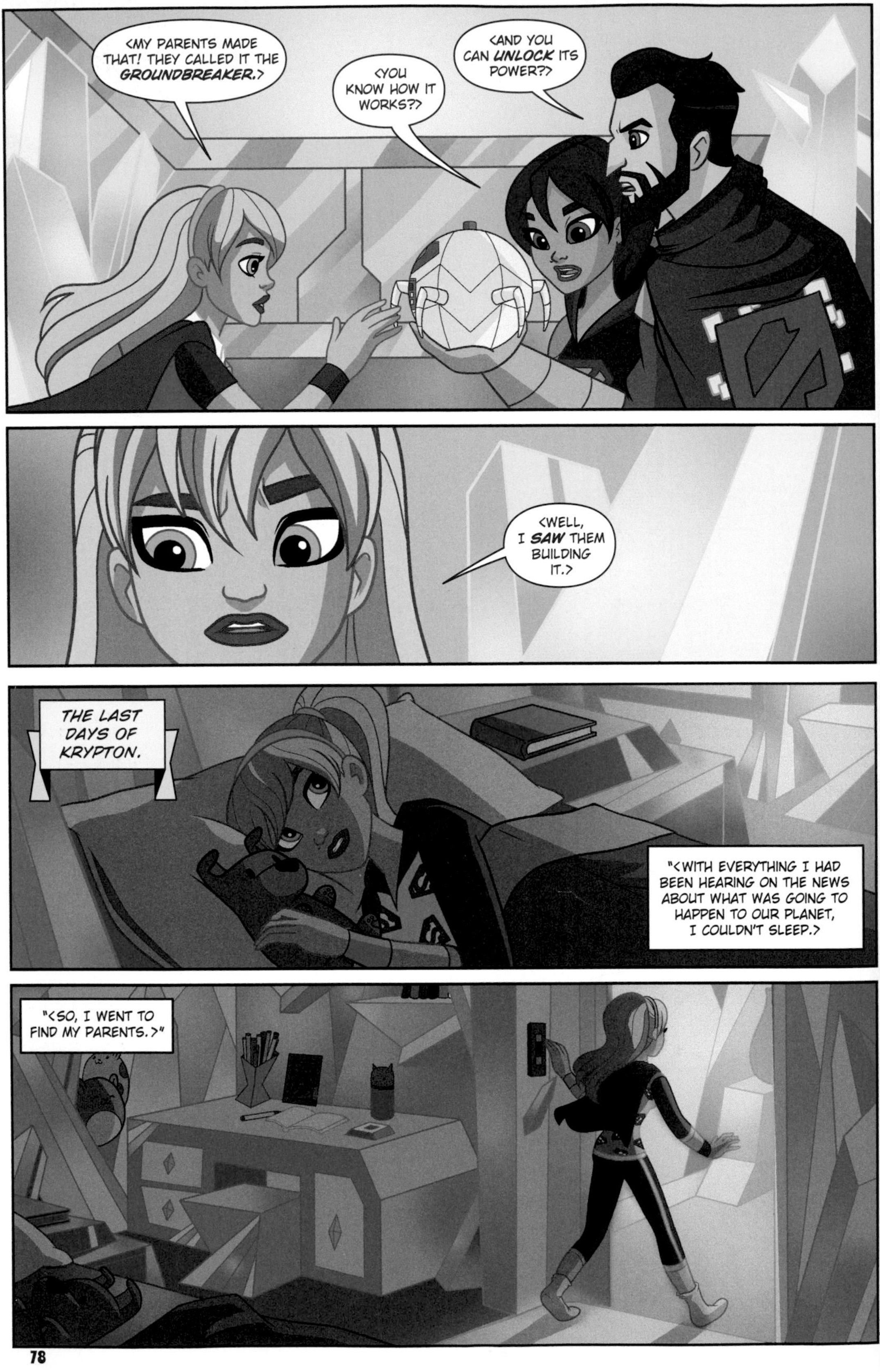

<MY PARENTS MADE THAT! THEY CALLED IT THE GROUNDBREAKER.>
<YOU KNOW HOW IT WORKS?>
<AND YOU CAN UNLOCK ITS POWER?>
<WELL, I SAW THEM BUILDING IT.>
THE LAST DAYS OF KRYPTON.
"<WITH EVERYTHING I HAD BEEN HEARING ON THE NEWS ABOUT WHAT WAS GOING TO HAPPEN TO OUR PLANET, I COULDN'T SLEEP.>
"<SO, I WENT TO FIND MY PARENTS.>"

‹MOM? DAD?›

‹KARA, YOU SHOULD BE IN BED.›

‹AS SHOULD WE, ZOR-EL. COME, KARA.›

‹WHAT ARE YOU WORKING ON?›

‹WE CALL IT THE GROUNDBREAKER. IT HAS POWER EQUAL TO THOUSANDS OF TERRAFORMING ROBOTS.›

‹JUST LOOK AT THE HOLO-SIM, DARLING!›

‹WITH THIS MACHINE, YOU CAN TURN WHATEVER BARREN PLANET YOU LAND ON INTO A HOME JUST LIKE KRYPTON.›

‹COOL!›

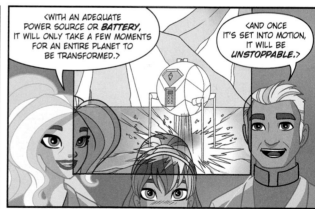

‹WITH AN ADEQUATE POWER SOURCE OR BATTERY, IT WILL ONLY TAKE A FEW MOMENTS FOR AN ENTIRE PLANET TO BE TRANSFORMED.›

‹AND ONCE IT'S SET INTO MOTION, IT WILL BE UNSTOPPABLE.›

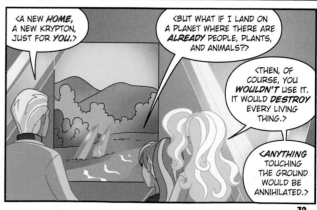

‹A NEW HOME, A NEW KRYPTON, JUST FOR YOU.›

‹BUT WHAT IF I LAND ON A PLANET WHERE THERE ARE ALREADY PEOPLE, PLANTS, AND ANIMALS?›

‹THEN, OF COURSE, YOU WOULDN'T USE IT. IT WOULD DESTROY EVERY LIVING THING.›

‹ANYTHING TOUCHING THE GROUND WOULD BE ANNIHILATED.›

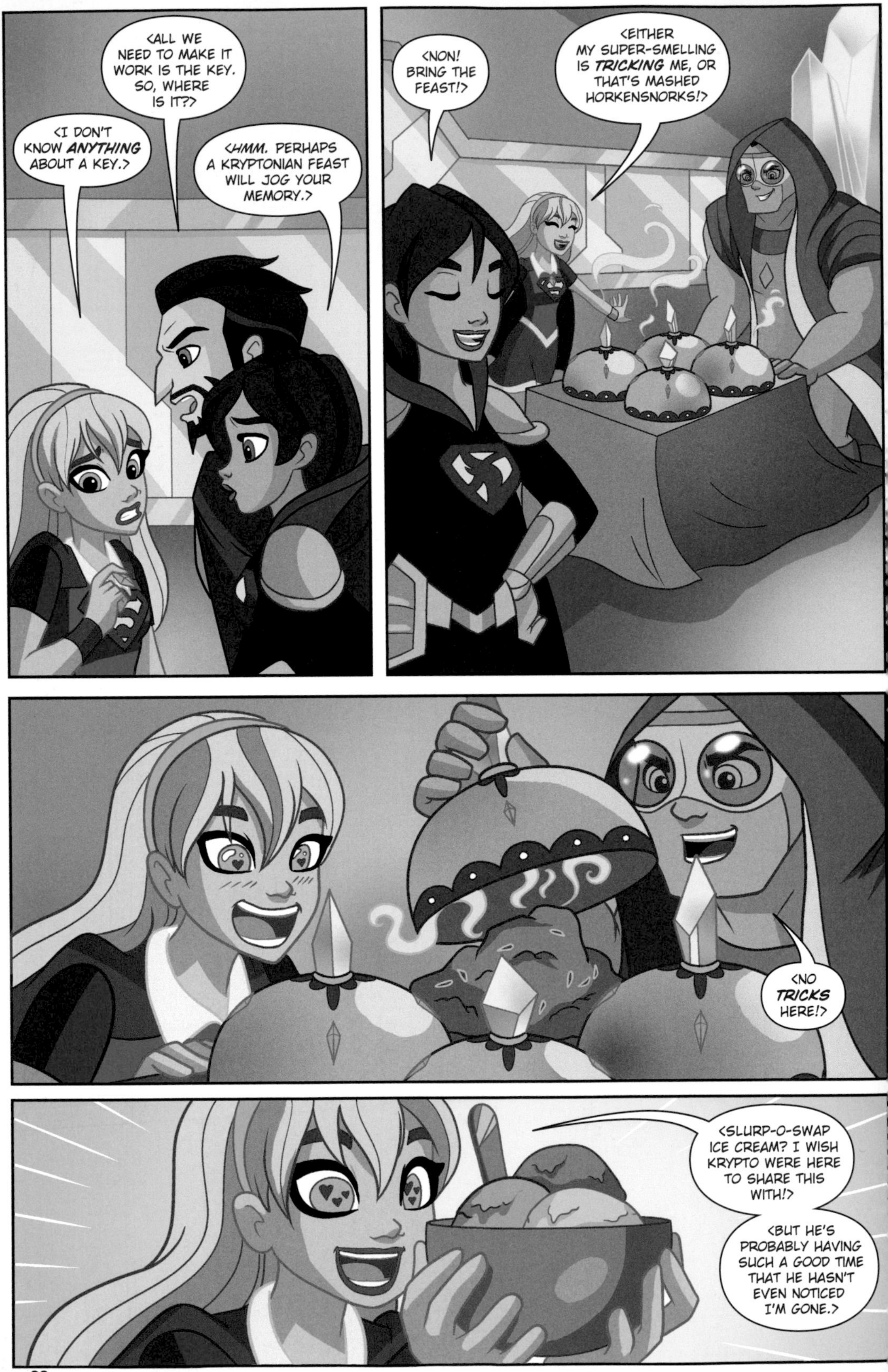
<ALL WE NEED TO MAKE IT WORK IS THE KEY. SO, WHERE IS IT?>
<I DON'T KNOW *ANYTHING* ABOUT A KEY.>
<*HMM.* PERHAPS A KRYPTONIAN FEAST WILL JOG YOUR MEMORY.>
<NON! BRING THE FEAST!>
<EITHER MY SUPER-SMELLING IS *TRICKING* ME, OR THAT'S MASHED HORKENSNORKS!>
<NO *TRICKS* HERE!>
<SLURP-O-SWAP ICE CREAM? I WISH KRYPTO WERE HERE TO SHARE THIS WITH!>
<BUT HE'S PROBABLY HAVING SUCH A GOOD TIME THAT HE HASN'T EVEN NOTICED I'M GONE.>

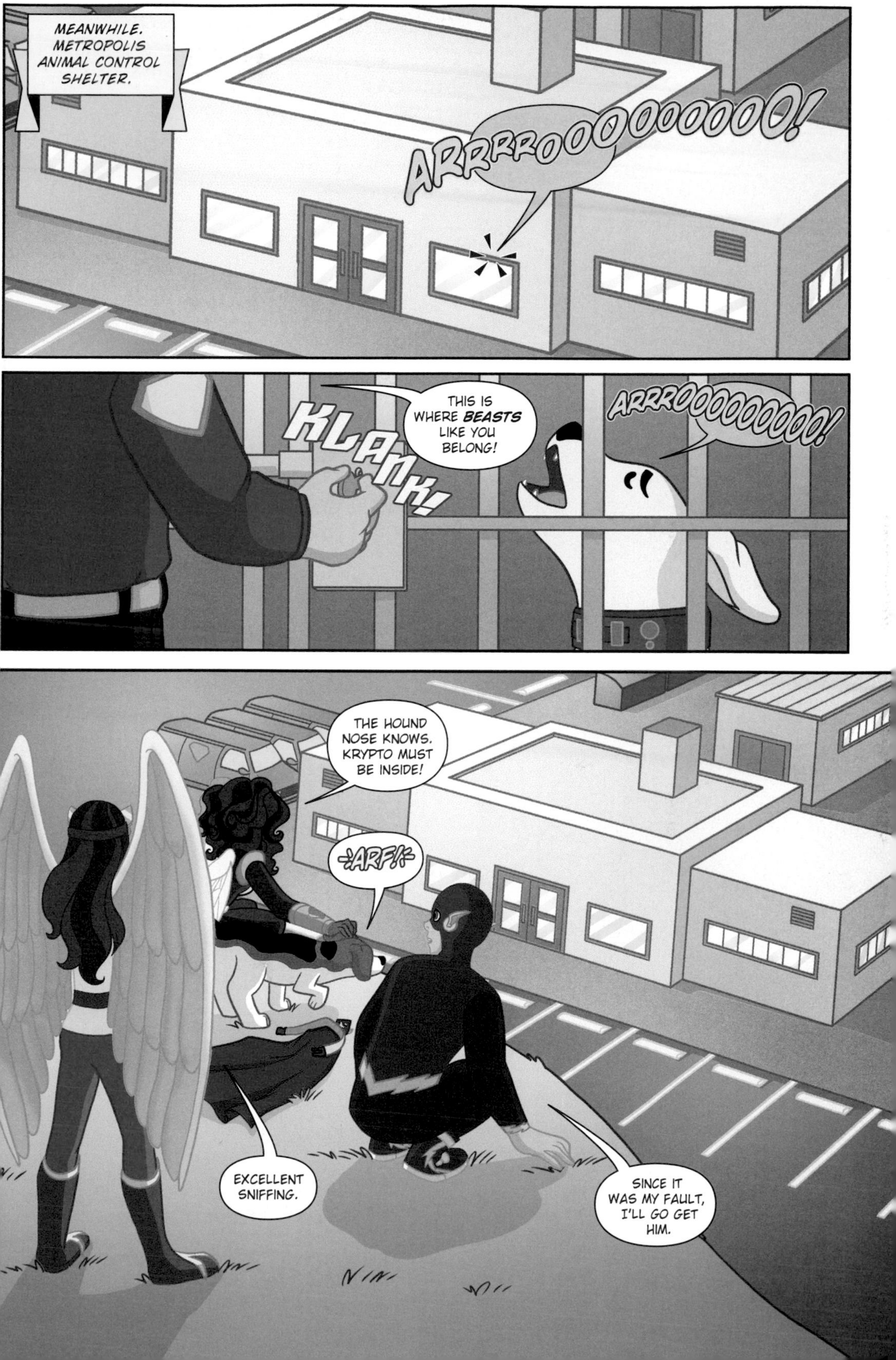
MEANWHILE. METROPOLIS ANIMAL CONTROL SHELTER.
ARRRROOOOOOOOOO!
THIS IS WHERE **BEASTS** LIKE YOU BELONG!
KLANK!
ARRROOOOOOOOOO!
THE HOUND NOSE KNOWS. KRYPTO MUST BE INSIDE!
-ARF!-
EXCELLENT SNIFFING.
SINCE IT WAS MY FAULT, I'LL GO GET HIM.

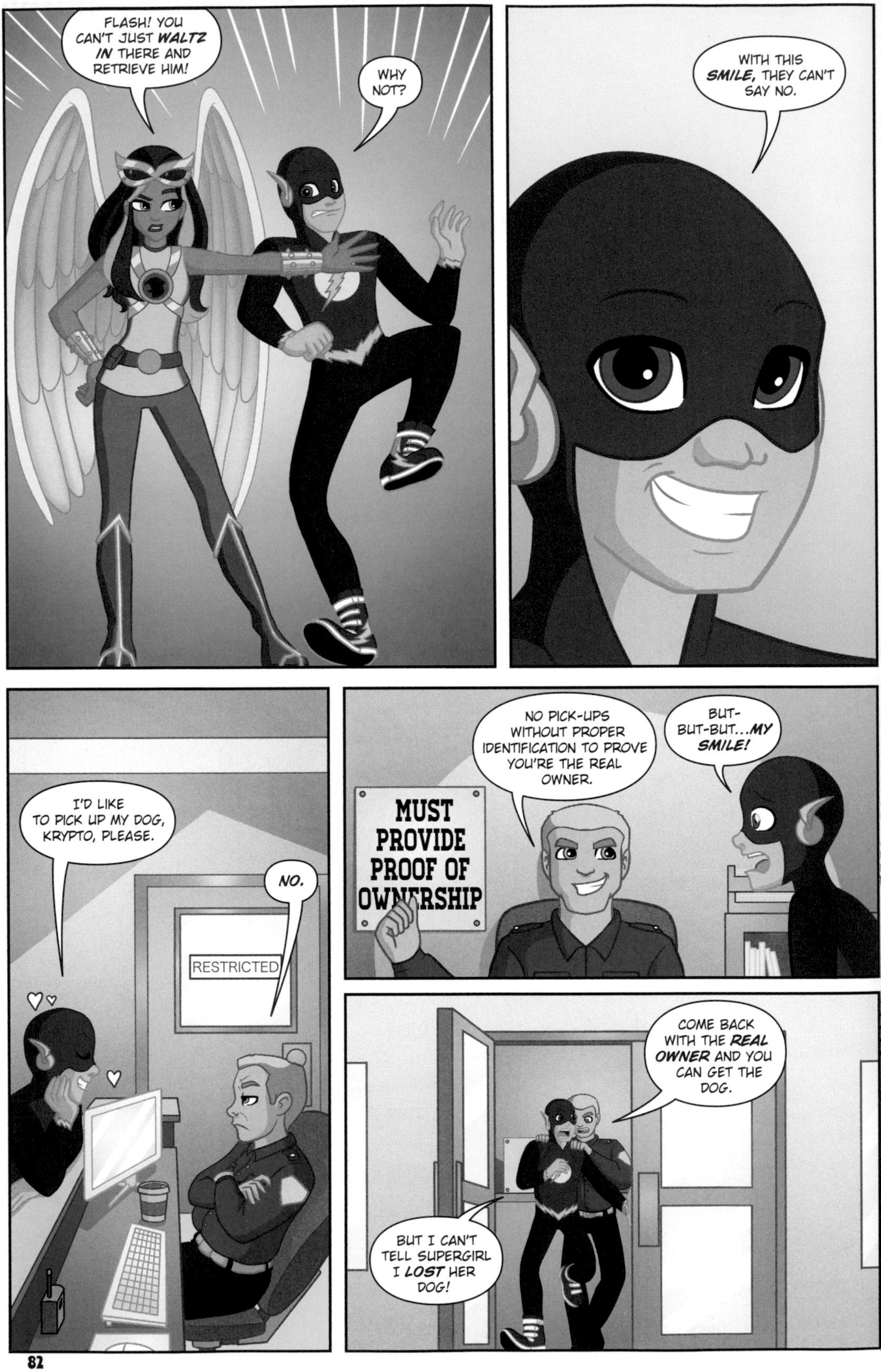
FLASH! YOU CAN'T JUST WALTZ IN THERE AND RETRIEVE HIM!
WHY NOT?
WITH THIS SMILE, THEY CAN'T SAY NO.
I'D LIKE TO PICK UP MY DOG, KRYPTO, PLEASE.
NO.
RESTRICTED
NO PICK-UPS WITHOUT PROPER IDENTIFICATION TO PROVE YOU'RE THE REAL OWNER.
BUT- BUT-BUT...MY SMILE!
MUST PROVIDE PROOF OF OWNERSHIP
COME BACK WITH THE REAL OWNER AND YOU CAN GET THE DOG.
BUT I CAN'T TELL SUPERGIRL I LOST HER DOG!

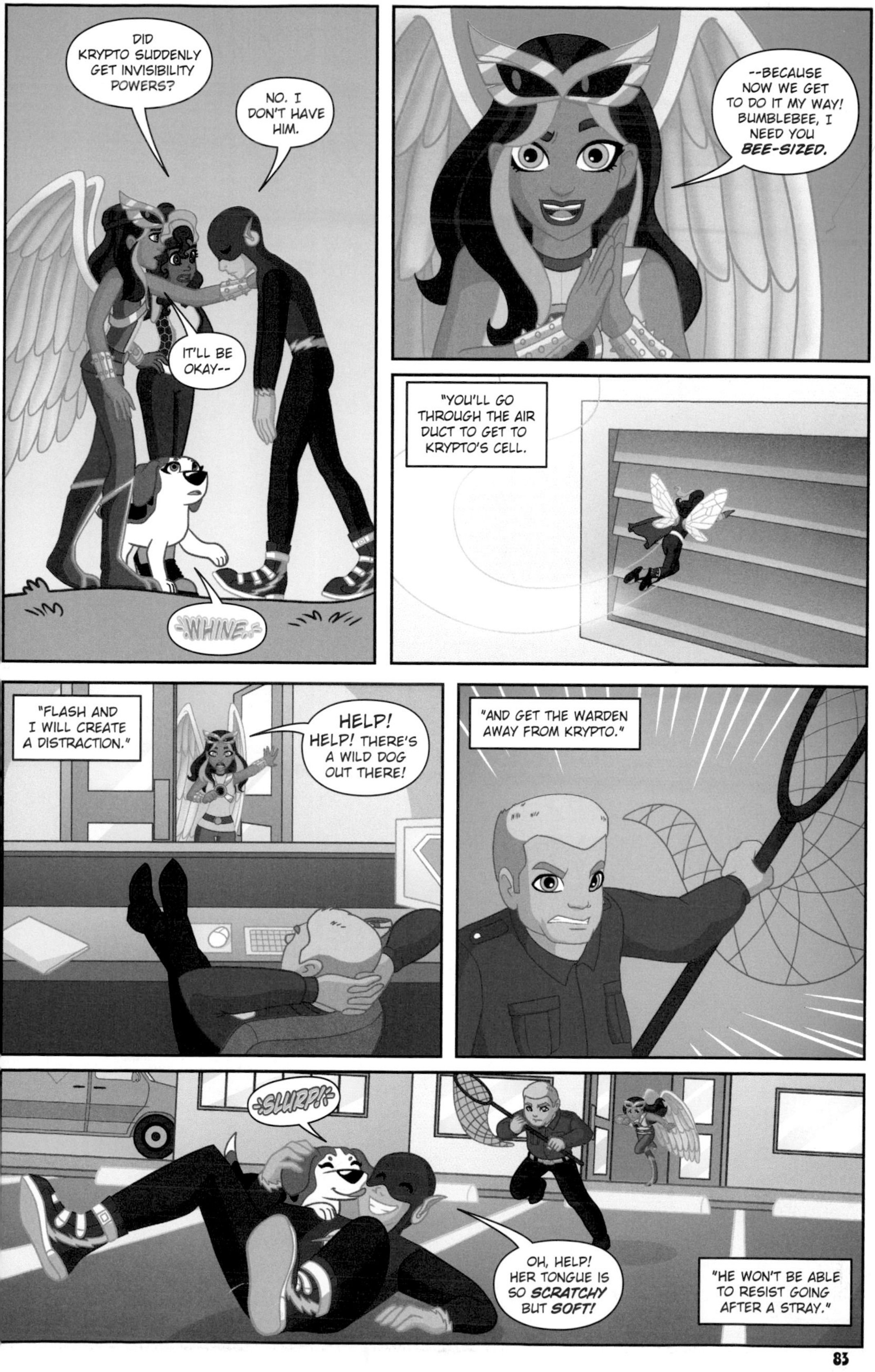
DID KRYPTO SUDDENLY GET INVISIBILITY POWERS?
NO. I DON'T HAVE HIM.
IT'LL BE OKAY--
WHINE
--BECAUSE NOW WE GET TO DO IT MY WAY! BUMBLEBEE, I NEED YOU BEE-SIZED.
"YOU'LL GO THROUGH THE AIR DUCT TO GET TO KRYPTO'S CELL.
"FLASH AND I WILL CREATE A DISTRACTION."
HELP! HELP! THERE'S A WILD DOG OUT THERE!
"AND GET THE WARDEN AWAY FROM KRYPTO."
SLURP!
OH, HELP! HER TONGUE IS SO SCRATCHY BUT SOFT!
"HE WON'T BE ABLE TO RESIST GOING AFTER A STRAY."

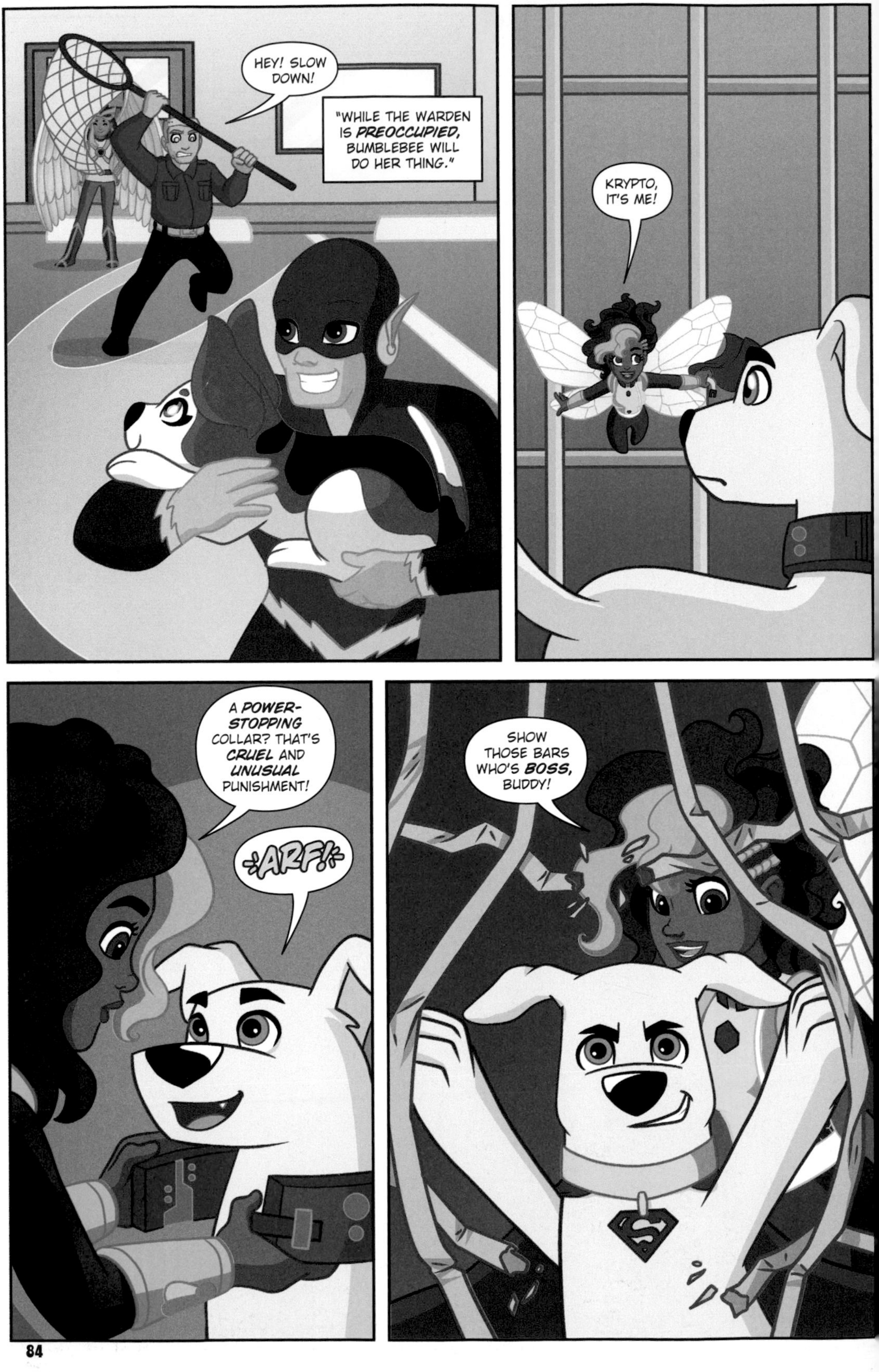
HEY! SLOW DOWN!
"WHILE THE WARDEN IS PREOCCUPIED, BUMBLEBEE WILL DO HER THING."
KRYPTO, IT'S ME!
A POWER-STOPPING COLLAR? THAT'S CRUEL AND UNUSUAL PUNISHMENT!
ARF!
SHOW THOSE BARS WHO'S BOSS, BUDDY!

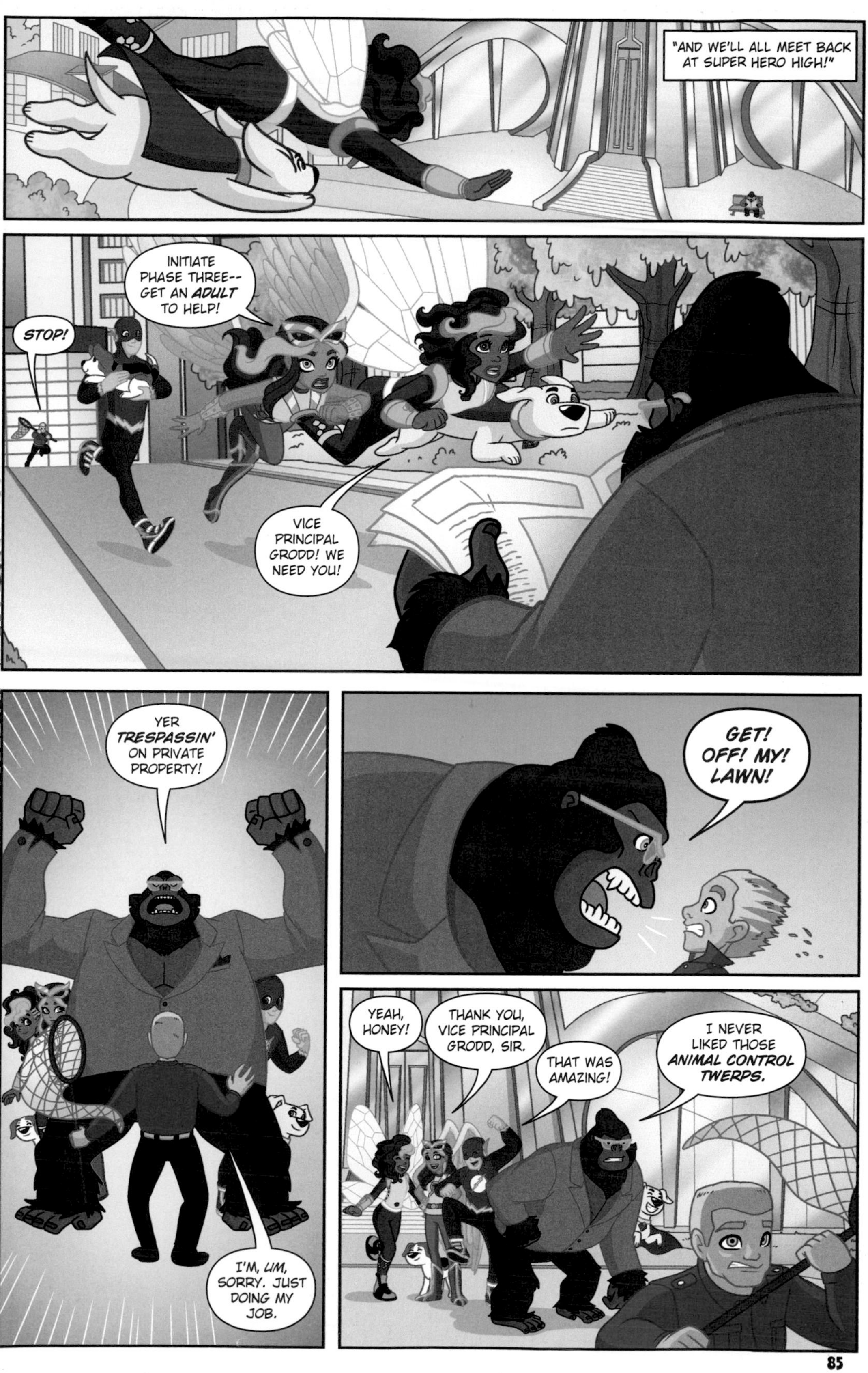
"AND WE'LL ALL MEET BACK AT SUPER HERO HIGH!"
INITIATE PHASE THREE-- GET AN *ADULT* TO HELP!
STOP!
VICE PRINCIPAL GRODD! WE NEED YOU!
YER *TRESPASSIN'* ON PRIVATE PROPERTY!
I'M, *UM*, SORRY. JUST DOING MY JOB.
GET! OFF! MY! LAWN!
YEAH, HONEY!
THANK YOU, VICE PRINCIPAL GRODD, SIR.
THAT WAS AMAZING!
I NEVER LIKED THOSE *ANIMAL CONTROL TWERPS.*

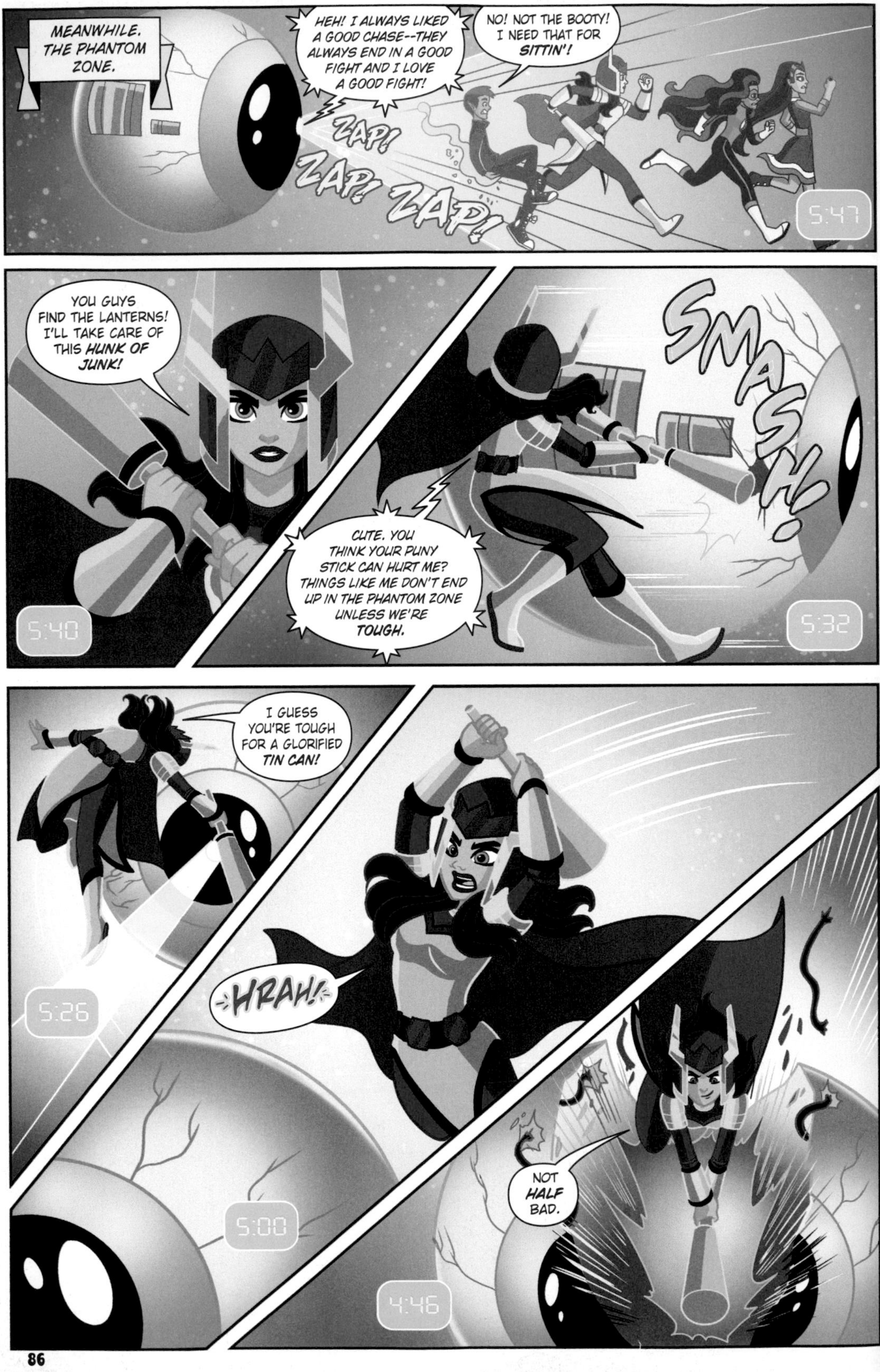

MEANWHILE. THE PHANTOM ZONE.
HEH! I ALWAYS LIKED A GOOD CHASE--THEY ALWAYS END IN A GOOD FIGHT AND I LOVE A GOOD FIGHT!
NO! NOT THE BOOTY! I NEED THAT FOR SITTIN'!
ZAP! ZAP! ZAP! ZAP!
5:47
YOU GUYS FIND THE LANTERNS! I'LL TAKE CARE OF THIS HUNK OF JUNK!
5:40
SMASH!
CUTE. YOU THINK YOUR PUNY STICK CAN HURT ME? THINGS LIKE ME DON'T END UP IN THE PHANTOM ZONE UNLESS WE'RE TOUGH.
5:32
I GUESS YOU'RE TOUGH FOR A GLORIFIED TIN CAN!
5:26
HRAH!
5:00
NOT HALF BAD.
4:46

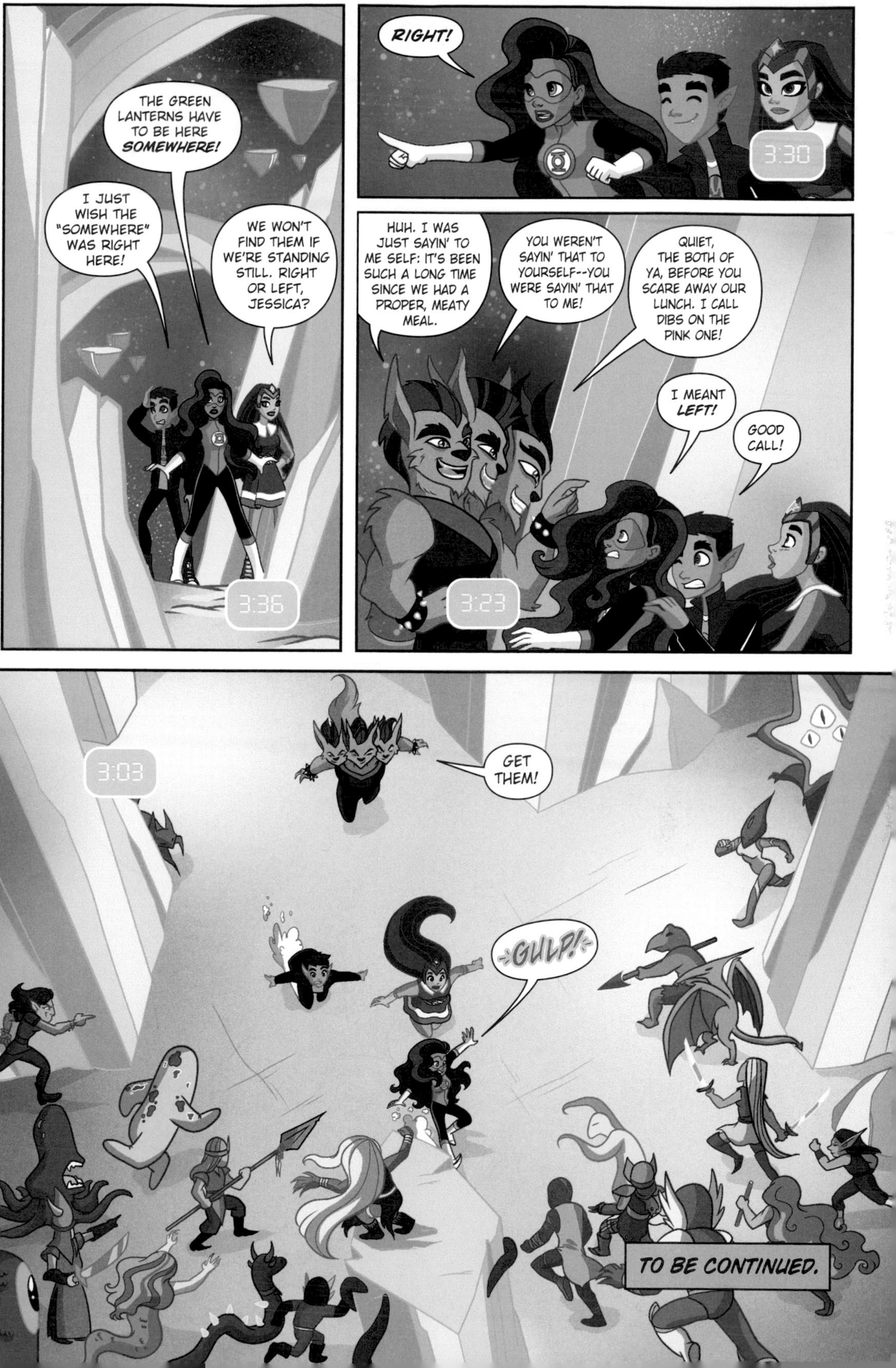
THE GREEN LANTERNS HAVE TO BE HERE SOMEWHERE!
I JUST WISH THE "SOMEWHERE" WAS RIGHT HERE!
WE WON'T FIND THEM IF WE'RE STANDING STILL. RIGHT OR LEFT, JESSICA?
3:36
RIGHT!
3:30
HUH. I WAS JUST SAYIN' TO ME SELF: IT'S BEEN SUCH A LONG TIME SINCE WE HAD A PROPER, MEATY MEAL.
YOU WEREN'T SAYIN' THAT TO YOURSELF--YOU WERE SAYIN' THAT TO ME!
QUIET, THE BOTH OF YA, BEFORE YOU SCARE AWAY OUR LUNCH. I CALL DIBS ON THE PINK ONE!
I MEANT LEFT!
GOOD CALL!
3:23
3:03
GET THEM!
GULP!
TO BE CONTINUED.

CHAPTER FIVE

LIGHT THE WAY HOME

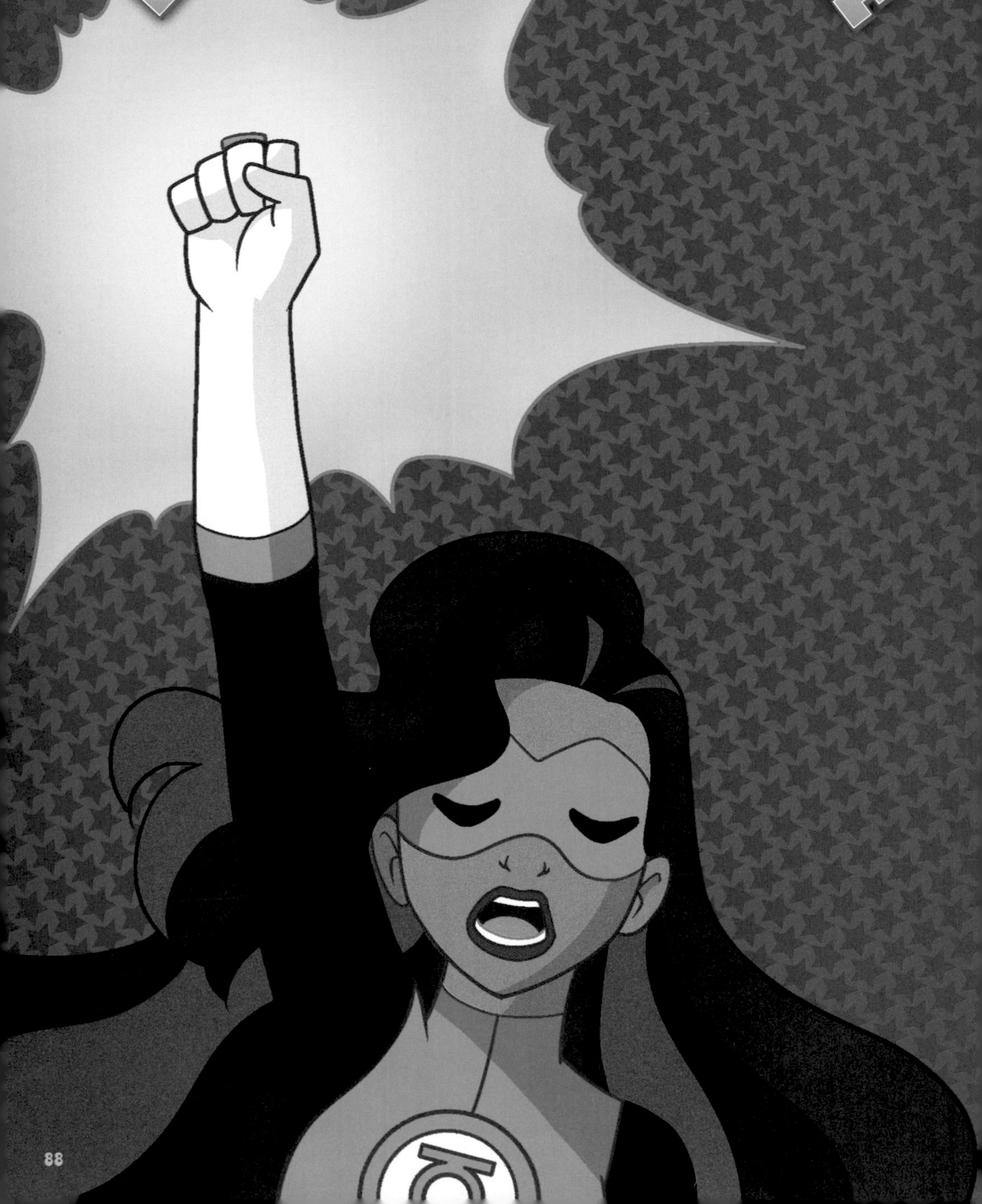

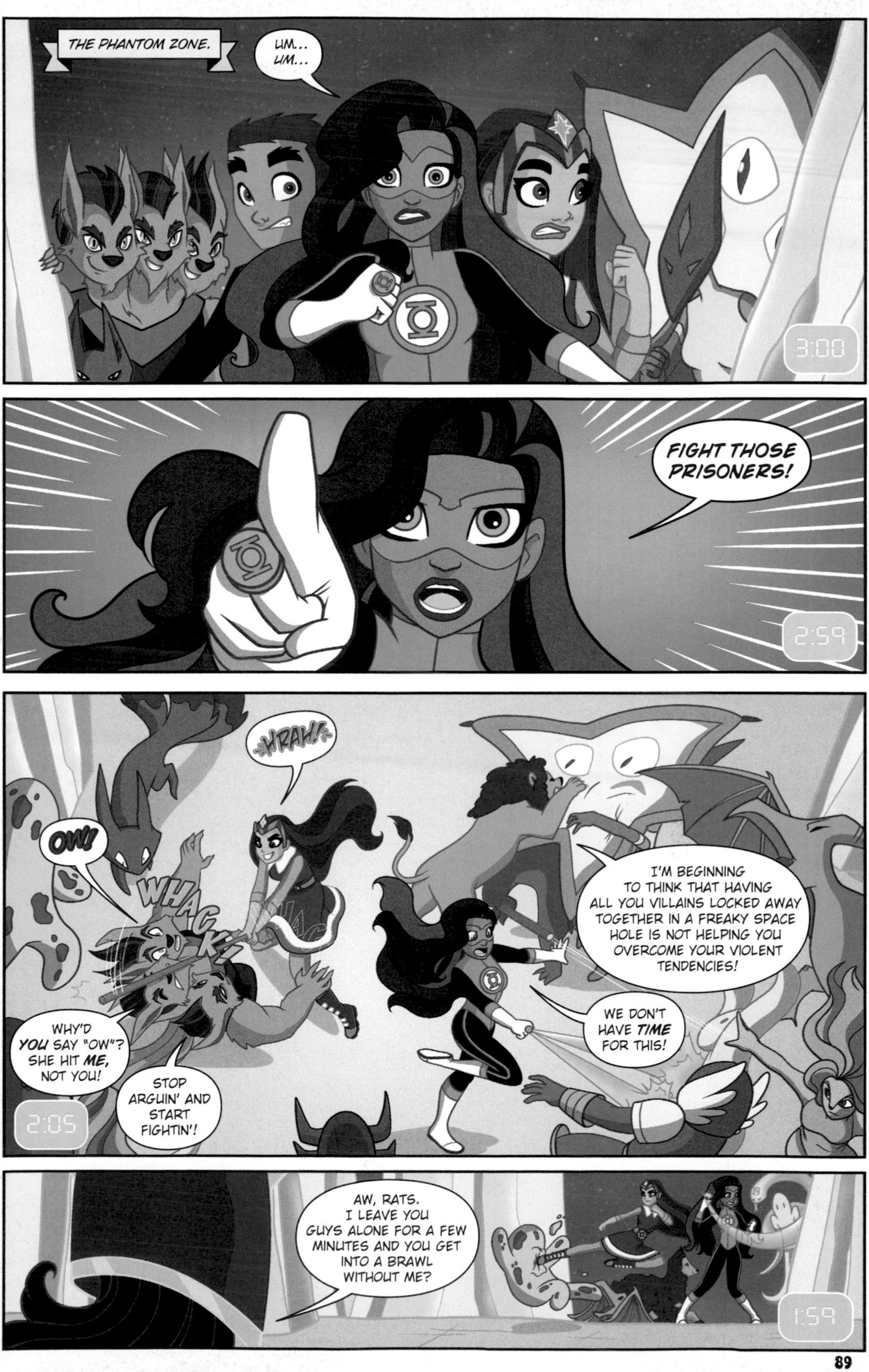

THE PHANTOM ZONE.
UM... UM...
3:00
FIGHT THOSE PRISONERS!
2:59
HRAH!
OW!
WHACK!
I'M BEGINNING TO THINK THAT HAVING ALL YOU VILLAINS LOCKED AWAY TOGETHER IN A FREAKY SPACE HOLE IS NOT HELPING YOU OVERCOME YOUR VIOLENT TENDENCIES!
WE DON'T HAVE *TIME* FOR THIS!
WHY'D *YOU* SAY "OW"? SHE HIT *ME,* NOT YOU!
STOP ARGUIN' AND START FIGHTIN'!
2:05
AW, RATS. I LEAVE YOU GUYS ALONE FOR A FEW MINUTES AND YOU GET INTO A BRAWL WITHOUT ME?
1:59

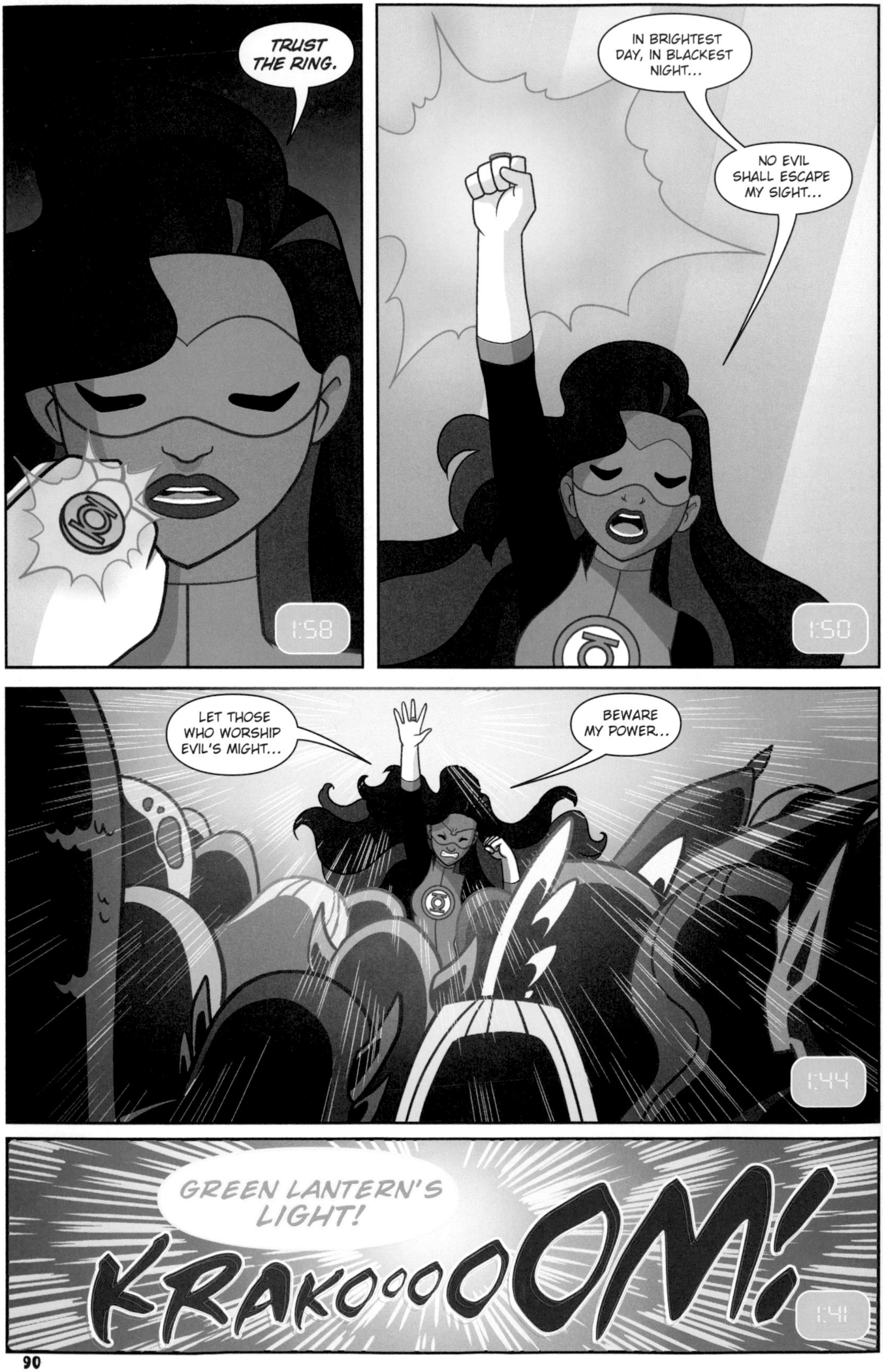
TRUST THE RING.
1:58
IN BRIGHTEST DAY, IN BLACKEST NIGHT...
NO EVIL SHALL ESCAPE MY SIGHT...
1:50
LET THOSE WHO WORSHIP EVIL'S MIGHT...
BEWARE MY POWER...
1:44
GREEN LANTERN'S LIGHT!
KRAKOOOOOM!
1:41

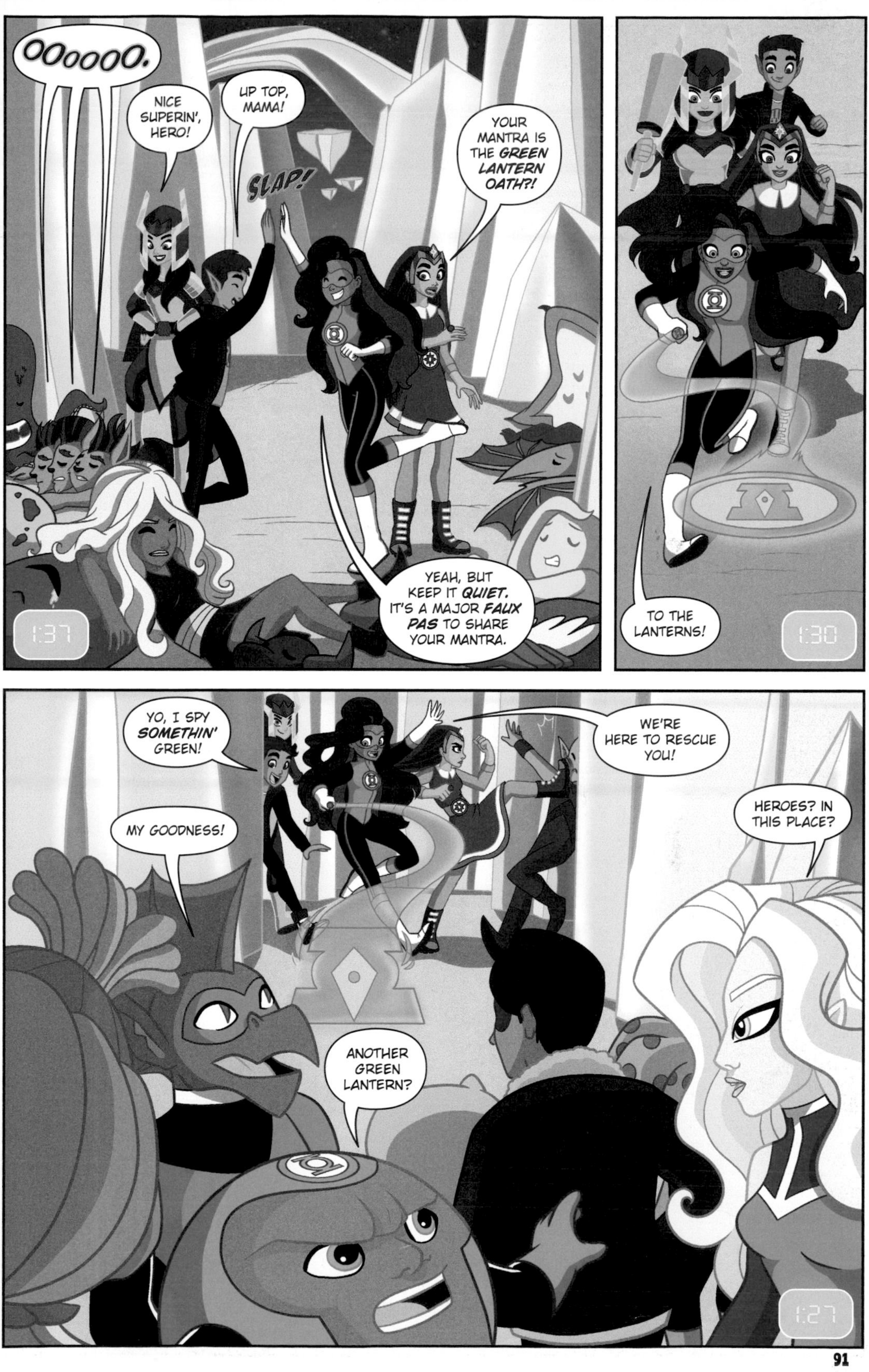
OOooooO.
NICE SUPERIN', HERO!
UP TOP, MAMA!
SLAP!
YOUR MANTRA IS THE GREEN LANTERN OATH?!
YEAH, BUT KEEP IT QUIET. IT'S A MAJOR FAUX PAS TO SHARE YOUR MANTRA.
1:37
TO THE LANTERNS!
1:30
YO, I SPY SOMETHIN' GREEN!
WE'RE HERE TO RESCUE YOU!
MY GOODNESS!
HEROES? IN THIS PLACE?
ANOTHER GREEN LANTERN?
1:27

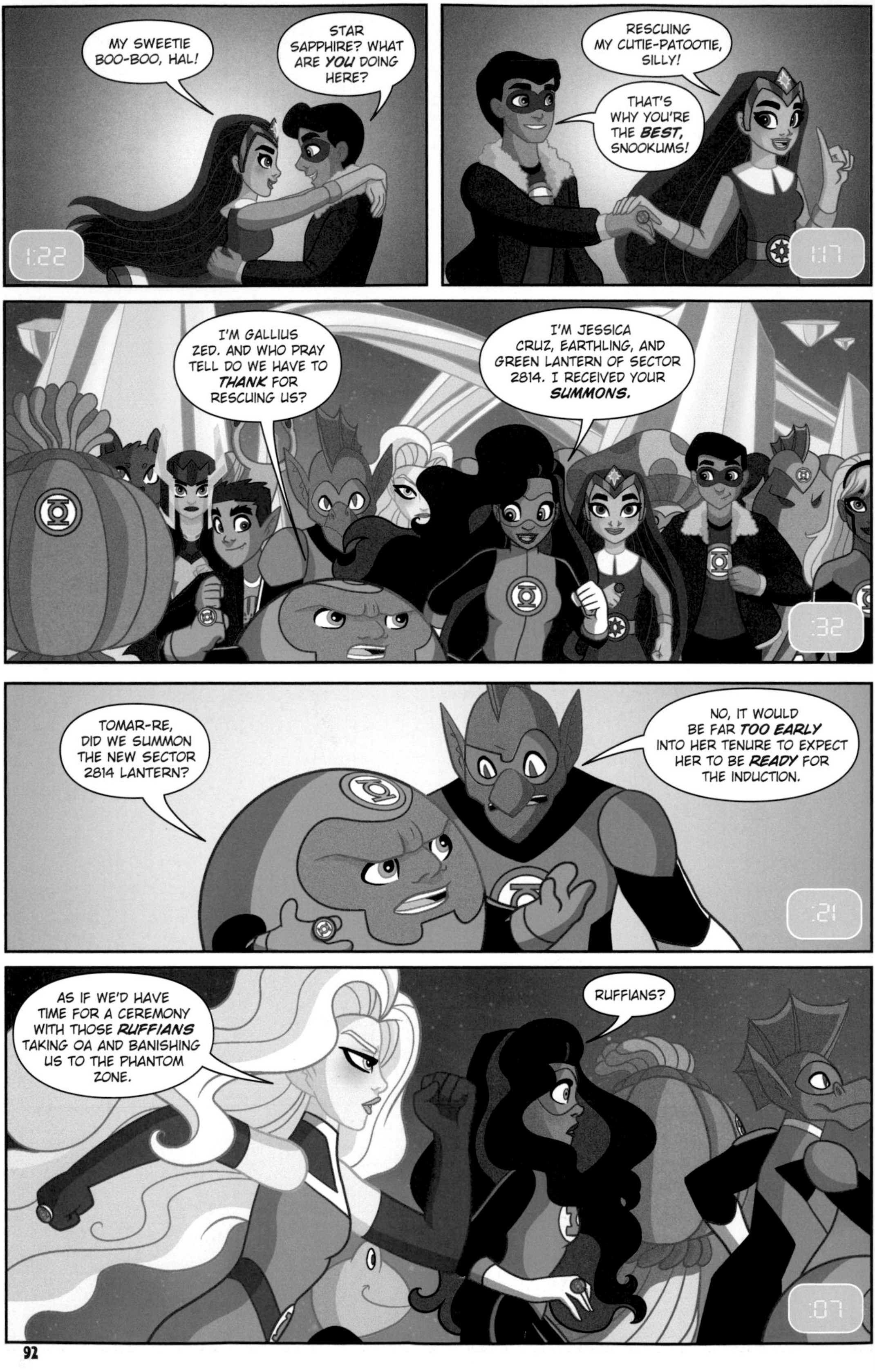
MY SWEETIE BOO-BOO, HAL!
STAR SAPPHIRE? WHAT ARE *YOU* DOING HERE?
1:22
RESCUING MY CUTIE-PATOOTIE, SILLY!
THAT'S WHY YOU'RE THE *BEST,* SNOOKUMS!
1:17
I'M GALLIUS ZED. AND WHO PRAY TELL DO WE HAVE TO *THANK* FOR RESCUING US?
I'M JESSICA CRUZ, EARTHLING, AND GREEN LANTERN OF SECTOR 2814. I RECEIVED YOUR *SUMMONS.*
:32
TOMAR-RE, DID WE SUMMON THE NEW SECTOR 2814 LANTERN?
NO, IT WOULD BE FAR *TOO EARLY* INTO HER TENURE TO EXPECT HER TO BE *READY* FOR THE INDUCTION.
:21
AS IF WE'D HAVE TIME FOR A CEREMONY WITH THOSE *RUFFIANS* TAKING OA AND BANISHING US TO THE PHANTOM ZONE.
RUFFIANS?
:07

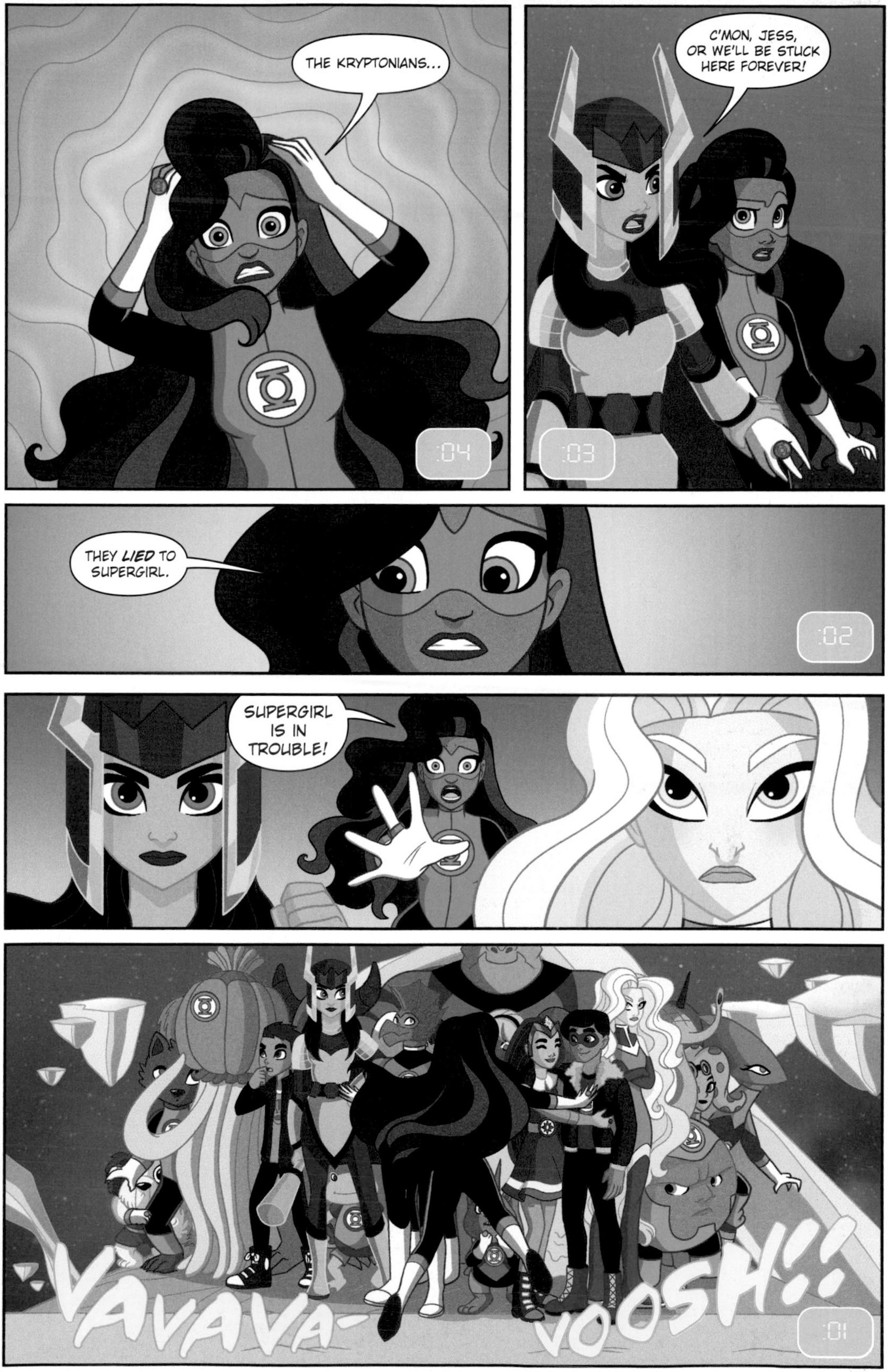
THE KRYPTONIANS...
:04
C'MON, JESS, OR WE'LL BE STUCK HERE FOREVER!
:03
THEY *LIED* TO SUPERGIRL.
:02
SUPERGIRL IS IN TROUBLE!
VAVAVA-VOOSH!!
:01

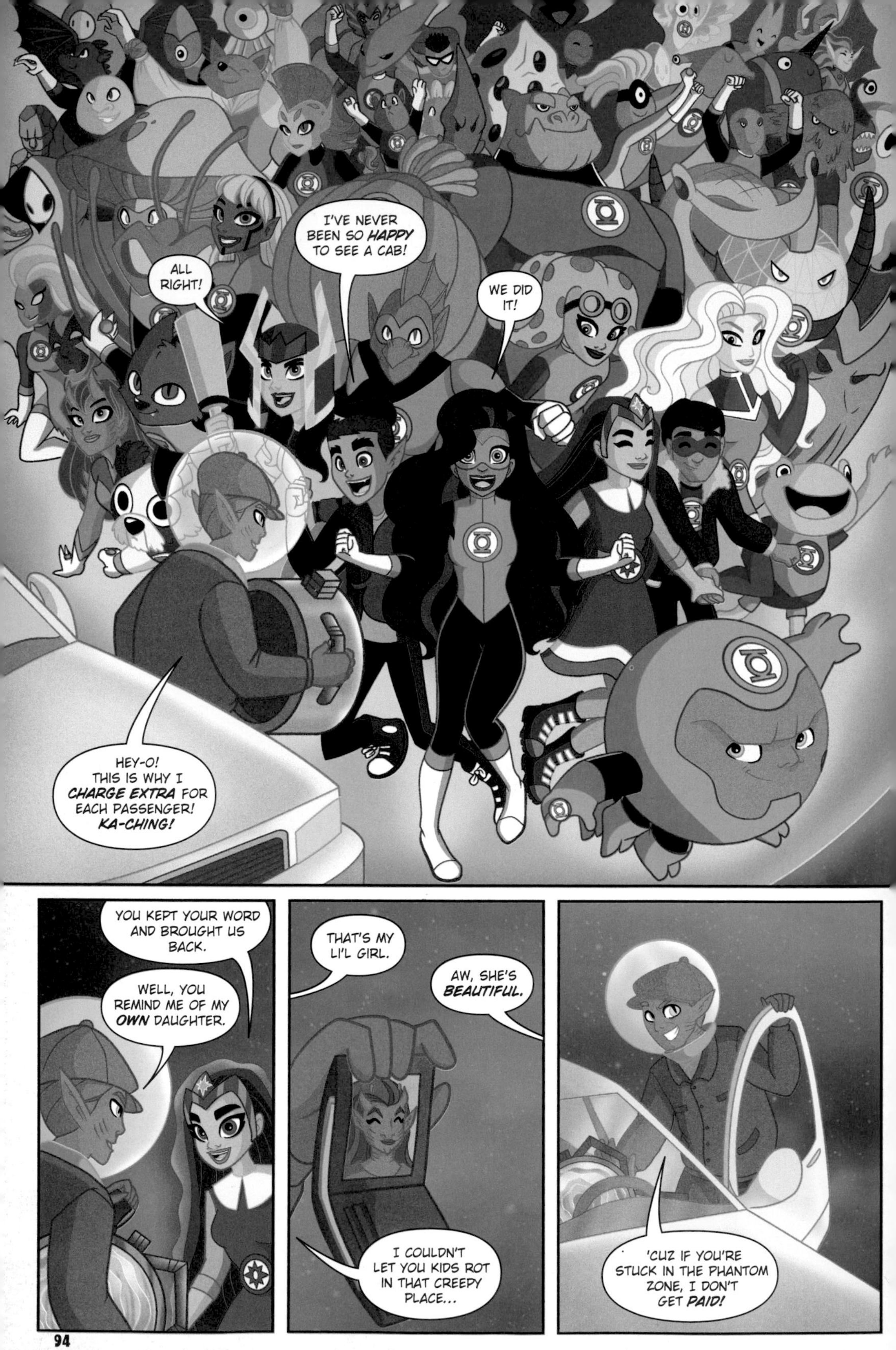
ALL RIGHT!
I'VE NEVER BEEN SO HAPPY TO SEE A CAB!
WE DID IT!
HEY-O! THIS IS WHY I CHARGE EXTRA FOR EACH PASSENGER! KA-CHING!
YOU KEPT YOUR WORD AND BROUGHT US BACK.
WELL, YOU REMIND ME OF MY OWN DAUGHTER.
THAT'S MY LI'L GIRL.
AW, SHE'S BEAUTIFUL.
I COULDN'T LET YOU KIDS ROT IN THAT CREEPY PLACE...
'CUZ IF YOU'RE STUCK IN THE PHANTOM ZONE, I DON'T GET PAID!

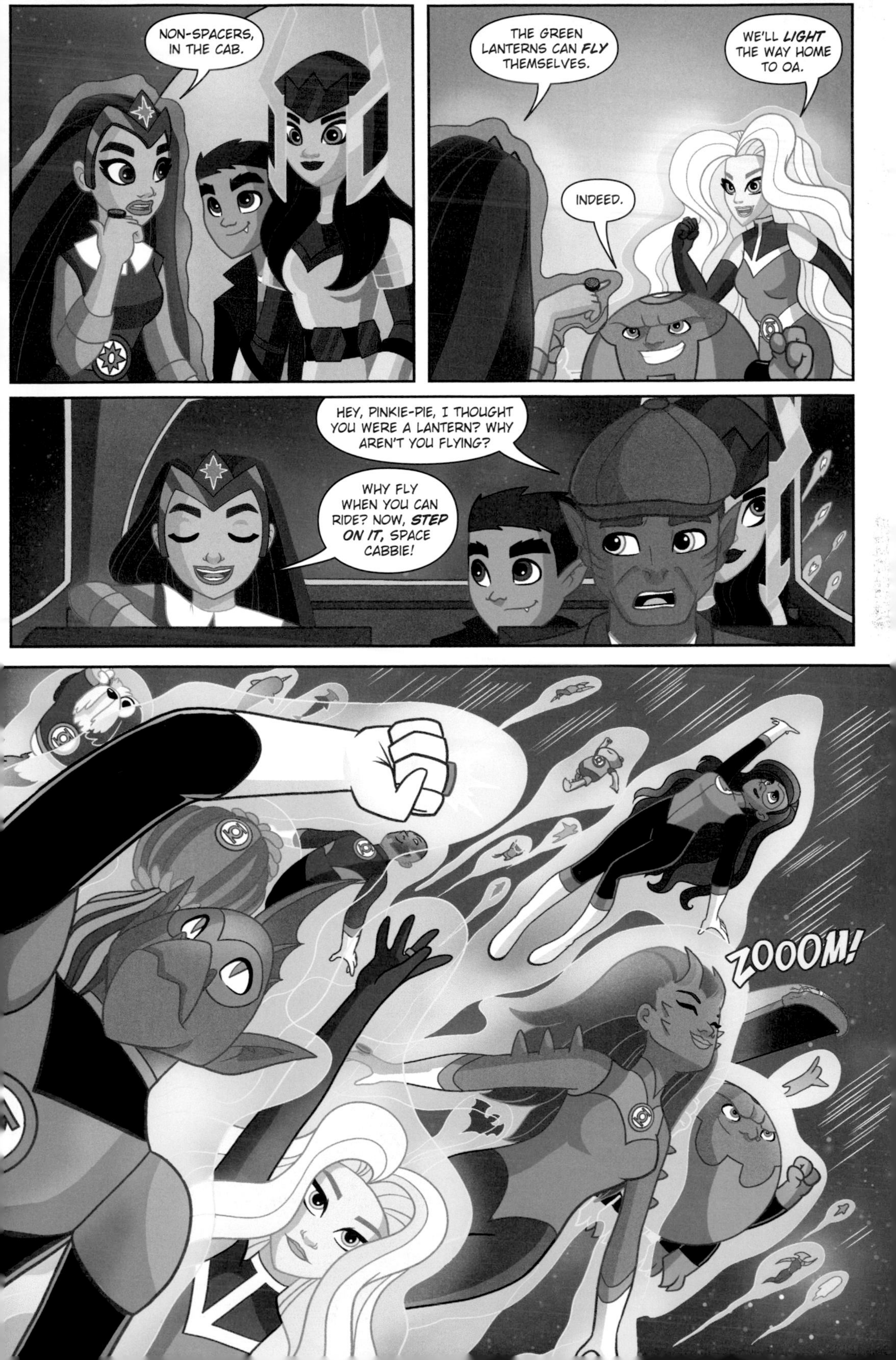
NON-SPACERS, IN THE CAB.
THE GREEN LANTERNS CAN FLY THEMSELVES.
WE'LL LIGHT THE WAY HOME TO OA.
INDEED.
HEY, PINKIE-PIE, I THOUGHT YOU WERE A LANTERN? WHY AREN'T YOU FLYING?
WHY FLY WHEN YOU CAN RIDE? NOW, STEP ON IT, SPACE CABBIE!
ZOOOM!

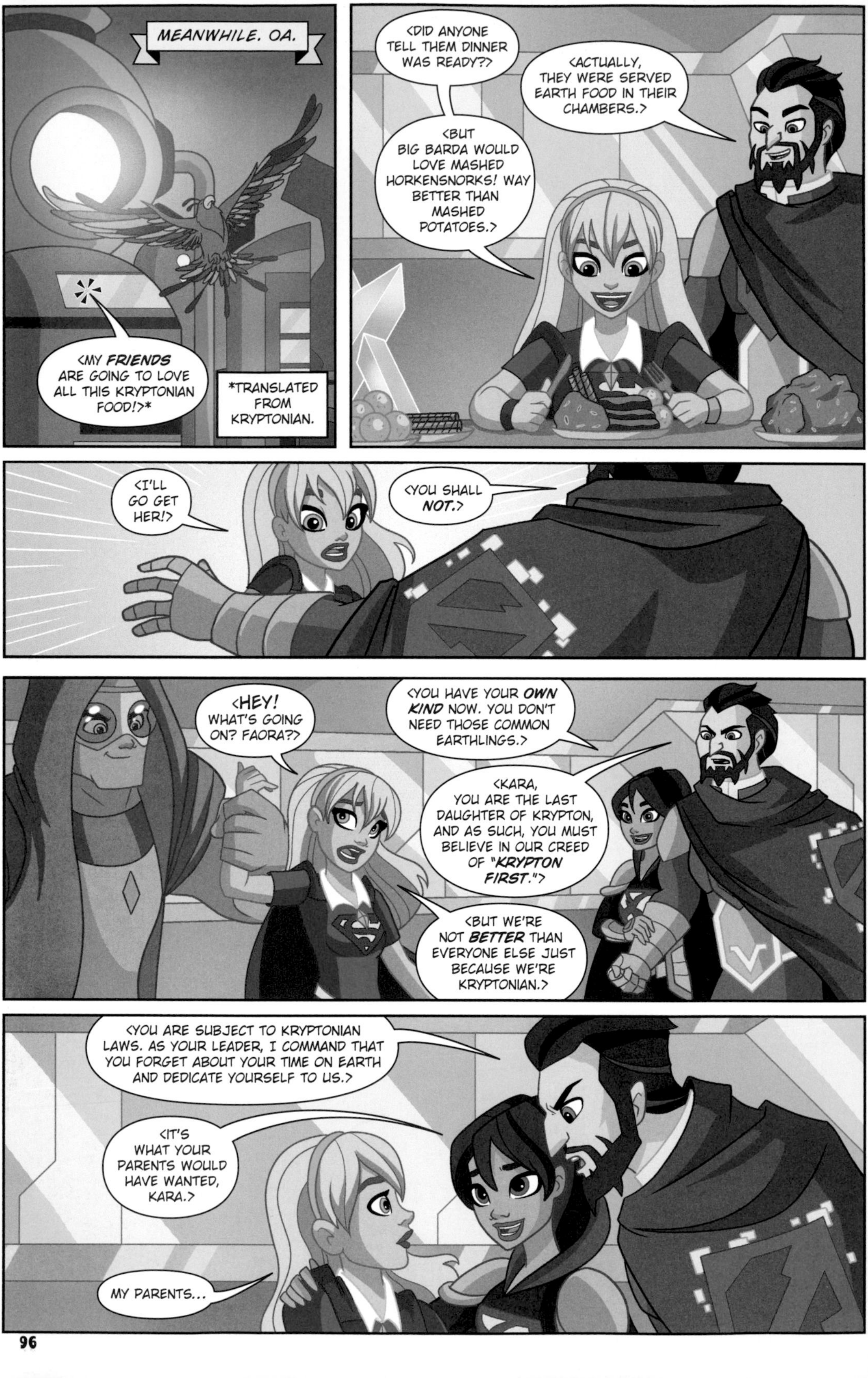
MEANWHILE. OA.
<MY *FRIENDS* ARE GOING TO LOVE ALL THIS KRYPTONIAN FOOD!>*
*TRANSLATED FROM KRYPTONIAN.
<DID ANYONE TELL THEM DINNER WAS READY?>
<ACTUALLY, THEY WERE SERVED EARTH FOOD IN THEIR CHAMBERS.>
<BUT BIG BARDA WOULD LOVE MASHED HORKENSNORKS! WAY BETTER THAN MASHED POTATOES.>
<I'LL GO GET HER!>
<YOU SHALL *NOT.*>
<**HEY!** WHAT'S GOING ON? FAORA?>
<YOU HAVE YOUR ***OWN KIND*** NOW. YOU DON'T NEED THOSE COMMON EARTHLINGS.>
<KARA, YOU ARE THE LAST DAUGHTER OF KRYPTON, AND AS SUCH, YOU MUST BELIEVE IN OUR CREED OF "***KRYPTON FIRST***.">
<BUT WE'RE NOT ***BETTER*** THAN EVERYONE ELSE JUST BECAUSE WE'RE KRYPTONIAN.>
<YOU ARE SUBJECT TO KRYPTONIAN LAWS. AS YOUR LEADER, I COMMAND THAT YOU FORGET ABOUT YOUR TIME ON EARTH AND DEDICATE YOURSELF TO US.>
<IT'S WHAT YOUR PARENTS WOULD HAVE WANTED, KARA.>
MY PARENTS...

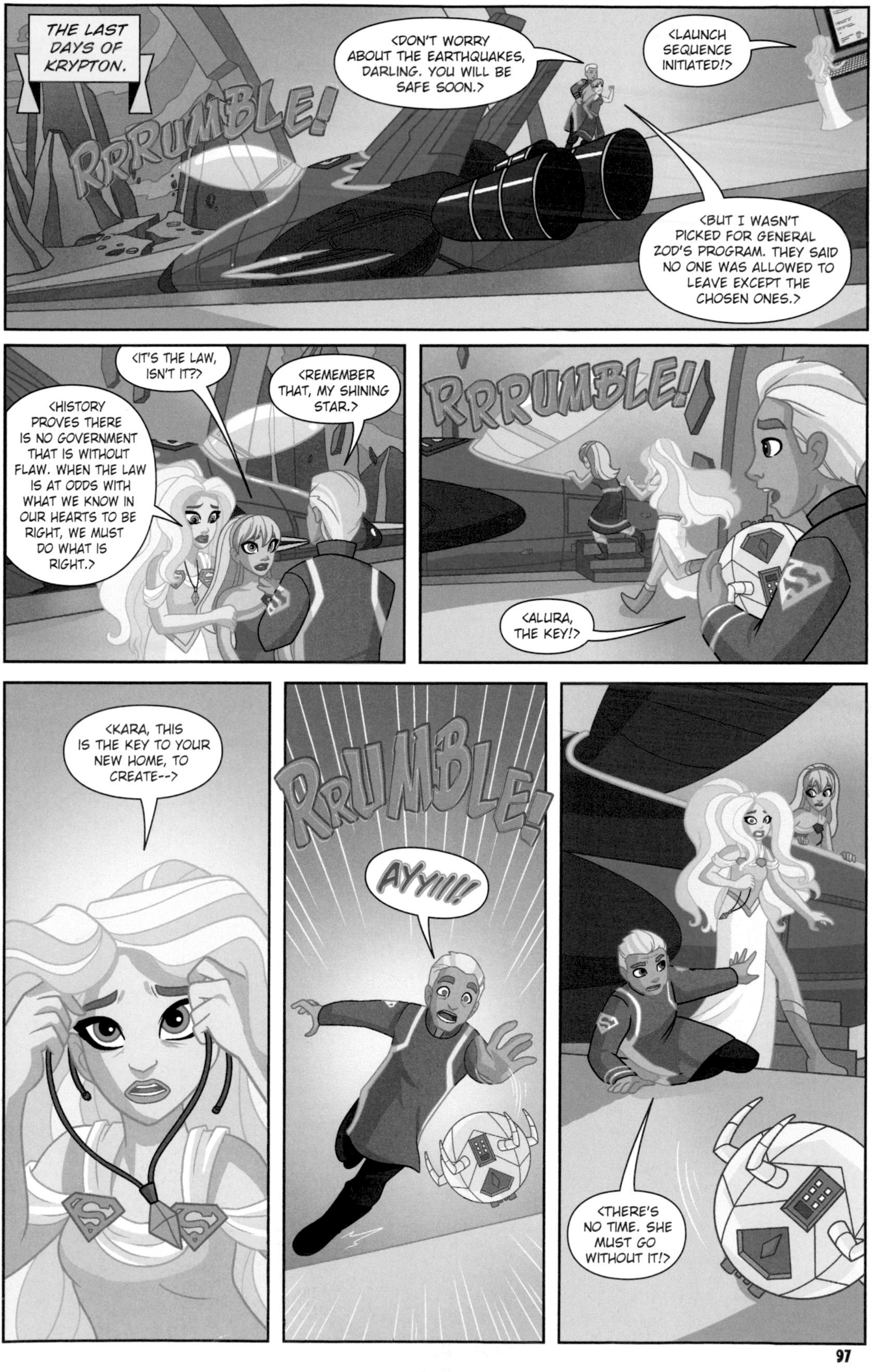
THE LAST DAYS OF KRYPTON.
RRRUMBLE!
<DON'T WORRY ABOUT THE EARTHQUAKES, DARLING. YOU WILL BE SAFE SOON.>
<LAUNCH SEQUENCE INITIATED!>
<BUT I WASN'T PICKED FOR GENERAL ZOD'S PROGRAM. THEY SAID NO ONE WAS ALLOWED TO LEAVE EXCEPT THE CHOSEN ONES.>
<IT'S THE LAW, ISN'T IT?>
<HISTORY PROVES THERE IS NO GOVERNMENT THAT IS WITHOUT FLAW. WHEN THE LAW IS AT ODDS WITH WHAT WE KNOW IN OUR HEARTS TO BE RIGHT, WE MUST DO WHAT IS RIGHT.>
<REMEMBER THAT, MY SHINING STAR.>
RRRUMBLE!
<ALURA, THE KEY!>
<KARA, THIS IS THE KEY TO YOUR NEW HOME, TO CREATE-->
RRUMBLE!
AYYIII!
<THERE'S NO TIME. SHE MUST GO WITHOUT IT!>

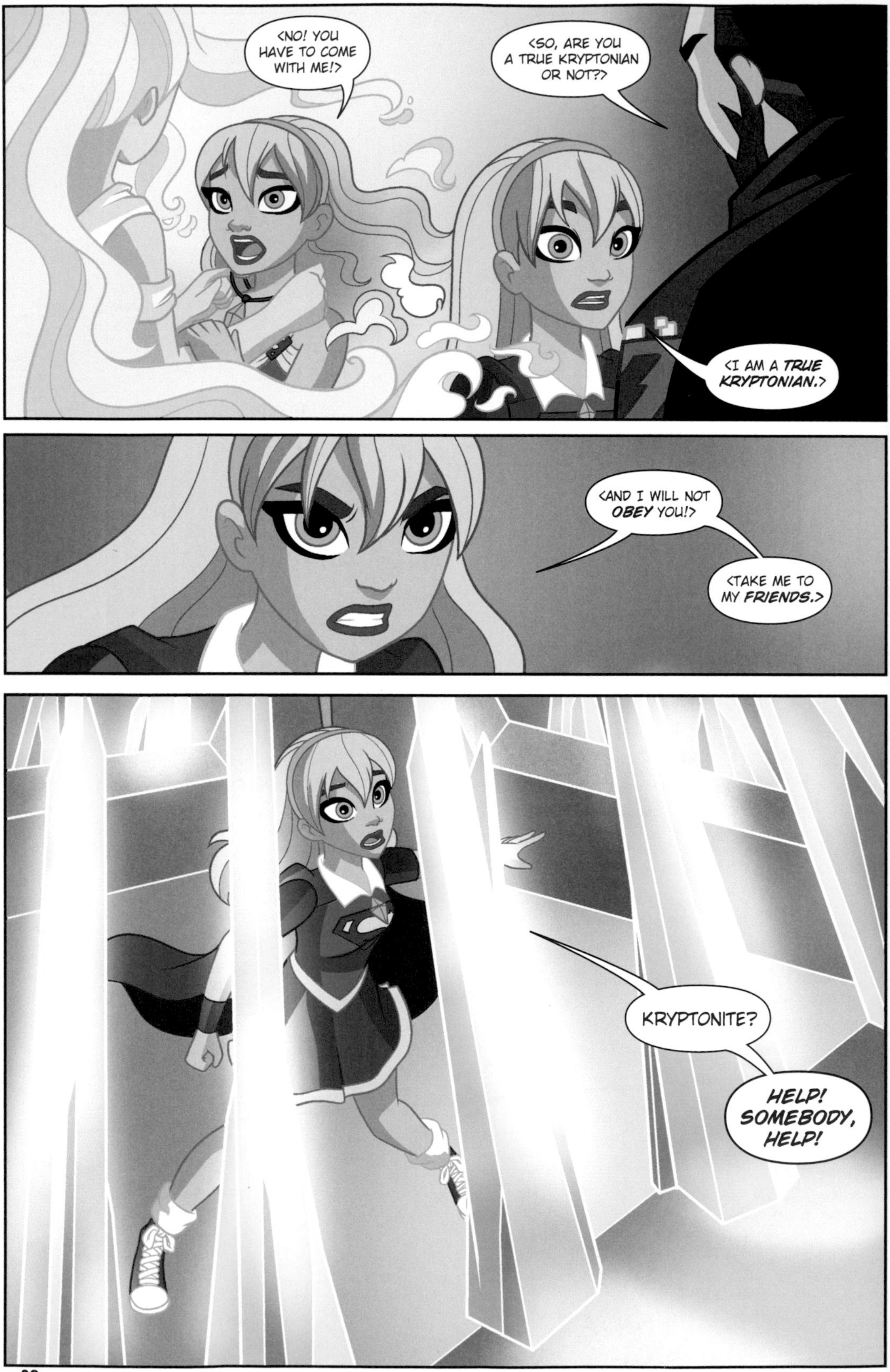
<NO! YOU HAVE TO COME WITH ME!>
<SO, ARE YOU A TRUE KRYPTONIAN OR NOT?>
<I AM A *TRUE KRYPTONIAN.*>
<AND I WILL NOT *OBEY* YOU!>
<TAKE ME TO MY *FRIENDS.*>
KRYPTONITE?
HELP! SOMEBODY, HELP!

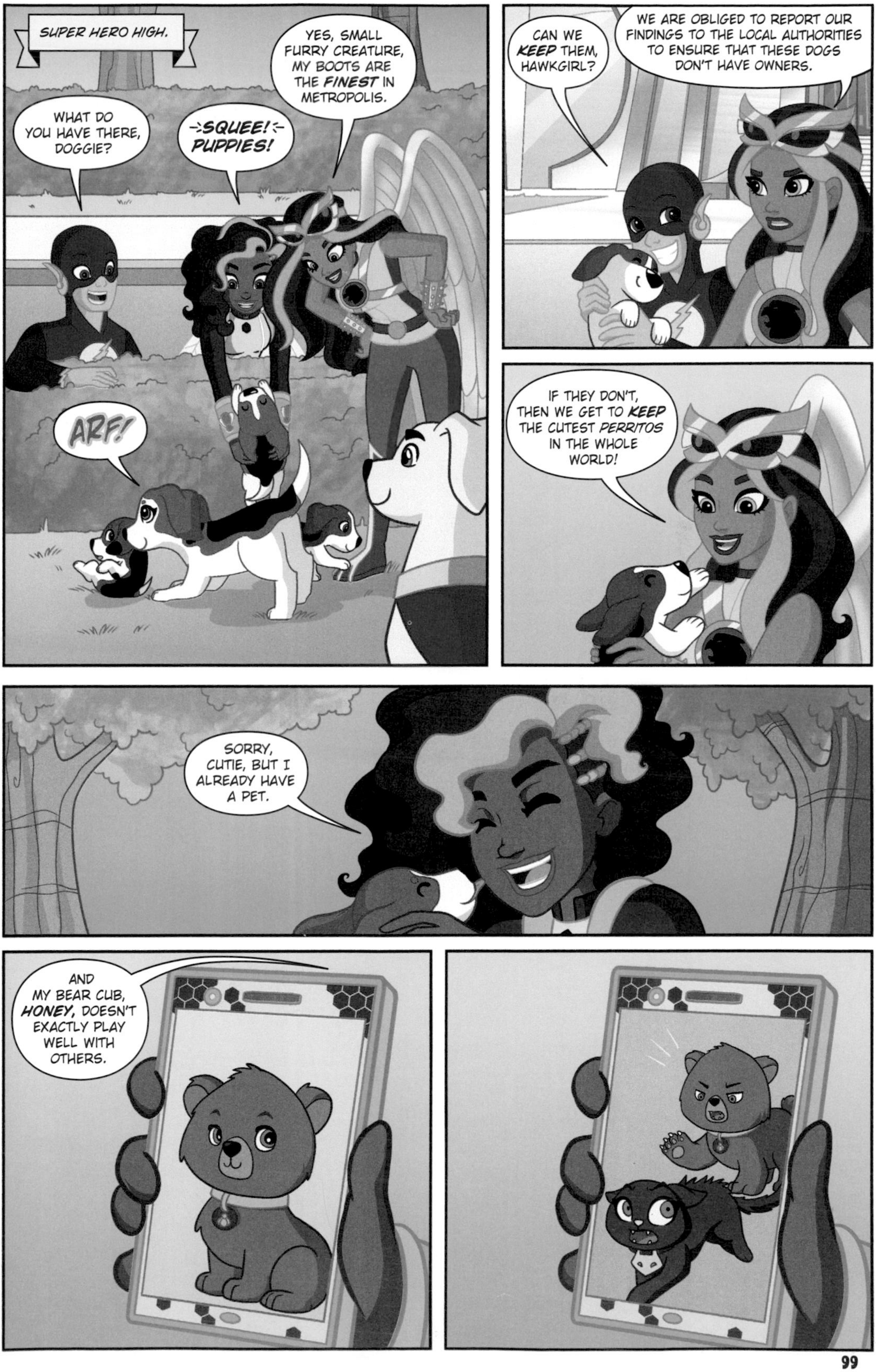
SUPER HERO HIGH.
WHAT DO YOU HAVE THERE, DOGGIE?
-SQUEE!- PUPPIES!
YES, SMALL FURRY CREATURE, MY BOOTS ARE THE FINEST IN METROPOLIS.
ARF!
CAN WE KEEP THEM, HAWKGIRL?
WE ARE OBLIGED TO REPORT OUR FINDINGS TO THE LOCAL AUTHORITIES TO ENSURE THAT THESE DOGS DON'T HAVE OWNERS.
IF THEY DON'T, THEN WE GET TO KEEP THE CUTEST PERRITOS IN THE WHOLE WORLD!
SORRY, CUTIE, BUT I ALREADY HAVE A PET.
AND MY BEAR CUB, HONEY, DOESN'T EXACTLY PLAY WELL WITH OTHERS.

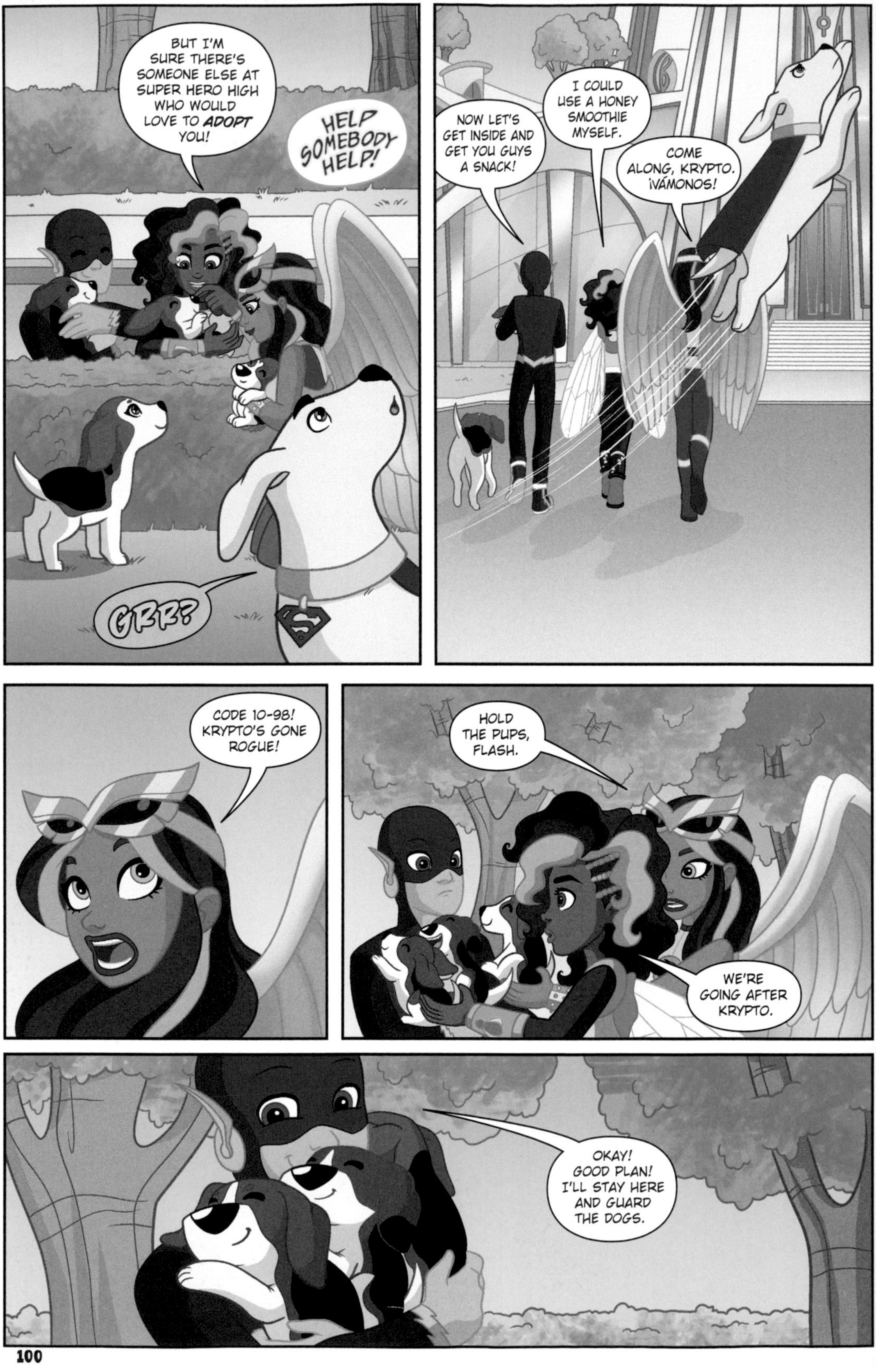
BUT I'M SURE THERE'S SOMEONE ELSE AT SUPER HERO HIGH WHO WOULD LOVE TO ADOPT YOU!
HELP SOMEBODY HELP!
GRR?
NOW LET'S GET INSIDE AND GET YOU GUYS A SNACK!
I COULD USE A HONEY SMOOTHIE MYSELF.
COME ALONG, KRYPTO. ¡VÁMONOS!
CODE 10-98! KRYPTO'S GONE ROGUE!
HOLD THE PUPS, FLASH.
WE'RE GOING AFTER KRYPTO.
OKAY! GOOD PLAN! I'LL STAY HERE AND GUARD THE DOGS.

COME BACK, KRYPTO!

AS HALL MONITOR, I'M OFFICIALLY ISSUING YOU A DEMERIT FOR THIS RUNAWAY BEHAVIOR!

HE'S FASTER THAN MY Nth METAL BELT WAS MEANT TO FLY!

-:KOFF!:- AND THE AIR UP HERE IS TOO *THIN!*

-:KOFF!:- I SHOULD'VE BUILT AN *OXYGEN PACK* INTO MY SUIT!

WONDER WOMAN!

-:HUFF:- 1,873. 1,874. 1,875--

WONDER WOMAN, COME IN!

WHAT'S UP, BUMBLEBEE?

WELL, WE FOUND KRYPTO AT THE POUND, BUT THEN LOST HIM *AGAIN,* AND NOW HE'S FLYING INTO THE ATMOSPHERE, AND I CAN'T FLY THAT HIGH. WE NEED YOU TO HELP!

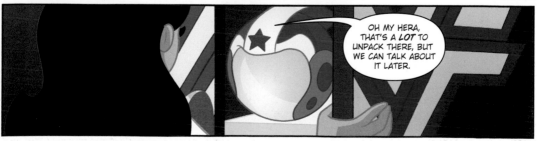

OH MY HERA, THAT'S A *LOT* TO UNPACK THERE, BUT WE CAN TALK ABOUT IT LATER.

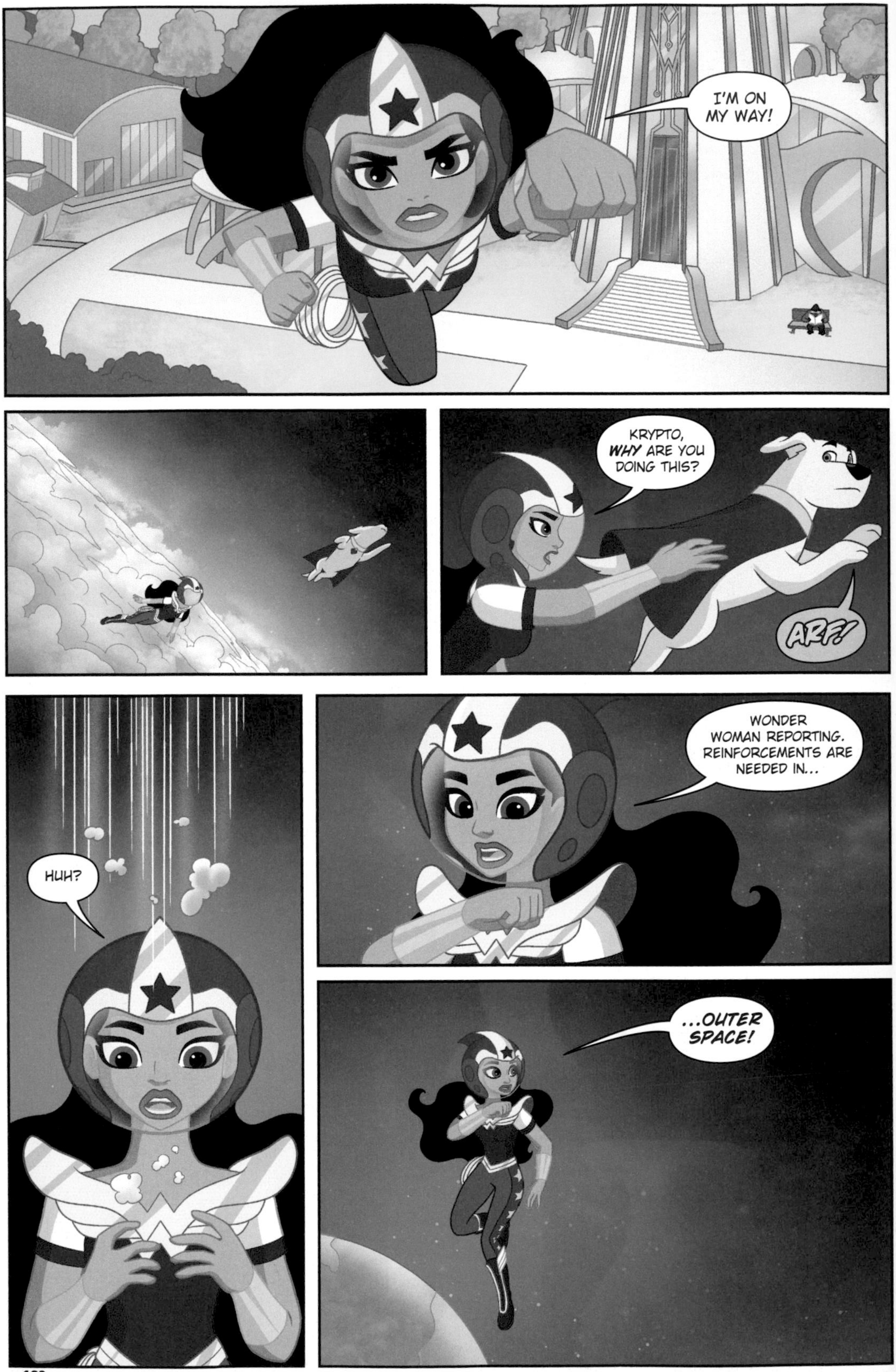
I'M ON MY WAY!
KRYPTO, WHY ARE YOU DOING THIS?
ARF!
HUH?
WONDER WOMAN REPORTING. REINFORCEMENTS ARE NEEDED IN...
...OUTER SPACE!

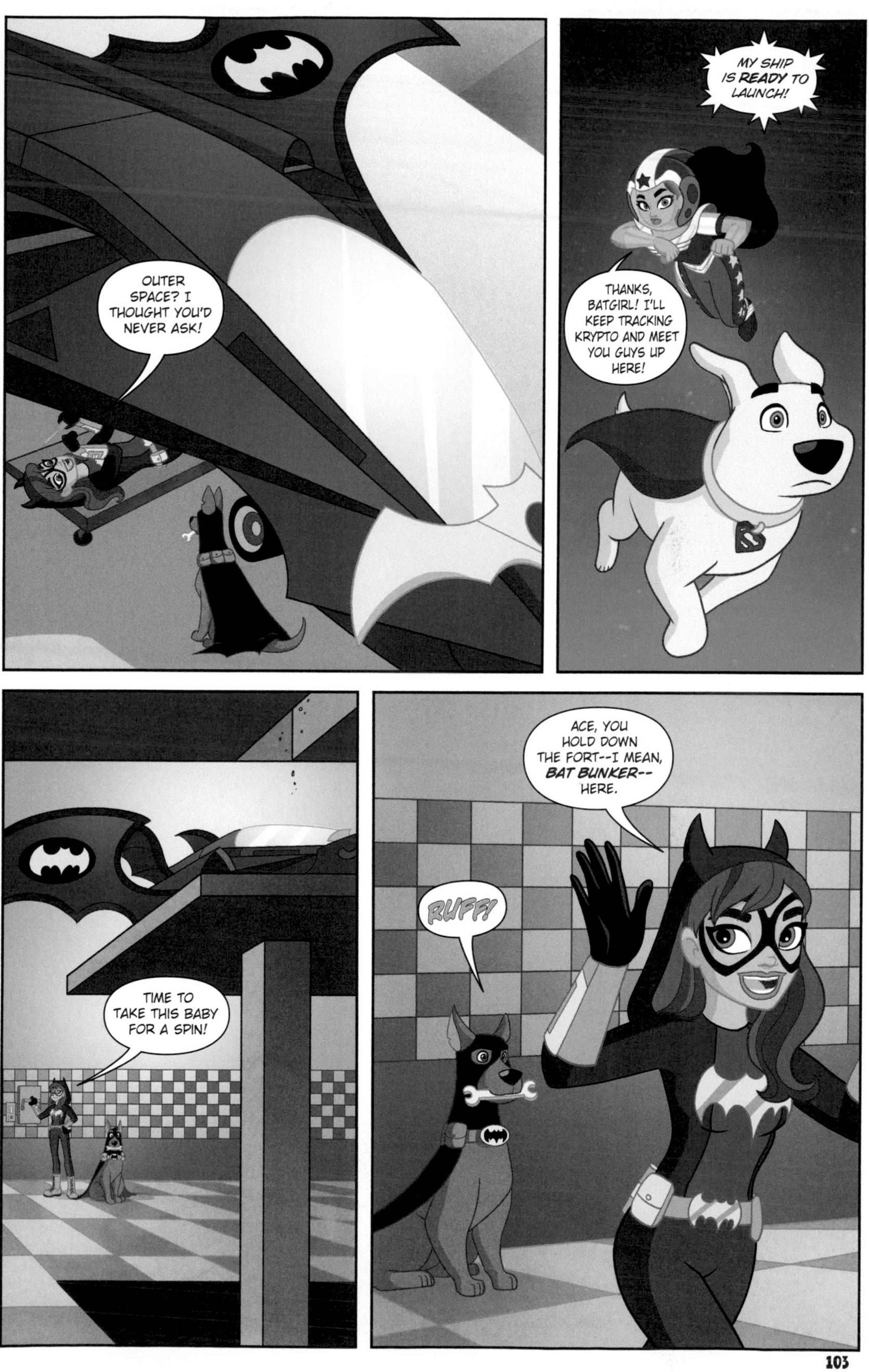
OUTER SPACE? I THOUGHT YOU'D NEVER ASK!
MY SHIP IS READY TO LAUNCH!
THANKS, BATGIRL! I'LL KEEP TRACKING KRYPTO AND MEET YOU GUYS UP HERE!
TIME TO TAKE THIS BABY FOR A SPIN!
ACE, YOU HOLD DOWN THE FORT--I MEAN, BAT BUNKER-- HERE.
RUFF!

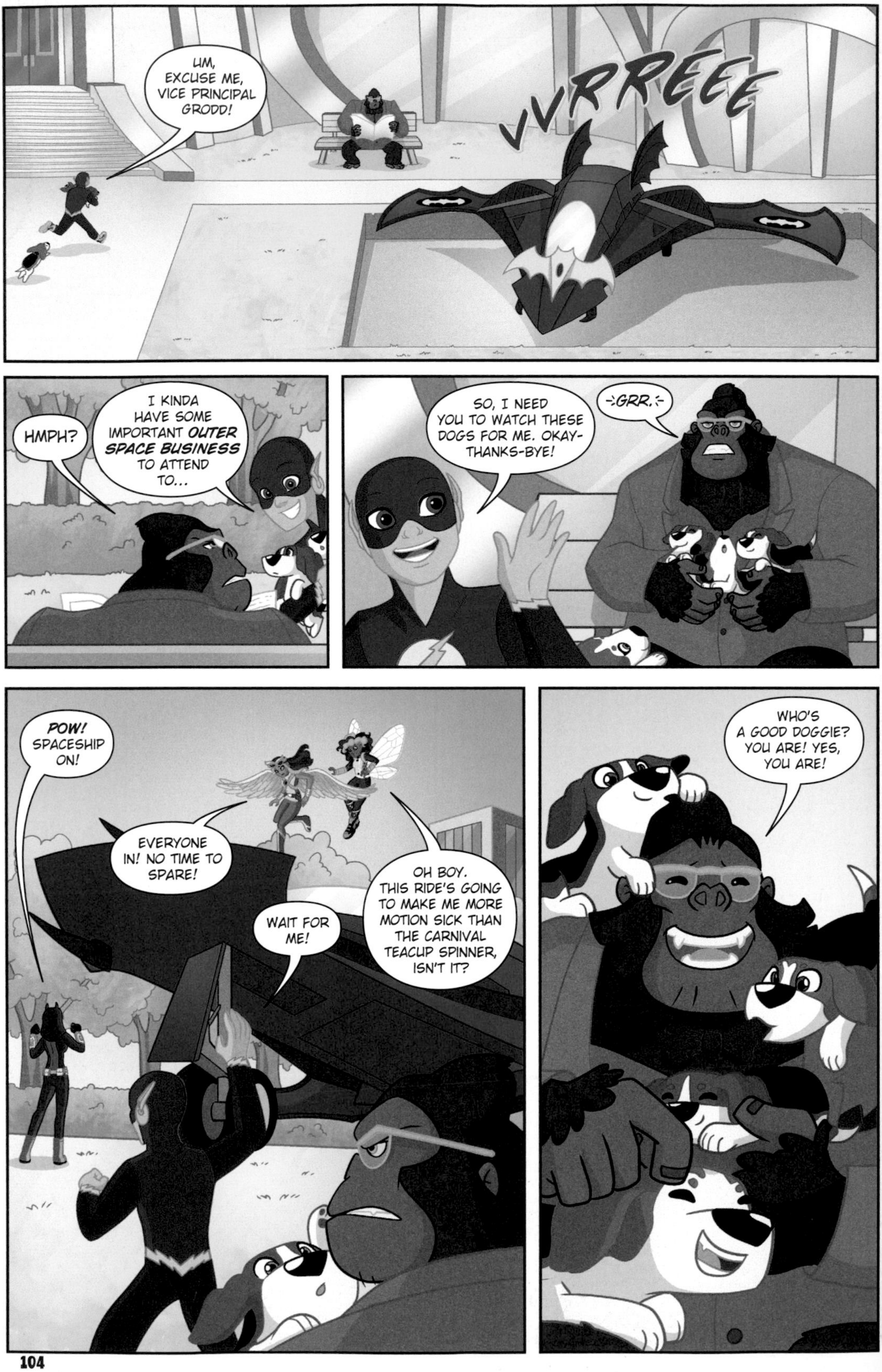
UM, EXCUSE ME, VICE PRINCIPAL GRODD!
VVRREEE
HMPH?
I KINDA HAVE SOME IMPORTANT OUTER SPACE BUSINESS TO ATTEND TO...
SO, I NEED YOU TO WATCH THESE DOGS FOR ME. OKAY-THANKS-BYE!
GRR.
POW! SPACESHIP ON!
EVERYONE IN! NO TIME TO SPARE!
WAIT FOR ME!
OH BOY. THIS RIDE'S GOING TO MAKE ME MORE MOTION SICK THAN THE CARNIVAL TEACUP SPINNER, ISN'T IT?
WHO'S A GOOD DOGGIE? YOU ARE! YES, YOU ARE!

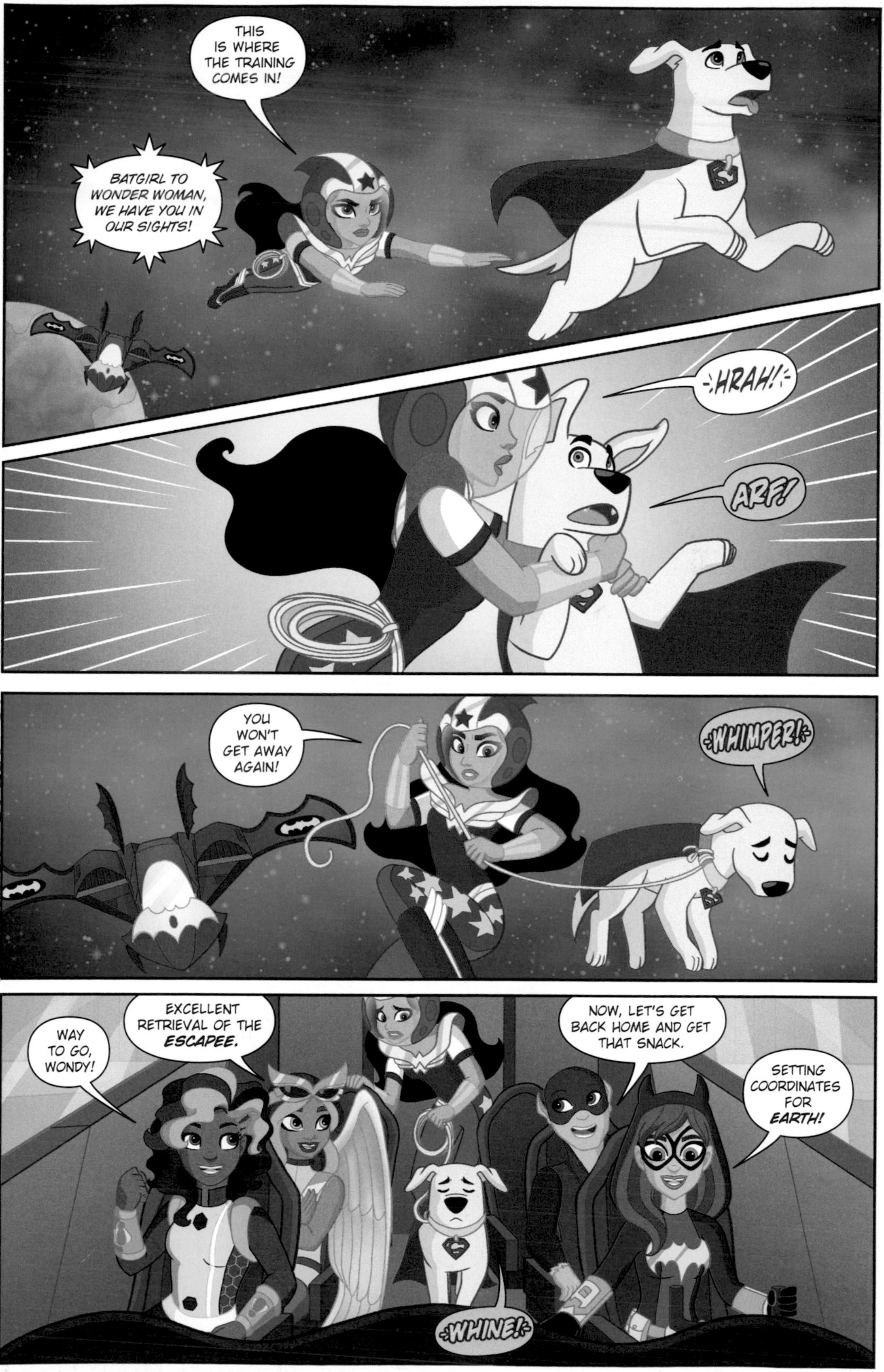
THIS IS WHERE THE TRAINING COMES IN!
BATGIRL TO WONDER WOMAN, WE HAVE YOU IN OUR SIGHTS!
HRAH!
ARF!
YOU WON'T GET AWAY AGAIN!
WHIMPER!
WAY TO GO, WONDY!
EXCELLENT RETRIEVAL OF THE ESCAPEE.
NOW, LET'S GET BACK HOME AND GET THAT SNACK.
SETTING COORDINATES FOR EARTH!
WHINE!

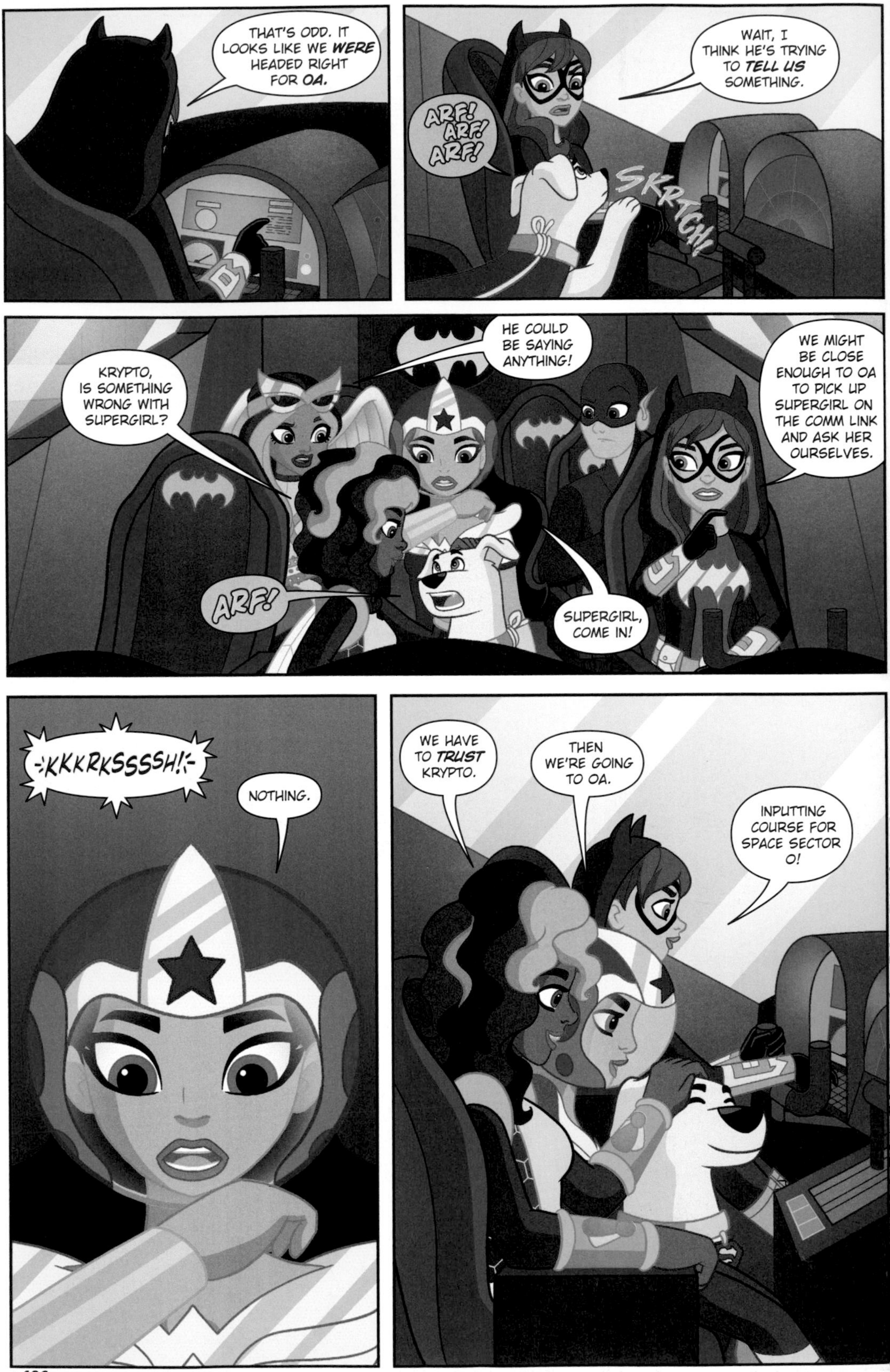
THAT'S ODD. IT LOOKS LIKE WE *WERE* HEADED RIGHT FOR *OA.*
WAIT, I THINK HE'S TRYING TO *TELL US* SOMETHING.
ARF! ARF! ARF!
SKRTCH!
KRYPTO, IS SOMETHING WRONG WITH SUPERGIRL?
HE COULD BE SAYING ANYTHING!
WE MIGHT BE CLOSE ENOUGH TO OA TO PICK UP SUPERGIRL ON THE COMM LINK AND ASK HER OURSELVES.
ARF!
SUPERGIRL, COME IN!
-KKKRKSSSSH!-
NOTHING.
WE HAVE TO *TRUST* KRYPTO.
THEN WE'RE GOING TO OA.
INPUTTING COURSE FOR SPACE SECTOR O!

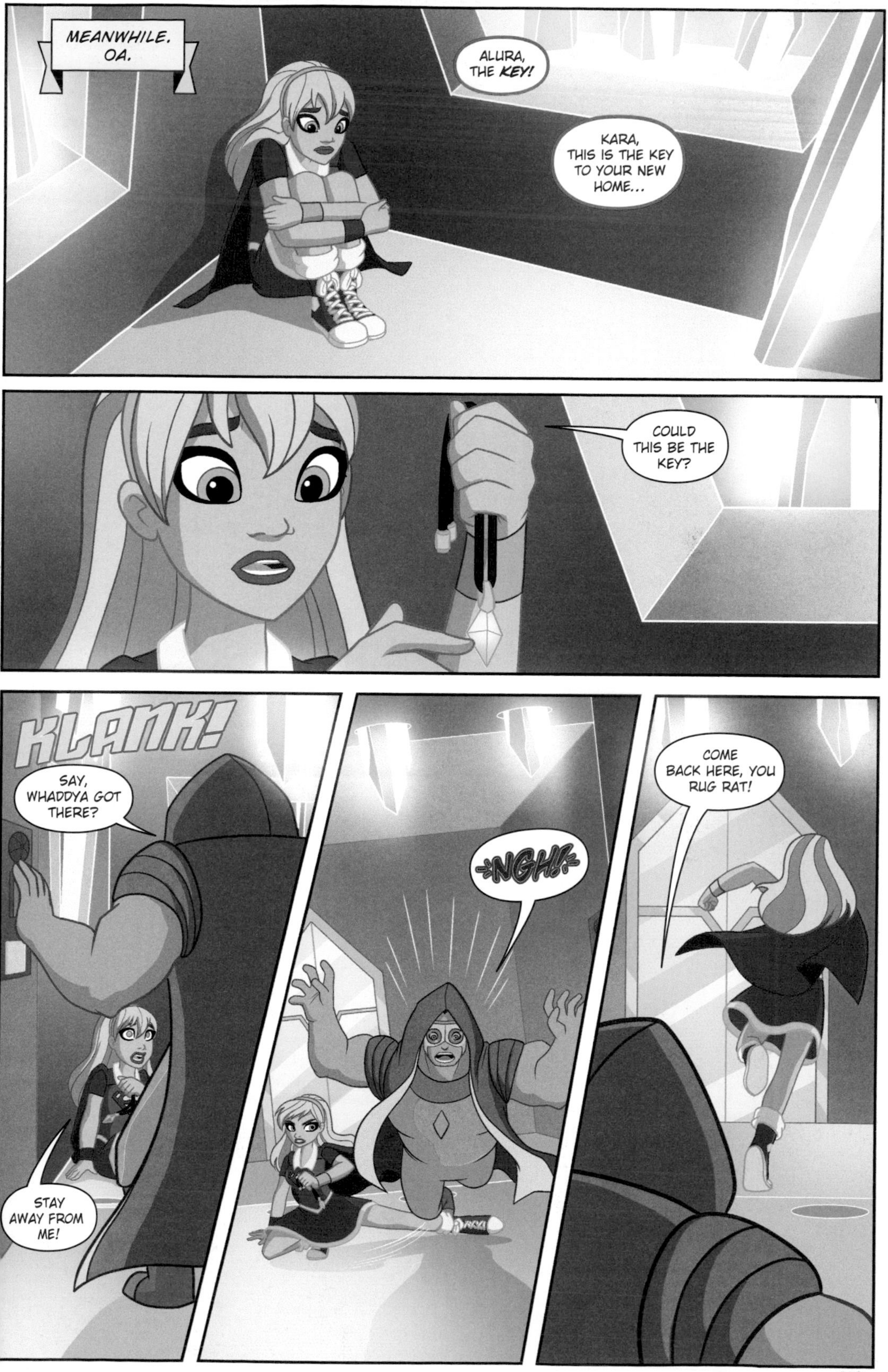
MEANWHILE. OA.
ALURA, THE KEY!
KARA, THIS IS THE KEY TO YOUR NEW HOME...
COULD THIS BE THE KEY?
KLANK!
SAY, WHADDYA GOT THERE?
STAY AWAY FROM ME!
NGH!
COME BACK HERE, YOU RUG RAT!

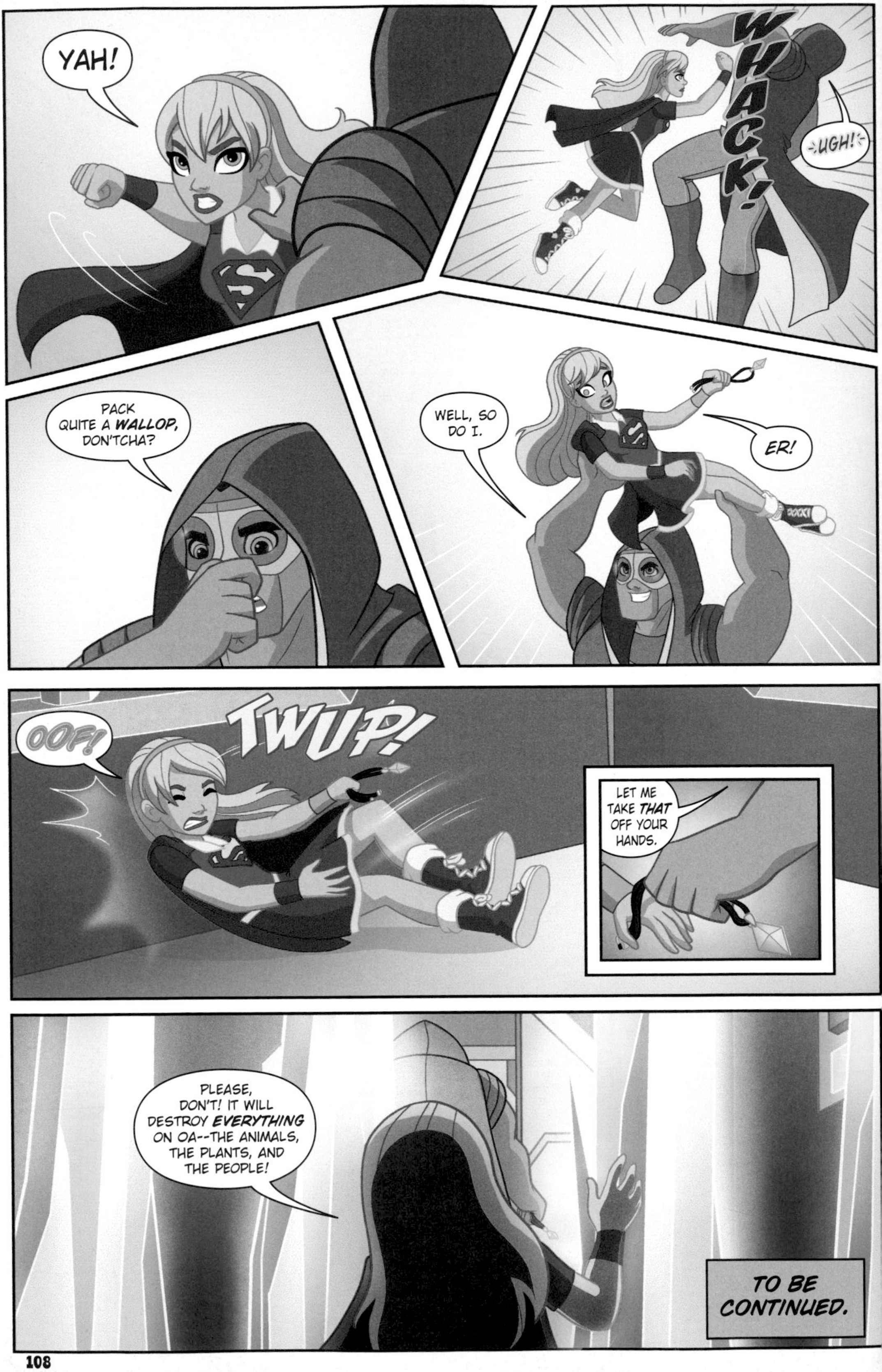
YAH!
WHACK!
UGH!
PACK QUITE A *WALLOP,* DON'TCHA?
WELL, SO DO I.
ER!
OOF!
TWUP!
LET ME TAKE *THAT* OFF YOUR HANDS.
PLEASE, DON'T! IT WILL DESTROY *EVERYTHING* ON OA--THE ANIMALS, THE PLANTS, AND THE PEOPLE!
TO BE CONTINUED.

CHAPTER SIX

THE FINAL FRONTIER

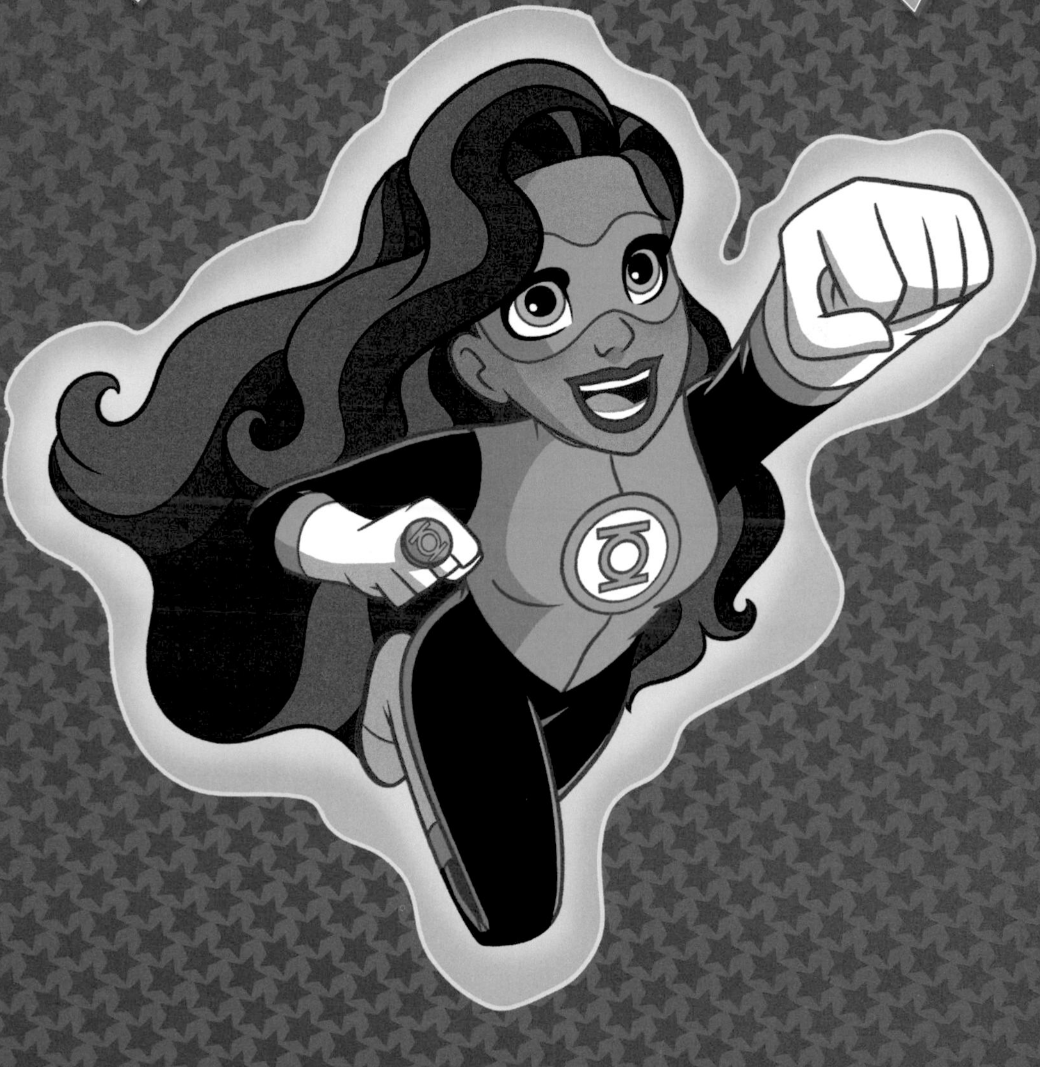

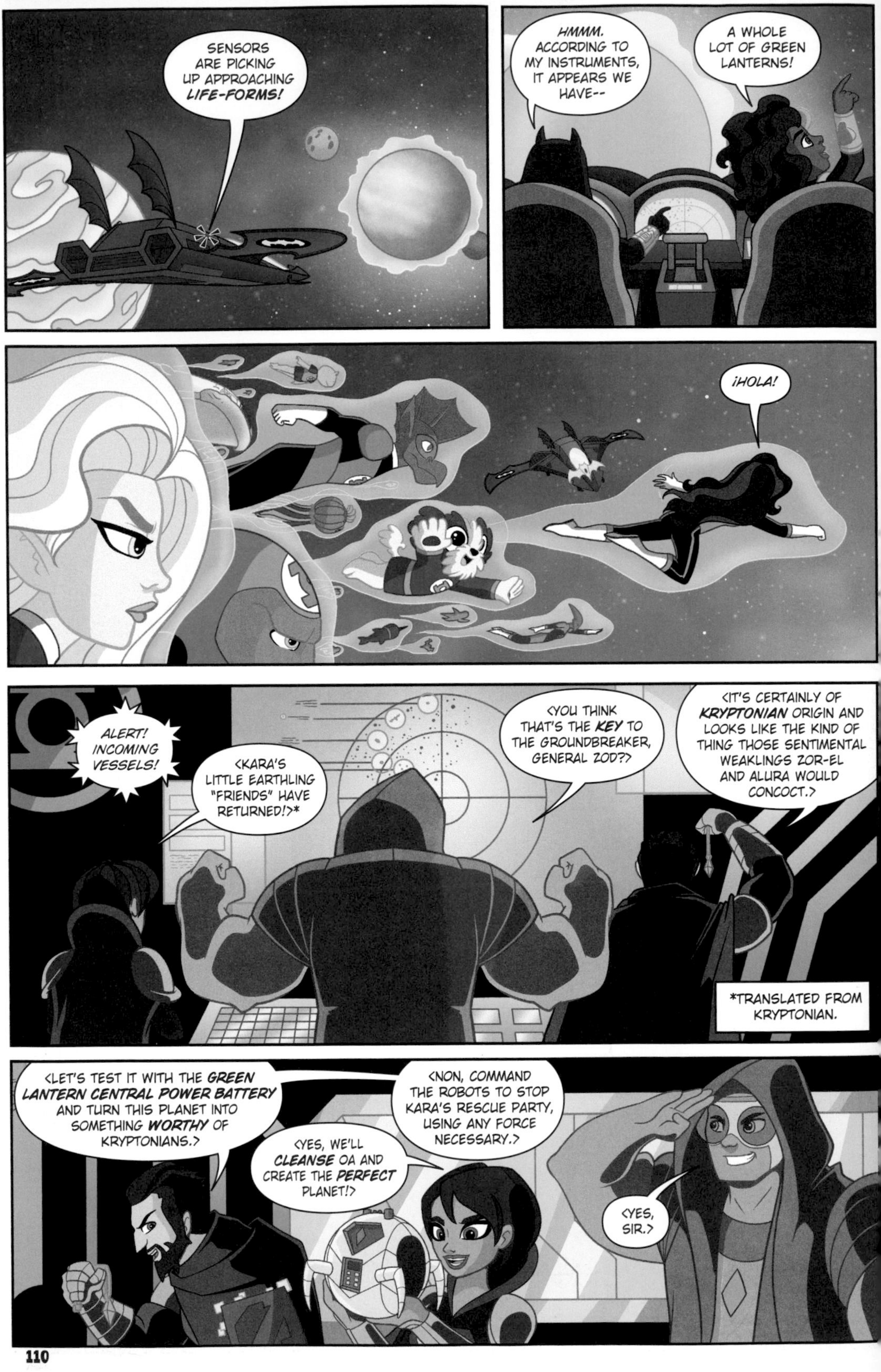
SENSORS ARE PICKING UP APPROACHING LIFE-FORMS!
HMMM. ACCORDING TO MY INSTRUMENTS, IT APPEARS WE HAVE--
A WHOLE LOT OF GREEN LANTERNS!
¡HOLA!
ALERT! INCOMING VESSELS!
<KARA'S LITTLE EARTHLING "FRIENDS" HAVE RETURNED!>*
<YOU THINK THAT'S THE KEY TO THE GROUNDBREAKER, GENERAL ZOD?>
<IT'S CERTAINLY OF KRYPTONIAN ORIGIN AND LOOKS LIKE THE KIND OF THING THOSE SENTIMENTAL WEAKLINGS ZOR-EL AND ALURA WOULD CONCOCT.>
*TRANSLATED FROM KRYPTONIAN.
<LET'S TEST IT WITH THE GREEN LANTERN CENTRAL POWER BATTERY AND TURN THIS PLANET INTO SOMETHING WORTHY OF KRYPTONIANS.>
<YES, WE'LL CLEANSE OA AND CREATE THE PERFECT PLANET!>
<NON, COMMAND THE ROBOTS TO STOP KARA'S RESCUE PARTY, USING ANY FORCE NECESSARY.>
<YES, SIR.>

<IT'S NOT JUST EARTHLINGS-- *THE GREEN LANTERNS* HAVE RETURNED!>

<WE GOT RID OF THEM ONCE AND WE'LL DO IT AGAIN!>

ARF!

=SNFFLE-SNFFLE!=

I THINK HE MIGHT'VE HEARD SOMETHING?

DOG-HEARING PLUS *SUPER-HEARING* MUST BE THE BOMB!

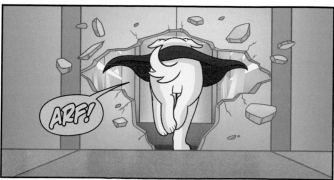

ARF!

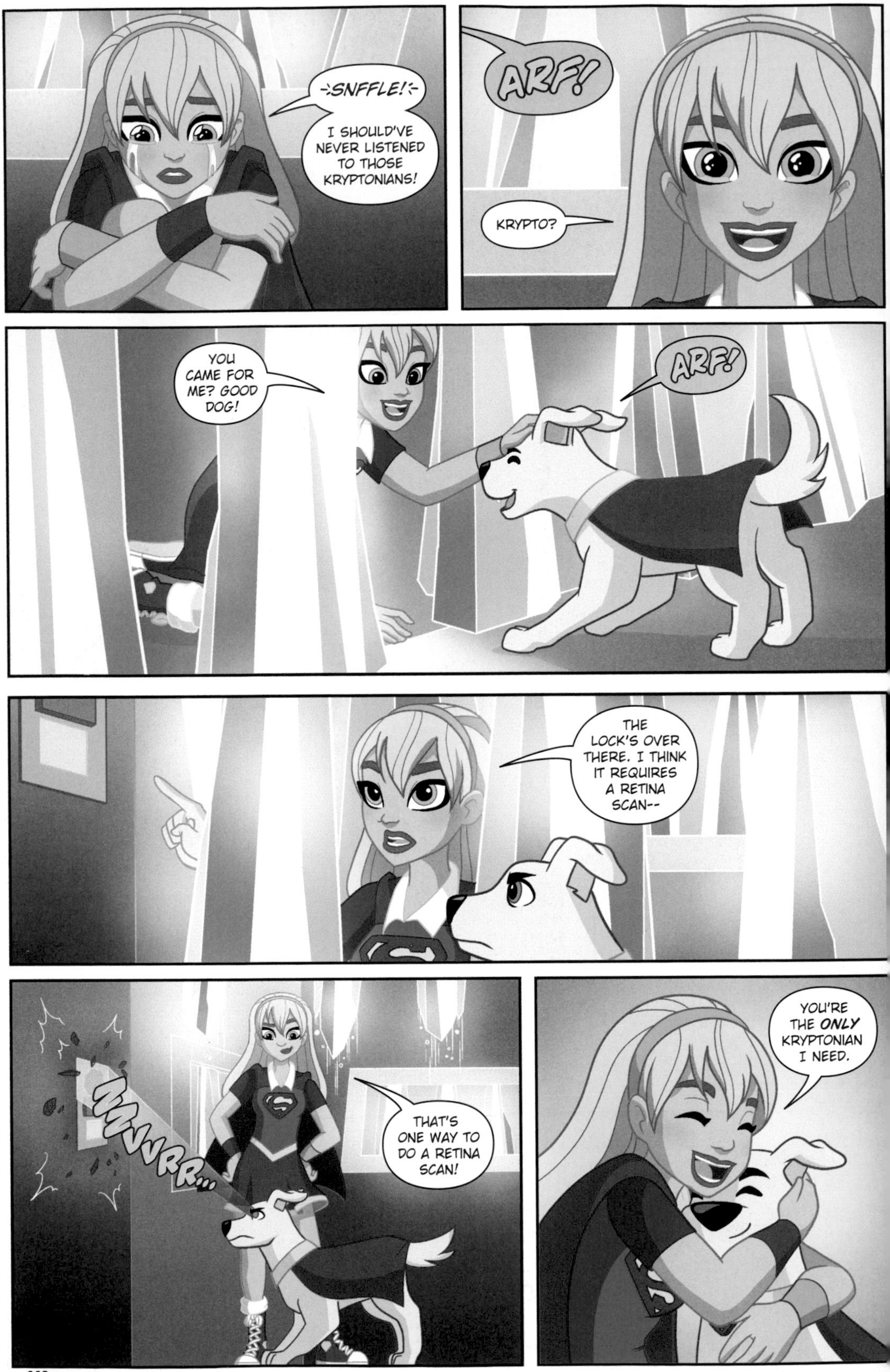
-SNFFLE!-
I SHOULD'VE NEVER LISTENED TO THOSE KRYPTONIANS!
ARF!
KRYPTO?
YOU CAME FOR ME? GOOD DOG!
ARF!
THE LOCK'S OVER THERE. I THINK IT REQUIRES A RETINA SCAN--
MMVVRR...
THAT'S ONE WAY TO DO A RETINA SCAN!
YOU'RE THE ONLY KRYPTONIAN I NEED.

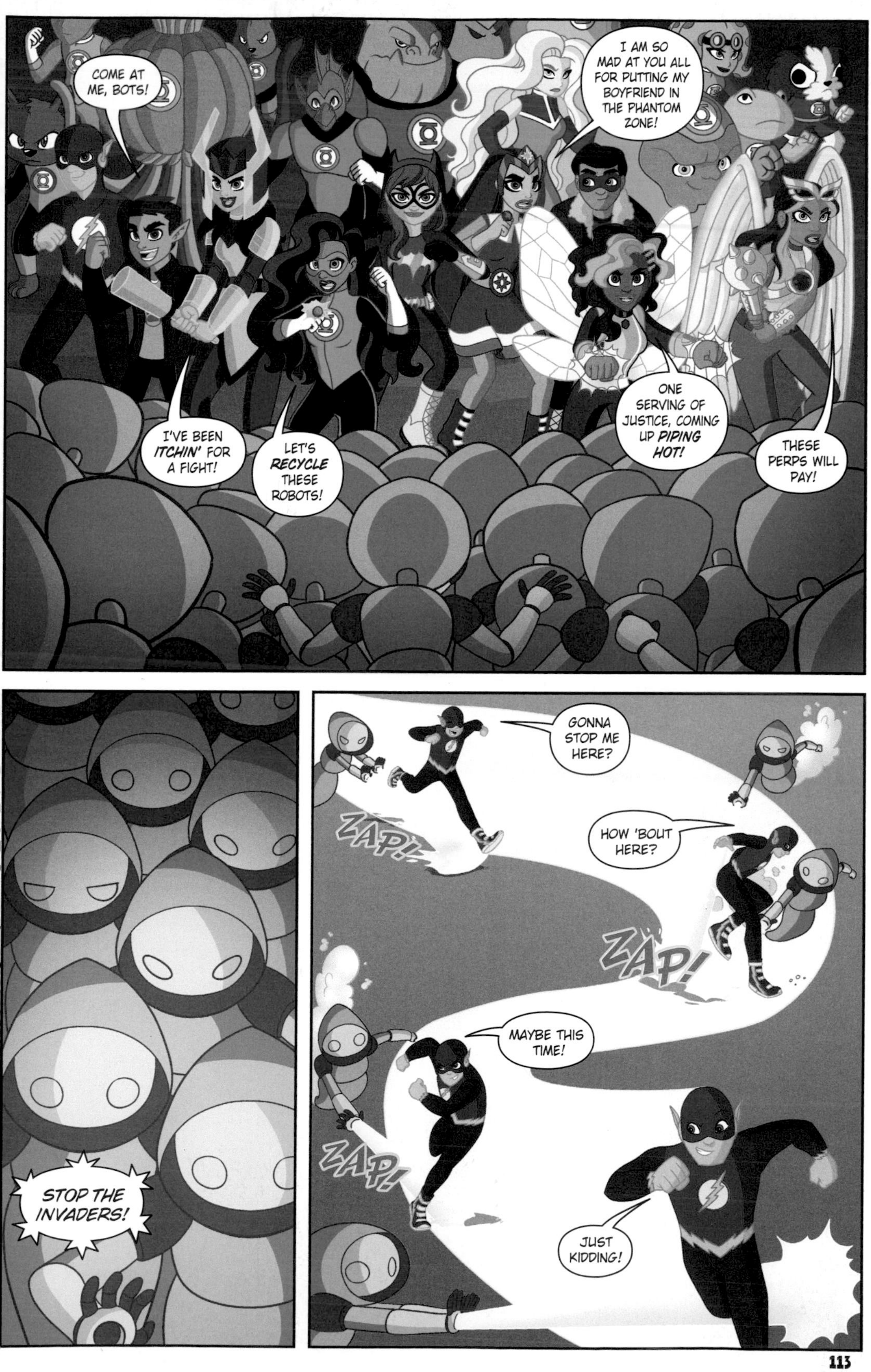
COME AT ME, BOTS!
I AM SO MAD AT YOU ALL FOR PUTTING MY BOYFRIEND IN THE PHANTOM ZONE!
I'VE BEEN ITCHIN' FOR A FIGHT!
LET'S RECYCLE THESE ROBOTS!
ONE SERVING OF JUSTICE, COMING UP PIPING HOT!
THESE PERPS WILL PAY!
STOP THE INVADERS!
GONNA STOP ME HERE?
ZAP!
HOW 'BOUT HERE?
ZAP!
MAYBE THIS TIME!
ZAP!
JUST KIDDING!

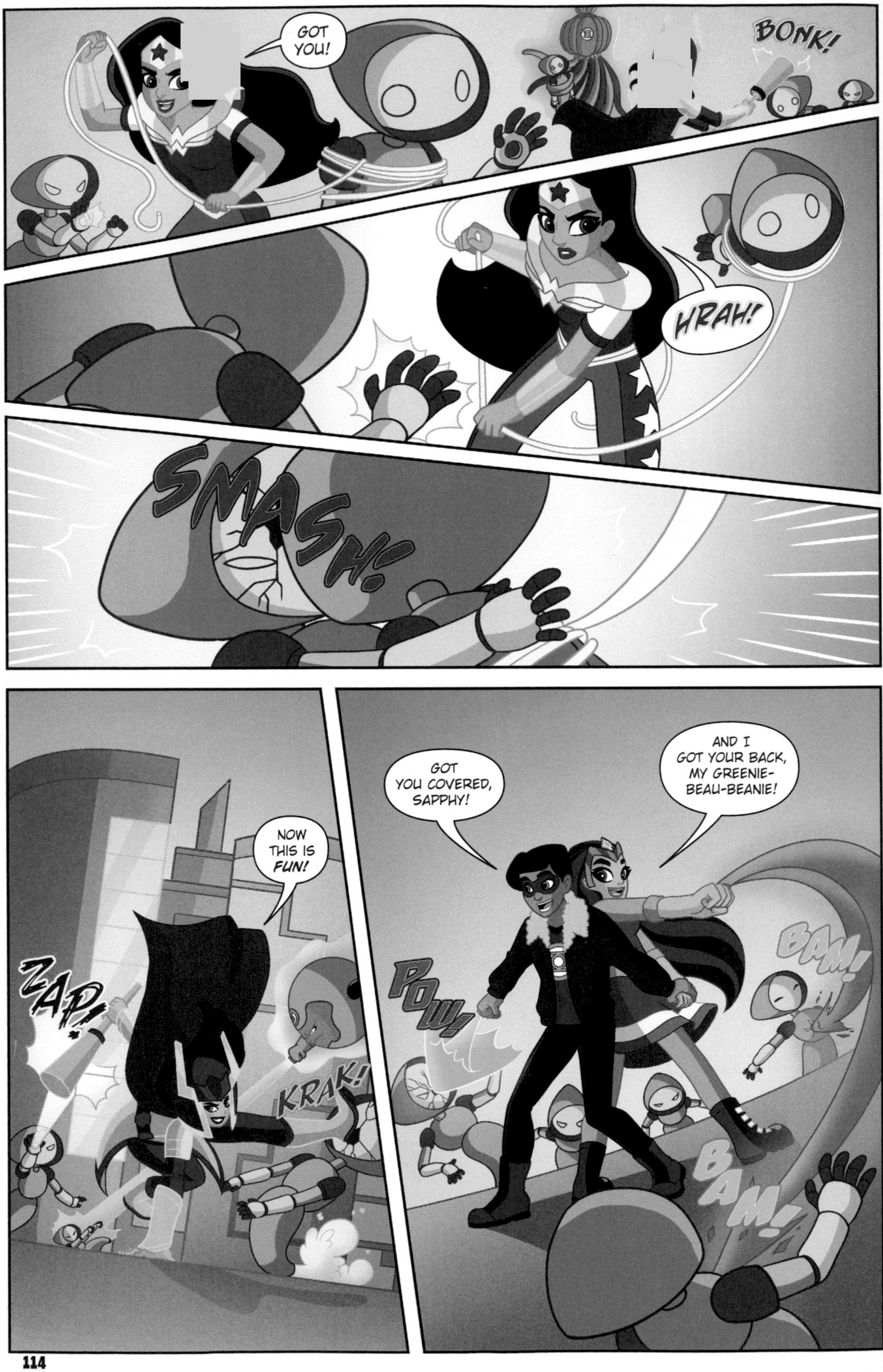
GOT YOU!
BONK!
HRAH!
SMASH!
NOW THIS IS *FUN!*
ZAP!
KRAK!
GOT YOU COVERED, SAPPHY!
AND I GOT YOUR BACK, MY GREENIE-BEAU-BEANIE!
POW!
BAM!
BAM!

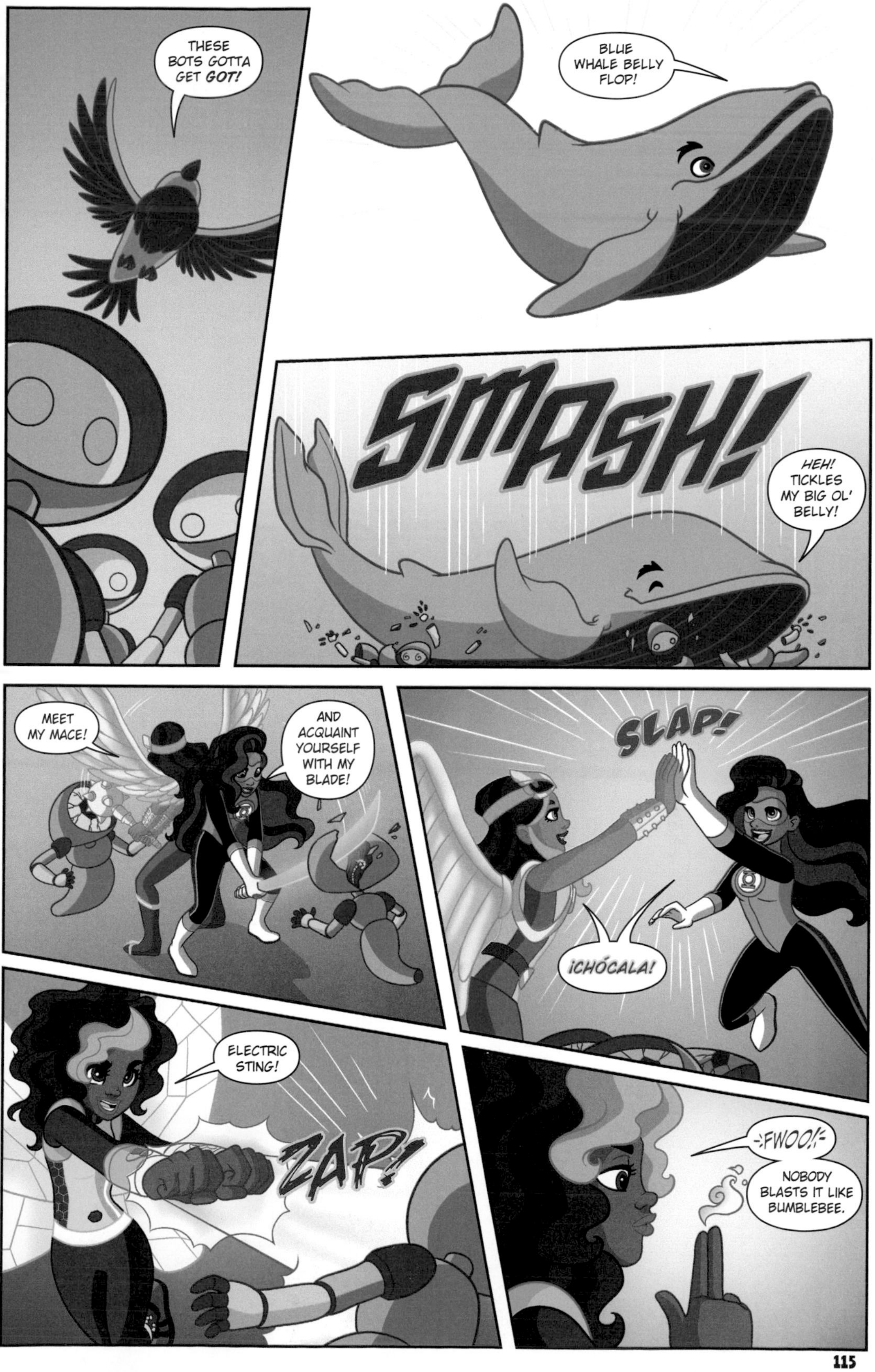

THESE BOTS GOTTA GET GOT!
BLUE WHALE BELLY FLOP!
SMASH!
HEH! TICKLES MY BIG OL' BELLY!
MEET MY MACE!
AND ACQUAINT YOURSELF WITH MY BLADE!
SLAP!
¡CHÓCALA!
ELECTRIC STING!
ZAP!
FWOO!
NOBODY BLASTS IT LIKE BUMBLEBEE.

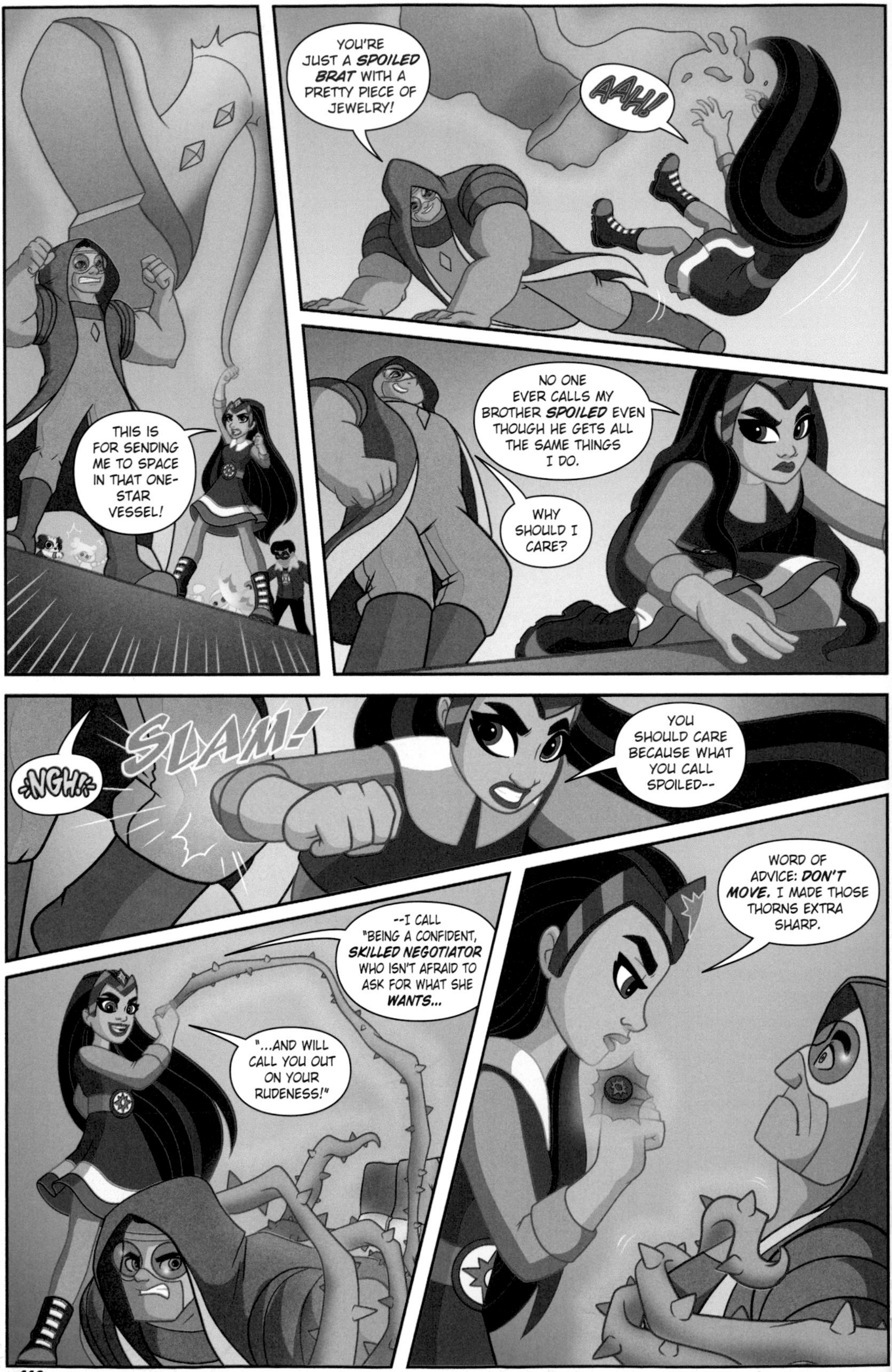

THIS IS FOR SENDING ME TO SPACE IN THAT ONE-STAR VESSEL!
YOU'RE JUST A **SPOILED BRAT** WITH A PRETTY PIECE OF JEWELRY!
AAH!
NO ONE EVER CALLS MY BROTHER **SPOILED** EVEN THOUGH HE GETS ALL THE SAME THINGS I DO.
WHY SHOULD I CARE?
SLAM!
NGH!
YOU SHOULD CARE BECAUSE WHAT YOU CALL SPOILED--
--I CALL "BEING A CONFIDENT, **SKILLED NEGOTIATOR** WHO ISN'T AFRAID TO ASK FOR WHAT SHE **WANTS...**
"...AND WILL CALL YOU OUT ON YOUR RUDENESS!"
WORD OF ADVICE: **DON'T MOVE.** I MADE THOSE THORNS EXTRA SHARP.

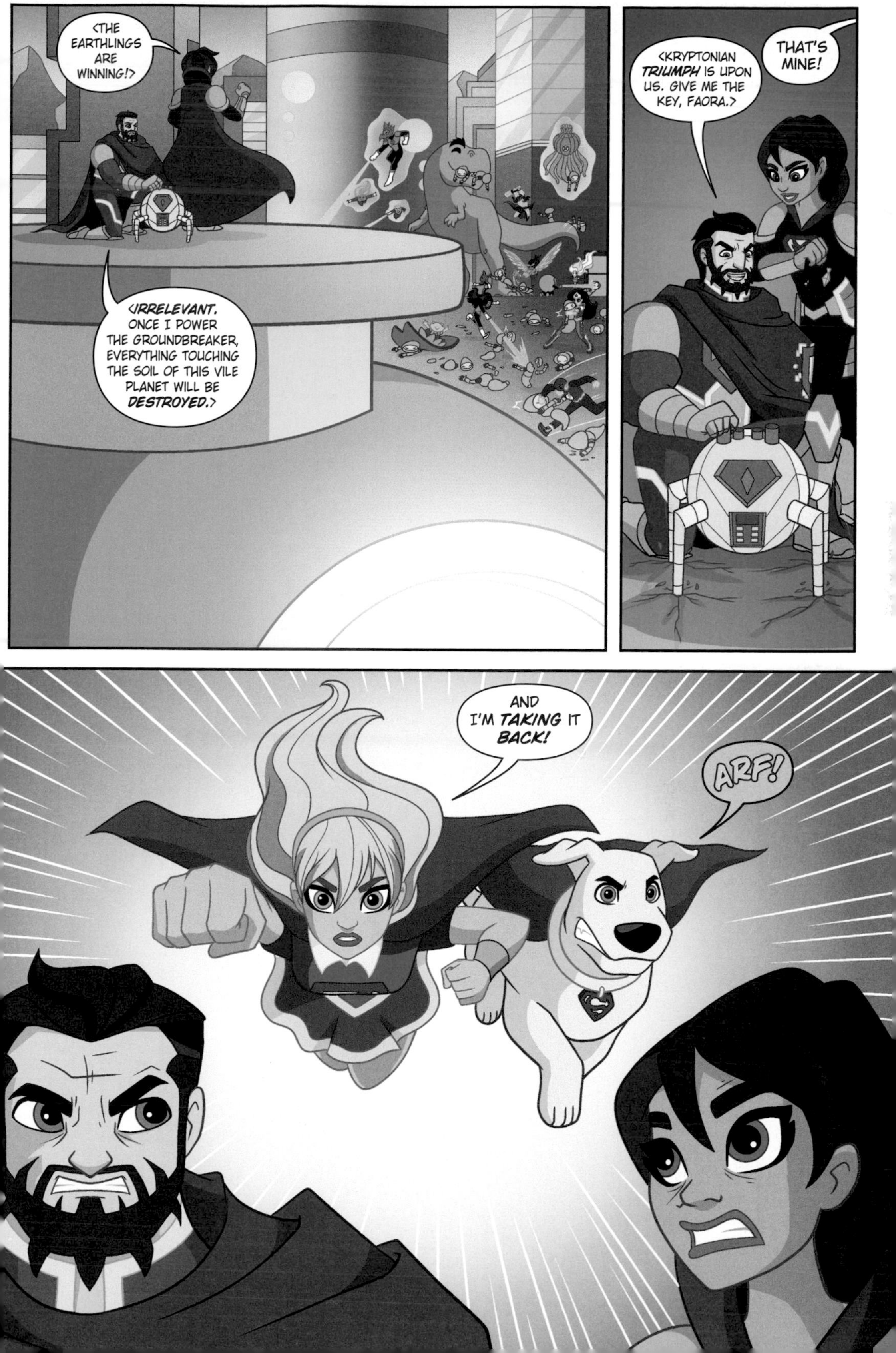

<THE EARTHLINGS ARE WINNING!>
<IRRELEVANT. ONCE I POWER THE GROUNDBREAKER, EVERYTHING TOUCHING THE SOIL OF THIS VILE PLANET WILL BE DESTROYED.>
<KRYPTONIAN TRIUMPH IS UPON US. GIVE ME THE KEY, FAORA.>
THAT'S MINE!
AND I'M TAKING IT BACK!
ARF!

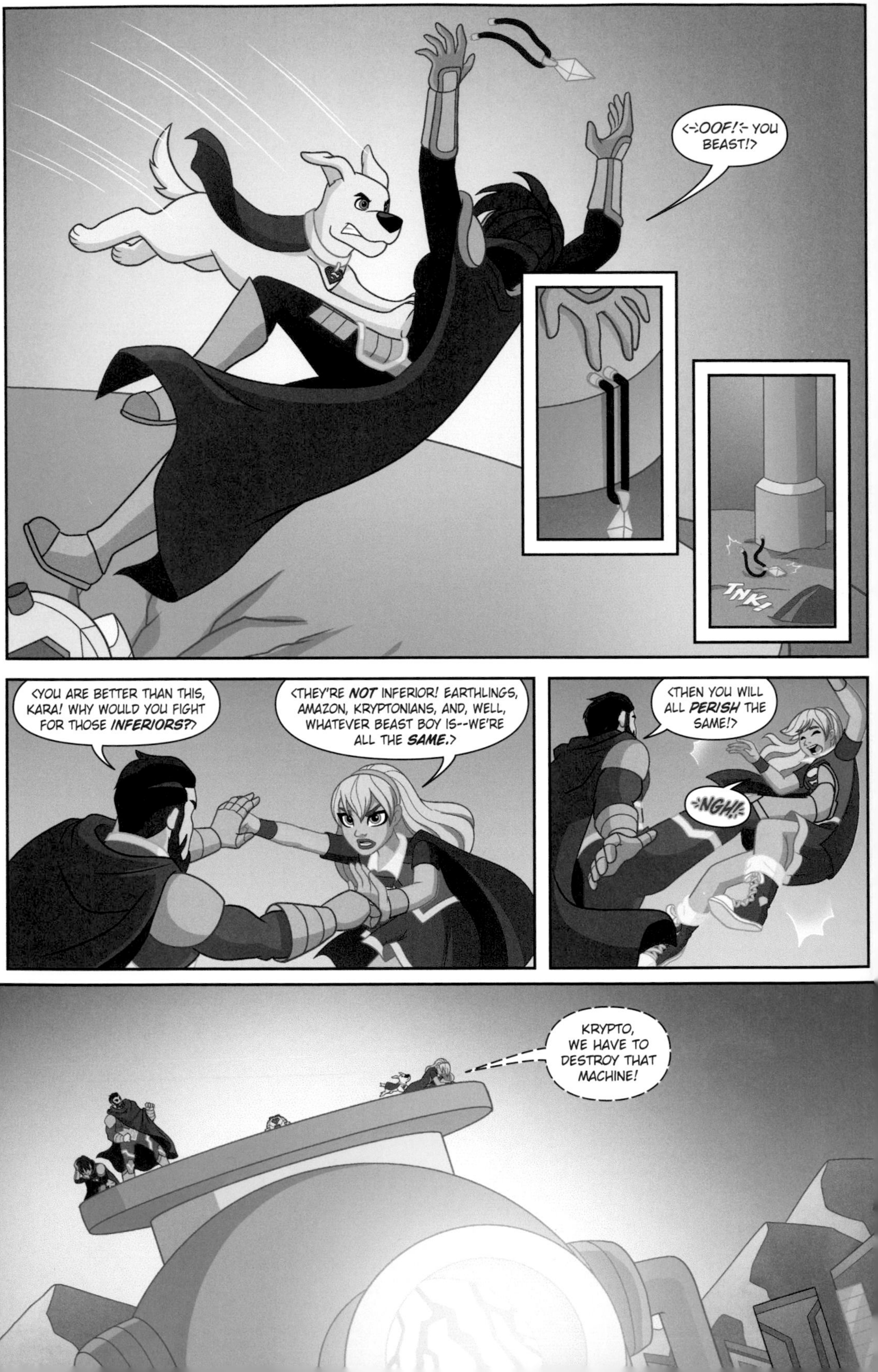

<–OOF!– YOU BEAST!>
TNK!
<YOU ARE BETTER THAN THIS, KARA! WHY WOULD YOU FIGHT FOR THOSE *INFERIORS?*>
<THEY'RE ***NOT*** INFERIOR! EARTHLINGS, AMAZON, KRYPTONIANS, AND, WELL, WHATEVER BEAST BOY IS--WE'RE ALL THE ***SAME.***>
<THEN YOU WILL ALL ***PERISH*** THE SAME!>
NGH!
KRYPTO, WE HAVE TO DESTROY THAT MACHINE!

<STAY BACK, TRAITOR!>

NO!

ZAP!

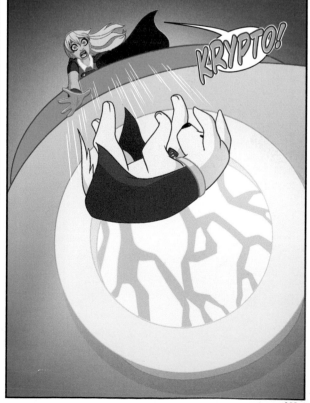

KRYPTO!

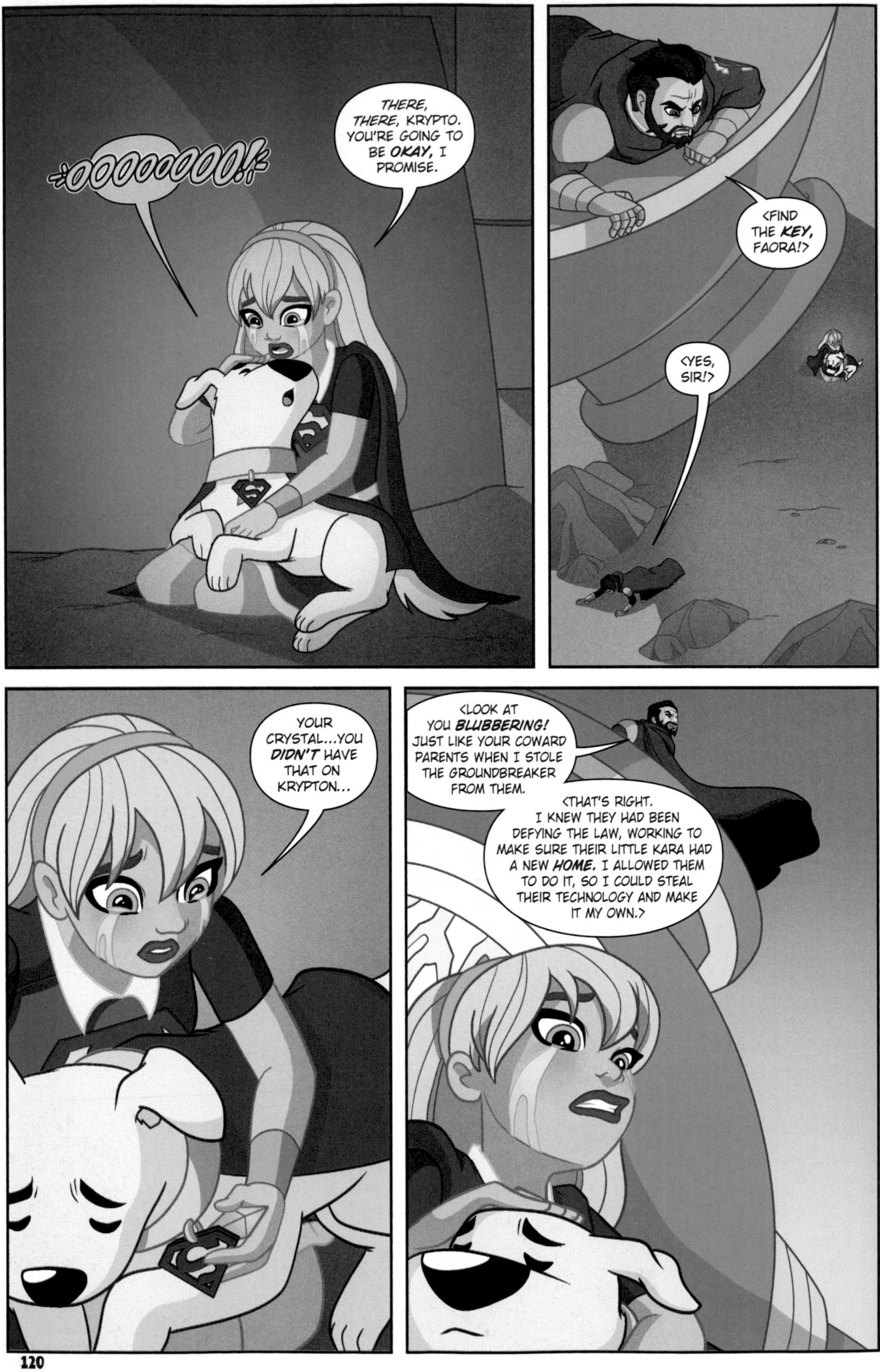
-OOOOOOOO!-
THERE, THERE, KRYPTO. YOU'RE GOING TO BE OKAY, I PROMISE.
<FIND THE KEY, FAORA!>
<YES, SIR!>
YOUR CRYSTAL...YOU DIDN'T HAVE THAT ON KRYPTON...
<LOOK AT YOU BLUBBERING! JUST LIKE YOUR COWARD PARENTS WHEN I STOLE THE GROUNDBREAKER FROM THEM.
<THAT'S RIGHT. I KNEW THEY HAD BEEN DEFYING THE LAW, WORKING TO MAKE SURE THEIR LITTLE KARA HAD A NEW HOME. I ALLOWED THEM TO DO IT, SO I COULD STEAL THEIR TECHNOLOGY AND MAKE IT MY OWN.>

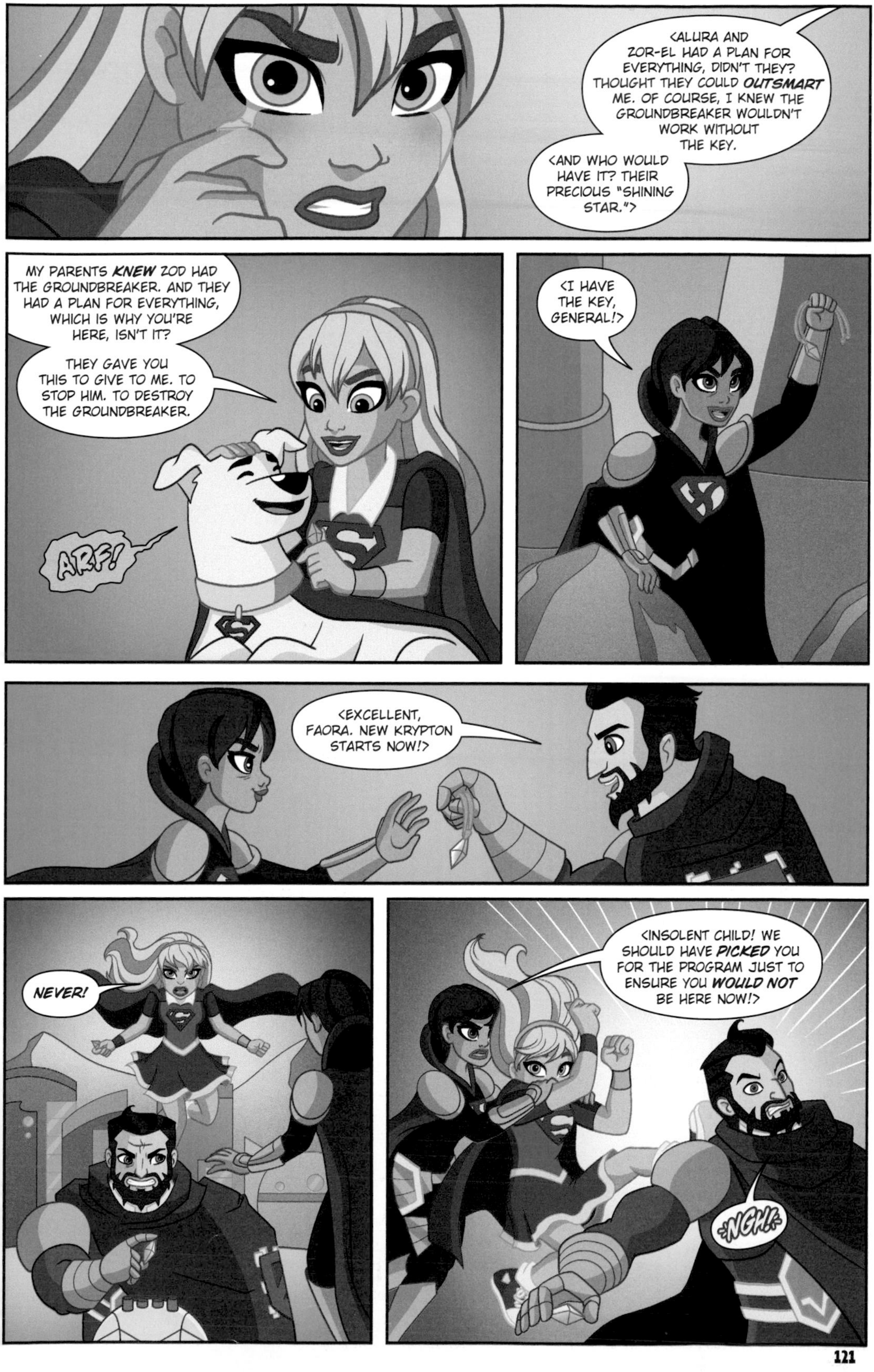
<ALURA AND ZOR-EL HAD A PLAN FOR EVERYTHING, DIDN'T THEY? THOUGHT THEY COULD ***OUTSMART*** ME. OF COURSE, I KNEW THE GROUNDBREAKER WOULDN'T WORK WITHOUT THE KEY.
<AND WHO WOULD HAVE IT? THEIR PRECIOUS "SHINING STAR.">
MY PARENTS ***KNEW*** ZOD HAD THE GROUNDBREAKER. AND THEY HAD A PLAN FOR EVERYTHING, WHICH IS WHY YOU'RE HERE, ISN'T IT?
THEY GAVE YOU THIS TO GIVE TO ME. TO STOP HIM. TO DESTROY THE GROUNDBREAKER.
ARF!
<I HAVE THE KEY, GENERAL!>
<EXCELLENT, FAORA. NEW KRYPTON STARTS NOW!>
NEVER!
<INSOLENT CHILD! WE SHOULD HAVE ***PICKED*** YOU FOR THE PROGRAM JUST TO ENSURE YOU ***WOULD NOT*** BE HERE NOW!>
NGH!

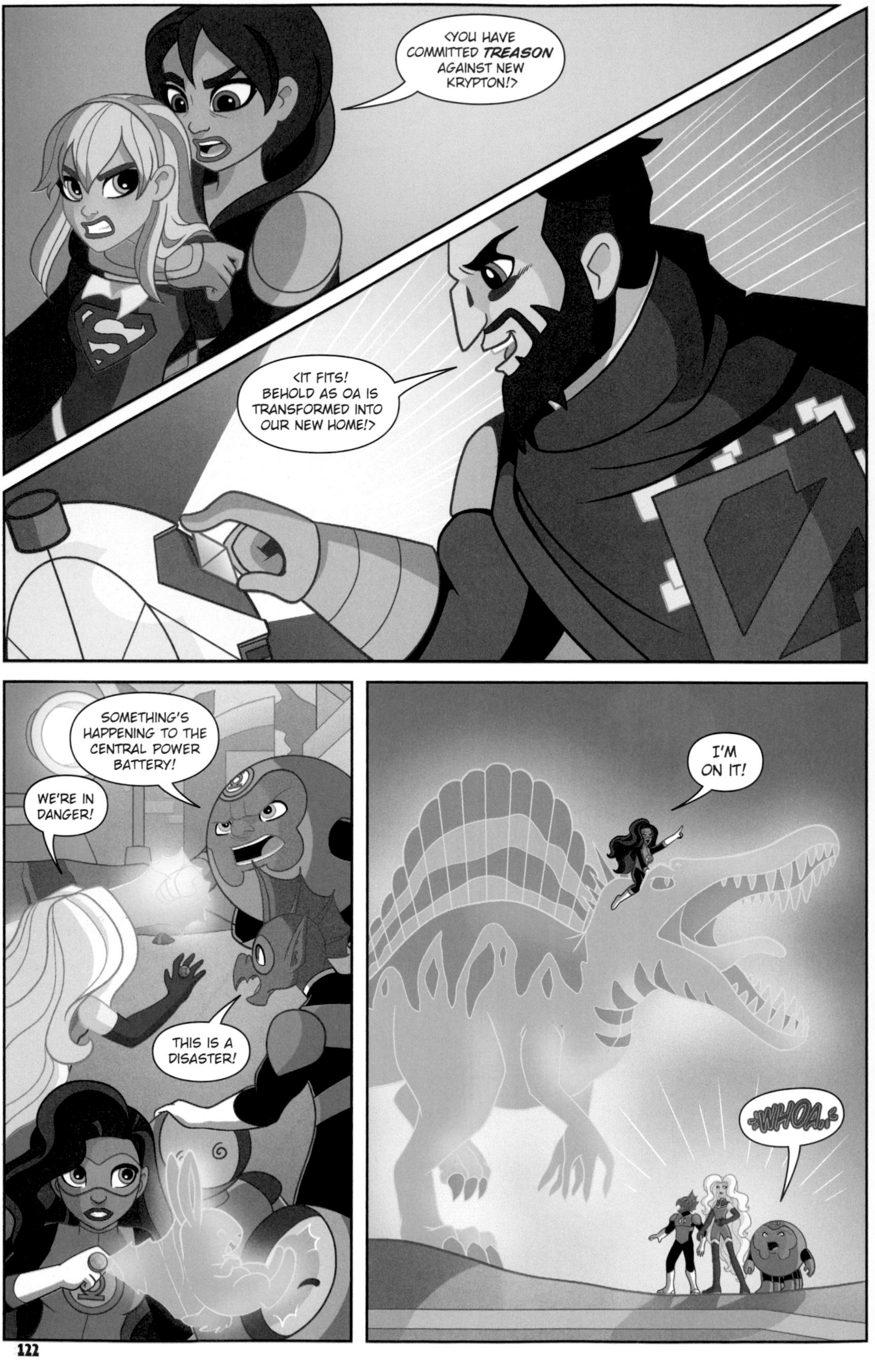

<YOU HAVE COMMITTED **TREASON** AGAINST NEW KRYPTON!>
<IT FITS! BEHOLD AS OA IS TRANSFORMED INTO OUR NEW HOME!>
SOMETHING'S HAPPENING TO THE CENTRAL POWER BATTERY!
WE'RE IN DANGER!
THIS IS A DISASTER!
I'M ON IT!
WHOA...

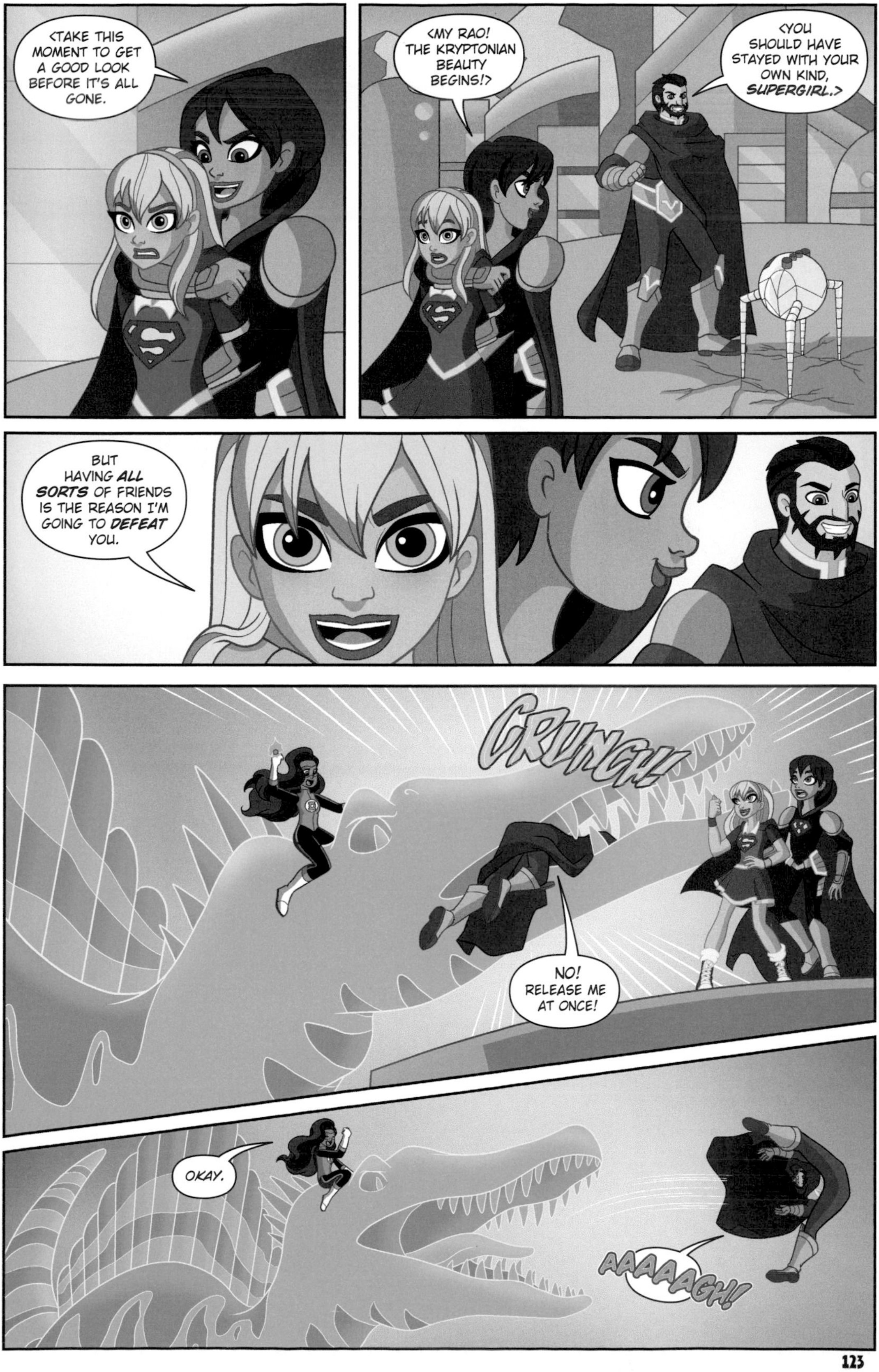

<TAKE THIS MOMENT TO GET A GOOD LOOK BEFORE IT'S ALL GONE.
<MY RAO! THE KRYPTONIAN BEAUTY BEGINS!>
<YOU SHOULD HAVE STAYED WITH YOUR OWN KIND, SUPERGIRL.>
BUT HAVING ALL SORTS OF FRIENDS IS THE REASON I'M GOING TO DEFEAT YOU.
CRUNCH!
NO! RELEASE ME AT ONCE!
OKAY.
AAAAAGH!

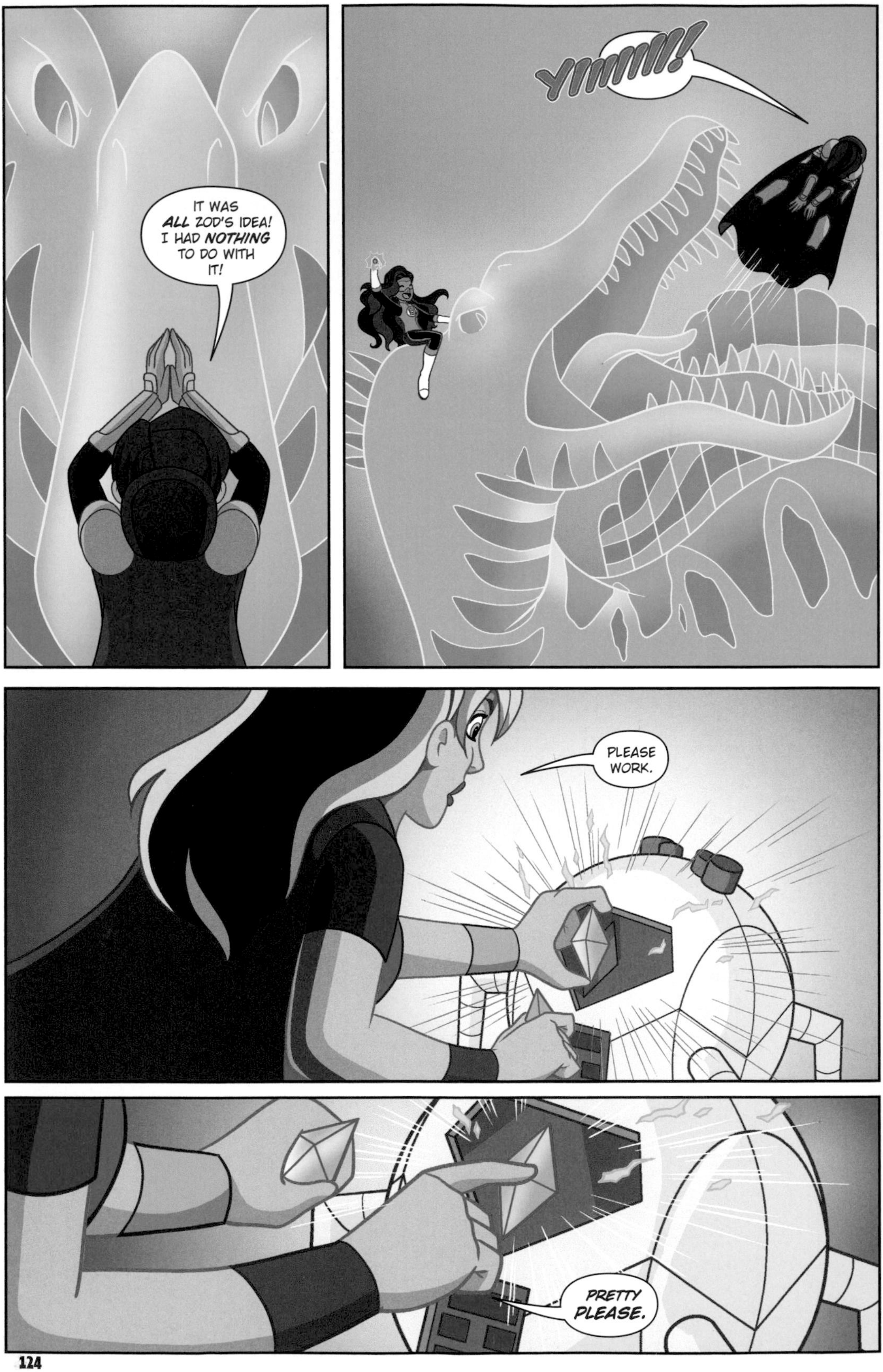
IT WAS ALL ZOD'S IDEA! I HAD NOTHING TO DO WITH IT!
YIIIIII!
PLEASE WORK.
PRETTY PLEASE.

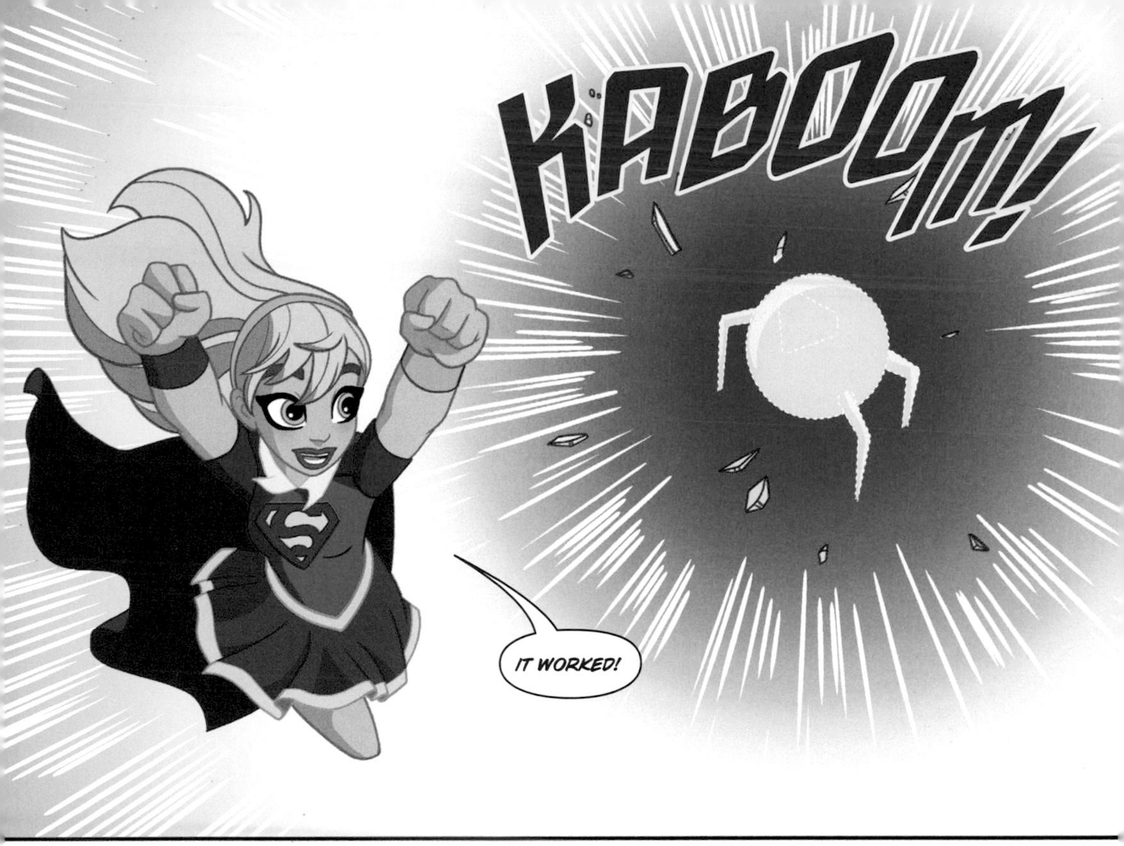
KABOOM!
IT WORKED!

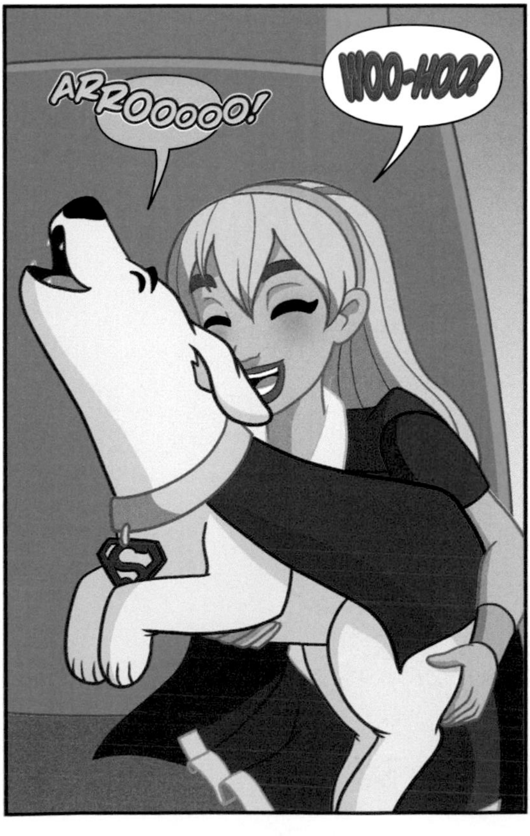
ARROOOOOO!
WOO-HOO!

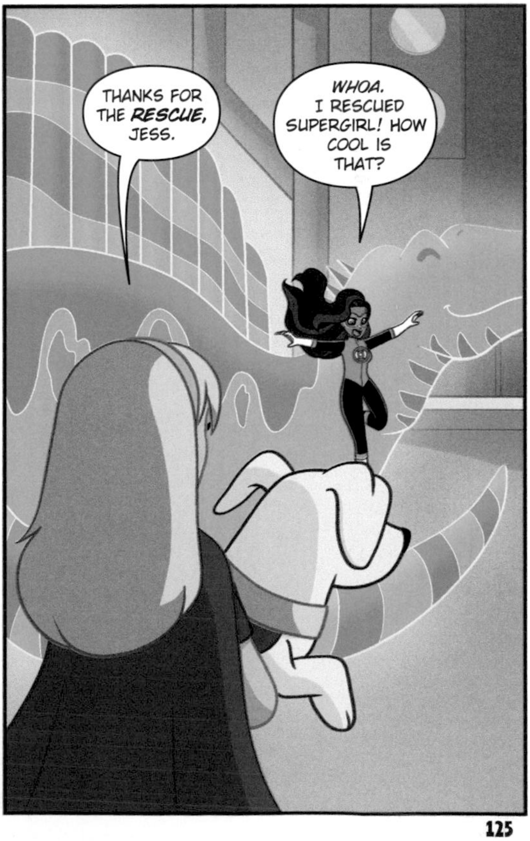
THANKS FOR THE RESCUE, JESS.
WHOA. I RESCUED SUPERGIRL! HOW COOL IS THAT?

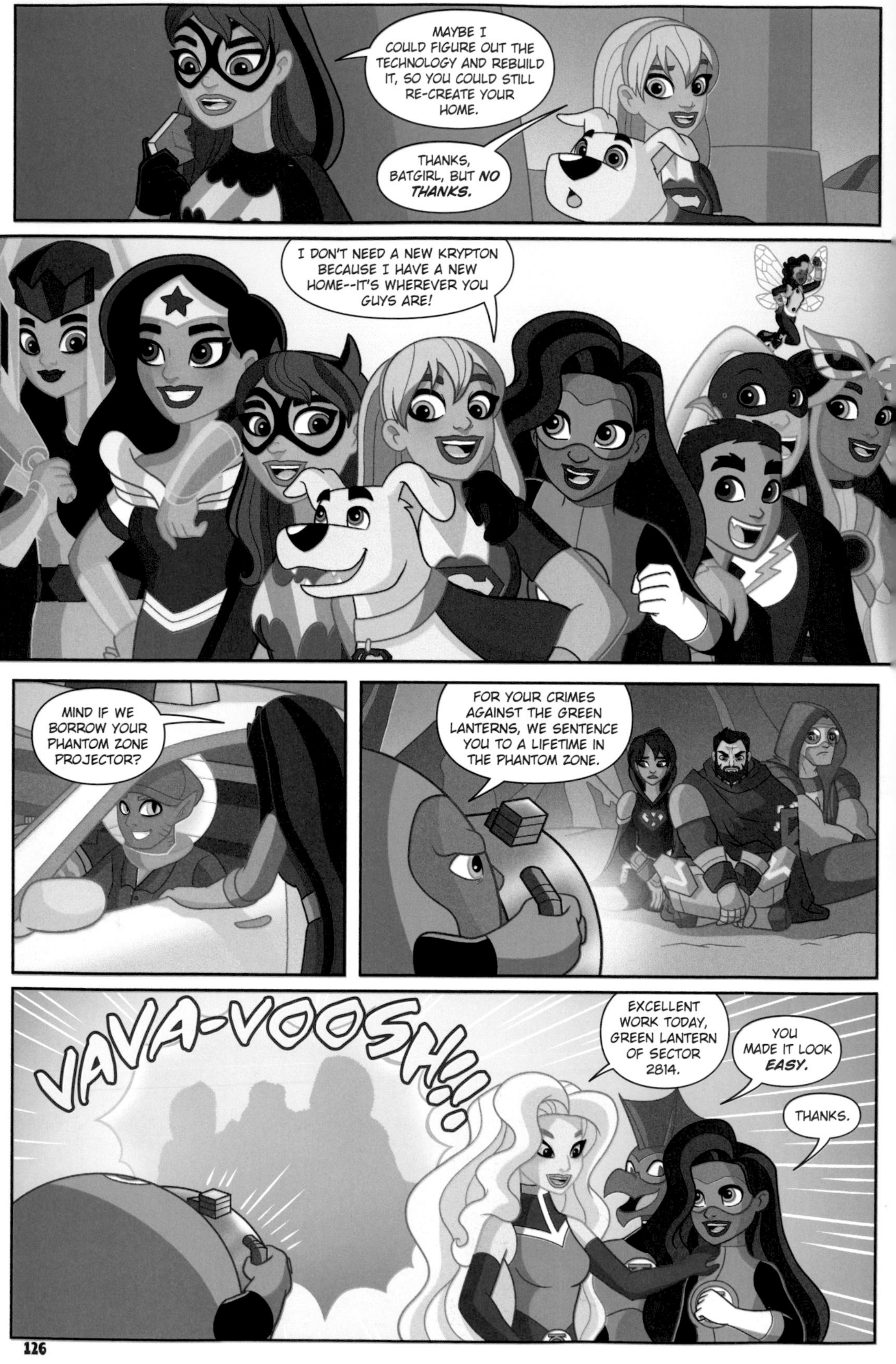
MAYBE I COULD FIGURE OUT THE TECHNOLOGY AND REBUILD IT, SO YOU COULD STILL RE-CREATE YOUR HOME.
THANKS, BATGIRL, BUT *NO THANKS.*
I DON'T NEED A NEW KRYPTON BECAUSE I HAVE A NEW HOME--IT'S WHEREVER YOU GUYS ARE!
MIND IF WE BORROW YOUR PHANTOM ZONE PROJECTOR?
FOR YOUR CRIMES AGAINST THE GREEN LANTERNS, WE SENTENCE YOU TO A LIFETIME IN THE PHANTOM ZONE.
VAVA-VOOSH!!!
EXCELLENT WORK TODAY, GREEN LANTERN OF SECTOR 2814.
YOU MADE IT LOOK *EASY.*
THANKS.

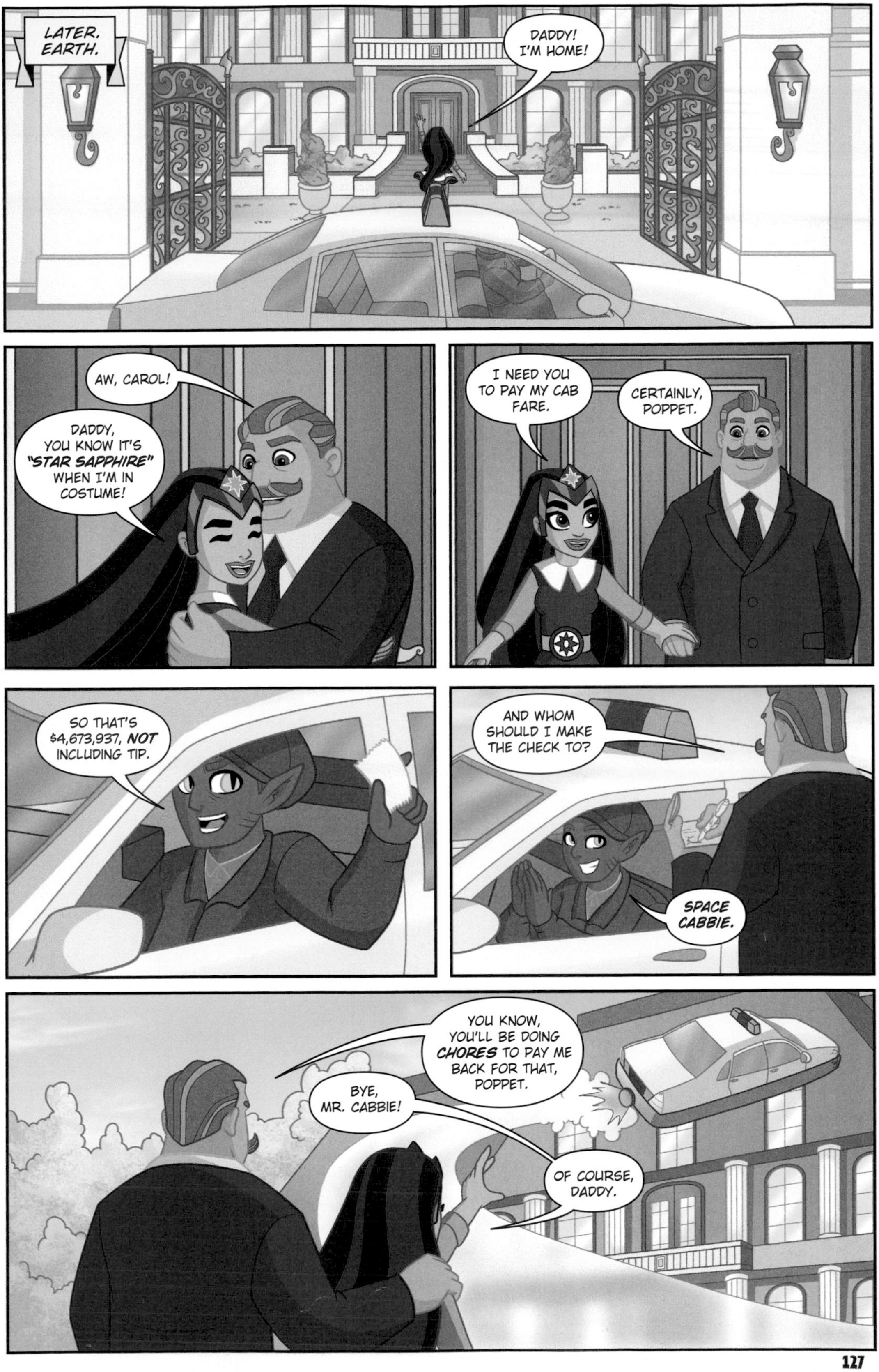
LATER. EARTH.
DADDY! I'M HOME!
AW, CAROL!
DADDY, YOU KNOW IT'S **"STAR SAPPHIRE"** WHEN I'M IN COSTUME!
I NEED YOU TO PAY MY CAB FARE.
CERTAINLY, POPPET.
SO THAT'S $4,673,937, **NOT** INCLUDING TIP.
AND WHOM SHOULD I MAKE THE CHECK TO?
SPACE CABBIE.
YOU KNOW, YOU'LL BE DOING **CHORES** TO PAY ME BACK FOR THAT, POPPET.
BYE, MR. CABBIE!
OF COURSE, DADDY.

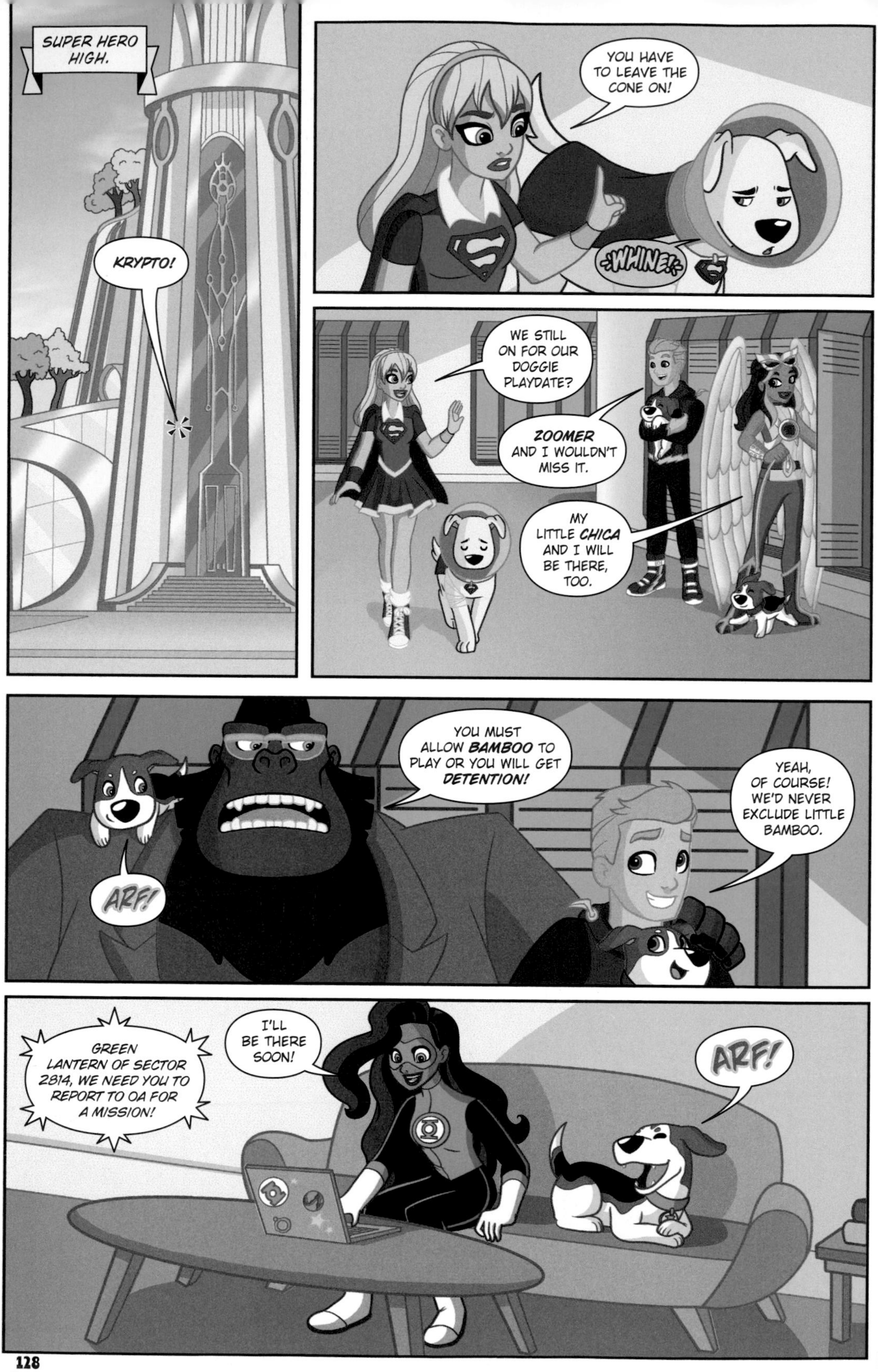
SUPER HERO HIGH.
KRYPTO!
YOU HAVE TO LEAVE THE CONE ON!
WHINE!
WE STILL ON FOR OUR DOGGIE PLAYDATE?
ZOOMER AND I WOULDN'T MISS IT.
MY LITTLE CHICA AND I WILL BE THERE, TOO.
YOU MUST ALLOW BAMBOO TO PLAY OR YOU WILL GET DETENTION!
ARF!
YEAH, OF COURSE! WE'D NEVER EXCLUDE LITTLE BAMBOO.
GREEN LANTERN OF SECTOR 2814, WE NEED YOU TO REPORT TO OA FOR A MISSION!
I'LL BE THERE SOON!
ARF!

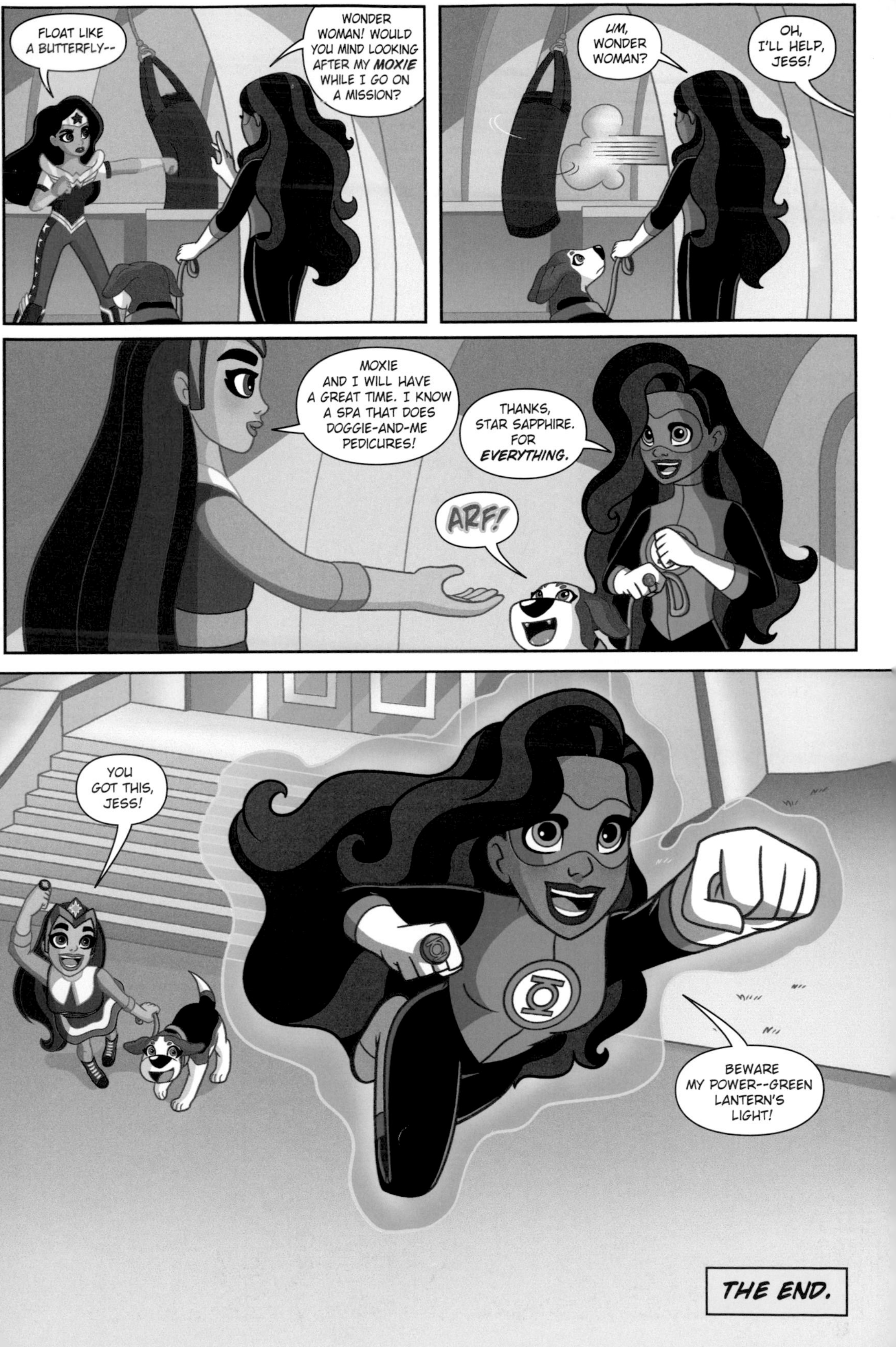

FLOAT LIKE A BUTTERFLY--
WONDER WOMAN! WOULD YOU MIND LOOKING AFTER MY *MOXIE* WHILE I GO ON A MISSION?
UM, WONDER WOMAN?
OH, I'LL HELP, JESS!
MOXIE AND I WILL HAVE A GREAT TIME. I KNOW A SPA THAT DOES DOGGIE-AND-ME PEDICURES!
THANKS, STAR SAPPHIRE. FOR *EVERYTHING*.
ARF!
YOU GOT THIS, JESS!
BEWARE MY POWER--GREEN LANTERN'S LIGHT!
THE END.

SHEA FONTANA is a writer for film, television, and graphic novels. In addition to the DC SUPER HERO GIRLS graphic novels, she also wrote DC SUPER HERO GIRLS animated shorts, a TV special, and movies. Her other credits include *Polly Pocket, Doc McStuffins, Dorothy and the Wizard of Oz, Whisker Haven Tales with the Palace Pets,* live shows for Disney on Ice, and some of DC's most iconic comic book series including WONDER WOMAN, JUSTICE LEAGUE, and the upcoming BATMAN: OVERDRIVE. She lives in sunny Los Angeles where she enjoys hiking tall mountains, tolerates running long distances, and loves snuggling her puppies.

AGNES GARBOWSKA was born in Poland and came to Canada at a young age. Being an only child she escaped into a world of books, cartoons, and comics. She is best known for her longtime work on *My Little Pony* (IDW Publishing). She has worked on many all-ages titles including *Jem and the Holograms* (IDW Publishing), *Transformers* (IDW Publishing), *Grumpy Cat* (Dynamite Entertainment), *Boo: The World's Cutest Dog* (Dynamite Entertainment), and *Sonic Universe* (Archie).

SILVANA BRYS is a colorist and graphic designer who has colored TEEN TITANS GO!, SCOOBY-DOO, SCOOBY-DOO TEAM-UP, *Tom & Jerry,* LOONEY TUNES, and many other comics and books. She lives in a small village in Argentina. Her home is also her office and she loves to create there, surrounded by forests and mountains.

JANICE CHIANG has lettered *Archie, Barbie, The Punisher,* and many more. She was the first woman to win the *Comic Buyer's Guide* Fan Awards for Best Letterer (2011), and was designated an outstanding letterer of 2016 by ComicsAlliance. She likes weight training, hiking, baking, gardening, and traveling.

Now that everyone's back at
Super Hero High, things are perfect.
Except for all the things that aren't, somehow.
When the girls experience a TEENAGE CRISIS,
Zatanna shows them a universe where things are very different,
leaving her friends to decide for themselves
where the grass is greener.

WRITTEN BY
Sholly Fisch

ART BY
Marcelo DiChiara

COLORS BY
Wendy Broome

LETTERING BY
Janice Chiang

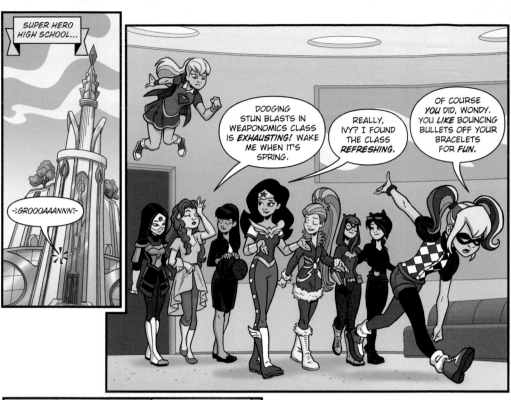

-:GROOOAAANNN:-

DODGING STUN BLASTS IN WEAPONOMICS CLASS IS *EXHAUSTING!* WAKE ME WHEN IT'S SPRING.

REALLY, IVY? I FOUND THE CLASS *REFRESHING.*

OF COURSE *YOU* DID, WONDY. YOU *LIKE* BOUNCING BULLETS OFF YOUR BRACELETS FOR *FUN.*

WHY CAN'T WE GO TO *NORMAL* SCHOOL, WHERE NOBODY FIRES RAY BEAMS AT YOU?

-:SIGH:- BECAUSE COACH WILDCAT SAYS "SUPER HEROES HAVE TO BE READY AT *ALL TIMES,*" FROST.

"EVIL COULD STRIKE ANYTIME, AT A *MOMENT'S NOTICE.*" RIGHT, BATGIRL?

UH, SURE...

BUT Y'KNOW, SOMETIMES, EVEN *I* WISH I DIDN'T HAVE TO BE A HERO *ALL* THE TIME. IT'D BE NICE TO BE SOMEONE *ELSE* FOR A WHILE...

WHAT'S WITH ALL OF YOU? CAN'T YOU JUST TAKE A *GOOD LOOK* AT YOURSELVES, AND APPRECIATE WHAT YOU HAVE?

HMM, ACTUALLY... MAYBE YOU CAN, WITH A LITTLE MAGIC. *LATROP RAEPPA!* *

*READ EACH ONE OF ZATANNA'S MAGIC WORDS BACKWARD.

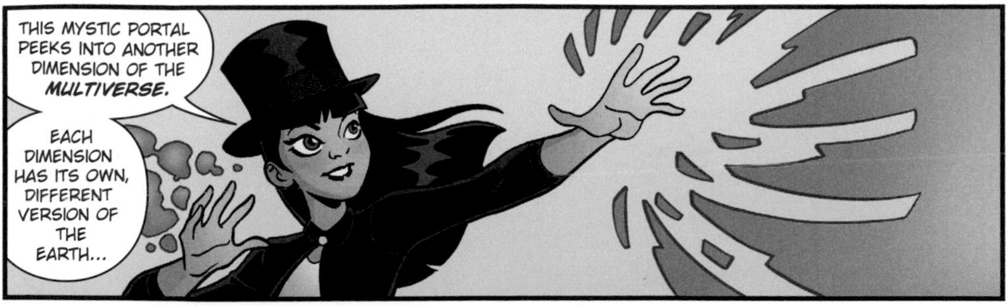
THIS MYSTIC PORTAL PEEKS INTO ANOTHER DIMENSION OF THE *MULTIVERSE.*
EACH DIMENSION HAS ITS OWN, DIFFERENT VERSION OF THE EARTH...

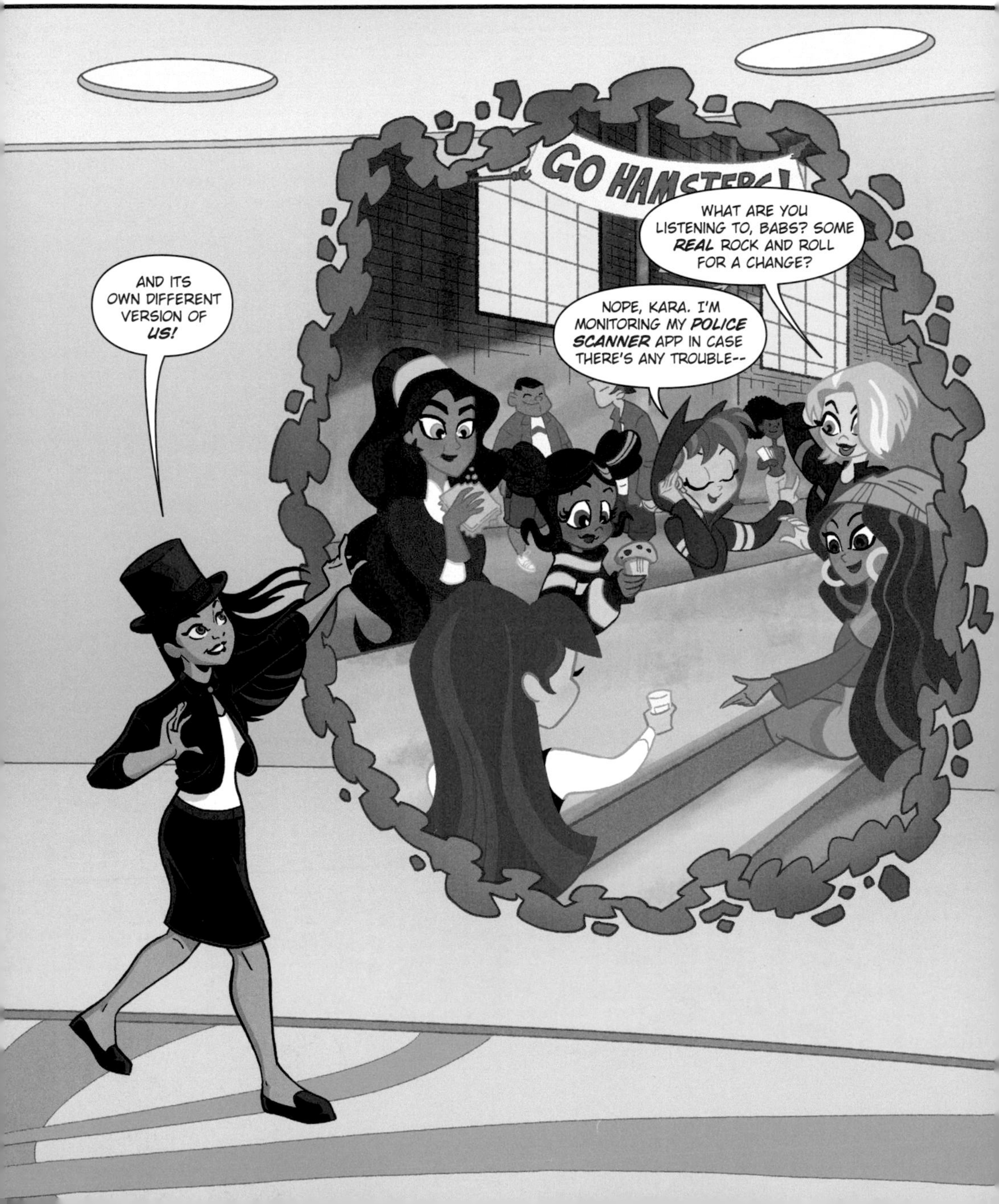
AND ITS OWN DIFFERENT VERSION OF *US!*
GO HAMSTERS!
WHAT ARE YOU LISTENING TO, BABS? SOME *REAL* ROCK AND ROLL FOR A CHANGE?
NOPE, KARA. I'M MONITORING MY *POLICE SCANNER* APP IN CASE THERE'S ANY TROUBLE--

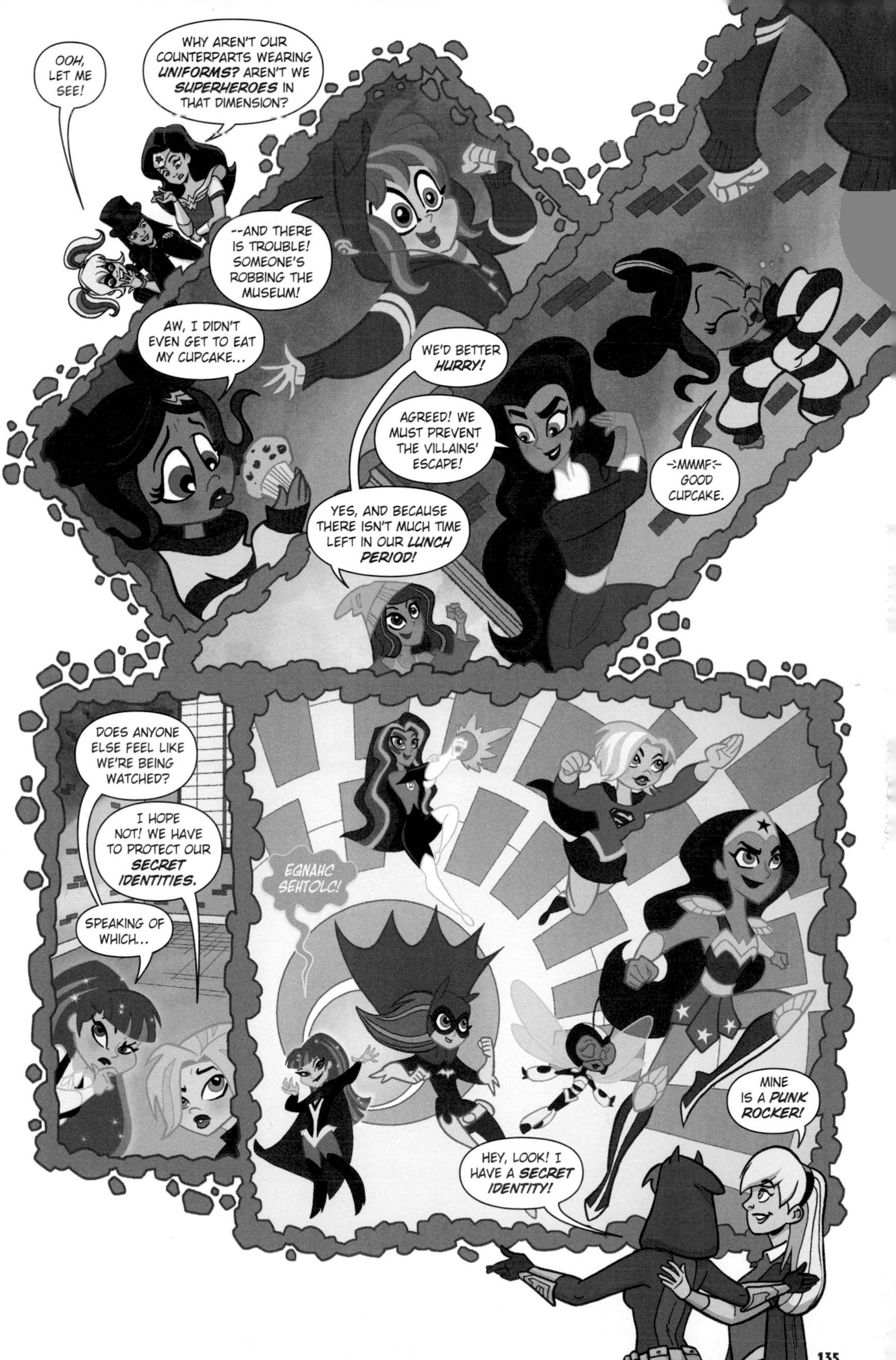
OOH, LET ME SEE!
WHY AREN'T OUR COUNTERPARTS WEARING UNIFORMS? AREN'T WE SUPERHEROES IN THAT DIMENSION?
--AND THERE IS TROUBLE! SOMEONE'S ROBBING THE MUSEUM!
AW, I DIDN'T EVEN GET TO EAT MY CUPCAKE...
WE'D BETTER HURRY!
AGREED! WE MUST PREVENT THE VILLAINS' ESCAPE!
YES, AND BECAUSE THERE ISN'T MUCH TIME LEFT IN OUR LUNCH PERIOD!
MMMF GOOD CUPCAKE.
DOES ANYONE ELSE FEEL LIKE WE'RE BEING WATCHED?
I HOPE NOT! WE HAVE TO PROTECT OUR SECRET IDENTITIES.
SPEAKING OF WHICH...
EGNAHC SEHTOLC!
MINE IS A PUNK ROCKER!
HEY, LOOK! I HAVE A SECRET IDENTITY!

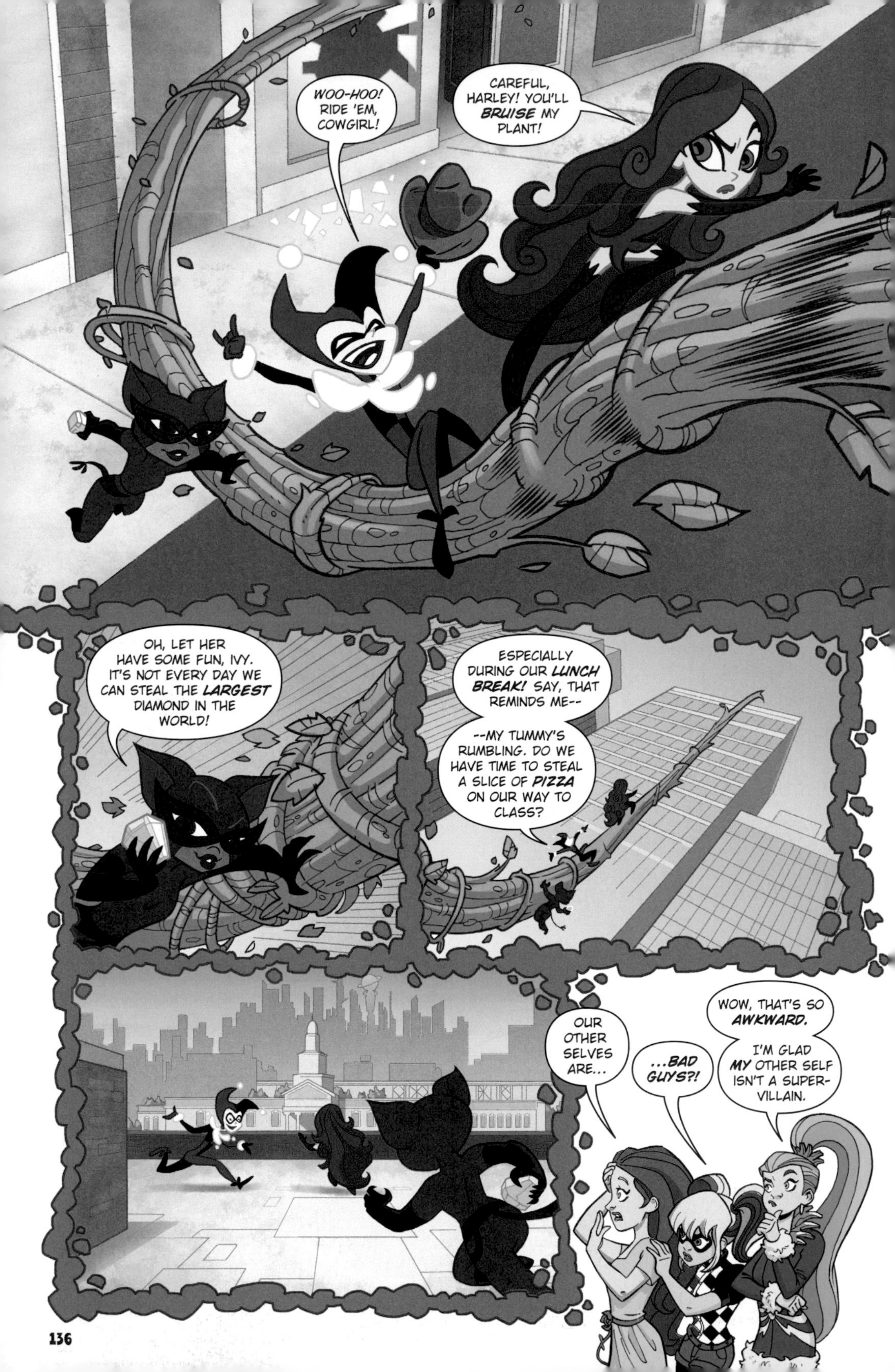
WOO-HOO! RIDE 'EM, COWGIRL!
CAREFUL, HARLEY! YOU'LL BRUISE MY PLANT!
OH, LET HER HAVE SOME FUN, IVY. IT'S NOT EVERY DAY WE CAN STEAL THE LARGEST DIAMOND IN THE WORLD!
ESPECIALLY DURING OUR LUNCH BREAK! SAY, THAT REMINDS ME--
--MY TUMMY'S RUMBLING. DO WE HAVE TIME TO STEAL A SLICE OF PIZZA ON OUR WAY TO CLASS?
OUR OTHER SELVES ARE...
...BAD GUYS?!
WOW, THAT'S SO AWKWARD.
I'M GLAD MY OTHER SELF ISN'T A SUPER-VILLAIN.

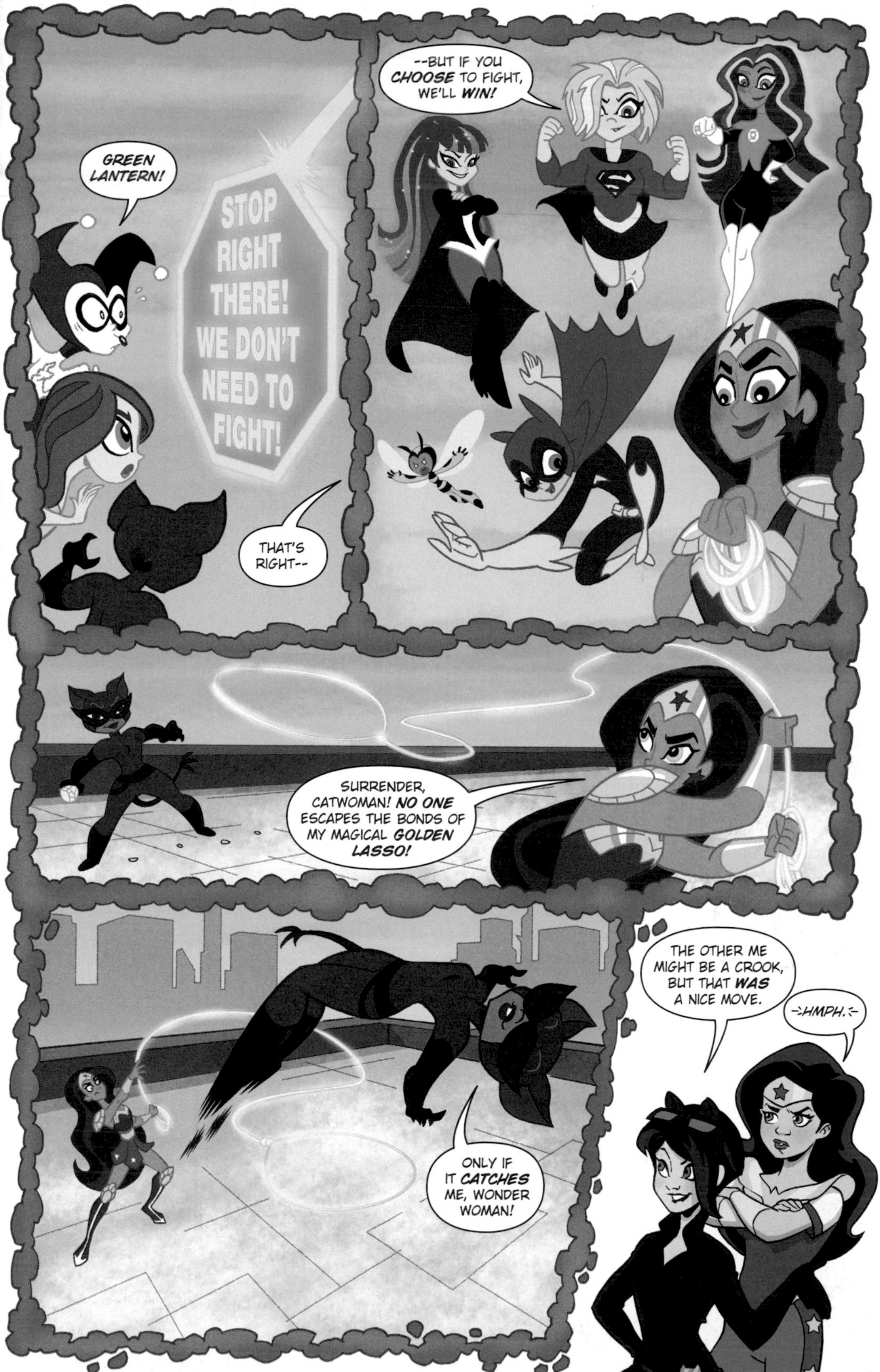
GREEN LANTERN!
STOP RIGHT THERE! WE DON'T NEED TO FIGHT!
THAT'S RIGHT--
--BUT IF YOU CHOOSE TO FIGHT, WE'LL WIN!
SURRENDER, CATWOMAN! NO ONE ESCAPES THE BONDS OF MY MAGICAL GOLDEN LASSO!
ONLY IF IT CATCHES ME, WONDER WOMAN!
THE OTHER ME MIGHT BE A CROOK, BUT THAT WAS A NICE MOVE.
HMPH.

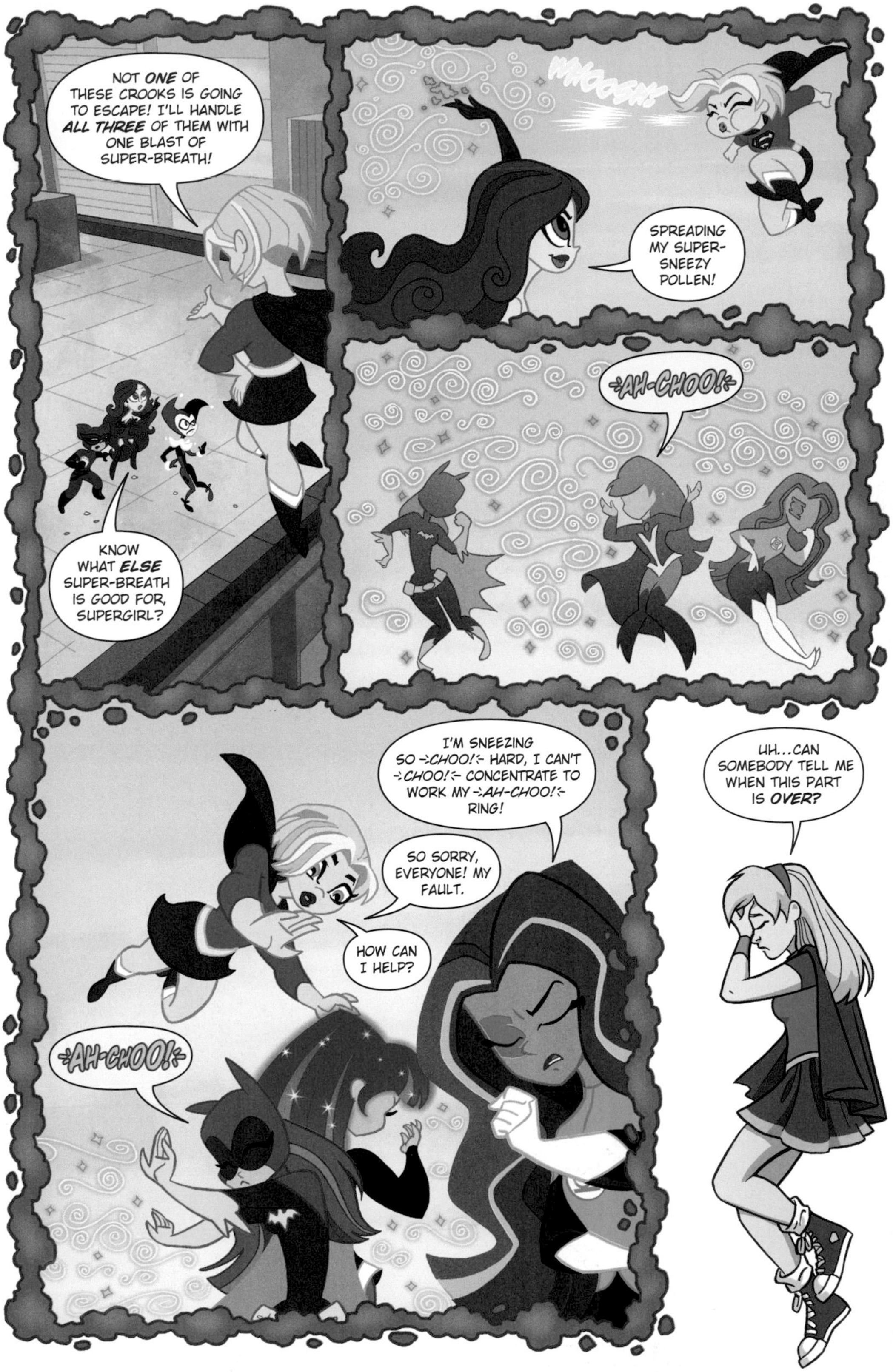
NOT ONE OF THESE CROOKS IS GOING TO ESCAPE! I'LL HANDLE ALL THREE OF THEM WITH ONE BLAST OF SUPER-BREATH!
KNOW WHAT ELSE SUPER-BREATH IS GOOD FOR, SUPERGIRL?
WHOOSH!
SPREADING MY SUPER-SNEEZY POLLEN!
AH-CHOO!
I'M SNEEZING SO -CHOO!- HARD, I CAN'T -CHOO!- CONCENTRATE TO WORK MY -AH-CHOO!- RING!
SO SORRY, EVERYONE! MY FAULT.
HOW CAN I HELP?
AH-CHOO!
UH...CAN SOMEBODY TELL ME WHEN THIS PART IS OVER?

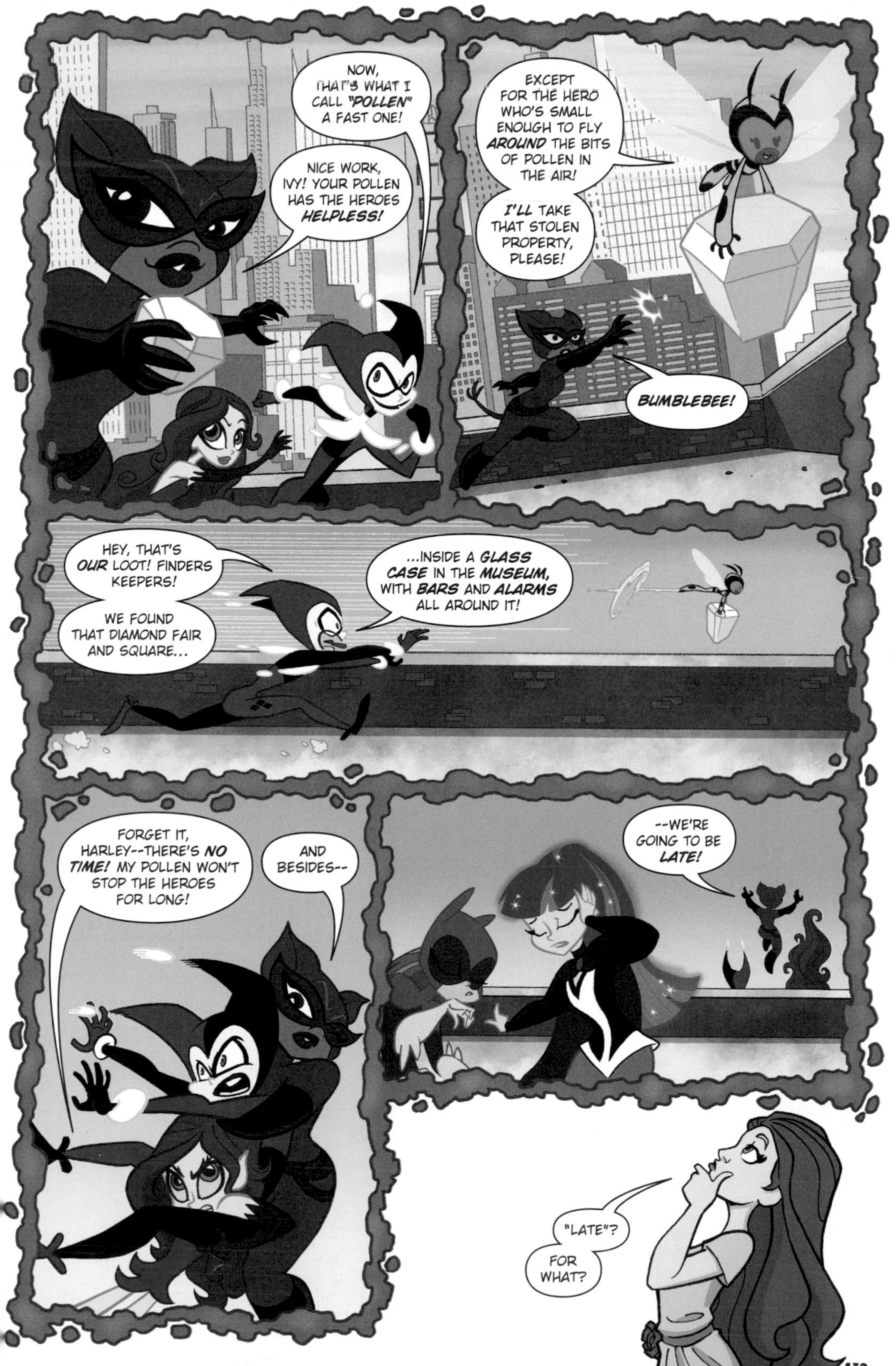
NOW, THAT'S WHAT I CALL "POLLEN" A FAST ONE!
NICE WORK, IVY! YOUR POLLEN HAS THE HEROES HELPLESS!
EXCEPT FOR THE HERO WHO'S SMALL ENOUGH TO FLY AROUND THE BITS OF POLLEN IN THE AIR!
I'LL TAKE THAT STOLEN PROPERTY, PLEASE!
BUMBLEBEE!
HEY, THAT'S OUR LOOT! FINDERS KEEPERS!
WE FOUND THAT DIAMOND FAIR AND SQUARE...
...INSIDE A GLASS CASE IN THE MUSEUM, WITH BARS AND ALARMS ALL AROUND IT!
FORGET IT, HARLEY--THERE'S NO TIME! MY POLLEN WON'T STOP THE HEROES FOR LONG!
AND BESIDES--
--WE'RE GOING TO BE LATE!
"LATE"?
FOR WHAT?

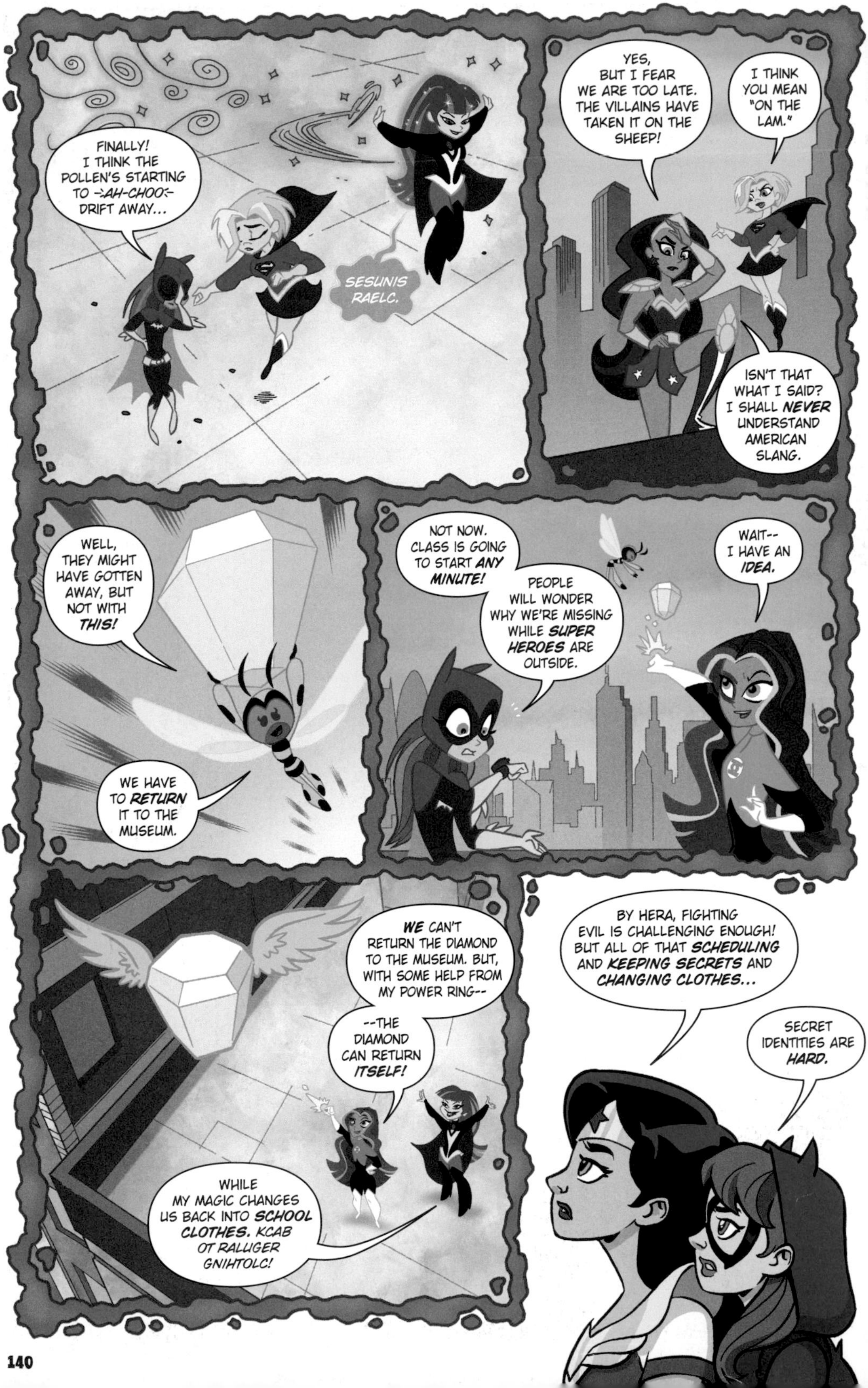

FINALLY! I THINK THE POLLEN'S STARTING TO -AH-CHOO- DRIFT AWAY...
SESUNIS RAELC.
YES, BUT I FEAR WE ARE TOO LATE. THE VILLAINS HAVE TAKEN IT ON THE SHEEP!
I THINK YOU MEAN "ON THE LAM."
ISN'T THAT WHAT I SAID? I SHALL NEVER UNDERSTAND AMERICAN SLANG.
WELL, THEY MIGHT HAVE GOTTEN AWAY, BUT NOT WITH THIS!
WE HAVE TO RETURN IT TO THE MUSEUM.
NOT NOW. CLASS IS GOING TO START ANY MINUTE!
PEOPLE WILL WONDER WHY WE'RE MISSING WHILE SUPER HEROES ARE OUTSIDE.
WAIT-- I HAVE AN IDEA.
WE CAN'T RETURN THE DIAMOND TO THE MUSEUM. BUT, WITH SOME HELP FROM MY POWER RING--
--THE DIAMOND CAN RETURN ITSELF!
WHILE MY MAGIC CHANGES US BACK INTO SCHOOL CLOTHES. KCAB OT RALUGER GNIHTOLC!
BY HERA, FIGHTING EVIL IS CHALLENGING ENOUGH! BUT ALL OF THAT SCHEDULING AND KEEPING SECRETS AND CHANGING CLOTHES...
SECRET IDENTITIES ARE HARD.

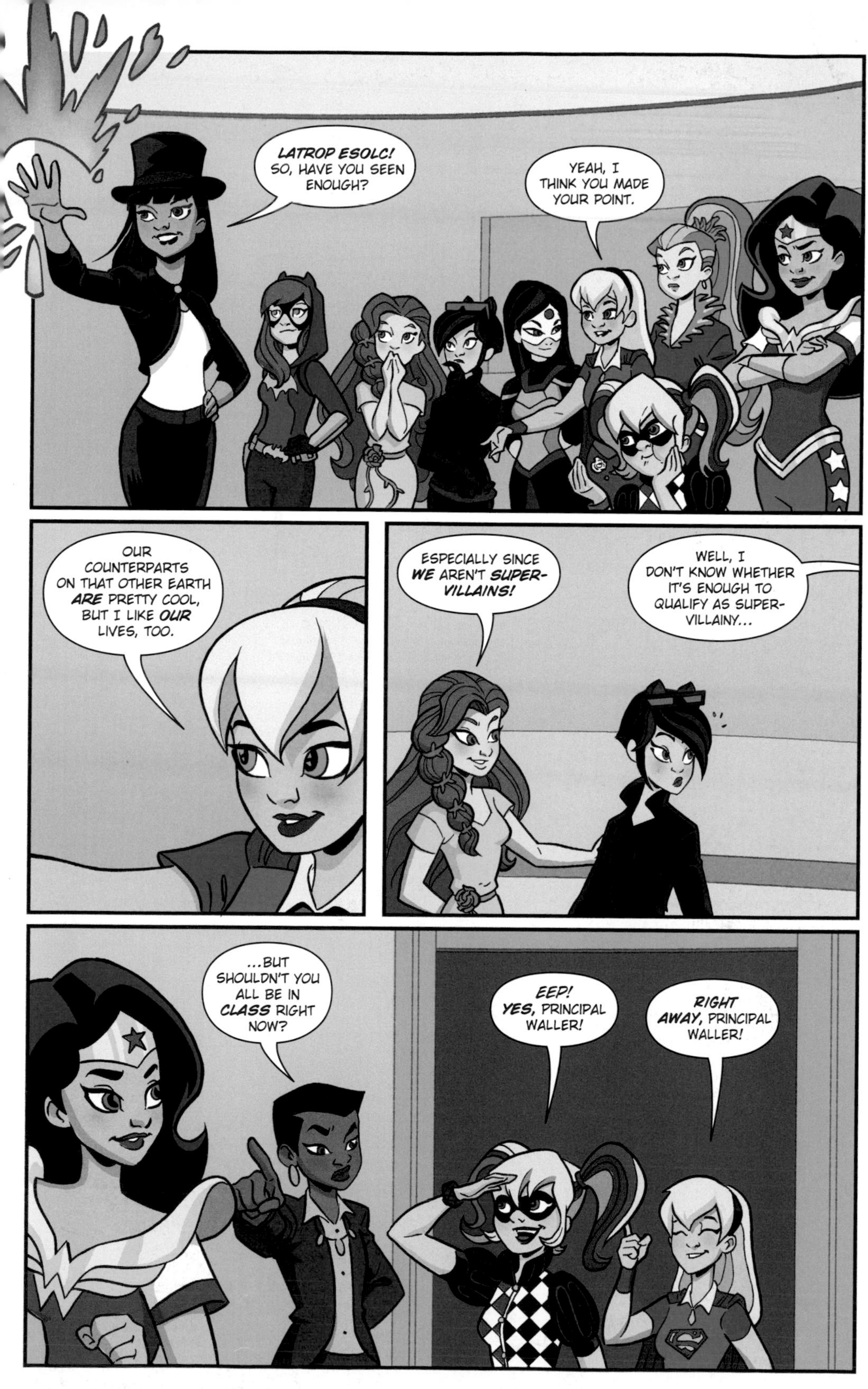
LATROP ESOLC! SO, HAVE YOU SEEN ENOUGH?
YEAH, I THINK YOU MADE YOUR POINT.
OUR COUNTERPARTS ON THAT OTHER EARTH ARE PRETTY COOL, BUT I LIKE OUR LIVES, TOO.
ESPECIALLY SINCE WE AREN'T SUPER-VILLAINS!
WELL, I DON'T KNOW WHETHER IT'S ENOUGH TO QUALIFY AS SUPER-VILLAINY...
...BUT SHOULDN'T YOU ALL BE IN CLASS RIGHT NOW?
EEP! YES, PRINCIPAL WALLER!
RIGHT AWAY, PRINCIPAL WALLER!

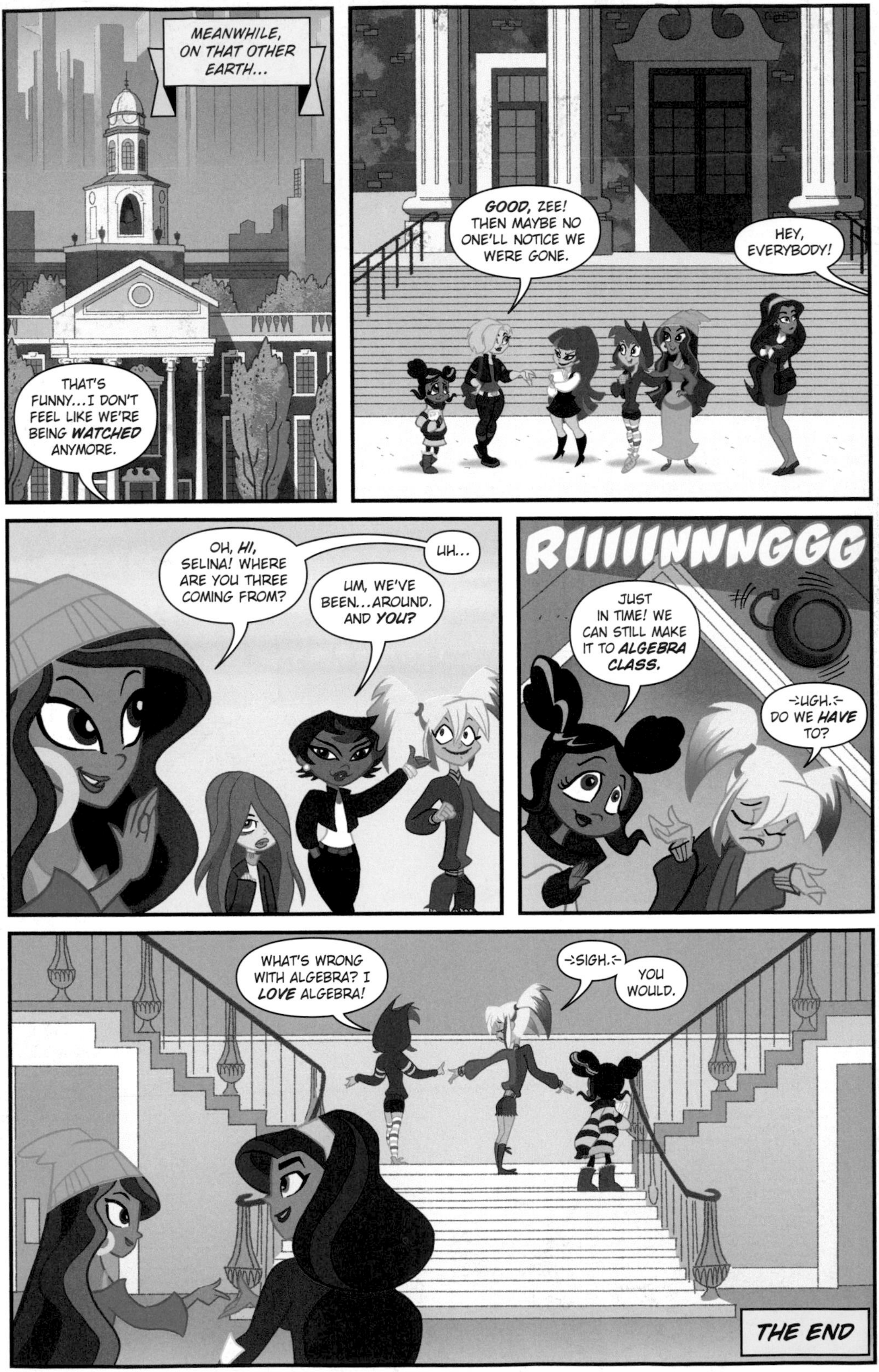
MEANWHILE, ON THAT OTHER EARTH...
THAT'S FUNNY...I DON'T FEEL LIKE WE'RE BEING WATCHED ANYMORE.
GOOD, ZEE! THEN MAYBE NO ONE'LL NOTICE WE WERE GONE.
HEY, EVERYBODY!
OH, HI, SELINA! WHERE ARE YOU THREE COMING FROM?
UH...
UM, WE'VE BEEN...AROUND. AND YOU?
RIIIIINNNGGG
JUST IN TIME! WE CAN STILL MAKE IT TO ALGEBRA CLASS.
-UGH.- DO WE HAVE TO?
WHAT'S WRONG WITH ALGEBRA? I LOVE ALGEBRA!
-SIGH.-
YOU WOULD.
THE END

...AND REVISIT OLD FRIENDS IN THESE GRAPHIC NOVELS, AVAILABLE NOW!

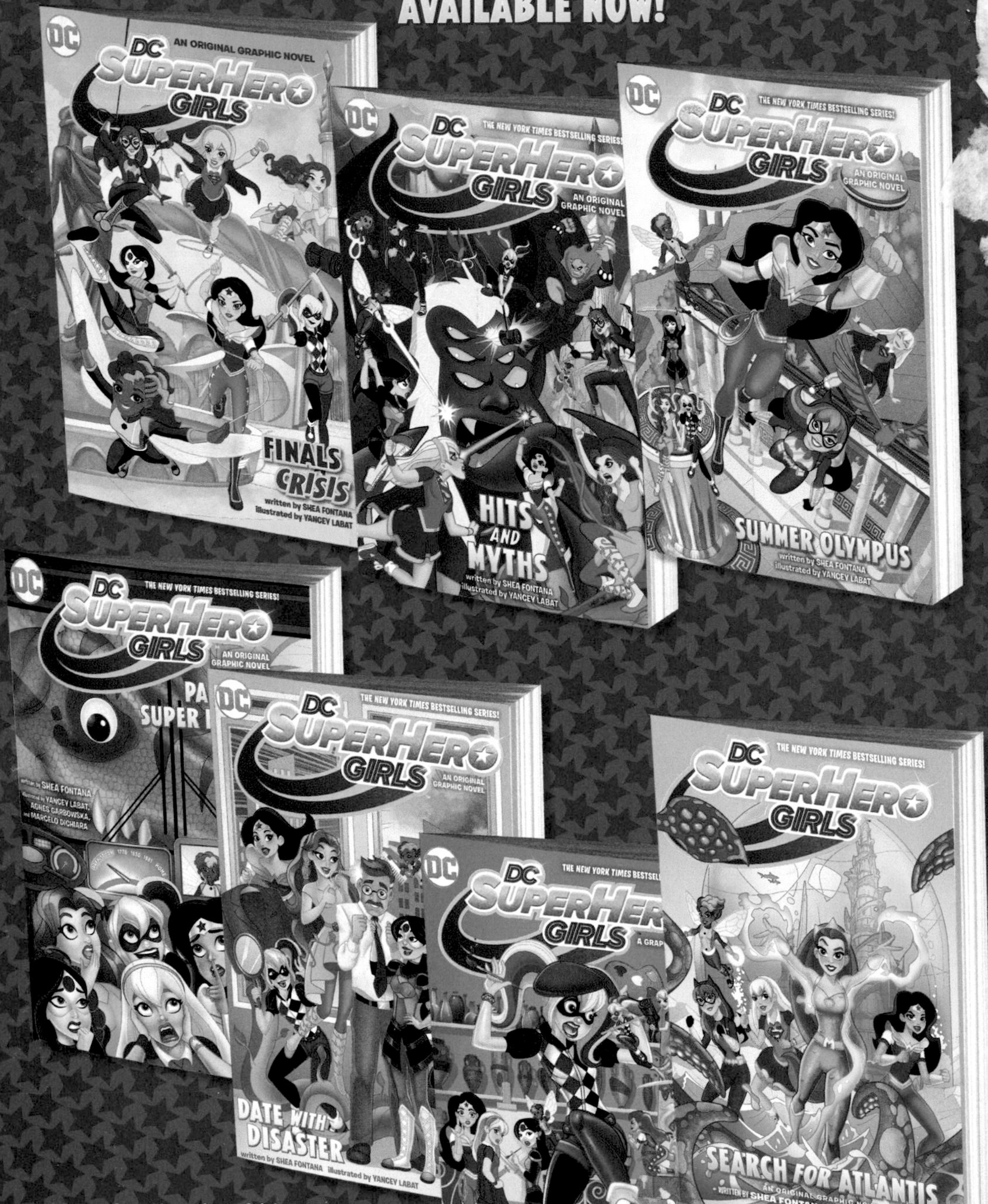
DC SUPER HERO GIRLS
AN ORIGINAL GRAPHIC NOVEL
FINALS CRISIS
written by SHEA FONTANA
illustrated by YANCEY LABAT
THE NEW YORK TIMES BESTSELLING SERIES!
HITS AND MYTHS
SUMMER OLYMPUS
DATE WITH DISASTER
OUT OF THE BOTTLE
SEARCH FOR ATLANTIS

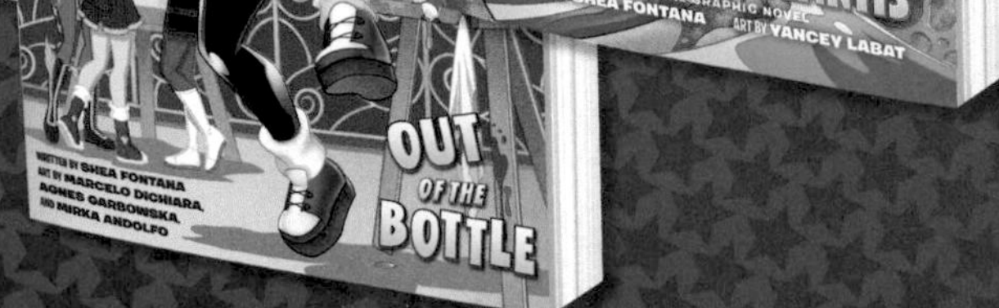

DC Super Hero Girls: Finals Crisis
DC Super Hero Girls: Hits and Myths
DC Super Hero Girls: Summer Olympus
DC Super Hero Girls: Past Times at Super Hero High
DC Super Hero Girls: Date with Disaster
DC Super Hero Girls: Out of the Bottle
DC Super Hero Girls: Search for Atlantis